Also by Heather Farmer

Of Dreams and Discoveries, poetry with the nature photography of Steve Parish, published 1979 and 1994.

The Longest Decade: A literary memoir of the 1940s, published 2015, shortlisted by the USA Memoir Magazine Prize 2022 and reviewed by Jerry Waxler, author of Memoir Revolution.

Collected Poems: A Life in Poetry, published 2021.

Praise for Shadows of Doubt

'In *Shadows of Doubt*, the main protagonist Jodie is a character I won't soon forget. She describes herself as 'a deaf, fat nerd who talks to herself'; she's a shoplifting teenager with a big heart and crushing anxieties. When she begins to uncover the dirty secrets in her dysfunctional family, I found I was holding my breath to the very last, tense page. I loved this novel. It's well-written and has a twist that will leave you gasping.'

Sally McDonald

In *Shadows of Doubt*, Heather Farmer takes us on a journey with Jodie, the central character, who doggedly attempts to unravel the dark mystery of her childhood, while simultaneously navigating fraught relationships with her mother and two older brothers, and experiencing painful first love.

At times written in a beautifully lyrical style, the reader is drawn into Jodie's deepest thoughts and feelings as she struggles to find her way to clarity, maturity and confidence. A complex, layered tale, with subtle twists and turns, the book climaxes with a stunning revelation, and an ending that will surprise even the most insightful of readers.

Shadows of Doubt is a gripping tale and a must-read for adults and adolescents alike. It is an immensely thoughtful, suspenseful and overall enjoyable book!'

Marilyn Venus

Some secrets shape you
Others consume you

SHADOWS OF DOUBT

HEATHER FARMER

First published in Australia in 2025 in conjunction with The Erudite Pen Independent Publishing.

This novel has been written in **Australian English** and uses Australian language, spelling, grammar and punctuation conventions. These are notably different to American, Canadian and British language conventions.

This is a work of fiction. Names, characters and incidents are a product of the author's imagination. Any resemblance to actual people, living or dead, is coincidental. Locales, products, titles of books and songs and public names have been used for atmospheric purposes.

Cover design by Judith San Nicolas
Typeset in Garamond 12 pt and Perpetua 26 pt
Printed and bound in Australia by IngramSpark
Prepared for publication by Dr Juliette Lachemeier at The Erudite Pen Independent Publishing: theeruditepen.com

I acknowledge all Traditional Custodians of this land and their forever connection to country, and pay my respects to Elders, past and present, especially the Bundjalung of the Northern Rivers of NSW. Grafton, on Boorimbah—the Big River—is the setting for my story.

A catalogue record for this book is available from the National Library of Australia

Shadows of Doubt - First edition.
ISBN 9780645187328
eISBN 9780645187335

For David, Ben and Janannie

Prologue

We're living in this ancient farmhouse, on *Gwongorella*, a property outside Grafton on the north coast of New South Wales, because of me.

Five years ago, when I was ten, we lived in the Blue Mountains. I returned home one Saturday morning after visiting my friend Sylvia next door. Dad usually worked Saturday mornings and Mum and my two older brothers I call 'the boys' had gone shopping, so I assumed no one was home and went upstairs to the playroom to watch TV. But guess who was sitting up there—he *never* sat up there that I could remember—my father, reading a letter written on pink paper, so engrossed he didn't hear me on the carpeted stairs or see me standing there.

I knew not to trust him. For years I'd watched my mother cry and heard her angrily accuse him of having affairs. He'd look her straight in the eye and tell her not to be so stupid, jealous and paranoid—that she was mad. To be honest, she was a bit crazy. I was always scared something bad would happen to her, that she'd disappear, or run away with the boys and leave me with Dad.

I was just a kid, but I knew business letters didn't come on pink paper and it wasn't likely to be from Mum. I rushed at my father, snatched the pink letter off him, bounded down the stairs and fled down our backyard into the bush. I kept running, sobbing and gasping and clutching the pink letter, until I reached the boundary separating our property from the Blue Mountains National Park. I crawled through the fence and scrambled into a rock overhang I don't think even my brothers knew about.

I read the pink letter. The woman who wrote it acted like she was my mother's best friend, but she was a traitor like my father. I hated her and I hated him. I wanted to throw up. I wanted to tear the letter into shreds, but I didn't. I decided to give it to Mum, so she'd know this woman was no friend of hers. Maybe Dad would feel so bad he'd stop what he was doing, and Mum would forgive him, and we could be a normal happy family. I felt powerful for once. I thought I was doing the right thing, but after Mum read the letter she fell apart, and although she says it's not true, it feels like everything bad that's happened since has been my fault.

Chapter One

Friday, 17 March 1995

Every now and then I secretly delve into Mum's filing cabinet. It's one way to find out what's going on in this family—I'm always the last to be told.

I've just found pamphlets on *Separation and Divorce, Property Settlement and the Family Law Act* and other forms to do with divorce in the Documents file. I feel weird and sick. I can't ask Mum questions as she'll know I've been snooping.

What makes me feel even weirder is a hand-written note: *'Under the Family Law Act child abuse can include physical or sexual assault against a child, or a sexual activity when a child is used as an object for sexual gratification or witnesses sexual activity between adults for the gratification of the adults.'*

My head has gone cold, the hair rising on my scalp and the back of my neck.

There's more: *'Is there a risk of sexual abuse occurring if custody or access is granted?'* I shudder and start shaking.

A few pages into the documents I read: *'It is a crime to have sexual intercourse with a child under 16 according to sections 66A, 66B, 66C, 66D of the Crimes Act 1900 (NSW). Maximum penalties: Child Under 10: Life Imprisonment, 15 years non-parole. Age 10 to under 14 years: 16 years imprisonment, 7 years non-parole. Child between age 14 and under 16 years: 10 years, nil parole.*' Now I feel even sicker—in my head as well as my gut.

I put everything back exactly where and how I found it. Then I just sit there, on Mum's office chair, waiting for the dizziness and nausea to subside and my heartrate to slow down.

In the *Family* file is *The Story of Jodie's Birth*. I find the big brown envelope and pull it out. Reading the story of my birth always helps me feel better. Mum wrote it a few hours after the event. She did the same after Dan and Billy, my older brothers, were born. The stories are all together in the envelope.

I'm so glad she wrote the story of my birth. It helps suppress the feeling I don't belong in this family. Not having seen them for the last four years, my brothers don't treat me like I'm their sister. Most of the time they ignore me, not just as if I'm invisible, but as if I don't even exist.

My father is worse. Late last year, Mum left him in the Blue Mountains, took me out of boarding school and moved with us kids to this property, *Gwongorella*, about thirty kilometres west of Grafton in northern New South Wales. Dad visited us for Christmas, driving up in a second-hand station wagon he bought Dan as a reward for getting his provisional licence. He drove me into town Christmas Eve for some last-minute shopping, and I was extremely nervous to be alone in the car with him after not having seen him either for the last four years. I was babbling, telling him how I had to wear my HAs—my hearing aids—all the time so I could hear conversations, understand the dialogue on TV, catch on to jokes and so on. When I sensed he'd switched off, I said, 'And the cow jumped over the moon' to test him, and he didn't bat an eyelid. He just said, 'Huh-huh,' and I knew his mind was somewhere else.

That same night, while I was in my room, supposedly asleep, he and Mum were sitting on the east veranda, talking. My south-facing window opens directly onto it. I still had my HAs on and

I overheard Mum explaining why she'd left him and come here to live. 'I would have relapsed, Hugh,' she said. 'I *had* to leave. I had to escape everything and everyone and leave the black memories behind.'

Hearing her say she would have relapsed really put the wind up me. Now I'm scared she'll relapse *here* and disappear like last time, and I'll be back with Dad, or in boarding school again.

In the same big brown envelope is a colour photo of Mum with the boys beside her. On the back of the photo it says Dan is two years and two months old and Billy thirteen months. Mum looks like she's swallowed a watermelon, and I tell myself the bulge really is me.

The Story of Jodie's Birth
Tuesday, 15 January 1980

Doc said he wasn't going to miss out on the action this time, not after Dan and Billy's high-speed performances. This time he wanted me to let him know at the first sign.

Late Monday afternoon, January 14, 1980, was a scorching hot day and I was ironing! Sweat poured off me, but I had this compulsion to finish things, to leave everything just right.

My back started aching, then my belly low down.

Dan arrived late and Billy was early, but this little one was right on time. I rang Hugh's mother Liz and warned her we'd need her for babysitting, possibly overnight, and then I rang Hugh's office and left a message with his secretary for him to come home ASAP. Finally, I rang the Doc. My bag, packed and ready to go, was by the front door.

I fed the boys, then bathed them, bending over the bath with a cast-iron belly and a backache that got worse by the minute. Afterwards, I had to sit down on the lino in the hallway and lean against the wall, the coolest spot, in a draught between the open back and front doors.

Dan brought me the 'baby book'. It's full of photographic-type drawings, prettied up, of embryos in the womb at different stages right up to birth, with graphic illustrations of the birth process itself. It's meant for Mums and Dads-to-be, but the boys have loved this book—it's been their favourite bedtime story for weeks—little Billy pointing at the pictures and Dan patting my tummy trying to feel the baby moving inside.

When an ultrasound revealed a girl, I was thrilled! I threw aside my feminist principles and decorated the bassinet with rosebud lace and net and pink ribbons!

Once Hugh came home, everything stopped. At ten o'clock we decided to go to bed. I was just about to climb in when WHAM—a vice around my middle started squeezing and my lower back felt like I'd spent all day shovelling sand. I rang Liz and the Doc between contractions while Hugh put my bag into the car.

On the drive down the mountains, she decided to turn over and take a nap. And in the hospital, in the delivery room, I was showered, in a white gown, ready and waiting and waiting and … nothing! Not even a twitch in her big toe.

Doc and Hugh sat outside so I could rest. Hah! They talked and talked about fishing and camping spots and four-wheel driving trails. Every now and then, Doc popped in for a listen with his stethoscope. Her heart was fine, her head was in position, and she was ready for lift-off. At 2 a.m., the Doc and Hugh looked in, bleary-eyed and disbelieving, and announced they were going home to bed.

'As soon as Sister thinks it prudent, she'll ring me,' Doc assured me.

'You get some sleep, and we'll be right back!' Hugh promised.

'Sure!' I sneered. 'Why don't YOU stay here and have the baby and I'LL go home!'

Not five minutes after they left, all hell broke loose. I sucked up Trilene gas and floated away with the birdies between contractions, but I knew what was happening. My baby would be born before those pikers got to the foothills. I thought I was going to split open at the end, but I didn't. Instead, this baby girl with a mop of curly black hair emerged. If she'd been born with pink ribbons in her hair, I wouldn't have been surprised, she was so gorgeous!

I instructed Sister not to call the Doc or the dad. 'Let the pikers sleep!' The truth was, I didn't want to be disturbed. I wanted to contemplate the miracle all by myself. It's wonderful to have a daughter. They left her with me until the nurses changed shifts at 7 a.m.

Hugh arrived after breakfast. We'd already agreed her name was 'Jodie', with 'Anne' her middle name, after me. I told Hugh 'Macleod' was his contribution!

Welcome, Jodie Anne Macleod, our precious little girl! Now the family is complete.

In a small white envelope labelled *Jodie's hair at birth* is a lock of black hair. I'm a golden blonde, but Mum's assured me my hair fell out a few weeks after I was born and thick, blonde hair pale as cornsilk grew in its place so fast it was down to my waist before I was two years old. And there's a photo of me taken in the hospital. I look like a fat little Eskimo. On the back of the photo, it says: *'Jodie Anne Macleod—a big little girl. 9 lb. 4 oz'.* It must have been a prophesy. I'm a big girl alright. I've stopped weighing myself and I've stopped looking at my body in the mirror, but my clothes are shrinking in the wash.

I replace everything in the brown envelope and put the envelope back into the *Family* section exactly where it was. I understand Mum's desire for privacy; her journals are in here. I would *not* want her to read *my* journal, that's for sure, nor the secret love letters I write to Shaun Marshall but never send.

Shaun lives on *Booyul*, the property next door.

I know it's wrong, but now I've discovered where Mum hides the filing cabinet key, I plan to go through every file in every drawer while my brothers are at school and she's in town and I'm left alone at home to do my lessons. Nobody tells me anything. Mum says it's because I'm hyper-sensitive and over-react, but if she won't tell me, I have to find out any way I can.

I'm studying through OTEN—the Open Training and Education Network—distance education through TAFE, for my Certificate in General Education, equivalent to the Year 10 School Certificate.

Cleo and Patra begin barking excitedly. Cleo is a golden Labrador with a bit of German Shepherd thrown in and Patra is her daughter, a black Heinz fifty-seven varieties bitzer. They're letting me know Mum has arrived home with Dan and Billy. She drives them to school and picks them up to save doubling up on petrol.

I close the file drawer, lock the filing cabinet and replace the key on the tack hidden under her dressing gown that hangs on a brass hook on the back of her bedroom door. I hurry into my room and open my loose-leaf folder at the last exercise I was doing; I straighten my doona cover, return the March issue of *New Woman* to her bedside table, then wait on the steps and watch the car roll down from the top gate, Cleo and Patra leading the way.

'Hi guys,' I say in my sunniest voice, with a big smile, hoping they'll be friendly. It depends on what sort of a day they've had. Fridays mean a weekend of sun and fun, surf and sand for them, so I'm optimistic.

Billy's already out of the car, fondling the dogs. 'You look very cheerful,' he says, his tone suspicious. 'Whatcha been up to!'

Mum climbs out, dragging her dilapidated, overloaded shoulder bag after her. She presses the lever by the driver's seat to release the Corolla's hatch.

'Dan? Billy? Could you grab some bags, please?'

Dan hasn't even noticed me. 'Did you have a good day?' I ask him.

'Huh!' he grunts. 'When is a school day ever a good day?' He lifts the hatch, picks up a bundle of grocery bags in his free hand and follows Billy inside.

Mum looks worn out. 'I'll get the rest of them,' I tell her.

'Thanks, Pet. How did you go with your lessons today?' She always asks me.

'Fine!' I lie. Apart from snooping in her filing cabinet, I spent the day reading her *New Woman* magazine and a Super Romance I stole from Book World, between vacuuming and tidying the house and making a sultana cake. I look into her eyes and smile sweetly as I pick up the leftover shopping bags. 'You look tired. Come inside and I'll make you a cuppa.'

'That'd be lovely, Jodie.' She closes the hatch. 'I'll just put the car away.'

Something's wrong, I can tell. She's more dispirited than usual.

Struggling up the back steps, I see Billy through the screen door as he goes into the kitchen. 'Hey, bro, open the screen door for me!' No answer. 'Billy?'

'What!' His mouth is stuffed full of something—probably the cake I've made.

'The screen door. *Please.*'

He comes to the back door and opens the screen door outwards. 'Great cake!' he says, spitting crumbs onto the mat I've vacuumed.

'Thanks, bro!' I'm looking at the crumbs, but he misses the sarcasm.

Mum comes in from the carport via the west veranda door and calls out, 'Gosh, Jodie, you've cleaned and tidied everything! It looks wonderful!'

After we settled in here, we had a family meeting and agreed on a roster system of inside/outside chores. I made a chart and stuck it on the fridge. I always vacuum on Fridays, but hearing

Mum sound so pleased makes me happy for a moment. She looks around the door of the kitchen and blows me a kiss. 'Thanks, Pet, I really do appreciate it. It's so nice to come home to a clean house after expecting to walk into a brothel!' Her eyes rest on Billy. 'Take note,' she warns him. 'You hear me, Dan?' she calls out as she retreats through the living room to her bedroom. 'Jodie's cleaned the house, and I want it kept that way or you guys can sleep in your tents! And you can both put the groceries away, okay?'

Dan replies and she laughs.

I turn up my Has, and Billy's voice in my ear a second later pierces my pleasant thoughts. 'She's a *good* girl. Mummy's *pet*!' He saunters out of the kitchen.

My stomach gets a knot in it when he starts on me. I fill the electric jug and while it's heating up, I put teabags into mugs, one for Mum and one for me, and cut two slices of the sultana cake and put them on a plate on the tray. I take a few deep breaths. It helps. I cut myself another slice of cake and eat it while I wait for the jug to boil. While I'm eating, I don't think. I just enjoy it.

Billy suddenly appears in the kitchen doorway as if he's been lying in wait for me. 'Sprung! Pigging out again! Oink! Oink!'

A surge of guilt rises in my throat like vomit, and I can't swallow what's in my mouth, let alone answer him.

'You don't need that!' He's always nagging me. 'Have you looked at yourself in the mirror lately? You'd think you'd quit eating and do yourself a favour!' Then he cuts himself another slice of cake and munches on it while he puts tins and packets and jars on the pantry shelves with his other hand.

The kitchen is suddenly drab and dim and everything's gone blurry. I take the second mug off the tray. I need to go to my room and shut the door.

I take the tray out to Mum. 'You're wonderful,' she says, seeing the cake. I turn to go. I don't want her to see my tears. 'Hey, Jodie, will you come for a walk after, to the road and back? I feel like a stroll, and you look like you could use some exercise.'

Her too. 'Okay. Call me.'

A decorated wooden door-hanger I stole from a bully in boarding school hangs from the doorknob on the outside of my bedroom door.

No moleste!

Do not disturb!

Bitte nicht stören!

Vennligst ikke forstyrr!

Ne pas deranger s'il vous plait!

In my room, door closed, I flop on my bed, angry and humiliated. Then I leap up—even fat frogs can leap—and go to my wardrobe. In a cotton shoulder bag, hanging between my clothes, is a secret hoard.

My diet, appearance, behaviour, weight and health are all Mum ever thinks about whenever she claps eyes on me. Between her and my brothers I'm under constant scrutiny, which is infuriating and demoralising. I'm so self-conscious, so aware of their critical eyes on me, I can hardly bring myself to eat a mouthful of food in front of them. The boys call me name, like 'front-end loader', 'porky pig', 'Venus de cocoa' or 'JAM-face'—my initials.

Mum refuses to give me pocket-money, so I can't buy 'rubbish' when we go to town. 'Junk food' is another phrase. She puts money into a bank account for me but she's the trustee, and I need her signature to take money out. She tries hard to look after me. Too hard.

Last week, after Dan was particularly patronising towards me about something, I raided his cashbox. He grows and sells baby zucchinis and button squash to teachers and mothers in the canteen for two dollars a bag. He's a real miser and even Mum has to pay. He's saving for a new 'stick'— a custom-built, limited-edition surfboard—so fast he'll need a seatbelt.

Saturday morning we all went to town, and the loot bought me Smarties, chocolate-coated almonds, a chocolate malted milk, and a waffle with strawberry syrup and ice cream.

I had to keep a wary eye out for Mum as she haunts coffee shops. She'd arranged to meet us for lunch at midday in the café at the RAG, the Regional Art Gallery, and we went our separate ways in the meantime. Because she thought I didn't have any money, she considered it safe to let me out of her sight. What a pig-out!

At the RAG café I said, 'I'll just have a mineral water, thank you.'

The boys looked approving, but Mum gets cross and worried when I pull that stunt. 'You must eat something!' she insisted. 'What about a salad?'

'Make up your mind! You get in a knot when I *do* eat, and you get in a knot when I *don't!*' All I wanted to do was throw up. 'I don't *feel* like eating, thanks all the same.'

Mum has a way of looking at me—the same way she used to look at Dad—as if she can see inside me, through my eyes.

'I just want you to be *normal*, Jodie. Just to eat normally, three proper meals a day!'

It felt good to be out of her control. I just wished she wasn't so sad about it.

The boys were pleased with me though. 'Good on you, Jode,' Dan said. 'Just keep trying like that, a bit at a time, and exercise—walking's good—and swimming in the creek. You'll soon get it off. You could be a really pretty chick, you know.'

That was the most he'd said to me in a week! I gave him a face-splitting grin and said, 'Thanks, Dan.' I was really thanking him for the money! I thought it was a great joke. I could have laughed out loud.

I rummage around in the bottom of the cotton bag and feel the shape of the packets, deciding with my fingers what I fancy. Smarties. Every colour of the rainbow, sugar *and* chocolate. The multiple hit. Guaranteed to make me see stars.

Dan doesn't seem to realise his cashbox has been raided. By the time he discovers he's twenty dollars short, I'll have forgotten all about stealing it. I'll be innocent and outraged to be accused.

I flop back down on my bed and tip Smarties into my mouth, savouring the flavours and sugary chocolate taste. Alone, I can daydream. And I do. A lot. I dream about Shaun Marshall. He makes my lonely existence bearable. Every weekday, Mum drives Dan and Billy to school on her way to the RAG or the TAFE, leaving me at home alone to do my studies, with two dogs, one frog and several snakes my only company.

We moved here in early December last year. All through the school holidays, the boys went camping and surfing, driving to the beach in Dan's car, a second-hand station wagon Dad bought him. Dad drove it up here from the Blue Mountains just before Christmas, stayed a couple of days, then flew back to Sydney. After the Christmas/New Year break, Mum constantly drove her car into Grafton, lining up tradesmen to build the dog enclosure and convert the shed between the west veranda and carport into an insulated, lined and air-conditioned studio, with big windows to let in the light. She needed to be able to paint and do her artwork in peace and listen to her preferred music, away from the noise of the TV or the boys' portable boombox thumping out music, or them strumming their guitars and singing, or wrestling each other, skylarking or arguing—when they weren't at the beach. Either way, I studied my Year 10 textbooks in my room or on the east veranda for something to do.

It was my choice to do home study. After four years in boarding school, the thought of going to a new school was just too scary. Dan and Billy weren't excited about school either, but they've made heaps of friends. Dan even has a girlfriend, Melanie. She's the lead female singer in the South High musical *Romeo and Juliet*, which opens in a couple of weeks. She's beautiful, with an extraordinary soprano voice. Thanks to her I managed to get to the beach occasionally during the holidays. Dan would con her into videoing Billy and him surfing, so they could 'study their form' (translate: study their beautiful bodies), but she'd be bored stiff watching them out on the waves. I was company for her and shared the videoing. We had some good talks, even though she's Year 12 same as Dan, and I'm only Year 10.

The boys started school at the end of January, and Mum's TAFE ceramics course started Wednesday, 1ˢᵗ February. It was a hot summer day and the house was stifling. Bored and restless, I set off down the paddock with Cleo and Patra towards Gwongorella Creek, the eastern boundary of *Gwongorella* the property. *Gwongorella* means 'dancing water'. The creek is clean and clear, running over smooth round pebbles, and there are pools with sandy bottoms. It's an idyllic place to swim and paddle the canoe and sit or lie on the grassy banks under the trees. The creek, and the billabong on *Booyul* swarming with waterbirds, convinced Mum to buy *Gwongorella*.

With the dogs for company, I wandered down the northern fence line separating our property from *Booyul*. There are cattle in our paddocks owned by a bloke called Joe Whittaker—Mum bought *Gwongorella* off him. Agisting the cattle gives her a bit of income and helps keep the paddocks under control. They were scaring me this day, the way they bunched up, facing the dogs, and moving closer to see what we were doing. I climbed through the barbed wire fence into the neighbours to escape them.

Whittaker owns *Booyul*—the Marshalls lease the farmhouse off him, along with part of the property for Shaun's organic market garden. Whittaker also owns—and lives on—the next property along, upstream from *Booyul* on the far side of the billabong. Because of the drought, he's had to spread his cattle out, which is why he asked Mum if he could agist some of them in our paddocks. He also warned her he was laying 1080 poison baits on his property, having lost calves to wild dogs, and he asked us to lock our dogs up at night and any time during the day when we weren't here to keep an eye on them. He told Mum he'd given all the neighbours in the area including the Marshalls next door the same warning.

'I don't want my cattle harassed and calves disembowelled,' he told her.

Mum was horrified. 'Our dogs wouldn't do that!'

'You better believe it!' he said. 'Dogs are cunning. They seem totally disinterested in the cattle by day and become murderers by night. They sneak out like delinquent kids in gangs, join feral dogs and roam around in a pack hunting until dawn. You wake up and find them on the doorstep, but check their paws and you'll know they've been travelling.'

Mum was pissed off, but knew she had no say in the matter, hence the dog enclosure.

I was wary of snakes too. The boys had already caught a red-bellied black snake frog-hunting half-in, half-out of the well near the back door. They warned me to be careful and to watch where I walked. I wasn't sure if they were trying to protect me—that was hard to believe—or just scare me into staying in the house.

On the Marshall side of the fence were rows and rows of vegetables. It all looked green and cheerful and healthy.

Irrigation sprays jetted around in shining arcs, creating rainbows in the hot air shimmering up from the earth. Seeing this market garden gave Dan the inspiration to become an entrepreneur himself. During the holidays, he cultivated one of the holding yards—the soil already well-fertilised—and grew his own baby zucchinis and button squash.

I could see a man, some distance away, walking through the rows with a large, leggy black dog prancing around him. Cleo and Patra saw them too and started barking like they owned the place. The dog bounded towards us in long-legged leaps barking fiercely. The closer he came, the bigger and louder he seemed. The man ran after him, whistling and shouting, but the dog ignored him. Cleo and Patra whimpered in trepidation, ears and tails drooping. Terrified I was going to be savaged, I folded my arms in front of my throat, pressed my hands over my ears, shut my eyes tightly and waited to be torn apart. The dog—a Doberman—jostled me, growling and snarling. I was shaking so much it's a wonder my blood didn't clot. Eventually, he left me alone and when I opened one eye, I saw Cleo and Patra acting submissive while he inspected them. They licked his muzzle and were disgustingly friendly.

The man arrived, offering apologies to me and swearing at his dog. He took off his battered, dirt-encrusted leather hat and belted him over the head with it. 'You're a mongrel, Saab. A disobedient, stupid dog!' His voice was deep, resonant and 'classy'. His hair, sun-bleached, dry-looking and untidy, fell across his eyes. Saab was unrepentant, leaping and barking, trying to snatch the hat in his teeth as if the whole thing was a game.

'I'm really sorry,' the man said. 'Just as well you're a girl—he doesn't like males, including me!' Saab was trying to bite the hand on his collar as he spoke. 'I'm Shaun Marshall,' he added, letting go of Saab so he could brush his unruly hair out of his eyes and plop his hat back on his head at the same time. He held out his right hand covered in dried mud. I shook it and told him who I was.

We stood beside the fence, buzzed by flies, surrounded by the panting dogs, the curious cattle creeping closer, while we told each other about our lives. I can be cheerful and humorous when I'm motivated, and with Shaun it was easy as he was so genuine and friendly himself.

He's taking a break between university degrees—he has an MSc and plans to start a PhD in climate science next year—this year being his second year on *Booyul*. He works in his organic vegetable patch all day most days, and his mother and casual labour he recruits from the CES, the Commonwealth Employment Service, help him harvest when the pressure is on. The produce has to be picked at just the right time, bagged or packed in boxes, and taken to the railway station to be freighted to the markets.

When he told me his favourite subjects were astronomy, physics, chemistry, and pure and applied maths, I asked him, 'Could you help me with my maths and science sometimes? Distance education is hard with no one to ask. Can you do quadratic equations?'

'Sure, I'll help you. If you come paddling with me. It's no fun paddling a Canadian on your own.'

'When?'

'On Wednesdays. The billabong or the creek—take your pick.'

'Okay.' I was so full of delight I thought I'd burst. But I had to tell him, 'Shaun, we'll have to keep our deal a secret.'

'Why?' He looked at me, one eyebrow raised.

'I guess what Mum and my brothers don't know can't hurt me.'

'You mean your mother won't approve of her only-just fifteen-year-old daughter hanging out with a twenty-seven-year-old male, especially a stranger she hasn't met?'

Clearly, in his eyes I was just a girl—and he was spot on about Mum. I nodded. 'She'll be at TAFE though, like today. She goes to town *every* day. She leaves at eight and drives my brothers to school and they don't get home 'til four. She does voluntary work at the RAG on Mondays, Tuesdays and Thursdays, and Ceramics at TAFE on Wednesdays. Fridays she lunches with friends and buys the groceries. I do my schoolwork on my own.'

He looked dubious. 'Okay. Bring your maths, a hat, water bottle and towel. Wear your swimmers under your clothes, put on sunscreen and mosquito repellent. And bring lunch!' He smiled at me, then walked off, whistling Saab. I whistled Cleo and Patra to come with me. They obeyed reluctantly, not wanting to leave their new playmate. I knew how they felt!

I was elated with the way my first day on my own had turned out. My face glowed, and I decided if Mum commented I'd tell her I'd taken the dogs for a walk, which was true enough! I'd just omit I'd met Shaun.

Chapter Two

Friday, 17 March 1995

The packet's empty. I can't believe it! I've been lying here munching Smarties and daydreaming about Shaun and I didn't even taste them. Why do I eat all these calories? It's such a *dumb* thing to do. I must be *stupid*. There really is something wrong with me!

I'm going to get my eating under control. I'll show them. I'll get so thin they'll start worrying about *that* and nag me to *eat*!

The sooner I go for a walk, the better, but I don't want to go with Mum. She'll pick up on how I'm feeling—same as I do with her—and ask me what's wrong.

I've told her before, 'It's my bloody brothers! You said they wanted to be with me, but they're always picking on me, putting me down, calling me names! They're so mean. I don't feel cared about at all! They want me to disappear!'

Problem is, she becomes upset—with *me*! 'Oh Jodie, stop exaggerating. They couldn't wait to be with you again after not seeing you for four years.'

'So why does Billy say, "Drop dead, Jodie" or "Piss off!" I feel like running away. Dan doesn't even *see* me. I may as well be dead!'

'Don't *say* that! Ignore their comments!'

'How *can* I?'

'They're just boys!'

'What do you mean "just boys"! Why are you letting them bully me?'

'Rise above it!'

'How can I when I feel like a cockroach crawling under their feet?'

She doesn't tell the boys to lay off, to pull their heads in. She doesn't get angry with *them*. She defends them, fed up with *me*! 'You give as good as you get, Jodie. You do and say mean things too. You're so hyped up and short-tempered—so easily hurt—you make mountains out of molehills. The only strategies they have for coping with you is name-calling or keeping out of your way since they aren't allowed to hit you. If you'd stop eating junk, you'd be so much calmer and easier to get along with.'

And we'd be back onto her favourite subjects: food, health, artificial colourings and flavourings and preservatives, kilojoules and kilograms, vitamins and minerals, sugar and fat, diet and exercise, diabetes, cholesterol, heart disease and mental health, all implying that I'm a disappointment to her, that I don't measure up to her ideal of a slim, healthy daughter, that I'm not perfect like the boys.

I go out onto the east veranda. Mum's absently stroking the white opal pendant she always wears, staring out over the shimmering paddocks down to the she-oaks and paperbark trees growing along the banks of the creek. She looks sad. She's a worry. Nothing I do cheers her up for long. I try and help her, and she's happy for a little while, but it doesn't last.

'Mum? I'm going for a walk now. It's the boys' turn to cook dinner.'

After all, I vacuum the house every Friday, including their room full of snakes in glass tanks—what a stink—cockroaches and tallyho papers and matches under their beds, little bags of dope and bongs under their mattresses, marihuana seedlings sprouting in a shallow plastic tray on top of their wardrobe, and her darling boys don't smoke dope? Hah!

'Can I come with you?' she asks.

'I'd rather go by myself. I'll take the dogs.' Shaun might be out walking Saab.

'Oh. I was hoping we could have a talk.'

That's why I'd rather go by myself. But I can't resist asking her, 'What about?' I feel dread and curiosity wondering what's on her mind. Does she want to discuss the Family Court documents I saw in the filing cabinet? Is she planning to divorce Dad? I have this terror that something bad will happen to my mother's mind again. She seems drained of energy. Dark rings circle her eyes. She's thinner and smaller somehow. 'What's up? What's the matter?'

She glances at me, her eyes dark, and shrugs slowly, drawing in a deep breath. She looks like she's about to cry. A tight, hot feeling crawls over me. Is she falling apart again? I need her to be strong; to be there for me. She drives me crazy, but if something bad happens and she gets sick again—it's too awful to contemplate. I give in. She looks like a child who needs a hug, and I reach out to console her.

'I'm sorry, Mum,' I tell her, though I'm not sure what I'm apologising for. 'Let's go for a walk, eh?'

We give each other a cuddle, which is nice, and I feel love for her, but she says, 'You smell of chocolate,' and withdraws. Guilt and irritation well up in me, but she doesn't pursue it. 'Let's get some shoes on,' she says. She goes inside and loudly reminds the boys it's their turn to make dinner.

In my room I pull on some socks and my Reeboks, another of Mum's bribes to encourage me to exercise, and brush my hair. I haven't seen Shaun all this week. Instead of our usual Wednesday up the creek, he had a bunch of school kids following him around his vegie patch and there were girls amongst them. I felt jealous and insecure. I did my lessons on the east veranda so I could keep an eye on him, and them, through Mum's binoculars.

I catch sight of myself in the wardrobe mirror. In my t-shirt and gathered skirt I'd scare away dingoes. My hair is my only redeeming feature. It's a honey-gold colour, thick and shiny, and tumbles down in waves past my shoulders.

'Pity about the face,' I tell myself cruelly, but Anne—my reflection, my middle name and secret friend—won't have it.

Your face is fine.

Anne is my alter ego, my better self. She stares back at me. Sometimes, when we play around with make-up, I can see I really do have striking eyes, big and widely spaced and very blue, with long, thick dark-blonde lashes. But I'm myopic with astigmatism and need to wear glasses. They are lightweight, rimless and expensive, but they are still glasses.

It helps if I smile; my teeth are straight and white. And despite my hearing disability and having to wear hearing aids, I speak well. Mum told me I was three before she realised my hearing was impaired. She used to leave me a couple of days a week at a childcare centre so she could have a break, and one day the supervisor told Mum she was sure I was deaf, but I could lip-read so well no one had picked it up. It also explained why I had so little to say and why I was unresponsive and disobedient sometimes. An appointment with an ENT specialist confirmed I had a 'moderate-to-severe hearing disability'.

After that diagnosis, Mum made sure I learned to speak properly and read and write well. She home-schooled me herself and enrolled me in speech therapy and elocution lessons.

In 1990, when I was ten, she disappeared. Nobody told me why. I can't remember anything about that year—it's like my mind disappeared too—but the following January I ended up in the best, and most expensive, boarding school in the state, in the southern highlands, where I was left for the next four years.

The boys call me 'Ms Lah-de-dah', because of the way I speak, but I'm glad I speak well, because Shaun has a rich, deep ABC announcer's voice. The boys never tease him about *his* voice, and they get on fine.

Shaun is scrumptious. He's *so* good looking! Not in a conventional sense. His blond hair is long and untidy, and he only shaves once a week—on Wednesdays! I like to think he shaves for me! He's tall and slim and muscular and his eyes are a vivid blue, like mine, and whenever he sees me, a wide elfin smile lights up his tanned face. I've only known him for six weeks or so, but we're soulmates, kindred spirits, best friends, secret companions. He's a man, not a boy, but I'm safe with him. He's always courteous and pleasant to me. I can't say, in all honesty, he's been anything more than that—courteous and pleasant— but it counts for a lot. He's never moody or mean. I can rely on him. I trust him. And I've fallen in love with him!

'Ready?' Mum is at my door, in shorts and running shoes. Seeing her, I feel frumpy all over again, but there's nothing I can do about that except go for a walk. Lots of walks.

As we set off across the dry yellow grass to the gate, the dogs appear, leaping and barking, eager to join us. I surreptitiously look out for Shaun as we walk up the slope to the lane that takes us to the Copmanhurst Road.

We walk in silence for several minutes.

'So, what's wrong, Mum? Just tell me! I *need* to know. Is it about Dad?' I sound croaky.

Mum nods. When she speaks, her voice is wobbly. 'He's not coming up here to live, Jodie. It's no use pretending anymore.'

'Are you sure?' I'm sad for her, glad and relieved for me, angry for us both. I try to stay calm and keep my reaction under control.

'There was a registered letter at the post office addressed to me. I had to sign for it. It was from a woman I don't even know! His latest f...' Mum suppresses an epithet, '...girlfriend. She somehow got to see my emails to him, and his emails to me, and she's realised from the contents he's two-timing her! *Her!* What about *me!* She writes like she thought I'd know all about her, asking is it over between Hugh and me, because he'd assured her it was, and now, since reading our emails, she's *confused!*' Mum's shaking her head, her voice rising. 'But he's never mentioned her! I truly believed he wanted to make a go of it, sell the business so he can come here and join us. A fresh start ...'

I feel sick and hot in my belly. Pictures flash across my mind, like slides flipping across a screen very fast, of my father having sex with a woman—I know her face and her voice and her laugh, though I can't name her, and I know the place, it's a place I've been in, but I don't know where, and I don't know if I'm remembering or imagining, and I feel small and frightened, anxious and angry, sick and horrible because I know it's wrong. Wrong and dangerous, then and now.

'... but I never learn! I'm such a sucker. I fall for his lies every time!'

'He'll *never* change, Mum. Can't you see nothing's changed? It's the same old story, lies, lies, lies, while he keeps you where he wants you, in case things don't work out for him and he'll still have you to fall back on. I *hate* him!' The Smarties have kicked in. I can hear myself shrieking. 'I just *loathe* the way he messes you about!'

'After we moved here, I went to the Family Court in Lismore for information about divorce, property settlement, access and contact, child support ...'

I couldn't tell her I already knew.

'… but it was so complicated I filed it away, hoping every-thing would get better.'

'It won't!'

'But if you feel like that about him, then I *will* file for di-vorce!'

Why can't I have a decent, loving, kind, honest father? Why is he such a cheat and a liar? A two-timing, uncaring husband? Why does he deliberately hurt my mother?

'What did you ever do to him, to make him be like he is!'

Mum stops walking. She stares at me, tear-streaked, disbe-lieving. 'God! Don't you *dare* blame me for your father's infidelities!' She's beside herself furious. 'I'm not responsible for the choices he's made or the lies he's told!'

'Mum! I didn't mean—'

She doesn't let me finish. She's beyond listening. 'Do you know what he said to me? "Make me happy and I'll be faithful." Can you credit that? And I fell for it! I tried—God knows I tried—for *years*, to make that man happy, but no matter what I did, no matter how hard I tried, it was never enough. It made no difference.'

'Divorce him then!' I don't want to hear any more. There's a black rock in my chest so heavy I can hardly breathe. Why do we always end up fighting when we talk? It's hopeless. She's walking fast, dismissing me, and I run to catch up, to say I'm sorry for whatever it was I said to upset her. I say sorry to my mother a lot.

As I draw alongside, she says, 'I'm finished with crying, Jodie. It's time to look after *myself*. It's time to make *myself* happy!' The expression on her face is hard and bleak. '*Never, ever* lay Hugh's atrocious behaviour onto *me*, okay?'

'I'm sorry Mum. I wasn't—I didn't mean it the way you thought.'

'I hope not!' she snaps. 'The man has problems of his own, Jodie, and the way he is, it's his problem from now on, not mine. He's just never worked out that a handshake, or a peck on a woman's cheek, or a friendly hug stops there. He just keeps going till he's in bed, as if he can't help himself—except he *can*. It is still a decision he makes. I should have been able to trust *him*, but no—I had to rely on the *women* to do the right thing by me—my so-called friends. I shouldn't have had to worry about *them!*'

I want so much to touch her, hold her hand, link arms or something, but another part of me is afraid to reach out in case she shrugs me off.

'It's an addiction, if you ask me.' I can hear the disgust in her voice.

'You mean he's addicted to women?'

'Yes. To women. To sex.' She sounds cold, contemptuous. 'To the thrill of the chase, the risk of getting caught. He's addicted to the secrecy, to lying and deceiving. Half his fun is playing us women off against each other. This latest self-deluded victim has ruined it for herself by writing to me and bringing it into the open. I'll photocopy her letter and post it to him. All the fun will go out of it for him.'

I'm like my father. I see Shaun in secret, binge in secret, shoplift in secret, read Mum's files in secret, steal from my brothers in secret, explore their room in secret and get a kick out of uncovering *their* secrets. I cover my tracks, tell lies, pretend to be what I'm not, pretend I'm not what I am. My whole life is a secret! No one knows who I *really* am, what I'm *really* like. They don't even like who they *think* I am!

'This time, *Hugh* is going to get a shock. *I'm* finished with *him*! It's over.'

That's how she'd feel about me if she really knew me.

'I'll tell him *I've* found someone else!'

'Mum! Have you really?'

She glares at me defiantly 'And why not!'

'Mum, that's so scary.'

'Well, get used to the idea, Jodie. I'm thirty-nine. From now on the rest of my life belongs to *me*! Don't look so horrified! I plan to find *myself* first.'

A strange man in my mother's life? In my mother's bed? Will he be good to her? What if she gets hurt again? What if he hates *me*?

'We'd better turn back,' she says. 'The dogs might go on the road.' She whistles and when they come to her, she pats and praises them.

We walk back in silence. The twilight is softening the edge of things. A curling twist of wood-smoke from Shaun's mother's slow-combustion stove rises like a genie from the chimney on the roof of their farmhouse, evoking images of homegrown vegetable soup.

'You know something, Jodie?'

'What?'

'Giving me that letter you snatched off your father five years ago was the best thing you ever did for me.'

The pink letter.

'A lot has happened because of it, but I thank you for it.'

I don't know how to respond. I'm sure the boys have never forgiven me for not minding my own business. I'm certain my father will never forgive me. The feeling it's all my fault has been with me for years, like a heavy backpack I've been carrying around for so long I just accept that it's there, a tired, tight feeling between my shoulder blades. Mum is offering to cut the straps, but it's too late; my family has disintegrated, and I don't know which weighs heaviest: my mother's breakdown, the family's break up, or knowing my father is a louse. I can't do anything to change him, or change what's happened, or make my mother happy again. It's all wrong. It's just not fair. I'm crying for what I've lost and for what I've never had. And I'm afraid. Something I don't want to remember is lurking in the shadows at the back of my mind. My feelings frighten me. I swallow them, stuff them down, smile at Mum a watery smile. I don't know what else to do.

Faigan is sitting on the plastic lid of the electric jug. He's a big, long-fingered, long-toed green tree frog. He lives above the sink where walls and ceiling meet, but at day's end he comes down to feed on the six- and eight-legged nasties that scuttle around our kitchen after dark.

'He maintains the ecological balance,' Mum says. Frog droppings on the bench top in the mornings are an acceptable, if overly optimistic, alternative to spraying with Mortein.

I pick up the jug with Faigan on the lid and carry it to the tap. I open the lid and Faigan tilts with it. I fill the jug, replace it gently on the bench, put the plug in and switch it on. The jug rumbles and vibrates and phlegmatic Faigan continues to squat, quivering with the beat, until the plastic lid heats up and he begins lifting his feet, one after the other.

Billy peers around the kitchen door frame. 'Wow! Yes please, Jode,' he says, in his oh-how-nice-of-you-to-do-this-for-me voice.

I succumb every time. 'What would you like?' I ask him, as if we're best mates.

'Ecco, thanks.' He eyes Faigan's antics on the jug lid. 'Mmm! Snake food!'

'Don't you *ever* dare!' I can't tell whether he's kidding or not. 'Faigan is on the endangered species list, didn't you know?' As if on cue, Faigan leaps from the jug onto the wall, *SPLAT*, and climbs out of reach. 'See, he knows you're not to be trusted.'

Dan appears. 'Wow, Ecco!' he says, in his fancy-meeting-all-my-best-friends-at-once voice. 'Thanks, Jode.' I take another mug from its hook, spoon in the brown powder, add milk and stir it *before* adding the boiling water, just the way he likes it. I make Mum's tea with a tea bag—she's a tea addict. Finally, I make myself hot milk Milo in the microwave.

'We need to set the mouse and rat traps. Carmen needs a feed,' Dan says to Billy. They head out to the east veranda with their mugs. Carmen is a diamond python. Dan and Billy have licences from the NPWS, the National Parks and Wildlife Service, to catch reptiles that need rescuing and release them as soon as possible into an appropriate environment. Dan rescued Carmen from someone's laundry. She's not venomous, but she can bite.

When they caught the red-bellied black snake frog-hunting half-in, half-out of our well Mum instructed them to release it on the far side of Rogan Bridge, on the other side of the Big River. She didn't want it coming back! They set off in Dan's car with the snake in a bag to do the deed, but a few days later, while I was vacuuming their room, I noticed a red-bellied black snake in the big glass-fronted cage—their show piece—decked out to emulate a snake's favourite environment.

Mum rarely enters our rooms. She says they're our responsibility and our private space; we're not to violate her privacy and she won't violate ours, which allows her to avoid facing reality and having to do something about it. She'd have a spack attack if she discovered what's behind our closed doors.

I carry Mum's tea and my Milo out to the east veranda. It's an after-dinner ritual, one of the rare moments when we feel like a family, a pleasant respite after the heat of the day. The boys loll on the steps, swotting mosquitoes that haven't been deterred by the mosquito coils. Mum and I sit together on the sofa. Cleo and Patra sprawl on the boards nearby.

The full moon has risen over the escarpment, so bright only a few stars, or planets, are visible. A fox screams down by the creek. Lapwing plovers on *Booyul* squawk a warning.

'It's time for bed,' Dan tells Cleo and Patra, removing a couple of biscuits from the dog-biscuit tin. They follow him around the house to their kennels, which are inside the roofed, timber-floored, fly-wired enclosure Mum had built between her studio and the carport, under the kitchen window, both structures shielded from the afternoon sun by a huge, spreading kurrajong tree.

Usually, I am calmed by the night air brushing my face and arms, but not tonight. Instead of peace, I feel rage. Outrage. Thinking about Dad, I want to smash something.

As if reading my mind, Billy asks, 'When is that man called *Dad* coming up again?'

'He's not!' I blurt out. 'He's a bastard…'

'Jodie! Hush!' Mum punches me to silence me, punching the mug in my hand as well, and the still-hot Milo spills down my front and burns my stomach.

'Ow! That hurt!' I yell at her. 'I *hate* him! He doesn't give a stuff about us! Well, he can get *fucked*, 'cause that's what he's done to me! Fucked up my life! And you should have *stopped* him! *Why didn't you stop him?*'

Dan leaps up the steps. 'What the hell? What's wrong? What happened!'

I've startled myself as much as them. Stomach burning, over-whelmed by feelings of danger and shame, rage and hurt, I rush into the house, escape out the back door and flee up the slope to *Booyul* and Shaun, as fast as I can run.

In the bright moonlight, the shadow of the barbed wire fence is charcoaled on the dry ground with cruelly exaggerated spikes. I open the gate and run across the bindi-eyes they call their lawn to the back door. Saab must be inside. Mum won't let our dogs in the house.

'Boo!'

I jerk with fright, but it's only Shaun, in the shadows in a deckchair, enjoying his own peace and quiet moon-gazing. His teeth glisten as he chuckles.

'Very funny!' Now I'm here I don't know what I want, or what to do, or say. I'm breathing fast in jerks, my heart thudding, my belly burning.

'What's up?' He hoists himself out of the low chair and comes over to me, replacing the plastic caps on the lenses of the binoculars, both ends.

'I'm sorry. I've spoilt your—'

'No, it's okay, it's really nice to see you.'

'Can I please talk to you for a few minutes?'

'Sure! Hang on.' He opens the flyscreen door, hangs the binoculars by the strap over a peg on the hat and coat rack on the laundry wall and disappears into the house. I can't hear anything except the murmur of their television. As he re-opens the screen door, Saab bolts through the gap, brushes past me and bounds down the track. Shaun swears, then whistles and calls to no avail. He sinks down on the steps and yanks at the socks stuffed into his boots, shaking them before pulling them on, muttering and cursing. I've ruined his night for sure.

'Pardon?' That's the most used word in my vocabulary next to 'sorry'.

'He's the stupidest dog I've ever had. Untrainable.'

Saab's not stupid—he's disobedient because he's too intelligent to take notice of mere humans. He doesn't love, honour and obey without question like Cleo and Patra. Mosquitoes are whining around my ears and I start slapping myself. Shaun digs into his shorts pocket and pulls out a small pink plastic container.

'Here.'

I'm glad his rejection of poisonous chemicals doesn't extend to mosquito repellent. He's planning to go for a walk. In the midst of my misery, I feel a pang of pleasure. I take the *Rid* and rub it on every exposed part.

'Do you need a jacket?'

'No, I'll be okay. Thanks.' I return the *Rid,* which he pockets. He sets off towards the stockyards and I follow him, glad to be going somewhere away from the houses, half-wanting Mum, Dan and Billy to show up chasing after me, looking for me, showing concern; half-wanting to avoid them if they do; knowing that they won't; wishing that they would so I could reject *them* instead of feeling like they don't care.

We arrive at the gate. Shaun opens it and waits for me to pass through the gap. He follows me, closes it and replaces the chain. We walk side by side, his thumbs jammed into the waistband of his jeans, his fingers hanging out. Saab is up ahead, a pouncing black blob with his delinquent shadow for company, on the hunt along the edges of the rows of vegetables.

Despite the moonlight, the track is treacherous. Shaun mooches along like he knows every pothole, but I stumble on the edges of the ruts and pebbles.

'Careful,' he says, as he grasps my left arm with his right hand, just above my elbow. 'You don't want a twisted ankle.'

He always looks out for me, but he's never touched me before for more than a moment. I've used his forearm as a brace to help me get into and out of the canoe, but that's been it. His hand holding my arm is new. I'm excited by it. I've written him—but not sent—passionate (read pornographic) love letters graphically describing imagined encounters and my intense desire for him, but right now I can't even say thank you because of the lump in my throat.

I stop, turn away and look back at our houses—at *Booyul* on the hill and at *Gwongorella* farther down the slope. From here they look far apart, roofed silhouettes with lights shining in them, which blur and ripple because my eyes are full of tears.

'You're very upset, aren't you?' He puts an arm around my heaving shoulders. 'What's happened? Tell me.' He gently turns me to face him, his other arm across my back.

'My fa-father's a rat—he's not coming up here and … Mum … Mum spilt a hot drink down my front … and it hur … hurts!' I rest my forehead on his shoulder and sob.

'Ouch!' His voice is gentle, his arms warm around me, his cheek against my hair. 'And why isn't your father coming up here?'

'Be … because Mum's going to divorce him. Because he's got someone else, which is nothing new. He's *sick,* he's a *turd* and I *hate* him! I ne-never want to see him again!'

Shaun digs into his jeans pocket and gives me a man-sized handkerchief, which I take, grateful but embarrassed. 'I c-can't stop crying!'

'It's okay to cry. It's therapeutic. You'll feel better afterwards.'

'But I *can't* stop!' I blow and blow my nose, but it just keeps streaming like my eyes.

'Don't try. You'll stop when you're ready. Let's keep moving.' With his right arm across my shoulders, he propels me forward. We walk slowly, me mopping up while he talks. 'Something's happening between my parents too. Mum's asked Dad to make a change.' He kicks a pebble ahead of him. 'But he's not prepared to throw in his job. He reckons there are too many middle-aged executives on the scrap heap, and he can't risk leaving the bank only to find things don't work out financially. We've cost him a fortune in school and uni fees.' He kicks another pebble, more viciously this time. 'Truth is, he's not into farming or country life. He prefers wheeling and dealing on the stock market, but Mum reckons when the world's major economies collapse, Dad's job and his shares won't be worth a crumpet, and only people able to grow their own food will survive.'

I'm listening, between nose blows and hiccups. I've stopped crying, miraculously. It has never occurred to me Shaun and his family might have problems too.

'We've never been a united family. I don't know why they bothered to have us, really.'

'Ouch!' I say, echoing him, while I very bravely wrap my left arm around his waist.

He responds by squeezing my shoulder. 'This is my second year on *Booyul* with Mum. Sally was in boarding school for six years before she went to Med school. I hardly know her.'

'I'm the same! After my four years in boarding school, my brothers hardly know me!'

He sighs. 'I just get on with my own life.'

'You sound like you accept it.'

'The serenity prayer helps. You know it?'

'Nope.' I shake my head. I don't like religion.

'It's on a card in my wallet. I'll give it to you.'

'Thank you.' I'm thanking him for the gift more than the prayer. I'm acutely aware we have our arms around each other—the first time we've been this close. The muscles over his ribs ripple under my fingers. I imagine stopping and kissing him, but fear of rejection over-rides the impulse. Something, adrenaline probably, is surging in my belly.

'We're going to get soaked!' he exclaims. 'We'd better make a run for it!'

The sound of the irrigation sprinklers, on our right and just ahead, enters my consciousness. Over to our left I can hear the irrigation pump and squawks from masked lapwing plovers on the stubble of the fallow corn paddock. The track is now wet and muddy.

'My Reeboks will be ruined!'

'Come on!' He grabs my left hand from around his waist and we sprint along the track. I feel incredibly light, springing into take off as soon as one of my feet touches the earth. We are in sync, like in a three-legged race, hands clasped together, adjacent feet touching down at the same time, arms swinging back and forth in unison, supporting and balancing each other as we almost fly over the mud. But we can't beat the sprinklers! The ones behind are swinging around, the ones ahead chugging inexorably towards us, seeming to pick up speed to catch us. I can hear the waterfalls coming. I can smell the heavy billabong odour and feel the cold, wet breath of the wind. I'm laughing and shrieking, anticipating the shock of the first sprays before they hit us—*splat-splat-splat-splat!*

Shaun yanks me towards him, pulling me sideways onto the billabong track, beyond the reach of the spraying water pistols.

'Whoopee!' he yells. He lets go of my hand to flick his wet hair out of his eyes.

'Yahoo!' I respond. I reach out impulsively and give him a hug. He immediately wraps his arms around me—just as birds on the billabong call out in alarm. One anguished cry can be heard above the rest. Wings thrash the water as they take off into the moonlit sky.

'Bloody hell! Saab's killing a bird!' Shaun exclaims, letting me go. He begins whistling and calling.

Saab has certainly killed the moment!

'I'll wait here while you go and get him and turn the pump off.'

'Are you sure?'

'Of course! I'm not like Saab—I won't run away.'

I watch him melt into the semi-darkness, heading for the billabong. Skeletal ghostly white gums stand in the shallow water, their hollow limbs shelter for nesting kookaburras, magpies, parrots and cockatoos, the billabong itself a sanctuary for herons, darters, moorhens, ducks, jacanas and many other species.

Our first paddle was on the billabong. Floating out in the middle, we noticed jacana chicks balancing on the waterlily pads. When we drifted closer, the fathers tucked the chicks under their wings and minced far away from us, on ridiculously long-toed feet across the round, flat leaves, until they felt it was safe to put their chicks down again.

The moon is ragged and colourful through the water drops on my glasses. My right hearing aid, zapped by the sprinklers, is hissing ominously. My HAs are my link to the world. They regularly need servicing or repairs by AHS—Australian Hearing Services. They are robust, but also delicate and touchy. I take the hissing HA out of my ear, release the battery and put it in my very damp skirt pocket. I'm relieved the left-side one is still working.

I gaze across the expanse of paddock towards the vegetable patch, where a white mist hovers between the still warm, wet earth and the now cold air. Chilled by the light wind, feeling isolated and vulnerable, I strain to hear Shaun's voice and the crunch of his boots on the stubble, but the *chug-chug-chug* of the motor running the pump and the *ch-ch-ch-ch* of the irrigation sprays overpower every other sound apart from the plaintive cries of water birds overhead.

The pump stops. The sprays die down. For a moment there is an illusion of silence. I cup my hands around both ears. Now I can hear the crickets under my feet scraping and chirruping. The wind whistles past my functioning hearing aid. A few frogs around the billabong and down by the creek burble and converse. A lone mosquito whines around my head trying to find an uncontaminated spot to land. I slap it into silence. Birds' wings *whirr-whoosh* overhead with urgent, rapid beats.

I gaze at the moon, rugged and shadowy, craters pocking its surface. It is higher now, but still huge and brilliant, reflecting the sun's light onto the dark face of Earth, onto my face, onto the billabong in a long shaft like polished antique silver, the still, black water reflecting the old, haggard face of the moon itself.

Shaun walks me home, his arm around my shoulders to keep me warm because I'm wet and cold. Something has shifted between us. Something good. He hugs me at the gate and his lips brush my cheek as he steps back and announces he's returning to the billabong with a torch to look for Saab. I watch his dark form retreating up the slope to *Booyul*.

I'm shivering. I take a deep breath, open the screen door, then the back door, slip into the laundry, turn and close the doors quietly, stand and listen. Music drifts faintly from the boys' room. Mum must be in her room or on the computer in the den. The kitchen is in darkness.

I sneak into the bathroom, which is off the laundry and behind the kitchen, and lock the door. First, I remove my glasses, left hearing aid and watch—it's just after ten—and rescue the right hearing aid from my skirt pocket. Then I sit on the edge of the bath and take off my Reeboks and socks. I pull the shower curtain around me, turn the shower on, knowing the sound of the pump kicking in will betray my presence, and undress. I wash everything, the mud sliding in sudsy swirls down the plug hole.

No one knocks on the door, or yells through the keyhole demanding to use the loo, or shouts at me to hurry up and stop wasting water. I wash and condition my hair. The steamy warmth is soothing, though my belly stings whenever the hot water strikes the red streak where the Milo spilt on me. It feels like bad sunburn.

I attack my Reeboks with the nail brush and soap, but they don't look new anymore. Finally, I scrub the bath like I've committed a murder and don't want to leave a single clue. I leave my Reeboks heel-side down on the windowsill against the fly-wire to drain.

Dd…d d dd…dd dd. That's Mum's knock.

'What?' I quickly put my left HA in my still damp ear.

'Do you want your dressing gown?'

I don't want her looking in my wardrobe!

'Because I've got it here if you want it.'

Shit! Too late. I unlock and open the door a crack. 'Thanks.' I take it and close and lock the door again without looking at her. I should be grateful—I've nothing else to put on.

'Would you like a cup of tea?' she asks, through the door.

I don't trust her when she's playing at being nice. At least I know how she *really* feels when she's screaming mad. This is her let's-sit-down-and-talk-reasonably-about-this tactic, and it makes me nervous. She'll ask too many questions; I'll feel I'm being interrogated. She'll try to intuit my thoughts and feelings, but she doesn't know everything, not by a long shot. Still, a hot drink sounds good.

'Okay. Thank you.'

'I'll put the jug on.'

I dry my hair with the hair dryer. Wrapped in my dressing gown, I emerge from the steam and drop my clothes into the washing machine—it's my turn to do the wash tomorrow. I prop my Reeboks on the shoe rack by the back door.

The bare floorboards in the kitchen are cold underfoot. The kitchen looks drab in the harsh light of the exposed globe in the middle of the red cedar ceiling. The wall of whitewashed bricks is the colour of nicotine, probably stained from years of smoke from the slow-combustion stove that nowadays gathers dust, newspapers, egg cartons and junk mail on its top while we use the electric jug, microwave, electric stove and oven Mum had installed. The other walls have a visible film of dust and grease. The floorboards are painted brown, the paint worn off by the constant traffic of those who lived here before us.

Mum's shown minimal interest in the house; her studio is her retreat. She wasted no time getting *that* fixed up into a home-away-from-home.

She was so busy with her artwork she forgot my fifteenth birthday on Sunday, fifteenth of January. The day before, she went to town without inviting me, and I presumed she'd gone in to buy me a present, but she came back with a whole lot of painting and drawing gear—for herself! It wasn't until a birthday card came in Monday's mail from *her* mother in New Zealand, which Mum opened 'by mistake' even though the envelope was addressed to me, that her memory was jolted.

'Don't give it a thought!' I told her sarcastically. 'I haven't had a birthday in years!' My stomach suddenly feels like someone's tied a knot in it. 'Where's Faigan?'

'I haven't seen him.' Mum glances around the walls and up at the ceiling.

Total pain smothers me in an instant. 'They've fed him to the snakes!' I rush towards my brothers' room and fling their door open. 'Where's Faigan!' I screech, barely controlling an impulse to rip the lids off their snake cages and smash every reptile against the walls.

'Chill out, idiot!' Dan yelps, plectrum poised, looking extremely alarmed.

Billy, lying on his back reading *Riptide*, bounces upright and reaches over to the tape recorder to press the Off button—Dan must have been recording. My voice will certainly add a surprise element!

'Haven't touched him, Jode!' Billy opens his palms towards me, fingers upright. 'He's probably gone lady-hunting.'

I stare at him, wanting to believe the soothing tones of his voice.

'Fair dinkum, sis! Don't worry. Really.'

Dan is staring at me, mute and wide-eyed. I withdraw, close the door quietly, rest my forehead on the red cedar panels. 'If you are lying to me, I'll kill every snake you own!' After a few seconds of silence, Dan starts plucking his guitar strings again. The notes sound plaintive.

I brush past Mum hovering in her bedroom doorway opposite, stalk past the piano in the living room, and head towards the dining room and kitchen.

She follows me. 'I did the dishes with them after you took off, and then they went to their room. I'm sure they wouldn't do that to Faigan!'

'Don't bet on it!'

She sighs and shakes her head. 'Bring our tea.'

Talkie-time.

I want to lie on my own bed, in my own room, door closed, curtains and windows open to the moon and the night sky, relive my walk to the billabong and back home again with Shaun; relive the experience of his warm, strong arms around me and embellish the way he responded to my hug. And imagine what might have happened—if Saab hadn't caused mayhem. Butterflies in my belly take flight again.

'Jodie? Did you hear me?'

'*Yes!* I *heard* you!'

I carry our mugs of tea into her room. It's on the south-east corner of the house opposite the boys' room. One window opens onto the east veranda, the other overlooks the south paddock with its stands of huge old eucalypts. Mum is already on her bed. She looks like an invalid under the doona, propped up on pillows. I place her mug on her bedside table.

'Shut the door,' she says.

I do so while she turns down the doona on the vacant side and pats the pillows. I put my mug of tea on the bedside table on my side and climb up next to her. She adjusts the doona over my legs. There have been occasions when I've enjoyed curling up with her like this, listening to happy stories about her childhood, but tonight I feel apprehensive and resentful.

We sip our tea in silence, until she puts her mug down and clasps her hands.

'Jodie … you said something tonight … about—about Hugh. I didn't know how to take it … what you meant … I've had the most terrible thoughts … that maybe you were trying to tell me something?' Her eyes are dark and dilated as she stares into mine.

'I don't know what you're talking about!' I snap. 'I don't remember *what* I said!'

Now her eyes glisten with tears and she looks away and down. I keep sipping my tea—it's the safest thing to do—but it's hard to swallow because the lump is back in my throat.

She asks my reflection in the wardrobe mirror, 'Has Hugh ever molested you?'

Tell her!

I *can't*! Tell her *what*? A prickly, hot, cold, creepy-crawly, goose-bumpy sensation runs up the back of my arms and neck and all over my scalp. I shudder so hard I almost spill my tea.

I shake my head. Part of me means no, but part of me doesn't know, because another part of me *feels* molested, feels violated and disgusted and appalled and sickened and enraged and ashamed, all mixed together, and my feelings are so confused and painful I don't want to think, or feel, or talk about any of it. I just want something sweet to eat, milk chocolate to drink. The tea tastes thin and bitter and offers no comfort at all.

'Are you sure?' Mum asks, ready to be relieved.

I've lost my voice. How can I tell her I *feel* molested, when I can't remember *being* molested? *How* molested? How can I tell her 'the truth' when I don't know what the truth is?

I lean over and kiss her cheek and whisper, 'I think I'll go to bed now.'

'I do love you, daughter. I just don't know how to handle you sometimes. I wish we could be friends. All I want is a peaceful life.'

I whisper, 'I know, Mum.' I still have no voice. 'I'll try. I love you too.' Sliding off the bed I escape with my mug of tea to my room.

Why do I feel like a traitor?

In bed, naked as usual, I quell painful, frightening thoughts by thinking about Shaun. I transport myself to the bank of the creek and imagine lying with him in the soft grass that grows there. And I dream-happen what might have happened if Saab hadn't killed a bird, while I stroke and caress myself, feeling both comforted and aroused. It will happen! It's started happening already. Sure, I'm only just fifteen and he is twenty-seven—but so what!

Chapter Three

Saturday, 18 March 1995

'Jodie—telephone!' Dan yells at me from the back door.

I didn't hear the phone ring. I'm sceptical, but I throw the towel I was about to peg onto the clothesline back on top of the basket of washing and hurry inside.

'Who is it?'

Dan's got a weirdo look on his face—a smirk, eyebrows raised, face framed by budding dreadlocks.

'Is it Dad?' I whisper. I don't want to, won't, talk to him if it is.

Dan shakes his head. I take the phone and wait for him to move away. He doesn't. I put my hand over the mouthpiece and hiss at him. 'Piss! Off!' He unglues himself from the wall and saunters towards the kitchen. 'Hello?' I say into the phone.

'Hi! I thought I'd ring and see if you caught pneumonia last night.'

Grinning, I take the telephone into my room and close the door.

'I've never felt healthier!'

'Any awkward questions?'

'No. At least … not really. Nothing I couldn't handle. Thanks for ringing.'

'That's okay.'

'Did you find Saab?'

'Not yet. I guess he'll come home when he's hungry.' He clears his throat. 'There's a top movie on at the *Saraton* tonight. *Gaia Strikes Back*. Mum wants to see it and I'm wondering if any of you guys would be interested? Hole in the ozone layer, global warming and all that.'

I'm so unsophisticated. I haven't heard of it at all. 'It must be good if you are recommending it! Do you mean—*all* of us? *Any* of us?'

'Yeah, anyone who is interested.'

'Did you ask Dan?'

'No, I thought I'd ask you first.'

He's asking me out!

'Um … how about I check with everyone and get back to you?'

'How about if I wander down—I've nearly finished my chores—and say hello? If no one else wants to go your end, you could still come with us.'

'Yeah, I could! See you soon then. For coffee?'

'For sure!' he says. 'Bye.'

'Bye,' I echo, and hang up. He could've asked Dan, but he didn't! He asked *me*!

I replace the telephone on the hall table and head back out to the clothesline. Dan is still in the kitchen, eating a chunk of my sultana cake.

'What did Shaun want?'

'Leave some cake for Mum!'

He points a sticky finger at me. '"Leave some for *me!*" you mean! By the way—' He points with the same sticky finger at Faigan in his usual corner near the ceiling.

I barely glance up before continuing to the screen door. 'I know. I checked first thing.'

'What did Shaun want with *you?*' he persists, following me.

I feel needled, but don't react. 'He's … he wants to see *Gaia Strikes Back.'*

'Good one! I've been wanting to see that.'

'We could make a family night of it. We could *all* go.'

'Yeah?' He's studying me. 'Are you being sarcastic?'

'No.'

'You're only asking me 'cos you want a lift in the old jalopy!'

I shake my head. 'Thanks for the offer, but I'm going with Shaun and Wendy. He's coming down for coffee soon. Discuss it with him. And don't eat any more cake!' I close the screen door in his face and float down the steps.

Next minute, Billy appears from around the east side of the house and starts helping me peg out socks! They're both being unusually friendly. Maybe Mum asked them to lay off after I disappeared last night. Maybe she told them about Father-dearest and they understand my feelings better. Maybe it was my threat to kill all their snakes. I have no idea, but I'll make the best of it and be pleasant back. It won't last long.

'What's the story? Did Shaun ask you out or something?' His nose is crooked front on, from dropping a barbell on it one time, and his spiky, sun-bleached hair looks like he's cut it without a mirror, but he's still good-looking.

'No! Not me—*us*! Okay?'

Mellow out!

'Thanks for helping me hang out the clothes.'

'We could *all* go,' he says. 'It's supposed to be deadly!'

My brothers are talking to me; they are being civil. They're willing to go somewhere with me; they're willing to be *seen* with me. According to Murphy's Law, if anything can go wrong, it will, and if everything seems to be going right, it means something has been overlooked. I'll need to get around Mum—and there's the question of money.

'Thanks, bro, that was quick.' I give Billy a genuine smile, pick up the empty washing basket and peg bucket and hurry inside before he can spoil the moment.

In my room, door closed, I rip off my grungy trackies and chuck them out of sight on the bottom of my wardrobe. I should have put them in the wash too. It's been a while since I've really looked at myself in the full-length mirror on the wardrobe door. Looking now, I hate the sight of myself—and I hate *myself* for letting me get this way. I locate my one-size-fits-all floral cotton shirt and my black stretch-cotton pants. My legs from the ankles up look okay till you get to my thighs and the shirt hides that part of my anatomy, but I still *feel* yucky.

Why do you always put yourself down?

I shrug at Anne, turn away from her. I don't know why I do it—criticise my appearance, my intelligence, my lack of knowledge, how poorly I do things—it's bad enough with the boys and Mum picking on me, without *me* adding to it. If I demean myself in front of Shaun, he just says, 'You look okay,' or 'You're doing okay,' and changes the subject.

Unconvinced, I look back at Anne in the mirror with a despairing expression.

Shaun likes you just the way you are, so stop worrying!

Anne—my reflection, my secret friend, my middle name, my inner better self—gazes back at me. She's kinder to me than I am. I need to believe her because I've run out of time. Cleo and Patra are barking a greeting, so maybe their playmate Saab is back! Shaun passes below my window, whistling. He flip-flops up the stairs onto the veranda where Dan and Billy are playing their guitars and singing Neil Young's 'Harvest Moon'.

I hurry into the kitchen to make 'real' coffee, Mocha Kilimanjaro blend. I spoon coffee grounds into two glass carafes and relive last night's conversation with Shaun on the way home.

You're so kind and understanding, Shaun. I'm so glad you're my friend.

Yeah, I was very lonely before you came along. I really do enjoy your company.

I slice up the last of the sultana cake on a plate and put five mugs on the tray.

You make maths fun; it's so much easier to understand when you explain it!

And you help me with written expression.

I fill a jug with milk, place it on the tray with a bowl of sugar and some teaspoons.

You help me with everything, Shaun. I'll miss you so much when you go away to uni.

That's a long way off! Let's make the most of NOW while we BOTH decide our futures!

I shiver, remembering how scared I felt when I heard him say, *My mother is feeling bad she hasn't introduced herself to your mother. She wants to do something about it.*

What has he told her about us? Will she blab to Mum? The jug comes to the boil.

My time with you is still a secret, Shaun—Mum will freak if she finds out!

I fill the carafes and replace the plungers and lids.

It's better to be open and truthful than secretive and having to lie.

Only if you're a twenty-seven-year-old male. It doesn't work for fifteen-year-old girls. Your mum might be tolerant, because you're her adult son, but mine will be a wet blanket because I'm her teenage daughter.

When Dan stays at Melanie's house, there's no way her parents allow him to sleep with her in her room—it's on the couch for him—Melanie's told me. That's why she prefers sleeping over at our place. Mum turns a blind eye because Melanie's not *her* daughter; she shuts her own bedroom door and Melanie's out of sight, out of mind.

I'm just not comfortable, Jodie, sneaking around behind your mother's back.

I can't tell him *I* get pleasure and satisfaction from the fact our relationship is a secret and I enjoy the excitement, risk and danger involved in maintaining it. I'm excited he's arranging this two-family outing, but I'm anxious and angry too. If Mum finds out I've been seeing him on the sly, she'll forbid me to spend time with him, and if I defy her, she could become *really* mean, convinced she's protecting me.

I call her through the kitchen window—she's in the studio. 'Coffee's ready, Mum!'

I take a couple of deep breaths to compose myself, then carry the tray out to the veranda. I acknowledge Shaun with a smile before placing the tray carefully on the tile and wrought-iron coffee table. Because of a defect in my eyesight, I frequently misjudge the position or distance of surfaces or objects, and put things down with a crash, or knock things over when I reach for them, because the surface of the table or the position of the object is closer than my eyes perceive it to be.

'Holy shit you're clumsy, Jodie!' I hear it all the time.

I sink back onto one of the single chairs.

Mum arrives, greets Shaun and chats with him as she pours the coffee. She's used to him turning up occasionally on weekends, or after the boys come home from school. Up till now he's maintained the charade, greeting me along with the boys like it's the first time we've seen each other since his last visit.

Now it's going to bust open.

He leans forward on his stool and asks me how many sugars I take.

'None!' says Dan. Shaun smiles at me, teaspoon poised over the sugar bowl.

'One-and-a-bit, thanks.'

'Just give her the bit!' commands Billy.

Shaun gives me one-and-a-bit, adds milk, stirs it, and hands me the mug.

'Thank you.'

He fixes his own mug, picks up a slice of cake and rests his back against the cast-iron railing, looking his usual, relaxed, long-legged self. I grin at him from inside my mug. The hot coffee steams up my glasses.

'Great brew!' he says. Then, 'Great cake!' He glances at me frequently as he talks with Mum and the boys. He's a turn on! Butterflies flutter, low down.

It's all arranged. Everyone's going to *Gaia Strikes Back*. Shaun asks me, in front of Mum, if I'd like to go in their car and I say, 'Sure!'

Mum starts to say something, hesitates, then says it will be nice to meet his mother and she's sorry she hasn't made herself known before this. Then she excuses herself saying she'd better get back to the studio.

Dan plucks at his guitar strings, wrestling with a melody— he's either composing something or it's an obscure song he's trying to recall. Billy asks Shaun for some help with his maths homework. Shaun agrees and Billy fetches his Adidas bag. Rummaging through it, he claps a hand to his head. 'Hey, man, I forgot! I have a letter for you!'

'Who from?'

'Emma-Sue. She's in most of my classes. She's one of the Joint Secondary School/TAFE students doing horticulture through TAFE and the rest of her subjects at school. She was in the group that came out to see your set-up. She's *very* impressed with your farming techniques ... among other things!' He's smirking at Shaun. 'How did you wrangle that? Bit young for you, aren't they?'

'One of my casual pickers is a high school student and he suggested to his Ag teacher that he bring his class out to *Booyul* to observe chemical-free horticulture at work, and when his teacher came to do a reconnaissance, he was so impressed he invited the TAFE horticulture teacher to bring her students out too. They helped me pick the last of the beans!'

I'm reliving the envy and jealousy I felt watching him through Mum's binoculars as he interacted with the students. Now a girl is writing to him! The same sharp pang is in my gut all over again.

'What's the difference between agriculture and horticulture?' Dan asks.

'Agriculture is the big, monoculture stuff like crop-raising, stock-raising, plantation forestry. Horticulture is the cultivation of vegetables, nuts, fruits, including berries and grapes, and flowers—usually for commercial purposes.' He's watching Billy scrabbling around in his bag. 'Can't you find it?'

'Patience, man!' Billy withdraws the letter from the depths with such a flourish it spins through the air. Shaun leaps up and catches it before it flies over the railing.

'Golly gosh! You *are* hungry for news!' Dan teases.

'For a woman, you mean,' Billy declares.

'Oh, shut up!' Shaun says mildly, blushing under his tan. 'I'm just curious, that's all.' He winks at me, maybe to reassure me, but watching his hands with their long, sinewy fingers opening the complicated folds of the note paper, I don't feel remotely reassured.

He leans back against the railing and reads, his face inscrutable. Billy tidies his maths folder. Dan plays a few bars, then jots down the notes in his music book. I don't know how Shaun can concentrate with my eyes boring into him.

I watch him attempt to re-fold the letter—the folds are intricate—and blurt out before I can stop myself, 'Can I read it?'

'Jodie!' Dan stops playing mid-bar.

'No, you can't!' Billy exclaims.

Shaun passes me the letter. It's dated Wednesday, 15 March 1995, Mum's thirty-ninth birthday. While she was in town, celebrating—or commiserating—with her TAFE friends over lunch, I was watching Shaun through the binoculars playing Mr Supercool with all those students, instead of taking me for our usual paddle up the creek to our secret island for our picnic lunch and my maths lesson. He must have given Emma-Sue *some* encouragement, for her to write to him. I *hate* her!

I read the letter and try to listen to their conversation at the same time.

Dear Shaun,

I'm writing straight away to thank you for today. Picking beans is heaps better than sitting in a classroom. What a life! I'd rather work outside any day.

'What does she look like?' Shaun asks.

'Nice,' Billy responds, leaning back on the sofa, hands clasped behind his head. '*Very* nice. I've thought of hittin' on her m'self.'

Thanks for showing us how to grow vegetables without using pesticides and inorganic fertilisers. Now I understand what companion planting means. I've tried to grow lettuces and tomatoes and other stuff at my auntie's place, but the bugs and wallabies eat them!

'Great tan!' Billy adds.

'That's 'cos she's original,' Dan says.

'Ah, okay,' Shaun replies, nodding.

I constantly have trouble following the boys' conversations. They talk too fast, mumble and interrupt each other, and if I ask them to slow down, or look at me, or talk a bit louder, or repeat something, they get impatient and ignore me. I still ask though.

'She's original?'

'You could say that,' Shaun responds, smiling at me. '*Aboriginal*.'

'Aboriginal? Really?'

'Yes,' Billy says, slowly and clearly. 'Really and truly.'

One of my OTEN subjects is *Aboriginal Studies—Contemporary Issues*, but the closest I've been to Aboriginal people in real life is in Shopping World, where they do their shopping and go about their business same as everybody else. When I've walked past Market Square, I've surreptitiously watched them sitting at tables on benches under shady trees. Little kids romp on the grass, and eat and drink, and splash and play under the taps. I'd *love* to know her … if I didn't hate her!

'Time I wasn't here,' Shaun says. 'I'd better go and see if Saab's come home.'

'Saab? Where's he gone?' Dan asks.

'Good question. He took off last night and hasn't come back.'

'That's a worry,' Billy says.

'Yeah.' Shaun looks at me. 'Come up just before seven.'

I hold the letter out to him.

'Keep it.'

A sick feeling invades my stomach. 'You *are* going to reply, aren't you?'

He shrugs, hesitates. 'No, I don't think so. I mean, no, I won't reply.'

'Why not?' A witch's brew of feelings is bubbling inside me. I should be pleased, but I'm not; I'm feeling what Emma-Sue would surely feel if she was me, rejected and discarded! I feel intensely and unexpectedly sad—a hollow, empty feeling—for *her!*

'What's it to you?' he says, his voice higher and louder than usual.

Males are hopeless. They have no idea how devastating it feels to be ignored. I hold the letter out to him. 'It's a lovely letter! She's written to you. She saw you, and admired what you were doing, and liked you enough to write to you and you're not going to reply to her?'

He's not looking at the letter, he's watching my eyes filling up. I'm thinking of the secret shoebox hidden in the bottom of my wardrobe, full of the love letters I've written to him, expressing my most vulnerable feelings, my secret erotic dreams and fantasies about him. Imagine if I sent one of those precious letters to him and he let someone else read it and then discarded it!

He's shaking his head. 'I don't even know her.'

'So? You could *get* to know her!'

'Lay off, Jodie,' Dan warns.

'Why don't *you* write to her?' Billy suggests.

'I *will!*'

Shaun walks along the veranda, his hands in his pockets, his usually straight shoulders hunched. He pauses to knock some sugar ants off the top tread with the tip of his thong, then walks slowly down the steps, returning along the outside edge of the veranda until he's level with me. He watches me through the old, ornate cast-iron railings, curlicues of peeling, once-white paint edging his face. I read his lips, 'Can we talk about it?'

It's hard to look at him, but I nod.

'See you tonight,' he says and mooches off.

'You can't make him do something he doesn't want to do,' Dan chastises me. 'Learn to mind your own business instead of trying to organise everybody!'

'Why *don't* you write to her?' Billy says. 'You need friends. Here's your chance.'

It's true. I do need friends. Shaun's a fantastic friend, but I'm totally dependent on him.

I need a *girl*friend. And an Aboriginal girlfriend would be perfect. But do I want a girlfriend who's crazy about Shaun?

'Oh, shit!' Billy exclaims crossly.

'What?' Dan asks.

'Shaun was going to help me with my maths. It's all your fault, Jodie!'

I could start a fight, but I've got more on my mind than I can cope with.

'I'm sorry, bro. Maybe he'll help you later this afternoon … or tomorrow. Remind him tonight. He's—I'm sure he'd be— very clever at maths.'

My bedroom door is closed, guarded by the *Do Not Disturb* sign on the brass doorknob. I sit at my desk with Emma-Sue's letter and try to enter her mind-space. It's a simple, open, honest, straightforward letter, in strong, clear writing. She likes Shaun and wants to know him better. The telephone numbers of 'Auntie I' and 'Nan and Pop' are with the date at the top of the letter. Maybe her parents don't have the phone on. Or she lives with 'Nan and Pop' or 'Auntie I'.

A *girlfriend!* Imagine all the things we could do together! But what if she's more interested in Shaun than in me—driving the tractor; walking alongside him while I'm on the other side of him unable to hear their conversations; her in the canoe, in *my* seat, paddling up the creek with him into the shadowy upper reaches, leaving me behind on the bank; two's company, three's a crowd.

Imagine meeting her in town, sitting with her under the trees at Market Square, meeting *her* friends, *her* family. But maybe they won't like me! I'd be on *their* territory, so maybe they'd resent me gate-crashing. She could visit me here—even stay sometimes—and I could visit or stay with her, like girlfriends do. But it's all wishful thinking.

Billy tells me, *'Get a life!'* But how? I'm so trapped out here, so isolated. It suits Mum. She feels safe thinking I can't get into trouble, that she can control me, save me from myself and the big bad world. But I need to get out and about like everyone else and handle myself. I *need* a life! And Emma-Sue represents a life I know nothing about. I so want to know her, but what if she rejects *me* the same way Shaun rejected *her?*

I can't sit still with these thoughts and emotions tumbling around inside me. I push my chair back and tidy up a bit, then sit on the stool at my dressing table.

'I've gotta *do* something about myself, before I can meet her,' I tell Anne in the mirror.

A girl with a pointy chin and a serious expression looks back at me. Her hair is pretty, falling past her shoulders in pale, honey-coloured waves. I scoop it up high on her head. Now she looks more mature. She has neat ears, but I can see her left-side hearing aid—the other one is dead after last night's episode with the sprinklers.

So what? What's wrong with seeing your hearing aids?

I don't share Anne's confidence. Maybe I can pull the hair around my ears more and hide my HA and still put my hair up. I fiddle around, chattering to Anne in a whisper and asking her opinion while I try to get it right.

I have a shoebox, shoeboxes come in handy, half-full of hair clips, ponytail holders, combs, headbands, wispy scarves and ribbons. I can't remember which items Mum bought for me at the Alumy Creek Reserve market and which ones I nicked from Suzie's Bazaar.

I shoplift when I go to town with Mum. She lets me 'do my own thing' because I have no money and she thinks I won't be able to binge, but more than once I've knocked off lollies and nuts from the Woolworths serve-yourself bulk foods section; one time I pinched a lamington roll from the rack outside Hank's Kitchen and ate the whole thing sitting on a park bench under a tree. Mostly, I shoplift items of clothing, or make-up, or hair stuff, or books, and hide the loot from Mum and the boys in my backpack before we meet up.

Anne feels bad about my thieving. When I arrive home from a shoplifting expedition, she confronts me in the mirror.

What are you angry about? Who are you trying to hurt? Who's going to be punished when you get caught? Who are you trying to shame?

The thrill of being daring and taking risks fades away, and I become depressed and scared instead. I hang the stolen items between my legitimate clothes in my wardrobe or hide them under other items in my chest of drawers. I put the stolen earrings with my other trinkets, and the make-up with other tubes and jars, with Anne's voice in my head saying *NO MORE!*

The Anne part of me doesn't want me to steal, for moral and ethical reasons and because the shit will hit the fan if, when—I get caught. The Jodie part of me, especially when I'm feeling pissed off, acts as if I *want* to be caught. I behave suspiciously sometimes just to give proprietors, sales assistants and store detectives something to do! The clothes I steal aren't even my size! They're not an incentive to lose weight so I *can* wear them one day, because once I'm home, excitement over, I hide them. I don't know what Mum would do if she knew. Maybe she does have her suspicions but chooses to turn a blind eye for the sake of peace, like she tends to do with everything else. I'm certain, if Shaun knew, he'd wipe me.

Anne eyeballs me in the mirror.

No more stealing. No more bingeing. No more lying.

I hurt Anne when I do stupid, destructive things. Tears glisten in her eyes. The lump is back in my throat again, and I try to swallow it down. We both stand up, sharing the shame. She turns away the same instant I do, and we retreat from each other.

I head straight for the kitchen, hungry for something. I peer inside the refrigerator. No 'goodies' in sight; nothing but fresh, healthy food. Just what I need for my reformed self.

Start now.

I put some eggs on the stove to hard boil and create a salad—lettuce, tomato, cucumber, capsicum, a few gherkins and black olives thrown in and slices of avocado on top—garnished with sweet basil, parsley and mint from Mum's herb garden by the tank stand. I lay the table and place a bowl of nasturtiums in the middle, then arrange the various items on either side: the salad bowl, crusty bread, butter, ham slices, hard-boiled eggs on a bed of lettuce, cheese and grapes. It's a feast. We've always got plenty of good food to eat; Dad transfers money from the business into Mum's bank account every month—I've peeked at her bank statements—but will he keep it up or be obstructive when she tells him she wants a divorce?

'Lunch is ready!' I call out.

Dan is the first to come wandering through. 'Wow!' he says, surveying the table. 'Expecting visitors?' He looks at me and whistles, 'Your hair looks nice.' A wave of pleasure surges through me—until he adds, 'But I like it better down.'

I retreat to the west veranda just as Mum appears at the studio door. 'Did I hear lunch?' Her crumpled smock has its own abstract design in paint, oil-stains, brush-streaks and charcoal finger-marks. 'Very elegant,' she says, looking at me appraisingly. 'Going somewhere?'

Unsure how to respond, I just shrug, but my heart lurches as Anne gives me a warning.

She knows more than you give her credit for.

Mum's studio is insulated and air-conditioned, so it's no wonder she practically lives in it. It has special lights, a sink, vertical mesh racks to hang her paintings on and wide shelves to hold her drawings. She works with 'mixed media': acrylics, oils, watercolours, ink-wash, charcoal, pencils, crayons and pastels. Even lipstick, nail polish, boot polish, wet tea bags, coffee grounds and beetroot have come in handy! I think her drawings and paintings are fantastic.

I enjoy watching her work. She tries to encourage me to have a go, but I resist doing anything in front of her, even though she says there's no such thing as a 'mistake' and it is fun whatever the outcome. I *have* done some drawings, using the sketchbook, coloured pencils and pastels she gave me to make up for forgetting my birthday, but I haven't shown them to her.

She's bent over a thin sheet of paper, moving a soft, dark pencil back and forth with rapid, even movements. Under the paper is a flat piece of wood and through the paper, through the graphite, the grain and nobbles in the wood are revealing themselves. She's filling in the larger-than-life, outlined face of a doll she's sketched. The eye-sockets are empty and it's beginning to look like a mask—an eyeless, wooden mask.

'That looks terrific,' I tell her. 'Spooky, but terrific.'

'You think so? Yes … it does look kind of interesting.'

The bench tops are cluttered with jars and tubes and wide-necked containers full of brushes. Flat tins and trays are filled with pencils, pastels, crayons and charcoal. Flat ceramic bowls and plates she's made at TAFE hold found objects she's picked up at the beach and on our walks along the lane.

On top of it all lies a baby-sized doll.

'Hey!' I pick up the doll. 'She's mine!' She's smaller than I remember.

'What's her name?'

I shrug. Shake my head. 'I dunno. I've forgotten. Where's she been all this time?'

'Packed away. I found her in a box in the shed. What *can* you remember?'

'I don't know!' I *could* remember—if I let myself. I lean on the bench and cover my eyes. Suddenly, I see my small-child self, pushing the doll in a doll-sized stroller across a patio towards a swimming pool. 'Oh no!' I uncover my eyes and look at Mum. 'I've tipped her into Poppy and Nan's swimming pool!'

'You did too! Dad had to jump in and rescue her.'

'Dad?' Now I feel dark and wary, ready to lose interest in the conversation.

'*My* dad. Your grandfather. Poppy.' She sighs. 'That was the summer he died.'

'Really? What from?'

'A cerebral aneurism, soon after your third birthday. Do you remember him?'

I clutch my baby doll, her blonde hair tizzy and matted, eyelashes missing, eyes staring, refusing to close though I'm laying her back. *She* looks dead. Drowned, to be precise.

'I remember Poppy holding me; his bushy eyebrows and white hair.' I'm feeling, twelve years later, a sense of loss, one of the nameless pains beneath my surface.

'You *do* remember him!'

'I missed him. One day he was there, then I never saw him again.'

'You were too young to understand.'

'No I wasn't! I didn't understand because nobody *told* me!'

'I'm so sorry.' Mum reaches out and takes hold of my hands and squeezes them, then lets them go to pull some tissues out of the box on the bench and pass them to me. 'He was a *wonderful* father and grandfather—a kind, gentle, honourable man. He loved my mother so much! He was romantic and affectionate towards her literally until the day he died. All I ever wanted was to marry a man like my father!' She gives me a wry, rueful smile as we both wipe our eyes. 'It was such a shock, him dying, no warning whatsoever. He was only sixty. I didn't handle it very well at all.' She sighs, gazing at the eyeless mask as if looking into the past.

'What are you going to do with that now?'

She sighs again as she re-focuses on the image she has created.

'I'm not sure where I'm going with it.'

I watch her work for a while, each of us silent in our own space, thinking our own thoughts, until she says, 'Don't forget to bring in the washing, Jodie.'

I follow Shaun as he weaves his way through the crowded foyer to join the queue at the *Saraton* box office. Billy grabs me from behind, and I swing around to whack him, but he fends me off.

'Don't look now,' he mouths at me, 'but Emma-Sue is on the stairs. The tall one.'

Of course, I look—and see her watching Shaun. She *is* tall. Slim, almost bony. Straight-backed and elegant looking. Her black hair is piled on top of her head, revealing dangly earrings, and she has bangles on her arms and rings on her fingers. The sleeves of her plain cotton top are pushed up her forearms. A colourful wrap-around skirt reaches mid-calf.

'Introduce me!' I beg Billy, but he shoves past me to join the queue in front of Shaun. I nudge Shaun's arm. 'Emma-Sue is on the stairs. When we get our tickets, can we go and say hullo and you can thank her for her letter and introduce me?'

He barely glances at her as he stuffs a twenty-dollar note into my hand. 'Buy our tickets, and I'll go get us some popcorn.'

So much for that idea! I dare myself to talk to her after I've bought the tickets. I surreptitiously check her out again. She would've seen me talking to Shaun, my hand on his arm. She probably saw him glance at her and give me the money before he moved away.

I lip-read the girl beside her, *'She's looking at you.'* I quickly lower my eyes, feeling stupid and shy. Maybe Emma-Sue is feeling the same way, especially with Shaun making no effort to acknowledge her.

After I've bought our tickets with Shaun's money—the ten-dollar note Mum gave me for my ticket now burning a hole in my pocket—I glance again in Emma-Sue's direction, but she's gone, probably downstairs to sit in the stalls where the high school kids usually sit. Billy has disappeared; he's probably sitting downstairs with the girls, maybe with Emma-Sue!

While I wait for Shaun, Melanie and Dan join me. I should've guessed Dan would ask her. She looks stunning as usual, her long, straight brown hair hanging down her back. She's wearing a white cotton-knit top under a black leather jacket and her matching leather miniskirt and high-heeled sandals show off her perfect legs. I'm wearing what I had on this morning, with my flat *Lois Lane* sandals.

'I love your hair up!' she exclaims. 'I can't do a thing with mine it's so straight and slippery.' Unfortunately, she reeks of smoke, and I'll probably be sitting next to her upstairs. Just as well I brought my Ventolin. When Melanie has a spliff or a cigarette on the east veranda I'm forced to close my bedroom windows because the smoke drifts in and makes me wheezy. I asked her once if it affected her voice, but she just shrugged and said, 'Maybe.'

Shaun joins us and we go upstairs. I make sure he's sitting on the end, on my left, so I won't be saying 'Pardon?' to him all the time. I also want to sit as far away as possible from Mum and Wendy, who are already in their seats, so I ask Dan and Melanie to sit between us and them, pissing Dan off no end—he hates me organising him. Mum and Wendy seem to have hit it off right away; they've been talking non-stop.

I don't know how much Shaun's told his mother about us. I want our time together to remain a secret, but him saying he prefers our friendship to be open and up-front has shattered that hope. Maybe *nothing* will be secret after this. Being with him in front of everybody feels a lot different than being alone with him paddling the canoe and doing maths on our secret island up the creek. I try to act like there's nothing significant between us. Dan, usually cool and detached, is holding Melanie's hand. Shaun isn't holding my hand—he's holding the popcorn—but he is resting his hand on my leg near my knee so I can get at the popcorn.

The movie starts. The *Saraton* acoustics are terrible, for me anyway, especially with only one HA. I'm having trouble deciphering the commentary, but I'm getting the gist of the story from the action. *Gaia*, the Greek goddess of Earth, mother of all life, has had enough.

The cinematography is brilliant, but the film's message about the many crises facing Earth is depressing and scary. Earth's climate is changing. Global warming is turning up the heat. More and more of the Earth is becoming scorched, waterless desert. Tornados, sandstorms and dust storms rip across landscapes. Crops are failing, animals are dying, whole communities are starving to death or migrating.

The footage is frightening because it's *real*. Drenching cyclones and hurricanes cause raging floods. Wildfires burn up forests and grasslands, killing the wildlife, destroying towns and villages, shrouding the planet in smoke. Various scientists explain how the ice caps are melting, glaciers are receding and exposed permafrost is releasing methane. One calamity leads to another, the narrator warns—rising seas are threatening Pacific islands *now*, and the world's leading scientists predict coastal cities and settlements on the continents will be inundated in a few short years.

Wars raging across the planet add to the displacement and misery of people. I cry silent tears as terrified children flee with their parents and grandparents.

Experts are interviewed. Outbreaks of ghastly diseases are occurring *now*, and they predict future pandemics of virulent *new* viruses.

The conclusion focuses on human waste: smoking mountains of detritus, vast quantities of plastics and other junk clogging rivers and oceans, piling up on beaches around the world, ingested by seabirds and marine animals, entangling and killing them. There are six billion of us; we've turned the planet into a garbage tip, and in another thirty years there'll be two billion more. We are a plague, and Gaia is striking back.

We end up at *Booyul*. It is the first time I've been inside Shaun's house. The living room is sparsely furnished. We sit around the dining room table, drink fruit juice with mineral water, eat crackers topped with cheese or avocado and black pepper, and talk about the movie until Wendy suggests *Scrabble*. 'Just one game,' she says, organising us into three teams: herself and Mum; Billy, Dan and Melanie; Shaun and me.

Shaun explains the rules according to 'the Marshal plan'. 'Take nine letters per team, instead of seven; dictionary perusal is allowed at any time without penalty. We're all geniuses with fantastic vocabularies and the challenge is to find the best spot on the board to get the highest score—if we can find a spot at all.'

For the record, Shaun and I won.

'It's so nice to have broken the ice, Anne,' Wendy says to Mum as we're leaving.

'Yes, we should catch up more often,' Mum responds.

Shaun says, 'I'll walk down with Jodie.'

'Don't catch cold!' Mum warns me, code for: 'Don't loiter!' Then she drives down to *Gwongorella* with Melanie and the boys, just like that.

Walking slowly down the moonlit slope, Shaun puts his arm across my back to keep me warm and to steady me on the uneven ground. I don't know what's going on in *his* head, but *I'm* imagining hugging him and kissing him goodnight.

We arrive to find Melanie huddled on the top step, smoking a cigarette.

Shaun says, 'G'night, Jodie, 'night Melanie.' And he turns and strides back up to *Booyul* without a backward glance. What an anticlimax!

Melanie is staying the night, and Mum's said nothing and closed her own door as usual. Mum's idea of sex education is to buy *Forum* or *Cosmopolitan* or *Cleo* or *Dolly* magazines and leave them lying around the place. To be fair, she did toss a couple of booklets at the boys recently, saying as she walked away, 'Here's something *every* male should read.'

Naturally, at the earliest opportunity, I invaded their room looking for them. One was called *The Modern Girl's Guide to Safe Sex* by Kaz Cooke and the other was a booklet, *AIDS Information for Women*, produced by the Women's Information and Referral Exchange. I read them both in one sitting, peeved that she hadn't given them to me first. She probably thinks I'm safely locked away and in no danger and don't need to be forewarned. Perhaps she thinks I'm not old enough to be interested. Or maybe, just maybe, she's a manipulative schemer and knows damn well I'll look for them and find them and read them and be more likely to take note of the contents *because* she hasn't given them to me with instructions that I become 'informed'.

I know what goes on. One midnight I got up desperate for a binge only to be confronted by Melanie and Dan hard at it on the lounge room carpet. I went back to bed and had nightmares instead. Now, when Melanie's here, it's Billy who sleeps in his sleeping bag on the lounge, banished. I'm sure it pisses him off, being kicked out of his own room and his own bed. Dan's relationship with Melanie is the only thing that's come between them.

Outside my window is an eerie patch-work painting. The trees are luminous, and the paddock with its dips and hollows seems to be breathing as cloud shadows shift across the landscape. Tiny bats flicker across the midnight air. The eucalypts reach up and the intermittent moonlight flows down them and spreads onto the short, pale grass. Clouds, heavy-bellied with rain, seem to be adrift, floating and bumping into each other, but it is unlikely the precious water will be released. It hasn't rained seriously since we arrived; from here west beyond the ranges is a declared drought area. Now and then, eddies of cold air flutter the curtains.

I undress and crawl into bed, naked. In the privacy, warmth and intimacy under my doona, I ponder my developing relationship with Shaun. Will we make love together? Will we make love *to* each other, or *with* each other? Do I need to worry about STDs and HIV and AIDS—meaning has he had unprotected sex with anyone else? It's sad and gruesome to think sex can kill. We're going to have to talk about it. And what about the risk of pregnancy? What a hassle! Should I buy condoms? Who's responsible for getting them anyway, him or me, and putting one on? If he hasn't had sex yet, we wouldn't have to use condoms at all if I was on the pill—but how can I get a prescription? I need to turn off my brain and sleep.

Something frightening is invading my dreams—a fearful rumbling vibrating in my bones, echoing on and on down the sky. Under my doona is warmth, but a cold wind chills my face. Flashes of light illuminate my room. The lace curtains billow and thrash, flicked and shaken by invisible entities. The house creaks as if bracing itself against the force. The trees' sway-and-whisper conversations have become a roar.

I'm closing my windows, opening the fly screens inwards first, lifting each one above my head to get at the old-fashioned window handles, fighting the north-east wind as it tries to slam the windows shut. The curtains cling to my head.

Trying the light switch to no avail, I grope my way along the hall, pausing at the entrance to the living room. The thunder is continuous, the claustrophobic darkness broken by bursts of lightning, the afterimage of the piano flash-burnt into my eyes. The house shudders and shakes with every savage gust. The rain is trying to punch through the corrugated iron roof. I need light! I'm terrified of the dark. Two candles and a box of matches are on the mantel piece above the fireplace; another candle is on the piano, also with a box of matches. I attempt to light the candle on the piano. The flame creates shuddering, contorted shadows on the walls before it is snuffed out by the draught.

A torch beam bounces down the south hallway. Mum's urgent, high-pitched voice mixes with Dan's deeper tones. Mum, Dan, torch and light disappear into the dining room.

I must have light! There is a torch amongst the junk on top of the refrigerator. I scurry with my fingers along the walls into the kitchen, scrabble around on the fridge top and find it. I point it in the direction of the laundry and the linen cupboard, but instead of seeing Mum and Dan gathering towels, I spotlight Billy. I don't know how he got there; Mum and Dan must have headed back towards the bedrooms while I was looking for the torch. Billy's arms are loaded with tablecloths and doona covers.

He turns towards the back door, and I shine the torch beam towards the bottom of the door where the rain is blowing in like someone's holding a hose to it. He stuffs tablecloths and doona covers into the gap under the door, and along the bathroom windowsill, guided by my torch beam. I'm glad I'm with him doing something, even if it is only holding a torch; it helps control my fear. The rain sounds like gravel being hurled against the windowpanes. The drumming on the roof is deafening.

Billy heads for the living room, guided from behind by my torch. Melanie is in there trying to relight the candle on the piano. She points at my belly, the whites of her eyes gleaming, her finger wagging urgently. Perplexed, I look at where she's pointing, and in the flare of a lightning flash I see I'm naked. *How could I not have noticed?* I retreat to my bedroom, shine the torch into my wardrobe where my track suit is lying on the bottom. I pull it on, then put on my socks and Reeboks, convinced the house is about to fly off its moorings and take off into the night sky with all of us in it.

Terrified of being alone, I force myself to follow my torch beam back into the living room. The candle on the piano has been extinguished again. I turn towards the hearth, considering whether I should try and light the candles there.

In that moment light bursts in my face from the fireplace, while a simultaneous explosion puts intolerable pressure on my eardrums. A surge of power flings me backwards against the piano, crackling miniature forks of lightning following me. Pain slivers through my head as I crumple onto the carpet beneath the keyboard. Dumb and numb with shock, I hold my head together with both hands. Blood, wet and warm, leaks through my fingers.

Forcing my eyes open, I see light bouncing off the piano pedals; Billy has picked up my torch. He's kneeling beside me, gently pulling my hands away from my head. He issues orders and Mum appears with a box of *Sure & Natural*. She holds the torch while he presses pads against the gash in the back of my skull and wraps something firmly around my head.

He signs me to stand up, then supports me as I walk towards his and Dan's room. My legs and feet tingle with every step. In the flare of a lightning flash, I notice Melanie lying on Dan's bed, under his doona, Mum and Dan sitting on the bed in front of her. Billy helps me lie down on his bed. He covers me with his doona, but I float out of my body and ascend to the ceiling, where I look down and see myself under the doona, Billy beside me, his arm supporting my back.

Chapter Four

Sunday, 19 March 1995

I wake up in my own bed, lying on my back. Billy and Dan must have carried me in here. Amazingly my head doesn't hurt. I reach up to feel the bandage, but there's nothing there. I lift my head and feel my scalp all over. My head is intact. I sit up, then check the pillow behind me to make sure my body sat up too. It did. And I'm naked, as usual.

The room is bathed in sunshine. The curtains stir and flutter, blown by a fresh, north-easterly breeze coming in the open windows. Didn't I close them? Who opened them again? I reach for my glasses, put on my left HA and listen, cupping my hands around my ears. The house is giving off the usual Sunday morning sounds and smells. The radio in the kitchen is chattering. I can smell bacon and eggs, freshly brewed coffee and slightly burnt toast—all the usual Sunday morning indulgences. I can hear Melanie's high, girlish voice and Dan and Billy's deeper tones. The dogs are barking, either demanding breakfast or to be let out. The west veranda screen door slams. Magpies are carolling on the south paddock.

There's a knock and I pull the doona up around my ears. The door opens and Mum peers around it. 'Breakfast is on the table, Jodie. Come now or you'll miss out.' She withdraws and closes the door again.

How could I have dreamt such terror, such horrifying noise and light and pain? I climb out of bed and peer into my wardrobe. My tracksuit is still lying on the bottom in a mouldering heap. My Reeboks are *not* in here; they're in the laundry on the shoe rack, where I left them on Friday night. I know that now, in the light of day. It was nothing more than a nightmare—but my *heart* is remembering. Thoroughly shaken, I put on the shirt and stretch pants I wore yesterday and last night. Why did I dream a nightmare like that? Maybe *Gaia* triggered it. Mum's always saying I'm 'too sensitive' and 'over-react'.

Everyone except Dan is sitting at the dining room table eating breakfast; he's in the kitchen making more toast. He brings it out as I sit down. Melanie says something, but I interrupt. 'Was there a storm last night?'

'Yep,' Dan answers. 'It *poured*. I checked the rain gauge, twenty-five millimetres.'

'That's an inch!' Melanie exclaims.

'With lots of thunder,' Dan adds.

'Any lightning?' Billy asks.

'There's no thunder without lightning, idiot.'

'Just asking, idiot! I was out for the count. Too busy dreaming. How long did it last?'

'I dunno, as long as it took.'

Mum gets up purposefully. 'Your turn to wash up, Billy.'

'Yeah, yeah, yeah …'

'I'll be in the studio if anyone wants me. But only if it's urgent!'

'Why do we dream?' I ask Dan. 'What do they mean?'

'Dreams are a window into the future, a glimpse, a prophesy,' Melanie says.

'Nah, they're nothing more than a series of metaphors reflecting what's happening in your life *now*,' Dan contradicts her.

'They're just chemical impulses that make pictures,' Billy adds.

'What do you mean, a series of metaphors?'

'Well, y'know, you might dream you're in a fast-flowing river heading for a waterfall and you've got no control, you can't stop it happening—a metaphor for what's maybe going on in your life. Everyone and everything in the dream is supposed to be a symbol or metaphor for something, linked together in a bizarre story indicating—maybe—what you fear, or what you already know but find difficult to face, or a solution to a problem even.' He glances at Melanie. 'More than a direct warning of some future event.'

'*I* think they're a warning,' Melanie insists, 'but who's to say what they mean!'

'Last night I dreamt I was on with the dolphins outside Yarra Point,' Billy interrupts. 'Man, those swells were frothing at the mouth outside, but inside the point they cleaned up and walled up and I caught this ripper and I'm on the peak with a ten-metre waterfall when seven dolphins drop in body surfing right next to me and I'm screaming down the line with them with the barrel closing in and the reef cod staring at me bug-eyed and then it fattens and flattens and lets me down real gentle right beside the bull-rocks and I swear I tipped the rigging of the *Cedar Venture* and saw the bones of dead sailors on that ledge. It was fan-bloody-tastic!'

Billy takes a breath and Melanie jumps in. 'I had an *awful* dream last night. I was in a supermarket between two huge dogs on leashes held by two guys, and the dogs started circling me, snarling at each other—they wanted to fight and they had big fangs and I could feel their hot breath on my legs.'

'Everything in the dream is supposed to represent an aspect of yourself,' Dan says.

'Thanks a lot! You think I've got big fangs?'

'Did I say that? I was thinking of your hot legs!'

Billy grins. 'It could mean you're scared of being the meat in the sandwich, y'know, maybe you've got a couple of wolves fighting over you and they *both* want your body.'

Melanie blushes.

'How come you know so much?' Dan growls.

It's time to interrupt. 'Billy, can I ask you something?'

'You can ask, but it doesn't mean you'll get an answer!'

'I'm serious.'

'Okay. Ask away.'

'If you dreamt a brilliant white light, a bolt of lightning, came down the chimney and struck you in the face and threw you backwards, like a great shove, and your head hit the edge of the piano keyboard and split open, and you had to hold the sides together with both hands so it wouldn't come apart—what would that mean?'

'Yuk! Brains for breakfast!' Billy makes vomiting noises.

'You sound like Kerry O'Brien; he asks long questions like that. By the time he gets to the end you can't remember the beginning!'

'I'm serious, Dan!' My voice breaks. The lump is back in my throat.

'Okay. Sorry. What would it mean? Alright, you seers, any ideas? No sneers!'

'You've seen the light and all will be revealed ...' Billy suggests theatrically.

'Could be someone musical has hurt you,' Melanie suggests. 'The piano is associated with pain—and your head is split in two, like you're in two minds ...'

Billy talks over her. 'You've seen the light. Something is becoming clear to you. It's blowing you away, knocking you for six, splitting your head open, it can't be contained any more—and the splitting means there are two sides, like a conflict of interests, or a dilemma.' He glances at Melanie. 'The piano *and* the bolt of lightning are significant, because they've *both* caused the injury, they're metaphors for something, but if you're supposed to be the piano as well,' he looks to Dan for confirmation, 'it means … I dunno what it means …'

'Maybe the piano simply represents an aspect of the dreamer's life,' Dan butts in. 'Think it through for yourself, Jodie. It's your dream. You're the one who knows.'

After breakfast the boys strap their surfboards onto Dan's roof-racks. Yarrawarra is their favourite surfing beach, something to do with the headland and a 'point-break'. It's also good for videoing because the waves roll in past the bull-rocks shelf and they can be filmed close-up as they go by. But when Dan comes out with the video camera, Melanie, already in the front seat, says, 'Dan, I *can't* video you guys today. I *told* you I've got an all-day tech and dress rehearsal for *Romeo and Juliet*. You never listen! I need to be dropped off at school and I'm going to be *late!* Can you *please* get a move on?'

Dan turns on his heel without saying a word and takes the camera back inside.

Melanie closes the car door and rolls down the window. 'The bard's turning in his grave, his greatest romantic tragedy turned into a musical with a happy ending!'

'I can't wait to see it!' I tell her. She's already bought our tickets for opening night on Friday the 31st of March—less than two weeks away. 'Can you possibly get me a spare copy of the libretto? It'll help me understand what's going on and I can learn the words of the songs.'

'Sure,' she promises. 'I'll ask the producer, and give it to Dan.'

After they drive away, I look around the outside of the house. Everything looks fresh. The grass glitters in the shady spots where the sun hasn't yet reached, soft under my bare feet. In the distance, the pale straw-coloured pasture radiates a hint of green. Shaun's vegetables seem to have grown overnight.

I go back inside. The torch is still on top of the fridge. There is no blood on the carpet. There are no candles or matches on the piano or above the hearth. I feel disoriented, between dimensions, between the world of the dream and the reality of the here and now.

The second movement of Beethoven's fifth piano concerto, Mum's favourite, wafts into the living room from her portable CD player in the studio. The familiar wistful notes take me to a lonely place and put me in a sad mood. She always puts on classical piano music when she's working in the studio—Bach, Mozart, Chopin, Rachmaninov. Whenever she sits at the piano and plays, I feel pleasure mixed with sadness, anger and grief.

For the first time since I cannot remember when, I lift the seat of the piano stool. I stare at Mum's sheet music and books of music inside it. I dig down and discover my first music book, John Thompson's *Teaching with Tunes: A Beginning Piano Book*. I sit on the stool, open the pages at the middle, and place the book on the shelf of the piano's music stand.

'Polly Wolly Doodle' and 'The Lady and the Tiger'.

I peer at pencilled comments: '*Susie semibreve swings by her hair while Minnie minim sits on a chair. One count, 4 counts, 2 counts, watch fingering. Fs are F#s'.*

Intense anxiety overtakes me. I cannot bring myself to strike a note. I cannot make sense of the written instructions. I cannot read the music. I've forgotten everything I ever learnt. Stalked by invisible ghosts, I close the lid of the keyboard sharply. The strings resonate, the hollow sound reverberating in the bones of my skull. I put the music book back in the piano stool. I need to get out of here.

I'm huddled on my outsized beach towel on the still damp grass under the twisted paperbarks beside the creek. The water level has risen, swirling debris floating rapidly downstream towards the Clarence—the Big River.

I remove my journal and pen from my backpack along with a writing pad, an envelope, a packet of biscuits and a carton of apple juice. Writing a love letter to Shaun will help block out the darkness, sadness and anxiety overwhelming me. I'll tell him what I want when we make love, when we are as close as two human beings can get. I'll write as if it's happening right now. I'll describe the intense pleasure overwhelming me as we kiss while he touches my breasts and strokes my skin and presses himself against me and into me. Writing it makes it real. I'll never give the letter to him—it will go in the shoebox with all the others—but whenever my feelings become unbearably painful, like they are right now, I'll soothe myself by re-reading them, reliving my fantasies of love and passion, innocence and joy.

But first, I need to write in my journal. I need to write what happened to me *before* I snatched the pink letter from my father's hands and gave it to Mum because I was sick of, sick of, SICK OF covering up for him. I'd kept his secret for *years*. I was only six when it started. How could he do that to me?

'It's our little secret. Don't tell Mummy. If you do, she'll leave us. She'll run away with the boys, and it will be all your fault. Here's ice cream, don't scream, with strawberry topping, and a Milo milk shake.' The bribe and the reward. I'm only six, seven, eight, nine, ten, terrified Mummy will find out. If she finds out, she will hate me. She will hate Dad too, but she will

hate me more, because I kept the secret for him and never told her. I feel so guilty.

Mummy is always unhappy. It's my responsibility to make her happy, to keep her happy.

I hate my father. I have no respect for him. He is weak and cruel and uncaring. The longer it goes on, the more dangerous it becomes, the more despair I feel. He knows how miserable I am, but he won't stop.

Every Tuesday he takes me to that woman's house for piano lessons. Every Tuesday she is ready—not for me—for my father, her husband at work and her children at school.

She sits me at the piano. 'Now you stay here and practise all your scales and all the pieces in your book!' Her voice is sharp and hard. Something awful will happen if I don't do what she says. My father won't protect me. He's already gone upstairs.

I sit at the piano and practise by myself. I watch the clock on the wall. The big hand moves very, very slowly.

The first time I crept upstairs, the piano stopped when I stopped playing and warned her. She came out of the bedroom and blocked the top of the stairs. Light shone through her flimsy dressing gown, and I could see she had no clothes on. She looked angry and fierce. She pointed her finger at me. 'Now you just go right back downstairs and sit at the piano, Jodie, like you're supposed to.' I know it's rude to point, but I obeyed her because I was scared of her. My father hid in the bedroom. He didn't come out.

Next time I crept upstairs, I heard her say, 'She's too smart. She'll find out.'

Was she talking about me?

'She'll hate me, Hugh. There'll be hell to pay. I'm supposed to be her friend!'

She was talking about Mummy.

'She'll never speak to me again! She'll tell Carl. He'll kill me! She'll leave you!'

'Yes,' my father said. 'If she finds out. But she won't find out. Jodie won't tell.'

Mummy is smart. She might find out. She says I talk in my sleep when I have bad dreams. I'm cheating my mother, and she'll find out and hate me too. I'm not worth loving. When I sneak upstairs and watch my father with that woman, I feel dirty and ugly and sick and ashamed and so guilty. I can't make him stop. I've begged him to stop, but he won't.

'Listen to me, Jodie. Are you listening? If you tell Mummy, she won't believe you. She'll think you're making it up. She'll think you're just being spiteful, to hurt her. If she does believe you, she'll leave us both. What she doesn't know can't hurt her.'

But I know. I know he's hurting Mummy. And he's hurting me. He doesn't love us.

It's his dirty secret, not mine. Why did he choose me to keep it for him?

Sometimes I creep upstairs and watch them. Mostly, he ignores me as if I'm not even there, as if I don't exist, but one time he beckoned me to come closer and when I obeyed him, he grabbed my arm and pulled me onto the bed with them. He thought it was funny … he laughed at me when I cried and struggled and tried to wriggle free.

I have bad dreams about a black rock in my chest so heavy I can hardly breathe. I nearly fall down. I know I will be crushed if I fall down. I wake up with asthma.

My father is supposed to love my mother, not betray her and cheat on her and lie to her. How can he prefer that woman to my mother? The boys say, 'Poor Dad,' when Mummy gets angry and yells at him and cries. If only they knew!

When that woman catches me watching them, she gets mad at me and upset with Dad. She tells Dad to send me back downstairs to sit at the piano and do my practice, but Dad says, 'Don't worry about her. Just ignore her.' I go back downstairs anyway and sit under the piano, and bang my head, and cry and cry, and refuse to play anything I AM SO AN-GRY!

When they come downstairs, she gives me ice cream with strawberry topping and a Milo milk shake, then a half-hour piano lesson.

On the way home, Dad says, 'Remember, it's our little secret, Jodie. Don't tell your mother what you had to eat today. Don't tell your mother ANYTHING about today. You'll make her VERY unhappy if you do, and she'll leave us, and it will be all your fault.' He doesn't care how I feel. I'm not worth worrying about.

I'm not allowed to cry. 'No tears! If you cry, Mummy will ask you what's wrong.'

The tears run down inside my nose instead. Mummy yells at me, 'Jodie! For god's sake stop sniffling! Blow your nose!' I cry and cry inside my nose and cannot make it stop.

I'm crying now on my towel beside the creek, my heart so heavy it hurts.

How can I write a letter to Shaun about love now?

Eventually I'm empty of tears, and empty of feeling. I can feel the chill of the water when I splash the snot and tears off my face, but inside me I can't feel anything. It's gloomy under the trees. Shadows are engulfing everything.

I can hear voices. I turn up my HA and cup my hands around my ears and realise my brothers are approaching. I place my journal, writing pad, envelope and pen in my backpack, put my towel, the empty biscuit wrapper and juice carton on top, and zip it up.

Cleo and Patra have tracked me. They appear over the rise of the bank ahead of the boys, noses in the grass. When they see me, they rush down the slope and leap on me, tails thrashing, whining greetings, licking my face with delight.

Dan arrives. 'Watcha doin'?' His voice is not unkind.

Billy is right behind him. 'Fuck!' he says, using his usual lyrical vocabulary, staring past me at the creek. 'See how much it's come up! First real rain since we've been here.'

Then, as if he's just seen me, he staggers back in mock-surprise. 'Well, look who's here, so far from home. You feedin' the mosquitoes or somethin'?'

I applied Rid when I came down here, but I can't be bothered telling him.

He dances about on top of the bank, swatting himself. 'I don't know how you can stand it! You'll end up with Ross River Fever. Or Murray Valley Encephalitis! Mum sent us all the way down here to find you and you're meditatin' with mosquitoes!'

'Mum was worried about you,' Dan says, as I approach him. 'Aren't you cold?'

I shrug. I'm numb. I don't know whether I'm cold or not.

I follow them over the upper bank, then trudge up the paddock towards the house. Shaun's vegie patch is on our right, but there's no sign of Shaun. Billy stops, turns around and watches me until I catch up. He puts a heavy arm across my shoulders. 'Hey sis! Whatcha so pissed off about, eh? Why don'tcha chill out, instead of makin' a Shakespearean tragedy out of every small thing?' He gives me what's meant to be a friendly squeeze. 'Don't let the dorks do you in. The world's a shit-can fulla turds 'n' toads—if somethin' good happens it's a bonus!' His tone tells me he's trying to be helpful.

'Thanks for the advice.' I shrug him off, gently, remembering how he helped me, not only in the nightmare itself, but in the interpretation of its meaning.

Dan waits for us to catch up. 'Life's a shit sandwich,' he says.

'Yeah—and every day you gotta take another bite!' Billy responds.

They quote shit jokes ad nauseum, plagiarising various sources of literary greatness.

'Eat shit!' Billy warms to his theme. 'Fifty billion flies can't be wrong!'

'Yeah, shit happens,' says Dan.

They are trying to cheer me up. 'Thanks for your concern,' I tell them.

Further up the paddock, Dan asks, 'Why should women stay out of the surf?'

I shake my head. I don't want to know. I cannot reconcile his apparent love for Melanie with his propensity for sexist and horrible jokes.

'Because they attract sharks?' Billy guesses. 'I know! Because they'd never find their way back to the beach. Most women don't know whether they're coming or going!'

'They know when they're coming alright! Because they're too good on a stick!'

I hate their sexual innuendos. Billy guffaws until he nearly falls over.

They move onto surfing, in a mostly incomprehensible argot, about how they copped a creaming, got chundered and sand-blasted, spinning down tubes and shooting out of barrels. I switch off and watch Cleo and Patra rabbit-hunting instead.

The dogs have separated, but it's co-operative. They cast about in the grass and when one is flushed out, the pursuing dog chases the bobbing white scut towards the other dog. It's a deadly game. The rabbits dive down holes and escape, but eventually one is trapped. It rushes backwards and forwards as Cleo and Patra close in. The rabbit squeals piteously. I cover my ears and shut my eyes and wonder if Saab has come home.

Mum is in the den on her computer, probably drafting an essay for her *Fine Arts* course. Dan and Billy are sprawled on the lounge reading magazines. I'm sitting on the carpet between them, using the lounge as a backrest while I prepare a plan and write preliminary notes for my *Aboriginal Studies—Contemporary Issues* assignment.

'Why did God invent men?' Billy asks. He must be reading Kathy Lette's article in the March issue of *New Woman*. I didn't find the jokes funny. They'll sound even worse coming out of his mouth.

Dan says behind his *Tracks* mag, 'To give women something to complain about?'

'Because He had no imagination!' I growl.

'Nup!' Billy delivers the punchline, 'Because dildos can't take out the garbage!'

'Bloody hell!' says Dan.

'Why are 'dumb blonde' jokes always one-liners?' Billy asks.

'Because you dumb guys can't put two words together to make a sentence, let alone remember more than one line at a time.'

'Close,' he says. He reads silently after that.

I return to my notes. I plan to research the impact of white settlement along the Big River, the Clarence, on the Bundjalung people and their culture. Shaun suggested I visit the Clarence River Historical Society. I'll also try the TAFE library and Grafton library.

'How do you get rid of cockroaches?' Billy interrupts again.

'Leave home,' Dan says, not looking up from *Tracks*.

'Leave Faigan alone!'

'Tell them you want a long-term relationship!'

Ouch! They're getting mean!

'You're telling them.'

Billy reads silently again. Dan turns the page of his *Tracks* magazine. I continue my notetaking, hunched on the carpet.

'Now it's *your* turn.' Billy taps my head. 'What's the definition of a woman?'

'The perfect model,' I suggest. 'Man is just a clumsy proto-type.'

'A wet blanket!' Dan says.

Billy chortles. 'Not even close!'

I stow my study notes in my folder. I'm feeling squeamish. It's time to go.

'A woman,' Billy declares, 'is something to lie down on while you're having a fuck!'

A wave of nausea surges over me in a hot flush. For sure I'm going to be sick.

'What's an anorexic woman with thrush?' he continues.

'A skinny, itchin', twitchin' bitch?' Dan offers.

I turn, begin to get up off the carpet.

'Nah, man,' Billy says, 'she's a quarter pounder with cheese!' And roaring with mirth he falls off the couch alongside me just as I throw up.

Mum comes tearing out of the den. 'You're over the top!' she yells. 'Do you think I want to listen to your obscenities? How can you say such things to her!'

'Fuckin' hell! They're just bloke-jokes!' Billy squawks. 'She spewed on me!'

Dan, hysterical, staggers off to the kitchen. He returns with the sponge and a towel. He's a basket-case, but I'm distraught with embarrassment.

Mum asks me, 'Are you okay?'

'*Sure* I'm okay!' I snarl savagely. 'I'm *fine!*'

'Go and have a nice warm shower.'

'*I'm* the one needs a shower!' Billy complains, stripping off to his underdaks.

'*You* can clean the carpet,' Mum commands Dan—he's still holding the sponge and towel. 'And make sure you do it properly. The pair of you got exactly what you deserved!'

She turns on her heel and returns to the den and her computer. Billy's already on his way to the laundry, gingerly holding his clothes in front of him.

'You can have the shower, Billy,' I call out to him, knowing he'll claim it anyway.

Dan has rapidly recovered from his hysterics, pissed off he has to clean the carpet. I pick up my *Aboriginal Studies* folder, relieved I didn't spew on that too, and retreat.

Later, after a mouth rinse at the kitchen sink, I sit at my dressing table in front of the mirror with a mug of Milo and a couple of—well, four—Arnott's Orange Crème biscuits, and read my draft notes to Anne in a whisper:

My Aboriginal Studies—Contemporary Issues subject is teaching me what Aboriginal people across Australia have suffered since the First Fleet arrived on 26 January 1788.

Two hundred years later, on 26 January 1988, the year of the Bicentenary, Australia celebrated 'the birth of a nation'. I was eight years old. There was a protest march in Sydney. Banners said: 'Two hundred years of mourning' and 'Australia has a black history'.

The High Court Mabo decision three years ago, 03 June 1992, overturned 'terra nullius' and recognised native title for the first time. Many conflicting views have been reported in the media.

A year after he became Prime Minister, and six months after Mabo, Prime Minister Paul Keating delivered a speech on 10 December 1992 at Redfern Park in Sydney. In an act of recognition, he said we'd dispossessed Aboriginal people, taken their land, destroyed their traditional way of life, brought diseases and alcohol, committed murders, removed children from their mothers, practised discrimination and exclusion because of ignorance and prejudice. ...

I need to keep an eye on the word-count, make every word relevant to the Bundjalung. I read through the notes again. Empathy, grief and guilt well up in me. I get up from the dressing table, sit down at my desk and write to Emma-Sue. If she doesn't reply, if she knocks me back, if she doesn't want to know me, I'll understand.

Sunday, 19 March 1995

Dear Emma-Sue,

I'm Billy and Dan's sister. I was there when Billy gave your letter to Shaun yesterday. Shaun doesn't want to write back, but Dan and Billy suggested I write to you myself, because I haven't met anyone my age (15) since we moved here late last year and I'm lonely. I'm studying Year 10 through OTEN instead of going to school. I have hearing difficulties and wear hearing aids. Billy or Dan will deliver your reply. I'd love to meet up with you.

Please write back.
Jodie

It feels good folding the paper, sliding it into the addressed envelope and sealing it. I prop the letter against my desk lamp.

My next challenge: how to overcome Mum's opposition to the pill. Apart from contraception, which could be useful, taking it might help reduce my period cramps and pain and my miserable, cranky, down-in-the-dumps feelings that swamp me before they come. I'm sick of feeling lousy every month.

I do know a doctor I could see. Mum made an appointment with her after we arrived here, worried I might have asthma attacks with the change in climate and environment. Turns out I'm fine outdoors. My *home* environment is the problem, like when Melanie smokes a cigarette or spliff on the veranda, or when Mum is out in the studio and the boys share a bong on the veranda, or when they smoke in their room and burn incense at the same time to disguise the smell. Mum thinks they burn incense to disguise the smell of the snakes! No one's asked me—or the snakes—what *we* think of the smell of incense, let alone marihuana!

I cross the hall to the door of the den and watch Mum pattering away on the keyboard. Billy's been pressuring her to convert this room into a bedroom for him. Sharing with Dan and a dozen snakes was tolerable, but Melanie's tipped the scales. I struck gold with my room—it's spacious, light-filled, airy, relatively private and I don't have to share it.

'Can I make you a cup of tea?' I ask Mum's back.

She looks at her watch. 'You should be in bed, it's late.'

'I need to talk to you for a minute.'

She swivels around and looks at me, lips pursed. 'I'll just save this on a back-up disc.'

I'm used to her promising to quit the computer only to emerge two hours later, so I'm not exactly counting on her, but she appears just as I carry our mugs to the dining room table.

Between sips of tea, I tell her about my need to visit the Clarence River Historical Society and the TAFE library to research my *Aboriginal Studies—Contemporary Issues* assignment. She's impressed! She agrees to take me into town tomorrow.

'I also need to visit AHS to look at one of my HAs.'

I won't mention Dr Lynne. I'll visit the surgery after Mum drops me off at one of the other places and try and get an appointment without notice. Dr Lynne might give me a prescription if I ask her myself, confidentially. It's worth a try.

Mum breaks the silence.

'Jodie, I don't want you taking the pill, if that's what you want to talk about.'

Where did that come from? She's a mind-reader!

'Why not?'

'You know why. There's a risk of blood clots when you're overweight.'

Stay cool.

'I'm *losing* weight. I'm not *that* big. The way you talk you'd think I was an elephant.'

'I noticed a packet of biscuits missing this afternoon when I came in to make myself a cup of tea. I can't keep up with what you get through. They were supposed to last a week.'

'I'd at least like to ask Dr Lynne for her opinion. I'm sick of cramps and pain.'

'I do *not* want you on the pill, Jodie. You're barely fifteen! Enjoy your childhood.'

I explode, white-hot with rage. 'Childhood? What childhood!' I point at her accusingly. 'I was *cheated* of it! You've been unhappy for as long as I can remember! And Dad—' I stand up to give space for my flailing arms and rising voice. 'For children to enjoy their childhood they need *happy* parents, who *love* each other, not a mother who ends up in the nuthouse and a father who…who….' and my yelling collapses into sobbing, because crying is safer than expressing my experiences, thoughts and feelings in words.

Dan and Billy emerge from their room. 'What's up? What's the problem?'

Mum gets up and goes to the fridge. She picks up something lying on the top of it and drops the mysterious item on the table. 'I found this in the clothes dryer.'

Have I missed something? What the fuck is she on about? Still sobbing, I pick up the green foil packet. It's a *Liaison Naturelle* condom.

I'm completely bemused by the turn of events. 'What's this got to do with anything?'

'Who owns it?' Mum demands, looking from the boys to me and back again.

Dan shrugs and shakes his head. 'Not my brand, sorry.'

Mum reaches out her hand for the condom, without looking directly at me. I give it to her. I'm still sobbing, but it's as if she hasn't noticed. She's looking at Billy now. I look from Billy to Dan and back again, trying to figure out what's going on. Billy is looking at Mum, his lips and ears twitching. He shakes his head. 'Can't help you, Mum, sorry.'

Glancing at Dan again I catch the last moment of a tiny smile. Mum apparently sees only bland innocence because she turns her disapproval and suspicion directly onto me.

'Why a condom, Jodie? Not to mention leaving it in the dryer to melt!'

'It's *not* mine!' I yell. I'm still crying. I can't believe she's ignoring my distress, swinging the finger-pointing around to me. And I'm totally outraged it's okay for the boys to be in possession of condoms, but not me. And because it *isn't* mine, and because Shaun and I have done *nothing*, not even kissed, I feel justified in attacking her. 'They're lying, Mum, and *you know it*! Why is it okay for them to have condoms and not me? I don't know who the fuck owns it, I don't care—but if it *was* mine, I'd claim it!'

'There's no need to be so aggressive!' she says, sounding aggressive herself. 'Dan and Billy are nearly eighteen and seventeen, you're barely fifteen!'

'If they're nearly eighteen and seventeen, then I'm nearly sixteen! What you're really saying is they're *boys* and I'm a *girl*. You think you can protect me by keeping me locked up at *home*. And you're horrified I might be protecting myself with a condom? Get real!'

Dan and Billy exchange looks.

I hold out my hand. 'Seeing as you think it's mine, give it back!'

She shakes her head. 'It's no good now.'

'I know that!' I'm still yelling and sobbing. 'I just want to own a condom!'

She goes into the kitchen, picks up a pair of scissors from the top of the fridge and cuts the packet in half. 'It needs recycling.' She drops the pieces in the rubbish bin.

'Uggh!' I want to smash something! 'You think you're protecting me,' I tell her, my voice loud, low and savage, 'but you failed to protect me when I most needed it!' I storm off to my room and slam the door. I wish I could lock it.

I dig deep into the cotton bag hidden in my wardrobe. Chocolate-coated almonds. Good brain food, nuts. I rip the packet open with my teeth, shove it under my pillow and flop onto my bed with the Harlequin Super Romance I stole from Bookworld. I'll suck, then chew, one almond every six pages, to maintain control. I'm way too enraged to sleep. *And* scared—I don't want to experience another nightmare like last night.

The door opens just as I'm feeding my face. It's Dan, shaking his head, a finger tapping his pursed lips to stop me from shrieking, *'GET OUT, YOU MORON!'*

He closes the door behind him, puts his hand in a pocket, and withdraws it, clasping something. He holds out a clenched fist. 'I thought you might like these.'

Infuriated with him, but curious, I wriggle into a sitting position and take the offering—a string of six Liaison Naturelle condoms in their shiny little green foil packets.

'You bastard!'

'I don't want my little sister getting into trouble.' His tone is bantering but not mean. 'They'll prevent pregnancy *and* protect you from AIDS and STDs, which the pill won't do.'

I'm speechless.

'Syphilis and gonorrhoea were deadly before antibiotics. But new, drug-resistant strains are developing. Chlamydia, herpes and warts are common as the common cold at South High.

Never let a guy talk his way out of using one. Tell him, "*If it's not on, it's not on!*"'

I nod dumbly.

To think sex can pass on such awful diseases!

It's enough to put me off.

'Can I have—?' He points at my pillow, then taps his teeth.

He paid for them.

I give him a chocolate-coated almond. 'Does this mean you and Melanie use condoms?'

'Of course. All the time.'

'D'you think you'll stay together?'

He shrugs, then shakes his head. 'I don't see how we can. She's going to the Con next year. And I wanna surf-travel before I go to uni—if I go at all.'

'Will you miss her?'

'Sure. But you have to roll with the punches. Go with the flow and all that.'

'Could you deliver a letter for me, Dan? Please? It's on my desk, against the lamp.'

He picks up the envelope, reads Emma-Sue's name and nods. 'Good one!'

'Thanks bro.' I wave the condoms at him before pushing them under my pillow.

'While you're there.' He holds out his hand, beckoning with his fingers. I give him two almonds this time. He pops them into his mouth.

I read his lips. 'You owe me!' Then he departs, closing the door behind him.

Chapter Five

I'm still furious with Mum because of the way she treated me last night, but I'm disguising my rage with courtesy and quietness. I have an agenda today, some of it secret, and I'm not going to risk it by fighting with her.

Being in her car with Dan and Billy is a rare experience. A part of me wishes I was going to school too, with them, like this, every day—but another part of me says, *No way!* If I had to choose between school every day, or Wednesdays with Shaun and being alone the other four school days, right now I'd choose Shaun and being alone.

I love maths and physics and chemistry thanks to his coaching. He doesn't do the work for me; he just shows me how to do the bits where I'm stumped. He tests me on things like the laws of physics, the periodic table, chemical formulas, definitions, theorems and so on, and I try to memorise everything beforehand because I want to impress him. He reads drafts of my English, Ancient History and Geography assignments and says *he's* learning from *me* how to write essays! I'm looking forward to discussing my Aboriginal Studies assignment with him.

If I went to school, I wouldn't hear half of what the teachers were saying, and they wouldn't have time to help me one-on-one like Shaun does.

At boarding school, the classes were small, the classrooms carpeted, and the teachers stood close to my desk when they were explaining things and made sure I could see their lips and hear them during lessons. Reading, studying, learning and making full use of the school's library helped ward off bad, sad thoughts and feelings. The downside: I was bullied for being 'a deaf fat nerd'.

The Clarence River is wide, brown and swirly, and Rogan Bridge is long, low and narrow, just two lanes, with no side rails. Debris is flowing swiftly underneath it and larger branches, fence posts and other chunks of rubbish are stalled against the bridge itself.

'You can see why they call it the Big River,' Mum says, slowing down—a small truck is approaching way too fast. It thunders past and she yells, 'Idiot!'

'If the water rises much more, the bridge will go under!' Billy exclaims behind me.

'Look at the blue sky!' I say, to join in the conversation. 'Not a cloud in sight.'

'You don't say,' he drawls, oozing sarcasm.

'It's still raining up in the gorge and over the catchment,' Dan explains.

After that unsuccessful effort, I ignore their mumblings in the back seat until Mum pulls up outside South High.

I look back at Dan as he opens his door. 'Don't forget—'

He barely glances at me. 'I won't.' And he's gone.

Billy reaches over the seat, pats Mum on the shoulder and clambers out. He slams the door, hitches his backpack over one shoulder and mooches off. I wind my window down and yell, 'Bye Billy!' but all I get is a backward wave and he's gone too. So much for that. A familiar sensation of emptiness, futility and disappointment overtakes me.

Driving back towards Grafton we merge with the traffic and cross the bridge, a double-decker, with footbridges and a railway line under the roadway. I overheard Dan telling Billy one time that people had suicided leaping from this bridge or drowned accidentally after jumping off it for a dare. I'd like to walk across it. I want to look down at the water swirling around the concrete piers and experience the torn feelings those people must have felt as they decided whether to jump or not.

'Could you drop me off at the PO, please Mum? And could you pick me up at TAFE Pound Street entrance this afternoon?'

'What time?'

'Three-ish. Or a bit after.' She turns into Victoria Street and pulls up at the post office.

'Oh, gosh, Mum! Can I have some money for lunch, please?'

'Why didn't you make yourself a sandwich?'

'I forgot. Sorry.'

She's clearly annoyed, but she rummages in her bag, finds her wallet and hands me a ten-dollar note. 'Buy something nutritious Jodie, and I want the receipt—and the change.'

'Will do. Thank you, Mum. Much appreciated.' I scramble out with my backpack. I push the ten-dollar note into my jeans pocket alongside the ten dollars she gave me on Saturday night to buy my movie ticket, unspent because Shaun paid for me. Twenty bucks! Enough money to cover any contingencies! I can feel my body relaxing as she drives away. I'm free! A day in town by myself. What a luxury!

Clarence River Historical Society is in a restored building called Schaeffer House. A volunteer historian very generously gives me well-thumbed, dog-eared copies of *A History of the Clarence River District 1837–1915* by John McFarlane, and *Rivers of Blood: Massacres of the Northern Rivers Aborigines and their resistance to white occupation 1838–1870* by Rory Medcalf, adapted from a six-part series published in *The Northern Star* newspaper. Both are exactly what I need.

At AHS the audiologist gives me a hearing test, replaces my right hearing aid with a new one, cleans and dries my left one, checks and adjusts both to fit the results of my hearing test, and finally hands me packets of batteries and a container to put my HAs in when I'm not wearing them—all for free!

At the Medical Centre, I discover Dr Lynne has just had a cancellation. Talk about lucky! She ushers me into her consulting room, where she asks me questions and takes notes while I tell her about my period pain every month.

'You're not alone, Jodie. Dysmenorrhoea effects about eighty per cent of women.'

'That's a *lot*! Why does it happen?'

'Sometimes we can identify causes—have you had sex yet?'

'No!' I sound like I'm shocked to be asked. 'No, I haven't.'

'Do you have heavy bleeding?'

'Um, no.' I shake my head. 'Not really. I wouldn't say heavy.'

'Pain?'

'Yes.'

'What sort of pain?'

'A heavy, aching, bloated feeling lets me know they're due. Then awful cramps.'

'How do you feel the week before? Some women feel uptight and irritable. They don't sleep well and feel unusually tired. Food cravings are common. They get body aches and pains. Does this sound familiar?'

I nod. 'Definitely!'

'Do you ever feel sad? Hopeless? Not in control of your moods? Have crying spells?'

I nod again.

'Do you ever feel suicidal?'

'Sometimes.'

I see a subtle change in her manner, a wary look on her face.

'It's just the cramps and the pain get me down.'

'Does it get so bad it stops you from going to school?'

'I don't go to school, because of my hearing impairment. I do distance education.'

'Really?'

'I'm doing very well with my studies though. I'm in year ten.' I shift in my seat, take a breath. 'I spend the day they're coming, and the day they start, in bed. Would it help me to go on the pill?'

'It could do. The pill lowers prostaglandins, and that can help reduce cramps.'

'I'd like to try the pill. See if it helps.' There! I've said it! I hold my breath.

'It's an option.' She takes my blood pressure, listens to my heart and lungs with her stethoscope, looks down my throat, looks in my ears and checks the inside of my lower eyelids.

After asking me to lie on the examination table, she pokes and prods my abdomen. 'I'll prescribe a low dose pill and see if it helps. Follow the instructions *exactly*; start on the first day of your next period. And *never* forget to take it—don't miss a day— especially if you're relying on it for contraception.' She begins writing on her prescription pad.

I shake my head, trying to imply contraception is not an is- sue. 'I won't forget.'

She hands me the prescription. 'There are five repeats, so it's good for six months, but I'd like you to come back and see me after three months, to check if it's helping pain-wise. If you ex- perience breast tenderness, or bloating,' she hesitates, 'or if you find yourself experiencing *big* mood swings; or you're *very* de- pressed, not just the week before your period, but all the time, come back and see me sooner rather than later. Keep a daily journal and record your symptoms, your ups and downs, your mood swings, especially in relation to your cycle and your periods, and bring it with you next visit.' She gently ushers me to the door. 'We're a bulk-billing practice, Jodie, so there's no charge for today. Just sign at the desk and make another appointment for before the end of June.'

'Thank you, Dr Lynne. You've been *very* helpful.'

I make the follow-up appointment, then walk—I want to skip but restrain my jubilation—to the pharmacy on Prince Street, the same one that dispensed my asthma medication and recorded Mum's Medicare card details. I'm worried they'll ask me for the card, or the details, or other awkward questions, but the pharmacist fills the prescription, no questions asked. I hand over my lunch money and pocket the change and the receipt. This receipt Mum will not get to see. I drop the packet of pills into my backpack and saunter out of the pharmacy, feeling older than when I went in.

I'm in the TAFE library. I've just photocopied a copy of the first known map of the Clarence River, dated 27 December 1838. The map has three cedar-getters' huts marked on it, downstream from what, in time, would become the village of Copmanhurst, about thirty kilometres upriver from Grafton. Grafton itself was founded in 1851.

I've discovered the Bundjalung name for the Clarence River is *Boorimbah*, and much of Bundjalung country used to be covered in rainforest, from the ranges down to the river's edge. The invaders were after the red cedar, which they called 'red gold', and they were soon in conflict with the original inhabitants on both sides of the river.

Maps in the *Encyclopaedia of Aboriginal Australia*, published last year, show the extent of Bundjalung country before the invasion. Food was so abundant they had semi-permanent camps. Today, apart from a few national parks preserving areas of forest and coastal heath, much of Bundjalung country has been cleared for its timber and to make way for beef cattle, dairy-farming, sugarcane growing, agriculture, horticulture and towns and villages.

In the early days after the invasion, there were confrontations and massacres and the Bundjalung were rounded up and ended up on missions and reserves. Later, they worked for inadequate rations as stockmen and domestic servants on cattle stations like *Yulgilbah*. Children were stolen. The displacement and trauma, loss of land and break up of families and communities interfered with the passing on of their language, traditional knowledge and culture. Reading what Emma-Sue's people endured, I can't think of one good reason why she'd want to be friends with me!

I'm reading about Baryulgil, a town segregated in the past, with an open-cut asbestos mine where Bundjalung were exploited for cheap labour. The workers, their wives, children and extended families became victims of asbestosis and mesothelioma, a terminal lung condition. In 1984, only eleven years ago, a Commission of Enquiry investigated the dangers. The mine has since been closed, but asbestos is everywhere in the town, incredibly dangerous for the Bundjalung families who continue to live there. Meanwhile, a site free of airborne asbestos was surveyed and the community of Malabugilmah was established ten kilometres north of Baryulgil. Most, but not all, Baryulgil residents relocated to Malabugilmah. I wonder if Emma-Sue has relatives still living in Baryulgil as well as Malabugilmah.

Mum picks me up across the road from TAFE as arranged. On the way to South High I dig into my pocket for the change from my visit to the pharmacy and drop it into her money purse, saying, 'Sorry, Mum, I forgot to get a receipt, but I had a ham and salad sandwich.' I don't give her airspace to respond, babbling about my successes at AHS with my HAs, and at the historical society and the TAFE library, as if last night's altercation never happened.

I do want to be happy. I don't enjoy being miserable, like Mum says. I can forget to be sad when I'm busy doing interesting, fun things (translate: when I'm with Shaun!) or lose myself in a book, or write, or re-read my secret writings, or immerse myself in my studies.

Sometimes I feel young and inexperienced around Shaun. He's so mature, thoughtful and well-informed, concerned about world issues instead of just himself. Mostly though, I feel we are on the same level, on the same wavelength. I read my assignment drafts to him, and he makes useful comments. He never criticises *me* or puts me down. He's given me *The Good Guide to Australian Universities*, which details university courses in Creative Writing, Journalism, Communication and Literature. He's suggested I talk to an adviser at the UNE, University of New England, Access Centre in Grafton and visit Southern Cross University—it only opened last year and has campuses in Coffs Harbour and Lismore. I'm developing a goal, a sense of direction, even though I know how easily something could happen to blow me off-course when I least expect it.

Right now, I'm re-reading happy pages in my journal to help me relax and fall asleep.

Our 'classroom' up the creek is a grassy little island, separated from the west bank by a narrow channel carved out by past floods. The island is held together by ancient grevilleas that grow on it, their gnarly, twisted roots partially exposed; the trees lie on their sides pointing downstream. They are covered in red flowers and tiny honeyeaters visit them.

Water dragons sunbake on the horizontal branches, watching us with beady eyes. They're well-camouflaged but lose their nerve and plop into the water if we come too close. The casuarinas on the west bank cast restless shadows on the grass of our island. I can hear a soft, faraway swishing sound when the wind blows through them …

On Wednesday mornings, when the rising sun lights up my walls and I hear the sound of carolling magpies and the laughter of kookaburras, I am consciously happy. As soon as Mum leaves to take the boys to school and go to TAFE to her ceramics class, I make huge sandwiches, piling on whatever I can find in the fridge. Shaun brings 'something special' like cashews, mangoes or avocados, and cheese with crackers. I can eat comfortably in his presence; he never notices what or how much I eat and enjoys his own share of the food to the last crumb.

I snuggle down under my doona, planning to fall asleep thinking about Shaun, but it is Saab who comes into my thoughts. *Has he joined a pack of wild dogs—or has he finally come home?*

Chapter Six

Tuesday, 21 March 1995

I'm sitting on the east veranda, peering through Mum's binoculars, watching Shaun working alone in his vegetable patch. Despite Saab's aloofness, he used to hang with Shaun all the time. Whenever I've watched Shaun through the binoculars, Saab's been there. Shaun must be missing him dreadfully. Fortunately, apart from our first memorable encounter, Saab has never growled or snarled at me.

I'm procrastinating getting on with my assignment, re-reading my journal instead, reliving our very first paddle up the creek and our first time on the island.

Along the banks, on both sides, the water-reflected light ripples and marbles on the trunks and the undersides of overhanging branches. Small birds flit in the undergrowth. The smell of eucalyptus blossoms, damp earth and leaf litter waft past my nose.

My polished wooden paddle dips into and slices through the glistening water. Droplets of silver fly off the lower edge as it arcs through the air for the next cleaving sweep. I sit up front, Shaun behind me, our synchronised strokes pulling the flat-bottomed canoe upstream. Between the long, tranquil pools are miniature rapids and we leap out and drag the canoe up and over the pebbly ledges…'

It won't be like that tomorrow, after the rain. Judging by *Boorimbah* yesterday, the creek will be up, the water muddy, swirly and moving fast. Maybe we'll paddle on the billabong instead. There are secluded, shady spots nearby for our picnic lunch and my 'lesson'.

'The first time we came across our little island we pulled the canoe onto the sand between fallen, but still living, grevilleas. We spread our towels on the soft couch grass, shaded by casuarinas, and protected from the cool breeze blowing along the creek. Sitting alongside Shaun in this very private place for the first time, with him wearing only his board shorts, I was very aware of him, wary even, and self-conscious too. I kept my big t-shirt on over my bikini, removing it only when I went for a dip, then putting it back on again as soon as I came out of the water. I soon realised I had nothing to fear. When he looked at me, he looked at my eyes, not my body. We solved algebraic equations and explored probability, and talked about astronomy and space travel, and forests and global warming …'

Since that first paddle up the creek with Shaun, and finding our island, and my first 'lesson' and picnic lunch with him, I've trusted him and felt safe with him. I was attracted to him from the start, and I was sure he was attracted to me, but apart from smiling at each other a lot, neither of us said or did anything to confirm it. With every meeting, my unspoken feelings for him intensified. My whole life is a secret, and my clandestine interactions with him and my feelings for him have been absorbed into that secret. Our relationship permeates every aspect of my being. It's an intense love affair, in my head and in my bed, whether I'm awake and stargazing, turning myself on thinking and imagining, or asleep and dreaming. The only way I can express my feelings—to him, for him, about him—is in secret, erotic, unsent, unseen, potent love letters and explicit, imaginative entries in my journal.

Last Friday night, when he held me for the first time while I cried on our way down to the billabong, something happened between us. He was so kind and gentle. I sensed he really cared, for me and about me. He truly listened to me, and I felt understood. I wanted so badly to kiss him when we were near the billabong, and I probably would have if Saab hadn't killed the moment. Saturday morning I'm sure he was flirting with me when he rang and asked me out to see *Gaia Strikes Back*, and afterwards while we were drinking coffee on the veranda. And at the movies our legs were touching—I don't think it was accidental—and when we walked down the hill from *Booyul* in the moonlight he put his arm around me, admittedly after I told him I was cold. I would have hugged and kissed him goodnight if Melanie hadn't been on the back steps smoking.

He's such a turn on! I want to take it further, in *real* life, not just in secret love letters and daydreams. I dream by night and imagine by day taking it all the way! We'll have to talk about it though, and the butterflies in my belly are frantic at the thought.

If I imagine the scenario first, it might be easier to manage when it happens. I flip over the pages of my journal past my last entry written on Sunday down by the creek—I do *not* want to re-read *that* entry again, not today or any other day—and begin writing on a fresh double page. I'll write as if it's happening *now*!

Our first time!

We are up the creek as usual, on our island, on our towels, but nothing is familiar. He is lying on his back, his arms under his head. I'm wearing my sarong, knotted above my breasts, and the thin straps of my bikini are showing above it. I undo the sarong and let it drop. My breasts overflow my bikini top, the cleavage between them deep and obvious. I notice his eyebrows flicker and his pupils dilate. His eyes are very blue, reflecting the sky.

I lie beside him for the first time. Two condoms are tucked inside the front of my bikini bottom, just below my navel. He puts his right arm around me, and I use his chest for a pillow.

'Why did you reject Emma-Sue?' I ask him.

'I'm the sort of bloke who can only cope with one woman at a time,' he answers. He moves his head so he can look at me. 'What do you want to work on or talk about today?'

'Can I ask you some everything-you-ever-wanted-to-know-about-sex-but-were-afraid-to-ask type questions?'

'Hmm.' He sounds doubtful. 'I guess so. What would you like to know, exactly?'

'Promise you'll tell the truth, and I will too.'

'Okay,' he says, slowly, his tone wary.

This is new for both of us!

'Do you masturbate?' I ask him.

'Good grief!' he exclaims, embarrassed, but amused too. 'Umm—yes, I do!'

'Do you?' I sit up, grinning, enjoying his honesty.

'Can I ask you questions too?'

'Yes. It's your turn.'

'Do you?'

'Do I what?' I'm teasing him.

'You know what—don't prevaricate!'

'Yes, I do!' I confess.

'Really?' He seems surprised. 'Does it work for you?'

'Best way to get to sleep I know and it's wonderful what a bit of imagination can do.'

'And what do you imagine?'

My heart is racing. It's the moment for revelation. 'I imagine making love with you.'

Just *writing* it is scary! What if he knocks me back, before we even get to first base? What if he says, 'I'm so sorry, Jodie, no offence, but you're not my type.' The thought of rejection makes me shiver and groan. I can't write *that*—it's too demoralising.

Cleo comes over and puts her head on my thigh and whimpers, like she's talking to me. I caress her around her throat and stroke her head.

'It's alright, Cleo,' I reassure her. 'I'm okay.'

Patra joins her and I pat and stroke her too. They are my only companions when I'm home alone. If they disappeared, I'd be beside myself with anxiety and grief. Shaun must surely be feeling the same way about Saab. He's lonely too, working by himself day after day with only his dog for company, and now he doesn't have even that comfort. I continue writing.

'What do you imagine doing, making love?' I ask him.

He strokes my face and hair in a loving way and says, 'How about if I show you, but you'll have to tell me whether you enjoy it—or want it—I can't read your mind. And if you don't like it, or don't want it, tell me to stop and I'll stop.'

'Promise?'

'I promise. And if there's anything you'd like that I haven't thought of, just ask!'

'I think I'll lie here like the Sleeping Beauty and pretend to be asleep.'

'Okay. I've no doubt you'll let me know when I've woken you up!'

I lie on my back, eyes closed. He rolls me onto my side, very gently so as not to wake me, enough to be able to undo my bikini top. He removes it and cups his hands around my breasts and kisses each in turn, his mouth so hot and the feeling so intense I want to cry, 'Stop!' But I don't—can't— because I'm asleep.

'Can I take these off?' His hands are on my belly, his fingers stroking me along the edges of my bikini bottom. Butterflies flutter deep inside me, low down.

I whisper, 'I'm asleep, remember?'

He chuckles softly, undoes the bows on my hips, and pulls the bikini bottom down and away, revealing two little green packets sitting on my belly.

'Hah!' he exclaims. 'What a sensible woman.'

I continue feigning sleep … I'm not responsible for what he's doing to me … for what comes next … it's not my fault it's …

I put my pen down. For some dark, unspeakable reason, I don't want to go there.

Chapter Seven

Wednesday, 22 March 1995

It rained again last night, but this morning it's sunshine and blue skies again. The creek will be too swollen to paddle upstream, but we can go on the billabong. Swimming in the billabong is a no-no, for lots of health reasons, but I still don my bikini. And instead of my usual t-shirt, shorts and sneakers, I wrap my sarong around me under my armpits and tie it in front of my breasts, then slip on my thongs. I tuck two condoms into my bikini below my navel, just as I imagined doing. I'm excited—but extremely nervous. Making our sandwiches, I notice a tremor in my hands.

When I arrive at his back door Shaun looks at me grimly. There's no smile of approval, no appreciative, or even quizzical, glance at my attire the way I'd fantasised.

'What?' I snap defensively, my tone bordering on belligerent.

'I've found Saab. Just inside Joe's fence at the north-west end of the billabong. He must have taken a bait. I need to pick him up in the trailer and bury him. I'll understand if you don't want to come. He's really on the nose—the maggots are having a field day.'

I'm shocked. Aghast. My stomach churns, but I don't hesitate. 'Of course I'll come.' I use my sarong to wipe away tears. 'Where will you bury him?'

Shaun points to the stand of tall eucalypts behind the stock-yards. 'A while back I discovered an old cemetery in there. Seems fitting.' He gives me a cursory glance, his expression un-readable. 'Best you wear jeans. He's in the blady grass, and you'll be cut to ribbons.' He notices my thongs. 'And it's boggy, so wear your old sneakers. Give me your backpack; I'll meet you by the tractor.'

I dash home, hurl my sarong and bikini—with the con-doms—on top of my tracksuit on the bottom of my wardrobe, and dress in bra and briefs, t-shirt and jeans, socks and sneakers, feeling strangely relieved. I arrive back at the lean-to, breathless after hurrying up the slope.

Shaun has hung our backpacks on a lantern hook hanging from a rafter. The canvas water bag, attached to the front of the tractor, is full. Two long-handled shovels, a coil of thinnish rope and a couple of gunny sacks are on the floor of the small trailer. He climbs up onto the tractor. 'We can share the seat,' he says, giving me a hand up.

I'm tearful, sad and sorry, sorry for Saab and sad for Shaun, but I'm also feeling intense pleasure pressed against him on the narrow tractor seat, my arm around his waist to stabilise myself. We don't speak on the way down to the billabong and have very little to say as we jolt along the track between the billabong and Gwongorella Creek, heading towards *Booyul*'s north boundary fence. Any other time and circumstance it would be an adven-ture, but Saab was Shaun's shadow, his daily companion, and the expression on Shaun's face is ineffably sad.

He pulls up at the boundary and manoeuvres the tractor so the trailer is close to the fence. 'Now we walk,' he says.

We each carry a shovel and sack; Shaun slings the coil of rope over one shoulder. He holds the strands of barbed wire apart for me, and I do the same for him. We set off in a westerly direction along the fence line behind the billabong, following a narrow cattle track between thick clumps of razor-sharp blady grass. The soft ground is pocked with hoof prints and puddles and my sneakers are soon saturated.

Shaun stops. 'Snake!' A long, thick red-bellied black snake is weaving through the tufts, moving away from us. I visualise Dan grabbing it by the tail, twisting it so it can't climb itself, and shoving it into one of the gunny sacks, held open by Billy, Saab forgotten.

'Saab's just up here,' Shaun says.

I smell the carcass before I see it. I start retching, nauseated by the stench and then by the sight of Saab, bloated and riddled with maggots, swarmed by whining, buzzing blowflies.

'Let's try and pick him up in one piece on the shovels, and move him over there, where it's drier, and get him into the sacks. That'll deaden the—'

'Good idea!' I interrupt.

Moving Saab's disintegrating remains is an extremely un-pleasant experience. I retch and spew a few times, but I survive the task. I even help Shaun get the stinking, fly-blown carcass into the sacks, to the disappointment of a million blowflies. Shaun ties the shrouded Saab onto the shovels' shafts with the rope. I hold the handle ends behind my back and lead the way, keeping a wary eye out for snakes, while Shaun holds the blade ends, the reeking burden heavy between us as we walk through the blady grass back to the tractor.

We drag Saab in his sacks, still tied to the shovels, under the fence. I help Shaun lift him, blade ends first, into the trailer and push him in. Shaun closes the trailer's gate. We drive along the eastern edge of the billabong, then up the slope alongside his vegetable patch, past the packing shed and towards the stock-yards, then behind the piggery, where he stops at a gate I haven't noticed before.

'I'll open it.' I climb down, my sneakers squelching. Shaun drives through and I close the gate behind him. He gives me a hand up onto the tractor, and again I sit close against him, my arm around his waist. He clears his throat. 'Thanks for your help today, Jodie. I really appreciate it.' His voice is gruff and cracked. 'It would've been so much harder without you.'

I rest my cheek on his shoulder and squeeze his waist where I'm hanging on to him. There's a recognisable, unpleasant odour of death around him and I'm sure I smell the same.

Both of us ward off prickly scrub leaning over the narrow, little-used track, which winds between tall trees, until we arrive in a clearing that still has a stand of spotted gums in the middle of it. A small group of wallabies flee as we approach. It is indeed a cemetery; half a dozen graves, each surrounded by bush rocks, are nestled amongst these trees. The wooden crosses, fashioned from the forest, have names and dates on them but they are indecipherable.

Three of the graves are very small.

'Probably babies, or young children,' Shaun says. 'Does that say 1887 to you?'

I peer at faded numbers on a grey cross and nod. 'Yeah— or 1889 maybe.'

'Shows how old our farmhouses are. They were probably built over a hundred years ago, with locally made bricks, and red cedar flooring, internal walls, ceilings and doors.'

We lift Saab in his shroud out of the trailer, still tied to the shovels, and lay him adjacent to where Shaun plans to dig the grave under one of the spotted gums. He releases the shovels and digs the hole while I collect bush rocks to use as an edging. I help him lower Saab into the grave, then stand back while he fills it in, the dirt dropping gently off his shovel.

'Rest in peace, dog,' he says. He speaks softly, but I hear him.

The bush is strangely quiet, as if it is listening too, and watching us. I see Shaun's grief—it's his turn to cry—but I know not to say anything. I'm an eavesdropper, a bystander, a witness, trying not to intrude. I watch him as he places the rocks I've picked up, not enough to finish the job, around the perimeter of the grave. 'I'll add more later,' he says.

We put the shovels and rope in the trailer, and he drives in silence back to the lean-to.

'I need a shower,' he says. 'I stink.'

'Me too.'

'And coffee. How about I meet you on your veranda and we have lunch there?' He holds out my backpack. 'I can still help you with anything you want to work on.'

'Okay. Are you sure you feel up to it?'

'Of course,' he says.

Our eyes meet, but I'm unable to hold his gaze more than momentarily before I look away and down, taking the backpack from him. I so want to give him a commiserating hug, but it's not the right time or place. 'See you soon, then.'

I wash my sneakers and socks, with the hose attached to the tank tap—Mum uses it to water her herb garden and the nasturtiums. I'm spreading out my socks and propping up my sneakers on the tank stand, when I glance across at the carport and see, with a whoosh of fright, Mum's car parked next to Dan's.

Holy shit! What's she doing home? I open the back door stealthily, sneak into the bathroom and lock the door. Where is she? I feel sick! She might be *in my room*, in my private space, *finding* stuff, reading my love letters to Shaun, reading my journal! She'll know I'm here as soon as the water pump comes on. My heart is racing. I'm convinced she's been snooping. Anticipating a confrontation I start to shake.

I soap myself all over, trying to neutralise the smell of death. I shampoo and condition my hair, but it's the shortest shower ever, I'm so worried Shaun will arrive and come face-to-face with *her* and I won't be there to defend him.

I can't put my stinking clothes back on. I'll have to go to my room with my towel wrapped around me, so I can put on something clean. I drop the clothes in the washing machine.

Where is she? What if she's in my room waiting for me! Or been in there!

I'll tell her my journal entries and love letters to Shaun are just wishful thinking, figments of my imagination, but for sure she won't believe me. Even if she *does* believe me when I tell her 'Nothing's happened!', she'll say, '*Yet!* Nothing's happened *yet!*' She'll consider my wishful thinking to be as bad as the act itself. She'll be convinced Shaun is grooming me.

Some of my journal entries *are* fiction, but other entries are true statements. For sure, she'll believe the fiction about Shaun is *the truth,* and the truth about Dad is *all lies!*

What if she's found the two condoms in the bottom of my wardrobe with my bikini and sarong? She'll consider it 'circumstantial evidence' that 'improper conduct' was being contemplated—and she'd be right—*but Shaun knows nothing about any of that!*

She might have found the rest of the condoms under my pillow. What if she's found the prescription for the pill and my first month's supply in my desk drawer?

If Shaun tries to defend himself, she won't listen to him or believe him. She'll accuse him of grooming me, of seducing me, taking advantage of me when I'm under-age. If she quotes my writings to him to prove her point, he'll think I'm totally crazy, utterly irresponsible, writing dangerous lies about our relationship, incriminating him. She could ruin his life. Our relationship will disintegrate, he'll hate me, and it will be all my fault.

I feel like the ten-year-old who gave Mum the pink letter. I remember Dad warning me for years she'd run away with the boys and leave me with him if she found out what he was doing. I can't remember anything else about 1990, but I can remember a man and a woman taking me to the boarding school early in 1991. During those four years at boarding school, never seeing or hearing from my father or brothers, seeing Mum only rarely, I grew up, but sometimes, often, like now—I still *feel* ten years old, even younger, scared she'll hate me, scared she'll run away again. I'm having a panic attack—the black rock in my chest kind.

She's *not* in my room. Nor is she on the east veranda. I peer through my lace curtains. I put on fresh underwear, T-shirt and shorts. I check everything is still safely hidden: my love letters to Shaun in their shoebox on the bottom of my wardrobe under other shoeboxes; the stolen garments hanging up between my clothes; the condoms under my pillow; other stolen clothing at the back of my bottom drawer under my jumpers and long-sleeved cotton tops; the pill packet in my top desk drawer; my journal behind my textbooks in the bookcase. As hiding places go, they are not remotely secure. They are only safe if I am at home to guard them.

I *think* everything is the way I left it, but *I'm not sure*. I *feel* violated—because even though I *think* everything is still in place, untouched, something *feels* different. I want to relax, but I can't. I no longer feel certain. Nothing feels safe.

I can handle: 'How come you weren't at home?' 'Where have you been?' 'What have you been doing?' 'Why were the dogs locked up?' It's everything else that's terrifying.

I pick up the phone in the hall outside my bedroom door and dial Shaun. He answers. 'Don't come down,' I whisper. 'Mum has come home. Catch you later.'

'Are you—?

'I'm okay.' I hang up.

I take the sandwiches from my backpack and arrange them on two plates. I boil the jug and make a pot of tea, put everything on the tray with two cups, and carry the tray out to the studio to face the music.

Chapter Eight

Saturday, 25 March 1995

Dan and Billy left for the beach before dawn. It never crosses their minds to invite me—it's Melanie who asks me to keep her company when she videos them, but she's busy with final dress and technical rehearsals for *Romeo and Juliet*; it opens next Friday night. My brothers would never think to invite me to the beach because I'm *me*, someone they value, someone they like to have around. And no reply from Emma-Sue, but Dan swears he delivered my letter to her on Monday. Clearly, she doesn't value me either, but why would she?

Since Wednesday, Mum's been in a strange mood, remote and weird. Maybe it's just my paranoia and feelings of guilt filling me with trepidation and making me miserable. When she questioned me about why I wasn't there when she returned home Wednesday morning, I burst into tears and told her the truth—the Saab part. I *was* genuinely upset about Saab, but I was crying and shaking thinking she'd invaded my room and my world was about to collapse! I'm still jittery. *Did* she find my journal and read at least some of the entries? She'd only have to read *one* letter, and keep it for evidence, and it would be enough to incriminate Shaun.

There's been no opportunity to commiserate or communicate with him since Wednesday. Mum stayed home Thursday and yesterday, and the boys had to catch the bus. She said she needed to work on her entry for the upcoming RAG exhibition, but I'm sure she was keeping an eye on me, constantly in and out, and on the phone—she has an extension in her room— talking to I don't know who. With her door shut I couldn't hear what she was saying. I did schoolwork both days to keep my mind occupied and stop me freaking out. At least now I'm ahead with everything.

This morning Mum asked me if I wanted to come to the Alumy Creek market with her, it's always on the last Saturday of the month, and I agreed. She's taken the Clarence Way route. It runs along the top of the escarpment and provides a beautiful view of our property. I peer out Mum's side at *Booyul* and then at *Gwongorella* as a panorama opens out. The billabong looks enlarged and fuller after the rain. The creek is swollen and brown. I can't see upstream to our island from this angle as the creek bends around at the boundary between *Booyul* and Joe Whittaker's place. Now I can see *Gwongorella* directly opposite us. Our quaint, old-fashioned homestead looks like a doll's house in the middle of the mostly cleared paddocks. It's good that several stands of big old trees remain. I practically break my neck looking backwards at Shaun's vegetable patch, hoping for a glimpse of him.

Noticing my interest, Mum glances to the right for a moment herself. '*Gwongorella* looks lovely, greener already. It's marvellous what a difference a bit of rain makes.'

We cut through Trenayr, past the timber mills. When a mill went up in flames recently, *The Daily Examiner* headlines declared: 'Sabotage!' It's a blackened shell, still smoking.

'Sad for the owners,' Mum observes.

'A reprieve for the trees, you mean.'

'That too,' she says shortly. Indicating she's not in the mood for debate, she adds, 'I just love this north coast autumn weather! Twenty-six degrees in Grafton, six degrees in Katoomba. Those cold, damp winters in the Blue Mountains rotted my bones!'

That's the closest she's come to talking about the past since my meltdown a week ago. It's as if there's an unspoken agreement between her and the boys not to mention the Blue Mountains, or Dad, though I'm certain there are all sorts of things going on to do with him that I don't know about.

We cross Alumy Creek bridge, pull up at the Lawrence Road junction, turn right towards town. On my left, a grey-trunked matchstick forest of poplars glows a pale, autumn gold. Dark green clumps of mistletoe cling to the trees' upper branches.

Before long we're forced to slow to a crawl, the road reduced to two narrow lanes, banks of cars parked rear-to-curb on both sides as we approach the Alumy Creek Reserve. Mum cruises between the vehicles expecting to miraculously find a vacant spot closer to the action.

'You're optimistic.'

'This little car is serendipitous.'

'How do you mean?'

She brakes suddenly. 'Like this!' A Toyota Landcruiser pulls out on our left, just in front of us. Mum waves cheerfully and next minute she's backing our filthy little Corolla into the vacant space between two polished town cars. 'Howzat!' she says, grinning at me.

I give her an answering smile, acknowledging her genius.

Directly across the road are huge old trees—oak, fig, black bean, cedar, flame trees and others—in various shades of green, red and gold against a startling blue sky. Cottonwool clouds float by. I should be enchanted, and part of me is or I wouldn't notice. Stalls, under striped awnings or colourful umbrellas, are in the shade under the trees.

After we cross the road, Mum does something unprecedented. She presses a fifty-dollar note into my hand. 'Go and buy yourself something. Anything except food.'

'Gosh! Thanks, Mum!' I feel a flicker of pleasure, despite her injunction not to eat.

'I'll meet you on that seat over there, or somewhere nearby, say in an hour, and we can enjoy a nice, healthy lunch together. I'm going to buy some native shrubs to attract honeyeaters. I want to paint birds!' She hurries away.

Feeling a burst of reciprocal generosity, I call after her: 'Come down to the creek if you want to paint birds!' Fortunately, she's out of earshot. I inspect the fifty-dollar note. Fifty bucks! Why would she do that? To stop me stealing? *Did* she look in my wardrobe? Did she see unworn clothes she knows she didn't buy for me in there? Did she notice the condoms on the bottom of the wardrobe with my sarong and bikini? A pang of fear stabs me.

Wylah clothing

I flick through the colourful t-shirts, shorts, skirts and long, loose-fitting pants, the soft cotton material screen-printed in pastel colours with contemporary Aboriginal designs. Emma-Sue would look stunning in them. I read a hand-printed sign: *Wylah—won't shrink, run or wash out. Completely user-friendly. Wylah is the black cockatoo that lives in our area.*

'They're lovely!' I tell the stall-holder.

Jacaranda Pottery

The mauve glaze is striking on plates, bowls, mugs, jugs, vases, plant pots and bread crocks displayed on strips of hessian on the grass.

Pint-sized hats just like Dad's.

Child-sized Akubras and leather hats lie next to adult ones on the table. Alongside them are straw concoctions draped with dried flowers, lace and ribbons. I try one on and check myself out in a mirror set up for the purpose. I can't help thinking it looks good on me, but it reminds me of Liz, my widowed grandmother, Dad's mother, another casualty in the family break up. I haven't seen her for years, but I can still remember her wearing a hat like this while she pruned shrubs and gathered flowers from her cottage garden in the Blue Mountains. Mum's mother rejoined family in New Zealand years ago. When the boys leave, I'll only have Mum.

'I put him back in his box, but he looks at me all sad and I can't resist the little fella!' She's holding a quivering puppy, which looks at me with anxious eyes.

'Emma-Sue!' I'm so overwhelmed I nearly burst into tears! I see silver earrings, studs and ear-cuffs—a frog, a lizard. Silver and leather bangles on her wrists. Black, crinkly hair scooped up and tied back with a red, black and yellow scarf. She's talking to *me*, smiling at *me*, though I can tell she's shy from the fleeting glances of her dark eyes and I recognise her speaking to me is an act of courage.

We gush over the puppy together. A man wearing a crocheted beanie in the Aboriginal colours wanders up to us, a little kid wearing a multi-coloured shade hat straddling his shoulders. The child reaches out to touch the puppy and when Emma-Sue raises the terrified morsel closer to him so he can stroke it, he laughs with delight. The man doesn't look at me, but he gestures towards the food van with its signs.

Fresh tropical fruit juice
Fresh fruit with cream and ice cream

I listen to them talking, trying to act nonchalant and not stare at them, fascinated by their differentness, entranced by the child. The man glances at me and nods as he moves away.

Emma-Sue says, 'My brother. They're gonna get something to eat.'

'Is it his little boy?'

'My older sister's little jarjum.'

'You got my letter?'

'Yeah.' She glances at the puppy's owner. 'I better put the puppy back. She'll think I'm trying to steal him. I'd love to buy the little fella, but I don't have forty dollars.'

I nearly offer her my fifty-dollar note. Mum did say, *Go and buy yourself something, anything except food!* But an image of her face, wrathful and disbelieving, intervenes.

'Thanks for reminding me!' I remove the hat from my head and return it to the stall.

I look where she's looking and see members of her family converging on the food van.

'Emma-Sue, please can we meet again somewhere?'

'Sure. I'm at TAFE Tuesday mornings. Twelve o'clock outside the canteen?'

'Okay. I'll try and be there.' I watch her go, with a sensation of anticipation and pleasure at having something to look forward to. I remember the same good feeling at the end of my first day with Shaun.

'She *chose* to speak to me! She's agreed to meet up with me again!' I mutter to Anne. 'With a *day*, and a *time* and a *place*!'

It can't get much better than that!

'Talking to yourself again?' I jerk at the unexpectedness of Mum's voice, higher and lighter than usual, right beside my ear. 'Who were you talking to?'

Does she mean Anne? Or Emma-Sue!

Be civil.

'Emma-Sue. She's in Billy's classes at school. She saw me with Dan and Billy at the cinema. See that little puppy in the box?' I pick up the puppy and give him to Mum to hold, then wave my fifty-dollar note at her.

'Can I buy—'

'No way!' She puts the puppy back in its box as if it's crawling with fleas.

'—you lunch?'

'I mean, yes, that would be very nice, thank you. Let's have a large apple, carrot, celery and beetroot juice, and fresh tropical fruit salad with cream and ice cream. I'll mind a table.'

We are soon sitting in the shade at one of the solid timber tables, eating delicious chunks of papaya, mango, pineapple, watermelon and strawberries and sucking up freshly squeezed juice through fat straws.

Mum tells me about birds that like grevilleas. 'They said all sorts of honeyeaters, including larger ones like Noisy Miners and Wattlebirds; Eastern Spinebills, finches, wrens.'

I blurt out, 'Can Emma-Sue come and visit one weekend?'

Everything changes. Mum's posture. Her breathing. The precise way she positions the plastic spoon in her fruit salad, before turning to me with a carefully composed expression. 'I'm not sure that's such a good idea, Pet—her coming to the house.'

Stay cool.

'Why not?'

'I'm not sure about that either.' Her neck is beginning to flush. 'I'm not racially prejudiced. It's not that.'

'No! Really?' I ooze sarcasm and contempt. We haven't exchanged two bits of information and already we're in total conflict. There's no way I can admit to her how desperate I am to have a friend; how lonely I feel. She'll see me as vulnerable, open to 'bad' influences, and use her concern as justification for keeping me even more confined and isolated—if that's possible—every aspect of my life under her control, so *she* can feel safe.

'Jodie—'

'Forget it!'

She explodes, quietly, because we're in public and she doesn't like to make a scene or attract attention. 'Why can't we have a sensible, mature conversation? Do you realise,' she snarls, her voice low, 'I am *never* allowed to have feelings of my own, or express an opinion you disagree with, without you jumping down my throat? Can't we at least *talk* about it?'

'What's the point? You've already made up your mind. You don't even know her, or know anything about her, but you're "not sure that's such a good idea".' I mimic her nastily. 'Well, thanks a lot for your confidence in my judgement.' I look straight ahead and suck on my drink like nothing's happening between us.

'I haven't made up my mind about *anything*!' she hisses. 'That's what "not sure" means, for godssake! It means I have anxieties and uncertainties, and I need to be allowed to express them, explore them, talk about them. It has nothing to do with your judgement. But if it comes to that, what *do* you "know" about her?'

I'm silenced by her challenge, defeated and deflated. When I do speak, my voice is tearful. 'She seems really nice.'

'So, it's a matter of trust, faith, hope and optimism. A good impression. And you pin everything on that. Women fall in love with charming men and find out too late they've married a bastard. Trust must be *earned*, Jodie, in any relationship, including friendship. I'm telling you, don't rush it. And I'm asking you not to rush me.'

'It *is* because she's Aboriginal, though, isn't it? You wouldn't hesitate if I told you she was the daughter of a doctor or a lawyer and she was *white*. That's true, isn't it?'

Mum is shaking her head *and* shrugging her shoulders, like she's struggling to answer me. 'I don't know! The implications frighten me—that it won't be just Emma-Sue.' She flicks her straw in the general direction of Emma-Sue's family. 'It'll be *everyone*. I'd worry about you. Alcohol. Drugs. Gambling. Violence. All those problems you hear about in Aboriginal families and communities. Child sexual abuse. The things any caring parent would want to protect their children from.'

'Yes, Mum, I agree! It is *very* important to be a caring parent and protect your child from sexual abuse!' I stare at her, daring her to look at me, but she's focusing on rearranging the chunks of fruit in her cardboard bowl with the plastic spoon. 'For your information, your *own* sons get drunk most weekends—and stoned out of their brains. I don't know about anything else.'

Now she looks at me.

Whoops! Big mouth!

At least I have her attention.

'If it makes any difference, Mum, Emma-Sue doesn't fit your stereotyped image. She's not into drugs, or alcohol, or violence. She's into education and good health and so is her family. One of her aunts teaches Pre-Voc at TAFE.'

Mum nods, raises her eyebrows and purses her lips, indicating she's impressed.

We start eating our fruit again. After a while, suppressing any challenging tone in my voice, I ask her, 'Have *you* ever had an Aboriginal girlfriend?'

'Yes, as a matter of fact. In primary school.' She examines the chunk of watermelon balanced on her plastic spoon. 'Her name was Lily. She was the best friend I ever had.' She raises the chunk of watermelon to her mouth.

'You've never told me that before.'

'You've never asked before.' She takes the chunk in her teeth, then into her mouth, chews, and swallows.

'Tell me about her.'

'We'd just moved to Sydney's north shore from the eastern suburbs. I was ten, in fourth class. So it was 1966.'

'The year after the 1965 Freedom Ride and the year before the 1967 Referendum!'

I'm astonished to realise that these events—historical to me—were in Mum's lifetime!

'What Freedom Ride and Referendum?'

'You don't know?' I'm shocked. 'How can you not know!'

'Because I'm ignorant!' she snaps, glaring at me. 'I was only ten. Aborigines were hardly talked about. I remember a photo, or drawing, in my Australian history textbook, of an Aborigine standing on one leg with a spear and a boomerang, but that was about it.'

'I'm sorry.'

'How come *you* know so much!'

'I've been learning about it in my *Aboriginal Studies—Contemporary Issues* subject.'

'So, explain. What Freedom Ride? What Referendum?' It's like she's testing me.

'In February 1965, Charles Perkins, he was the first Aboriginal person to go to university, and Jim Spigelman and a bunch of university students went on a bus trip around northern New South Wales to investigate racial discrimination and protest against it and show Aboriginal people how to put a stop to it.'

'What sort of discrimination?'

'They weren't served in shops; they had to sit separately in cinemas; they weren't allowed to swim in local swimming pools or go into pubs or clubs. They couldn't get decent, well-paid jobs. It didn't matter if they were clean or dirty, drunk or sober, educated or uneducated, old or young, they were discriminated against. They couldn't vote. Their living conditions were terrible. They suffered from poor health. Their educational opportunities were limited. It was like *Apartheid* in South Africa.'

Mum nods slowly, pulling a face. 'And what about the Referendum?'

'On May 27, 1967, there was a national referendum to amend two things in the Constitution, so the federal government could take over responsibility for Aboriginal people in all the states and territories and have the power to make special laws for them, and so Aborigines could be counted as citizens in national censuses, instead of just being considered part of the flora and fauna. And over 90 per cent of the people who voted, voted Yes.'

'So less than thirty years ago they weren't even counted as citizens! Is that when they finally got the right to vote?'

'Sort of, but it wasn't *compulsory* for Aboriginal people to vote, like it was for other Australians, until 1983.'

'Only twelve years ago!' She stands up. It's end of conversation. Time to go.

I stack the cardboard containers and cups and take them over to the bin. When I return, the box of grevilleas is on the table.

'Would you mind?'

I dutifully carry the plants to the car. In my pocket are the leftover banknotes and coins from buying lunch. I won't be offering Mum the change! After all, she gave me fifty dollars to spend on myself, but I didn't get to see much of the market. And I *did* use it to buy food after all! That makes me smile. I've still got the ten dollars she gave me for the cinema. Enough to buy my second month's supply of the pill *and* replace the money I stole from Dan's cash box.

In Shopping World we load a trolley with groceries. Mum usually does the shopping on Fridays, but she didn't go to town yesterday.

We drive home in silence and eventually pull up in the carport. Mum lets the dogs out and they dance around us, tails wagging, whining a greeting. She removes her box of grevilleas and disappears with them, probably to park them under the tank stand and give them a drink.

It takes me three trips to unload the groceries and take them into the house.

While Mum is working on her creation in the studio, I'm lying on my bed writing in my journal about my encounter with Emma-Sue. It makes me want to hear Mum's story about her own childhood experience of an Aboriginal girlfriend in 1966, when she was only ten. I'm amazed and intrigued. If I make her a cup of tea and persuade her to take a break on the veranda, she might be willing to tell me about Lily. Right now, though, I can't be bothered moving.

I turn my HAs up and listen. When I turn them off, or take them off, the world around me dies in that one sense. Sounds indicate life.

The wind-chimes on the west veranda ping a delicate, melodic, unfinished song. Today my tinnitus sounds like drumming distant cicadas or chirping crickets. Sometimes it's a whooshing or hissing and I imagine I'm on a beach, waves surging, pebbles rolling back and forth on a rocky shore.

I force myself to get up. I put on a pad, just in case, then head for the kitchen, where I make Mum a pot of tea, go out to the studio, invite her to take a break and come and sit on the east veranda.

She tells me she'd rather stay put. 'But come and join me in here,' she says.

So I do.

When we are settled opposite each other, with our cups of tea and crackers with cheese, I ask her, 'Please tell me about Lily, the best friend you ever had.'

She sighs, sips her tea. Many seconds elapse, maybe half a minute, before she puts down the cup. 'It's not the easiest story to tell, Jodie. It doesn't have a happy ending.'

Mum's stories have been about the good times in her life when she was a child. Stories about not-so-good times remain locked away, which is why I haven't heard this one before.

'Tell me, anyway,' I beg her. 'Please. I really want to know.'

She sighs again, deeply. 'Lily's circumstances were dire. Back then, as a child of ten, I certainly noticed, but I don't remember ever questioning *why*. When we moved to the north shore, I started a new school. I was with my mother, waiting outside the principal's office. An Aboriginal girl was there, also waiting to see him. Maybe she was in trouble. He kept her waiting while he interviewed us, then he introduced me to her—her name was Lily. He told her to take me around and show me where everything was—toilets, library, play areas, no-go zones, tuckshop—and then take me to her classroom and introduce me to her teacher. He also told her to look after me at recess and lunch time.'

Mum pauses, eats half of her cracker with cheese, sips her tea. I wait.

'Lily seemed nice.' She gives me a half-smile, as if acknowledging I'd said those same words to her about Emma-Sue. 'She was quite beautiful really, in an uncared-for sort of way. She had unbrushed, badly cut, sun-bleached hair, deep dark eyes and very white teeth in her brown face. She wasn't *very* dark. More like she was tanned. She had a soft voice—with a different way of talking. She was thin, with skinny legs; they had what looked like the scars of sores on them and I thought they were healed insect bites or paspalum sores, but I found out, much later, they were scars from cigarette burns inflicted by her father.' Mum looks and sounds disgusted. 'He wasn't Aboriginal. At least, he didn't *look* Aboriginal to me.'

She pauses again to sip her tea.

'Lily was the only person I knew in that whole school. I soon noticed other, snotty kids looked down on her, but it was too late for me to join them and snub her like they did as we were already friends. We needed each other. She was my *only* friend in that school for the next three years, but she was my *best* friend. I could rely on her. I never doubted her loyalty. I knew she'd never dump me like other so-called friends in the past who drifted off when they found someone better to play with.'

Mum looks sour for a moment, but then her expression softens, and she chuckles.

'What's funny?'

'Lily already had breasts, and I had this fantasy that the reason she had breasts was because she didn't wash very often, so whenever I had a shower or a bath, I made sure I didn't wash my very flat chest!'

My mother amazes me sometimes, the things she comes out with. 'Did it work?'

'Sadly, no!' She grins, then drifts away again as she cuts another piece of cheese and puts it on a cracker.

'Tell me!' I demand, not wanting to miss a single memory.

'Lily liked coming to my place to play after school—'

I don't know if Mum realises what she just said, but I'll remind her Lily was allowed to visit *her* house, when I ask her again if Emma-Sue can come here.

'—but I preferred to go to *her* place. It was much more exciting than mine. They had a cow and a calf, and hens and chickens and a scary rooster, and a dog and puppies, and her father kept homing pigeons. They lived on the edge of the Lane Cove National Park, not far from the Lane Cove River, where she swam with her brothers and sisters, and fished, and caught yabbies and eels and turtles—to eat! Lily knew great places to play in the bush—flat rocks with emus and kangaroos carved into them; rock shelves and shallow caves with paintings on the walls; trees to climb; cicadas to catch. We'd scoop up taddies from a nearby creek with a small net and put them in a bucket and watch them gradually turn into frogs. We picked blackberries when they were in season and filled billy cans for our mothers to make into pies, or jam.

'I remember the first time my mother let me go to Lily's place after school. It was on the proviso I was home before dark, and I wasn't to get my uniform dirty. We got off the bus at Lily's stop—she had several brothers and sisters who got off too—along with other kids, and we walked down a track into the bush. The area wasn't built out in those days. Eventually, we came to a cluster of dilapidated houses, low on the ground, made of grey weatherboards or fibro, and corrugated iron. There was flaking paint on window frames, broken panes, rusty iron roofs. Dogs yapping. Hens with chickens scratching around. Old car wrecks rusting away in the long grass.

'Inside Lily's house, I'll never forget the flypapers—incredibly sticky strips of brown paper hanging from the rafters—covered in trapped, buzzing flies, above a stained, round wooden table with a pail of cow's milk standing on it, the cream thick on top, and lots more flies! A few chairs. A bare wooden floor. The kitchen was small, with corrugated iron walls, and you had to pass through it and go down some wooden steps to get out to the back yard. Between the sink and the stove was a bread-cutter, screwed to the one and only bench in a nest of breadcrumbs.

'Lily turned a handle while she pressed the loaf against a whirling sharp disc, and it sliced the bread in thick slabs. We only had a bread knife at our place! And they had crusty loaves of *white* bread! We only had brown. And they had homemade blackberry jam, in a meat safe hanging off a hook so the ants couldn't get at it. Lily spread the jam thickly on our slabs of bread—*much* thicker than Mum ever let *me* spread jam—then she scraped cream off the top of the milk in the pail and smeared it over the jam. I was in heaven! It was the ultimate luxury, white bread with homemade blackberry jam and cream.

'The house only had two bedrooms, and one was the parents' room, with a baby in a cradle and a toddler in a cot in there as well as the parents' bed. Lily slept in the other room with her younger siblings, in double bunks, two to a bed, with stained old mattresses and pillows, no sheets, just grey blankets. I remember the smell of stale urine from the wet beds of the little kids. Her older brothers slept in a shed out the back.

'The dunny was a thunderbox down the back yard. There was also a corrugated iron lean-to near the back steps, with a laundry tub, which only had one tap—there was no hot water, though I think there was a copper. The shower was a galvanised bucket with small holes in the bottom of it and the big boys had to fill the laundry tub, then fill the bucket with water from the tub and quickly lift it onto a hook hanging down from the rafters and have a shower before all the water ran out through the holes. I understood why Lily didn't wash very often!

'Her mother looked old enough to be her grandmother. She was nice to me, but very shy. Lily's father was a horrible man! I learned to stay out of his way, when he was around.'

'Why was he horrible?'

'His homing pigeons were confined in a smelly, three-sided shed, with chicken wire across the front of it. He invited me in, saying I could hold a pigeon while he put a ring around its leg. Lily whispered, "Don't go!" but I ignored her because I was curious about the pigeons. But then he started nuzzling my neck and put his hands up the skirt of my uniform! I was petrified! I didn't know *what* to do!'

I stare at her, appalled. 'What *did* you do?'

'Lily suddenly ran up to the chicken wire, screaming hysterically, "Dad! Come quick! The welfare's here! They're taking the little kids away!" And he bolted out of the shed and started running towards the house. I followed him out, Lily latched the door, grabbed my hand, and *we* ran—in the opposite direction! We climbed down the cliff and escaped into the bush.'

Mum leans back, shaking her head. 'He was *furious*! He stood at the top of the cliff, in a rage, yelling, "Get back here!" And when she refused, "Don't say no to *me*! Who do you think you are? Do what I tell you and pronto! You want a flogging?"'

'While he was carrying on, Lily showed me a path to follow along the base of the cliff, which would take me up to the house. Then she slowly climbed up the cliff towards her father, keeping him distracted, while I escaped. I could hear her screaming. It was *awful*! It was my first experience of violence; my first realisation not all fathers were kind and decent! I couldn't tell Mother—I knew she'd stop me from going to Lily's place again, and I had too much fun playing with her and her younger siblings in the bush. I went back to Lily's many times after that, but I made sure I steered clear of her father.' Mum raises her teacup to her lips. 'After it happened, I asked Mother if we could adopt Lily.'

'What did she say?'

'"Absolutely not! There's far too much of that going on—children being removed from their families. It's wrong!"'

'The Stolen Generations?'

'I guess.'

We are both quiet for a while, until she says, 'One of my deepest regrets involves Lily. It's haunted me all my life, my betrayal of her.'

I wait for more. I can hear the silence. Eventually, I urge her, my voice low. 'Please tell me what happened. How did you betray her? What do you regret?'

She draws in a deep breath, releases it. 'It was January 1969, the summer holidays. We walked down the track at the end of Fiddens Wharf Road to the Lane Cove River. The wharf was built in the 1820s, primarily to ship timber down river to Sydney. The Bradfield Park Housing Settlement and Migrant Hostel was nearby, and kids used to come down to Fiddens Wharf to swim. The river wasn't polluted in those days.

'A gang of older boys were watching us. I didn't know if they were migrant kids or locals, but there were no adults around. I said to Lily, "Let's go!" But it was her turn to ignore me. She wanted to swim. I told her I was going home and set off up the track. I looked back. She was on her feet, as if she'd decided to come with me, but the boys had surrounded her. I called out, "I'll get help!" and took off up the track, terrified they'd chase *me*. I ran all the way home. The awful thing was, once I was home, I *didn't* get help for Lily. I did *nothing*! I didn't tell *anyone*! It was as if I *forgot*!'

Mum looks like she's begging to be forgiven. 'I didn't see Lily for the rest of the holidays. And she wasn't at the high school I went to. I assumed she'd gone to a different high school. But one afternoon, looking for the comics in the *North Shore Times*, a news item caught my eye. I was on the Persian rug in our living room, surrounded by three of Mother's elegant friends sipping tea from fine bone china teacups, when I asked, "Mother, what does carnal knowledge mean?" I remember the silence, before she replied, "Carnal knowledge, Anne, is when a man has sexual intercourse with a girl under the age of consent, which is sixteen." The news item stated that five youths aged sixteen to eighteen had been charged with carnal knowledge of a thirteen-year-old Aboriginal girl at Fiddens Wharf, and they'd pleaded not guilty, alleging she'd consented and told them she was sixteen.

'One of Mother's friends said, "I saw that article. Those darkie girls *are* very promiscuous and precocious." I was outraged! "She *didn't* consent!" I contradicted her, very loudly, "And she *was* only thirteen!" Mother tried to smooth things over, saying, "With or without consent, she's under-age, Anne, and it's a crime and they'll be punished." But she was *not* happy with me! It was not a fit subject for a thirteen-year-old, especially in company. I'd embarrassed her in front of her friends. I'd spoilt their afternoon tea.' Mum shakes her head. 'I don't know to this day if Mother realised—or at least suspected—the article was about Lily. She probably didn't *want* to know!'

That sounds familiar.

'I never saw Lily again.' Mum looks directly at me. 'Twenty-one years later, *my* daughter, aged ten, gave me a pink letter she snatched from … from my husband, containing irrefutable evidence he was having an affair with her piano teacher.'

I'm startled by the shift in topic—not that it's unusual; it happens frequently, as if disparate things get connected in her brain. But it's also weird to hear her talking *to* me, *about* me, as if I was somebody else, in another time and place.

'I'd suspected, for *years*, there was something going on between those two, not to mention various others, but Hugh was a consummate liar. He'd undermine me, tell me I was jealous, crazy, hysterical and absurd, when my intuition screamed the reality!'

Now she looks at me directly. 'When you are chronically lied to, Jodie, when the truth is constantly denied, you lose your sense of reality! Reading between the lines of the pink letter, I was certain it wasn't the *only* letter; it wasn't the *first*. There were subtle references to previous correspondence in it. I begged Hugh to be straight with me, but he swore it was the only one.

So I drove to his office while he and his secretary were at lunch, and I looked in his desk drawers and found what I expected to find, at the back of the right bottom drawer, a *bundle* of pink letters—'

I shiver involuntarily.

'—and I drove to a park and spent the afternoon reading every one of them. They were in order, all dated from beginning to end. Then I went home and arranged a babysitter and rang Hugh and told him I'd booked a table for dinner in a local restaurant, and to meet me there, so we could talk.'

'What happened?'

'He turned up, and after we were both settled, I placed the pink letter, the one you gave me, on the table, and I asked him again to please tell me were there any more letters. I begged him to be real. I told him I couldn't live without reality, that I needed to make decisions based on reality. I needed *truth*. But he insisted, no, there were no other letters. She'd only recently become infatuated with him, he said, and it was all imagination on her part. He was suggesting that *she* was mad! For the first time in years, I knew *I* wasn't! I removed the bundle of pink letters from my handbag and laid them on the table and asked him was he *still* going to deny it? Were *these* letters a figment of my imagination too? That blew him out of the water! The problem was, once I got it straight that I *wasn't* mad, I had a nervous breakdown! I couldn't handle the reality. I couldn't handle the truth. I realised, from reading those letters, that you'd witnessed their affair—at some level—for *years*. She expressed anxiety in several of the letters that you would spill the beans and the shit would hit the fan and it would ruin everything—for her and Hugh!'

Mum is focused on herself, but my brain has homed in on one statement of fact.

I realised … you'd witnessed their affair—at some level—for years.

'I was devastated how little regard she and Hugh had for *me*. She was supposed to be my *friend*! He was *my* husband! Hugh was always telling me I was mad, but he was *driving* me mad! Still, my leaving him—and you and your brothers—the way I did was gutless and cowardly.'

She's crying, and all I can do is pass her tissues. I can't touch her, or forgive her, or console her, but I keep giving her tissues and I keep listening, because I want to know what belongs in the blank spaces in my mind. I want my wiped-out memories to be restored.

'I didn't know what I was doing. I no longer knew what was real, or what to believe. I'd only had my intuition to go by, and I'd stopped trusting it. I no longer knew the difference between truth and lies, between reality and deceit and duplicity.'

A cramp hits me, low down, like a red-hot washcloth being twisted and squeezed and wrung out, slowly and cruelly inside me. I breathe through it. Mum doesn't notice.

'One day ... afterwards ... in the clinic, in a group therapy session, the group leader said, "Imagine you're a child aged ten or eleven, playing with your friends." Some members of the group started zooming around, playing at being children, but one of the participants, a woman, asked me, "Do you want to go for a swim?" It triggered a flashback of Lily being attacked at Fiddens Wharf and I fell apart, I relapsed severely, because everything *else* fell into place. I remembered Lily's father, my first nightmare realisation that not all fathers could be trusted— and just as I ran away while he gave his daughter a flogging, and just as I "forgot" to get help for Lily when I ran away from those boys at Fiddens Wharf, I realised I'd done the same to you. I "ran away" and left you with Hugh, "forgetting" what had happened to you—was maybe *still* happening. When I came to my senses, I tried to remedy the situation with help from my lawyer. He had Power of Attorney for my affairs, and I gave him permission to enrol you in the boarding school on my behalf. I didn't know what else to do.'

Meaning you put me in the boarding school to protect me from my father.

'Eventually, I checked out of the clinic and returned home, and Hugh made me so many promises! He said he didn't want the family to break up, but the only time I saw him cry was when he thought he'd lose *the business*—when *his* identity, *his* ego, *his* self-esteem, *his* wealth, were at risk. The issue of property settlement loomed large because the business, our properties and shares and investments, insurance policies and bank accounts were all in joint names. I had a half-share claim to *everything*, plus the business was financed with part of my inheritance from my father's estate. Hugh convinced me co-operation was better than revenge. He started courting me again. It was so hard to let go. I so wanted to believe him. I guess I still loved him.'

So, while I was in boarding school, out of sight, out of mind, you returned to my father.

'I don't know why we women do that—keep loving our abusers. It's as if we can't let go of the dream, the romantic dream. We're not in love with who he *is*. We're in love with who he *could* be—*if only he'd change!*

'Why was I isolated from Dan and Billy for those four years?' I try not to sound accusing. 'I remember lunches with you in cafes near the school, but I have no memories of seeing my brothers, or Dad, or coming home for holidays in all that time.'

Mum hesitates. She looks awkward. 'I had no control over the boys. I still don't. Your father took possession of them during my absence in the clinic, and when I returned home, I had no influence over them at all. He'd take them away every weekend and for the entire school holidays, on road trips, camping and fishing and what have you. It was like he was keeping them to himself. I'd drive down to the boarding school to see you on my own. But when I decided to move here with you, your brothers insisted they wanted to come too, to be with you. Not with me especially. With *you*! They said they'd lost you and they wanted you back!'

'That is so hard to believe!'

'It's true! I agreed they could come here to be with you. Hugh was upset they wanted to be with you and not him. I hoped he'd miss them and join us out of loneliness. I was sure, if the boys stayed in the Blue Mountains with him, the family would be permanently split. He *said* he wanted to join us but needed to sell the business first. I can't believe I kept dreaming it would all work out, that we could let go of the past and make a fresh start.' She sighs heavily. 'I'm the winner, at the end of the day. I ended up with my children, my family.'

I want to ask her, 'What do you think happened to me, Mum, during those years before you abandoned me? What do you think happened to me after you disappeared from my life and left me with Dad?' But I'm too frightened to ask her; too frightened to tell her what *I* remember, or what I *think* I remember; too scared to share my confused reality with her. What if she believes me and falls apart again? And if she *refuses* to believe me, *I'll* fall apart! I cannot risk disclosing *anything*.

Another cramp grabs my belly low down. I try not to gasp. I stack the cups, plates and teapot on the tray and retreat to the kitchen, almost doubled over with pain.

Chapter Nine

Sunday, 26 March 1995

I've started the pill, but I know it won't relieve my period pain. Not this time anyway. Panadol has barely taken the edge off it. I've been in bed all day with a hot water bottle, reading, writing and snoozing between cramps, Mum in and out of the studio, on the phone in her bedroom, her tone elevated, probably talking to Dad. I hope she's told him she wants a divorce. There's no way I want him to come and live with us. I don't even want him to visit. If Mum takes him back after this last episode, I'll be the one running away from home.

Melanie kept her promise to give Dan a copy of the *Romeo and Juliet* libretto. He picked it up on his way home from the beach.

To understand where, when and how tragedy was averted in this musical rewrite, I'll read Shakespeare's version first, so I know what *really* happened, then read the libretto and discover how the musical version deviates from Shakespeare's version of events. Instead of having to concentrate on the actors' lips during the performance, I'll be able to enjoy the costumes and scenery and follow the action, *remembering* what they're saying. I'll memorise the words of the songs too, so I can really get into the music on the night.

In Mum's copy of *The Complete Works of William Shakespeare*, *Romeo and Juliet* begins on page seven hundred and sixty-four. It's heavy, the book I mean, and the print is small, the pages thin, the language ornate.

Right at the start, a sonnet by the chorus explains how the two noble families, Montague and Capulet, bear a mutual, ancient grudge of unknown origin, and their feud is only finally healed by the tragic deaths of their children, Romeo Montague and Juliet Capulet, who fall in love despite the hatred between their families.

The first thing that gets me mad is the way the male characters threaten warfare and revenge, including the rape of the women and servant-girls of the opposing family.

In the beginning, Romeo is in love with a disinterested girl called Rosaline, the niece of Lord Capulet. Romeo gate crashes a masked ball at the Capulet's, hoping to get a glimpse of her. He is suicidally depressed by Rosaline's rejection of him, but not to worry, he switches off that unrequited love and all its associated despair from the moment he sees Juliet! He falls madly in love with *her,* based on what she looks like!

As far as I can work out, Romeo and Juliet meet on a Sunday evening. On Monday afternoon they are secretly married by a friendly friar. By Monday evening Romeo has killed Juliet's cousin Tybalt, avenging the murder by Tybalt of Romeo's friend Mercutio, and Romeo is banished from Verona by the prince. After spending the night with Juliet—okay because they've been secretly married by the friar, never mind the fact she's only fourteen—Romeo leaves early Tuesday morning to go into exile in Mantua, leaving Juliet behind to face all sorts of appalling difficulties.

Juliet's father is horrible! He decides to marry her off to Paris, another suitor, and when she refuses to marry Paris—she can't tell her father she's already married to Romeo—he tries to intimidate her into submission with insults and threats of abandonment.

'You green-sickness carrion!' he screams at her. 'Out, you baggage! You disobedient … wretched … puling … whining mammet.' Juliet is a possession her father considers he owns and can do what he likes with. 'An' you be mine,' he declares. 'I'll give you to my friend … an' you be not, you can hang, beg, starve, die in the streets … for by my soul, I'll ne'er acknowledge thee.'

I hurl the *Complete Works* into my waste-paper bin. The spine breaks with the impact. I only pull it out again because I want to learn how Juliet resists her father's attempts to coerce her into doing what he wants.

Juliet resists him by taking poison, given to her by the friar, which knocks her out like a zombie for a couple of days. Only when her family thinks she's dead do they realise they love her and mourn her. They place her in the family vault. Romeo is supposed to be there with her when she regains consciousness, ready to whisk her off to Mantua, but unfortunately there's a communication stuff-up and believing what he hears, that she's dead, he buys poison from an apothecary in Mantua and returns to Verona, where he kills Paris—who happens to be mourning beside the Capulet vault—then swallows the poison and dies alongside the unconscious Juliet. When she revives and finds Romeo dead beside her, she takes up his knife and kills herself.

The families arrive at the tomb and the friar describes the tragic series of events. So great is their sorrow at the death of these 'star-crossed lovers', the Montague and Capulet patriarchs decide to end the feud once and for all.

Where Hate reigns, everybody loses. And Love doesn't conquer all—Death does.

Chapter Ten

Monday, 27 March 1995

This morning, I weighed 70.40 kilograms on the bathroom scales. I've lost three kilograms in ten days, taking my premenstrual bloat into account. I tried on my shrinking-in-the-wash jeans, and they fitted me again. I left them on, and between cramps went out to the kitchen with my t-shirt tucked in, hoping Mum or the boys would notice I looked thinner. They didn't notice of course as mornings are chaotic. Dan usually gets up at dawn to pick his produce to take to school and then the kitchen rush is on while they make their lunches and eat breakfast on the run. I usually keep out of their way. Some days, I don't even bother to get out of bed until after they've gone. Today they at least said goodbye, despite Mum yelling at them to hurry up.

I'm sitting at my desk, journal open in front of me, nursing a hot water bottle. The house is silent, not even a creak. It is as lonely and as empty as I feel.

I haven't seen Shaun since Saab's burial last Wednesday. Mum coming home unexpectedly was an omen, a warning. I need to destroy my journal and the love letters, especially if she's found them and read them already. I can't put my finger on it, but my room *feels* different. She says our rooms are our own private space, but I don't trust her—probably because *I'm* not trustworthy, snooping in *her* filing cabinet, delving into *her* documents, planning to read *her* letters and journals. She's moody and strange. One minute she's talking to me, over-sharing even, like telling me about Lily, then next minute she acts preoccupied and remote. Maybe she's ruminating about Dad and it's not about me at all.

Fragments of memories have been rising to the surface of my mind, like bubbles of noxious gas in a bog. They're a serious turn-off. Last night, on the edge of dreaming, I thought I heard someone coming into my room, but when I woke up, heart thudding, I couldn't hear *anything*, even if someone *was* coming, I am *so* deaf in the dark without my HAs. Out here in the middle of nowhere, when there is little or no moon, the sky is awash with stars, but their light fades, lost before it reaches Earth. In the darkness, in the silence of my deafness, I am totally vulnerable.

Cleo and Patra begin whining on the east veranda, and I hear a familiar whistle.

Shaun! An adrenaline rush makes me tremble as I go to the veranda doorway, clutching the hot water bottle against my stomach. I watch him as he walks along the grass to the steps.

'Okay if I come up?'

'Sure.' I'm shaky and short of breath.

'I've been worried about you since Wednesday, when you rang to say don't come down. I noticed your Mum was home Thursday and Friday too.'

'She was busy with her artwork and lots of phone calls.'

'Are you expecting her back this morning?'

'No. At least, I don't think so.'

'Can we sit out here and talk for a bit?'

About what?

'Sure. Would you like coffee?'

'Not right now, thanks.'

I sink into the single chair while he sits on the sofa. He gazes at me steadily, hands clasped. He looks different—very tidy. He's had a haircut, a proper one, and a shave. His white t-shirt is tucked into neat grey chinos. His boots are still dirty though, which I find oddly reassuring. I wait for him to speak, he looks like he has something to tell me, but he's waiting for *me* to speak first, and I don't know what to say. I'm jittery and tearful, my painful period adding to my distress.

'A tummy ache?'

I nod.

'Cramps?'

I nod again.

'Ouch,' he says, his tone sympathetic.

My eyes fill with tears. I wish he'd hug me.

'So, what happened Wednesday?'

It bursts out of me. 'I had a huge anxiety attack thinking Mum invaded my room while I was with you and found, and read, my … my secret writings.'

'Secret writings?' He looks bemused. 'So what if she read them?'

The flood-gates open and I can't hold back the tears, or the rush of feelings—the panic I felt then and am reliving now, the guilt I've betrayed him, the fear I've incriminated him.

Shaun drags his handkerchief from his pants pocket and hands it to me. 'What secret writings can turn you into a nervous wreck thinking your mother might have read them?'

'I've fallen in love with you, Shaun!' I'm sobbing. 'I've fantasised about us making love and … and … I've written graphic descriptions in my journal, and written love letters to you, but never sent, about us having sex. If Mum's found them and read them, she'll believe it's all *true*! She'll think you're a very b-bad person because you're an older man and I'm an under-age girl. She'll report you to the *police*.'

"Struth, Jodie, that is scary!' His face has paled. 'Are you saying she's read them?'

'I don't know! She was in her studio when I got home, but she *could* have read *some* of the letters and *some* of my journal entries while I was with you. She's been acting really weird.'

'Jesus!' he mutters. 'Is there anything else I should know about?'

I tell him about getting the pill behind Mum's back and Dan giving me condoms.

'Even your brother thinks I'm …' He's shaking his head, his face white under his tan, his t-shirt quivering. 'I'm about to make a speech, Jodie, so hear me out.'

Whatever he has to say can't make me feel worse than I feel already. Holding the hot water bottle against my belly with my elbows, I blow and wipe my nose with his handkerchief.

'For sure your mother will think I'm guilty, even though I've done *nothing* because you *are* under-age and it's my responsibility to maintain proper boundaries because I'm the adult. Now I'll *never* be able to convince her I'm behaving appropriately.' He sounds angry, but he looks scared. 'The law will take a *very* dim view of me if she alleges I've been doing the wrong thing. The police only need to *believe* her, and they'll charge me.'

He's sweating and quivering. I've ruined everything! He'll never forgive me.

A trace of colour is returning to his face. He leans forward, he clearly has more to say, and I shrink back from the coming rejection. 'I've tried to keep my feelings under wraps, too afraid to admit I've been attracted to you too, from the first day I saw you. I think about you constantly. I dream about us. I try to talk myself out of it because I *know* I—we—can't *do* anything about it. But it doesn't change how I *feel* about you.'

Joy surges through me. Is he saying he loves me?

'But you know what? Even if you turned sixteen tomorrow, I'd *still* want us to keep our relationship platonic because I'm *leaving* you. I'm going away to uni, maybe Antarctica, sooner rather than later.'

Now I feel joy and grief together. '*When?* When will you leave?'

He shrugs. 'I don't know, exactly.'

The tears flow again. 'Will you write to me?'

'Of course I'll write! I just hope not from a prison cell.'

'I'll miss you so much, Shaun!'

'I'll miss you too, Jodie, I know I will, but we both need to experience more of the world, and the people in it, and pursue our studies, and develop careers we're passionate about, before we commit to each other. You'd think I'd know by now what I want to do with my life, but I *don't*. I'm *still* trying to work myself out, and I'm twelve years ahead of you.'

Relief is mixed with a searing sense of deprivation. I'm thrilled *and* devastated *and* confused. He's attracted to me, he cares about me, maybe he even loves me—but he's willing to leave me. I just don't get it.

'Right now, we need to figure out what to do about your writings. If I'm accused of, or worse, charged with being a paedophile—it's horrendous, Jodie—it will ruin my entire life! Destroy *everything* you've written about me, and promise you won't write another word!'

I'm gutted he thinks my love letters are dangerous pornography that could ruin his life!

'Can I trust you?'

I nod.

'Let's be optimistic she hasn't read *any* of it.'

'But she *might* have!'

'She *might* have. But let's assume she *hasn't*. Either way, we get rid of *everything!*' Silence ensues while he gazes into the distance, his expression implacable. But when he looks at me again, he says, 'Let's bury everything, in a suitable container, near Saab. Even if your mother *has* read some, or all, of it, without tangible evidence to back up her allegations, it will be her word against ours.'

I breathe again. He's not demanding I destroy everything. There's something romantic about burying my writings, rather than burning or shredding them. It sounds like a reprieve. 'Ten years from now, we could resurrect the container and read the letters together!'

'We could! You'll be a famous writer by then!'

'We'll be like Elizabeth Barrett and Robert Browning. They were the truest of friends and wrote letters and poems to each other for years. And eventually married.'

He ignores that comparison. 'First thing Wednesday. Don't let *any* of it out of your sight between now and then!' He releases a noisy sigh. 'I'm glad we've got that sorted.'

He stands up, stretches, goes to the railing and leans on it, his back to me, taking in the vista before him. I gaze at his long, lean, male body, his broad shoulders. He is clearly a man.

I stand up, place the hot water bottle, now lukewarm, on the chair behind me, step towards him and touch him lightly on his left shoulder. He slowly turns to face me, his back against the railing, his hands holding it on either side. I move in close and hug him, my left cheek against his chest, just below his throat. I can feel and hear the strong, rapid beat of his heart. He folds his arms across my back and rests his cheek against my hair. He holds me, and I hold him, until our hearts slow down and beat to the same drum.

Chapter Eleven

Tuesday, 28 March, 1995

I'm sitting in the TAFE library, working on my *Aboriginal Studies—Contemporary Issues* assignment. Beside me, in my backpack for safe keeping, are my journal and letters, condoms and pill packet. My mother can accuse me of being a thief, which I am, and use the stolen items in my wardrobe and chest of drawers as evidence against me, but she cannot accuse Shaun of being a paedophile and use my writings as evidence against him. I will fight her to the death.

'Jodie?'

I look up and recognise the girl I saw standing next to Emma-Sue at the *Saraton*, the one I lip-read, *'She's looking at you.'* My heart lurches.

'Em asked me to give you this.' She offers me an intricately folded piece of paper.

'Thank you.' I'm excited and nervous. I open the note. And read it.

Hey Jodie, meet me at Market Square 12.30. Bring lunch. Em.

'Do you know what it says?'

She nods.

I re-fold it, put it in my jeans pocket. 'I don't know *your* name, sorry.'

'Jacinta.' She glances at her watch. 'The canteen will be full in a minute.'

'I've brought a sandwich from home.' I remove the sandwich container from my backpack, and place my loose-leaf folder, study notes and the three books I've borrowed by special dispensation as an OTEN student on top of my journal and letters. 'Is there anywhere I can leave this? Mum's picking me up here this afternoon.'

'I've got a locker, near the canteen. You can put it in there.' She waves her key at me.

We walk to the locker together, then go into the canteen. 'Emma-Sue's note said to bring lunch. Did she mean for me to buy lunch for her? Have you got any lunch?'

'I got an account. So's Em. I'll get hers.'

It looks like Jacinta is coming downtown too. Now I've got *two* new friends!

She greets the canteen manager by name. 'Hi Larry!' When she asks him to book up their sandwiches, he doesn't hesitate, writing the details in a well-used exercise book. They must pay up or he wouldn't be so willing. I buy myself a bottle of water.

As we walk to Market Square, Jacinta tells me she's doing the TAFE TPC—Tertiary Preparation Certificate—hoping to get into the Bachelor of Business in Tourism at Southern Cross University's Lismore campus as a mature age student.

'Are you thinking about the kind of tourism where … where you tell visitors about culture and history and special places?'

'Yep. Our art and crafts, music and dance, stories and song-lines, language, bush medicine, bush tucker. About country, sacred sites, culture, land care. Before and after.'

I know what she means by 'before and after'. It feels awful to be on the wrong side.

'I'm reading about the history of Grafton, about, you know, what happened to … to … to the Bundjalung people after …

after it was settled—' I'm stuttering because I'm anxious I'll say the wrong thing, ask the wrong questions, use the wrong words— 'for an assignment for my *Aboriginal Studies—Contemporary Issues* subject.'

'After we were invaded?'

'Yes. About what happened after the … after the invasion, y'know, the impact on the Bundjalung, then and now. Do you think I could ask you and Emma-Sue a few things?'

'Sure,' she says. 'That's cool.'

I'm not sure if it is cool, though.

Market Square is a well-kept park with grass, flower beds, big shady trees including jacarandas, solid wooden tables and benches. Going there with Jacinta is a dream come true. Em, Jacinta told me to call her that, is sitting on a bench, beside a table. In her mini-skirted South High uniform she looks like she's wagging it. That's another good thing about TAFE: no uniforms.

Em and Jacinta greet each other. 'Jingi-wahla,' she says to me, smiling with shy eyes.

Once I'm sitting down, and we're eating our lunches, I feel more at ease, though I don't know what to say, so I listen to them instead, concentrating on hearing and understanding them. One question pops out of my mouth though. 'What's the significance of Market Square?'

'It's still our place,' Em says. 'Over there,' she points and waves an arm indicating she means beyond the railway viaduct that forms a barrier north of the park, 'is our waterhole, where our people used to camp. A spring. Never dried up. Beautiful water back then. Rainforest all around. River not far away. When yidligan came, for the red cedar, they found the waterhole. Real soon they come with cattle and horses and bullocks to drink the water and camp there.'

'It's clay,' Jacinta adds. 'They dug out clay to make bricks. And they built a place on the creek to boil down cattle for tallow, for soap and candles and stuff.'

'More yidligan come,' Em says. 'They chop down trees, clear the land, build houses, make gardens, plant vegetables, fruit trees ... Bundjalung always camped by that waterhole.'

Jacinta takes over. 'They took our water, our land, hunted our game, but if blackfellas took *their* fruit and vegetables, the gubbas shot the blackfellas.' She sighs heavily. 'So, one time a blackfella kills a whitefella and then—a *big* massacre.'

Em says, 'Bundjalung leave here after that, join our people in the mountains, but yidligan come into the mountains too! Make tracks in the forest for bullocks to haul the red cedar, build towns, roads, put up fences, poison us and shoot us ...'

Jacinta helps her out. 'Now—here is still our place. Elders come to town from the communities, Baryulgil, Malabugilmah, Jubullam, Jubal, Tabulam,' she's pointing towards the ranges, 'and from all around. The Baryulgil and Malabugilmah fellas meet up with the Grafton fellas and have a yarn. Dubay with jarjums wait for their rellies and friends to come.'

Em says, 'The Grafton Training and Employment Centre has a new program. For early leavers and long-term unemployed. They're gonna clean up the water hole. Get rid of the lantana and weeds. Plant rainforest trees. Revegetate the area. Poppy used to swim there when he was a kid. Reckons it's full of stolen bicycles!' She grins, but only for a moment. 'And maybe human bones.'

I can't possibly ask her whose bones.

Jacinta screws up her lunch papers and scores a direct goal in a nearby waste bin. 'Gotta go! Can't miss class. *Language and Learning Skills.* How to write essays! You comin'?'

I nod. 'Are you going to school this afternoon?' I ask Em.

Yep.' She looks at the clocktower. 'I gotta go! The bus comes in three minutes. You comin' Friday night?'

'Yeah, I can't wait to see it!'

'It'll be deadly!' She heads for the bus stop.

Walking back to TAFE, Jacinta says, 'Talking about the past makes us sad.'

'I'm so sorry it happened.' Lame words for the empathy, and guilt, I feel.

'Acknowledging the truth is the first step towards reconciliation,' she responds.

At TAFE we go to her locker to get my backpack. 'Thanks Jacinta, I've had the best time! Can I meet up with you and Em again?'

'Sure! Tuesdays are best. I'll give you my phone number.'

'I'll give you mine, too.' We scribble our numbers on bits of paper and exchange them.

'Seeya Friday night.'

'You bet.' I watch Jacinta as she walks away.

TAFE is where the friends are.

Or I could go to school … but I'm not ready. Not yet.

Chapter Twelve

Wednesday, 29 March 1995

Last night in bed I recorded my meeting with Em and Jacinta in my journal. It was after midnight when I wrote:

Another burial day today. It makes me cry. I know the letters must go. But I can't let this journal go. I won't write fantasy stuff about Shaun anymore. I won't write any more letters. I'll find other ways to keep the good things and the bad things separate.

Shaun hasn't made any promises about the future. He says he doesn't know what he wants, and I think he means our relationship as well as life generally. He did agree we could resurrect the evidence in ten years' time and read the letters together, but I think he's hoping, once he leaves here, that I'll forget about him—and the letters.

Right now, I cannot imagine life, or living, without him ….

Re-reading this latest journal entry in the light of day, especially the paragraph about Shaun, I can hardly see what I've written for tears. I leaf through the journal's pages. Sometimes there's something compromising written on one side of a page, and something harmless and innocent and 'literary' written on the back of the same page.

I look through my letters and find the one I want to keep, *the* one, so I can read and re-read it when I can't think of a single good reason for staying alive. I don't *need* to keep it—I know what it says, word for word—but the feel of it in my hands, being able to *read* it, is what matters. I attach the letter, in its envelope, to the inside of the back cover of my journal with a paperclip and return the journal to its hiding place behind the textbooks in my bookcase.

If Shaun finds out you've kept the journal and letter, he'll go ballistic!

'I know!' I don't need Anne to rub it in. He'll despise me if he discovers I've broken my promise. But it's imperative I keep them—the journal and this one letter—for my sanity.

Anne is agitated!

What if it all goes pear-shaped! What if he ends up in jail because of your selfishness! His life will be ruined. He'll never forgive you, he'll ....

'I know, I know, I *know*!' I whisper, equally agitated. 'Get off my back! I *need* to keep them for *my* self-preservation. I'll be super careful.'

Secrecy, risk-taking, lying, breaking promises, you're just like ...

I shrug, shudder, shake my head to get her out of my mind and off my back as I tie the rest of the letters together with a ribbon, and attach the bundle to a new, unused journal. I know how disingenuous and deceitful I'm being, but it doesn't stop me. I slide the bundle into a plastic bag and seal it with lots of Sellotape. Finally, I wrap a flimsy silk scarf around the parcel, slide it into another plastic bag, then place the package in one of Mum's Tupperware containers and close the lid. I make our sandwiches and stow them in my backpack, along with my water bottle and the 'coffin', lock up Cleo and Patra and set off up the slope to *Booyul.*

Who knows what the future will bring? I'd visit and ask the psychic fortune-teller in town if it wasn't for the incense she burns in her little shop.

The 'grave' is under the same tree as Saab's. There's a star picket at the head of Saab's grave with his collar and nametag wired to it. More bush rocks are around the perimeter and Shaun has placed a large rock with a natural hollow in it, filled with water, on the grave itself, 'So birds by day and creatures by night will visit him, for a drink.'

It's a painful experience, burying my love letters to Shaun, with Shaun. He trusts me and I'm deceiving him. He's holding the 'coffin' now, no doubt aware of its weight as he lowers it into the hole he's dug, while Anne is whispering in my ear.

You don't deserve his trust.

I shrug her off with a shiver. It's too late now. I'll be *super*-vigilant about protecting my journal and letter from prying eyes.

I gently fill in the hole, then spread a mulch of dead leaves and twigs to disguise it. 'How will we know where to find it in ten years' time?'

Shaun looks up. 'We're directly under that big branch.' He strides towards the trunk. 'And three paces out from the trunk. We'll find it.'

We'll find it. He said 'we'. We will find it.

'Can I hug you, Shaun?' I beg him. 'Please?'

'Sure.' He moves towards me. I drop the shovel, and we wrap our arms around each other. I look up at his face; he looks into my eyes. I kiss him, gently. I feel desire for him, our bodies close together, and for sure he's feeling the same way about me—I can tell.

'This is dangerous!' he says softly. 'Let's eat our sandwiches before the ants find them!'

'Okay.' Half-elated, half-deflated, I let him go and step away. I pick up my backpack, no ants, while he examines a hollow grey log nearby and inspects the inside of it.

'It's all clear,' he declares. 'No goannas, snakes, echidnas, termites, bull ants, spiders, centipedes or cockroaches that I can see!'

'What about wasps, hornets, mosquitoes, sandflies, March flies or blowies?' I add. I sit alongside him and pull out the sandwiches. 'Salad with ham and mustard.'

'Great! I only brought mixed nuts and an apple each.'

We munch our sandwiches in silence. Then he says, 'I can't hang around today, I'm sorry. I've got so much to do I can't keep up.'

A pang of disappointment spreads through my gut.

'The sow farrowed last night. Eight little piglets. Would you like to see them?'

'Yes, please!'

'I'm selling Big George, as he's getting too big for his boots, but I'll keep Mama and the weaners for now. I haven't enjoyed pig farming. It was just an experiment.'

A breath of cold air raises the hairs on the back of my neck.

Sandwiches eaten, Shaun takes the packet of mixed nuts and two apples from his backpack. He passes me an apple, opens the nuts and shakes some into my open palm. 'They go well with apple,' he says.

'Thank you.' There's a tremor in my hands. I put the apple on the log beside me, pick out a cashew from the nuts in my palm, and chew it slowly until it's a paste in my mouth. I swallow it past the lump forming in my throat. 'It's *all* an experiment, isn't it? Are you bored with your vegetable patch too?' My voice sounds raspy, gravelly.

Shaun takes a deep breath. 'There's something I need to tell you, Jodie. It doesn't matter how I feel—committed and enthusiastic, or bored, disillusioned and tired—it's out of my hands. My father rang last night to tell us he's decided 'the experiment' isn't economically viable and he wants us to return home as soon as the lease runs out. He's threatened to pull the pin financially if Mum doesn't agree, but I think she's glad he's made the decision.'

A chill runs down my spine and I shudder. 'When will the lease run out?'

Shaun wraps an arm around my shoulders as if to warm me, or maybe support me. 'End of May. I'll harvest what's left, but I won't be planting any winter vegetables.'

'May?'

Only two months from now!

'I've also applied to join the Australian Antarctic Division's Science Program at Mawson Research Station in 1996.'

'Why?!' I'm really asking, *Why are you leaving me?*

'Mawson's the best place to study the impact of climate change, including its effect on the habitat of seabirds. There are huge colonies of Emperor and Adelie penguins, all sorts of Petrels, and Skuas. The research facilities are amazing, apparently. I'd like to study ice-core changes, and Antarctica's role and influence on global climate systems—and the effects of climate change and global warming on Antarctica itself. Ice reflects the sun's energy much more effectively than land or water. If there's less ice, the earth will heat up faster. Not to mention the fact more methane will be released into the atmosphere as the permafrost melts. It's a vicious circle.' He squeezes my shoulder. 'I'll start my PhD at Sydney University next semester instead.'

Chapter Thirteen

It was my turn to cook dinner tonight: grilled lamb cutlets with root vegetable mash and steamed greens. I push the peas and broccoli around my plate, too miserable to eat anything. Mum and the boys are so engrossed in the nightly quota of misery on TV they haven't noticed. I pile their empty plates on top of mine and escape to the kitchen. Better not to eat anything, than eat and throw up.

You're starving yourself—not eating, eating and vomiting, bingeing and throwing up.

Anne's nagging does my head in. I'm running out of time. I need to look halfway decent if I'm to be seen with my brothers at their school. And I want to impress Shaun, though he's never commented on my weight or appearance. I stow my uneaten cutlets, mash and greens in a Tupperware container at the back of the fridge.

TV news over, Mum and the boys come into the kitchen to do the dishes.

I tell them, 'I'll have Milo thank you,' and retreat to my room. This afternoon, before Mum and the boys arrived home, I raided Mum's wardrobe and found her silvery-grey stretch pull-on pants. They're sleek and silky-feeling, with a darker, subtle leopard-skin pattern shimmering through the weave. Mum wears them with a black silk blouse and looks stunning. I pulled them on and they fitted me—with a bit of persuasion. I'll ask her if I can wear them tomorrow night. I've got a black t-shirt and a silvery-grey satin jacket that matches the pants perfectly and covers my bum, and I'll wear my soft, flat grey Lois Lane shoes Mum bought me on our way here.

I dress up, put on lip gloss and brush my hair while Mum and the boys are in the kitchen. When they plonk themselves down again with their hot drinks to watch more TV, as it's too chilly to sit outside, I'll make a grand entrance and see what reaction I get.

'Your Milo's ready!' Dan calls out.

'Thank you.' I give them a minute to get settled, then sweep out before I lose courage.

'Bi-bip!' Billy says, staring at the TV, craning his neck to see around me. He says that to the dogs when they're in his way. 'Move, willya.'

'Sorry.' I move. No point getting him off-side. But Confidence is wavering. Feeling Foolish is coming up on the inside.

'Welll!' says Mum. 'They fit! Almost.'

Dan's glazed eyes, staring beyond the TV through the walls into some distant out-of-it realm, gradually focus and bring me into the foreground of his attention. 'You look great, Jode!'

Billy sees me now and whistles. 'Yeah! Turn around!'

I do so, as gracefully as possible. Confidence takes a flying leap forward.

'Just a bit more off the bum,' Billy says. 'And here.' He grasps the outside of his own lean, taut, muscly thighs to indicate the spot.

'And here,' Dan adds, pinching his own midriff, which is as hard as the torso of Michelangelo's David, 'and you'll be perfect!'

'Yeah,' Billy nods in agreement. 'Just a bit more, Jode, and you've made it.'

'You'd better get out of them,' Mum says. 'You'll stretch them.'

'They're stretch pants. They're meant to stretch.'

'Yes, but not that much. If you really like them, and lose a bit more, I'll buy you a pair of your own! Is that a deal?'

She is making me a generous offer. She is taking control of my weight-loss program. She is offering me a bribe and if/when I lose the weight, she will take the credit.

'Thank you, that's very kind of you.' I speak with the utmost courtesy as I retreat to my room, my heart a heavy black rock pressing down on my empty belly.

In the mirror, Big Bum and Feeling Foolish are vying for first place. I can see the ugly bits now. Massive Midriff and Thunder Thighs wide on the outside.

Just a bit more … and you'll be perfect. Just a bit more …

They're meant to stretch … yes, but not that much. Lose a bit more …

I take everything off. I pull on my sloppy tracksuit pants; pull on, over my tear-streaked face, over my drooping, heavy breasts, my loose-fitting stained tracksuit top with the smelly underarms. I put my feet into my rank, gross, Ugg slippers. Now I am 'normal'. Normal for me. Normal for them. What they expect to see. I haven't made it yet. Not yet. I can try and try to be perfect, to make them happy with me, to make them love and accept me, but I'll never quite get there. I just know I'm never going to make it.

I'll show them! I'll starve myself, occupy minimal space, fade away until I disappear. 'Drop dead, Jodie.' I hear that, often enough.

But I'm invisible now and I don't like being invisible. I'll become very visible. I'll spread my edges, extend my boundaries, occupy more and more space, cushion myself against their put-downs, keep them at a safe distance, so they can never again reach the core of me. Fuck them! I'm awash with anger, sweating in the heat of my rage. I can smell it in my armpits. Fuck them! Fuck the whole fucking lot of them! I'll eat myself into oblivion. I'm already revolting. I'll demonstrate, with my physical bloat, that I am revolted by them!

I return to the loungeroom. Nobody notices. Seething, I pick up my mug of Milo from the tray and retreat to the kitchen. I down the Milo while I make thick toast, with lashings of butter and strawberry jam—and no one had better try and stop me! Including Anne!

You're over-reacting.

'Shut up! How would you like to be treated like that!'

Confront them.

'What's the point?'

Tell them how you feel.

'They don't care how I feel. They're telling the truth.'

Every time you binge, or starve yourself, or throw up, you're punishing ME!

'Too bad!'

And you know what? I refuse to be punished. I deserve respect.

I falter. Torn.

Don't sabotage us! Do something unexpected, but never self-destructive.

I return to the loungeroom, put the plate of toast on the tray in front of them, an offering.

'Toast anyone?' I turn away, walk towards my room. 'Good-night. I'm going to bed.'

'Yumm-eee!' Billy exclaims, reaching for it.

'Wow! Thanks, Jode!' Dan says, scrambling to grab his share.

'What's that all about?' I hear Mum ask them.

I enter my bedroom, and gently but firmly close the door.

Chapter Fourteen

Friday, 31 March 1995

Romeo and Juliet the musical is fantastic. The set is essentially a spring garden with a stone wall and a balcony, but changes in the lighting turn it from daylight to moonlight, from indoors to outdoors, from ballroom, to Juliet's balcony and bedroom, to church, to alley, to tomb. The director has changed the time and place; it's set in the heart of a modern city. The characters are wearing exaggerated versions of the latest trendy clothes. The poor, unemployed street-people—the chorus-singers—are sporting pink or purple dyed wigs, the guys in tattered, grungy, baggy jeans, striped t-shirts and tennis shoes, the girls in mini-skirts, black goth and fishnet stockings, while the rich, noble types look like fashionable yuppies.

Romeo is a hunk in an open-necked silk shirt with voluminous sleeves. His voice is rich, deep and powerful. He reminds me of Kamahl.

The first act is non-stop action. After the masked ball, Romeo and Juliet sing a love song duet, closing with a passionate kiss. Melanie must have had fun rehearsing *that*! There's something going on between the two of them; something electric in the body-language. It's not acting—they're *really* attracted to each other. Watching Dan out of the corner of my eye I feel sorry for the poor dude. I'd be jealous too!

Shakespeare's original sword fight between Mercutio, Benvolio, Tybalt and Romeo is now a confrontation with flick-knives. Juliet's cousin Tybalt kills Romeo's friend Mercutio, so Romeo kills Tybalt. It's one thing to watch a Shakespearean fencing duel, or a swordfight in armour and feathers in an exotic setting; it's something else to see a fight with flick-knives between teenagers in familiar clothes in an inner-city alley. The scene is choreographed, the fight very realistic. The only change in the violence department is the weapons; otherwise, it's still macho hatred, murder, revenge and bloodlust. The first act concludes with Juliet's father trying to force her to marry Paris. The audience is going berserk, booing and hissing, and I'm joining in! I'd *love* to be in a show like this!

Everyone has come outside for interval excited and steamed up. It's an absolute crush trying to buy drinks and cake. Shaun is being gallant, buying mine for me. I watch Emma-Sue approaching, Jacinta close behind, and grin a welcome.

'What d'y'think of Rambo?' Em asks, sounding proud. 'Deadly voice, eh!'

'Rambo?' I didn't know that was Romeo's name.

'Roger! Rambo's his nickname. Him and Troy sing and play together sometimes.'

Dan and Billy emerge from the crowd with their drinks and chunks of cake and join us. I'm looking out for Shaun while trying to listen to and hear what everyone's saying at the same time. He emerges from the crowd and walks steadily towards us, clutching two cardboard cups of coffee by their handles in one hand and two pieces of cake on one paper plate in the other. He could be one of the teachers, he looks so mature.

Em nudges me. 'Got yourself a SNAG, eh!' She grins at me and moves sideways towards Billy, making room for Shaun to stand beside me.

'Thanks, Shaun.' I extract one of the coffee cups from his fingers, taking care not to spill a drop on my grey satin jacket or shrinking-in-the-wash jeans.

'I'll hold the plate while you have a bite of cake, then you can hold it for me, right?'

I take a small bite out of my slice of cake, then take the plate off him to free his hand so he can have a bite of his slice too. We smile at each other as we take it in turns to hold the paper plate and I realise I'm happy! I'm on a date with Shaun and he's looking after me. He knows I love him, and I know he at least cares for me, even if he *is* leaving me—well, leaving the farm; I'm just collateral damage. I swallow my feelings of abandonment with the cake. Right now, I'm enjoying being surrounded by so many excited, happy people my age, feeling like I'm part of it. I could belong here, have a life, and friends. I introduce Shaun to Jacinta. 'You already know Emma-Sue,' I add lightly. He nods and smiles at them, then returns his attention to me as we take it in turns to eat cake.

Gazing around between bites, I see Mum and Wendy standing nearby with their coffee and cake. I instantly look away, but I've taken it all in.

Wendy is smiling, talking animatedly, focused on Mum.

Mum, sleek and elegant in her shimmering grey stretch pants, appears to be listening, but she's staring at Shaun and me and whatever she's thinking or feeling, it isn't benign.

In the second half of *Romeo and Juliet*, building up to the climax, there's plenty of dramatic suspense. Romeo's servant arrives and breathlessly tells his master that Juliet is dead in the family vault. Romeo, beside himself with grief at the news, is all for stabbing himself on the spot, never mind buying poison to do it, but thank his lucky stars, the fat friar's other half arrives—a tall, skinny basketballer in a clerical collar—with a letter from the friar, which Romeo reads aloud. It seems Juliet is only temporarily zombified and Romeo had better hurry if he wants to be there for her when she wakes up. He wastes precious time singing a fantastic solo about how lucky he is, because the next scene is in the tomb with Juliet just as she wakes up, and unsurprisingly Romeo is running late.

Melanie, Juliet, sits up in spooky blue light, surrounded by ancestral skeletons. Convinced she's already dead, she sings a heart-rending solo unaccompanied, until suddenly the bones of her ancestors leap up and rock and roll around her, accompanied by *Rock Around the Clock* belted out by the school band. It's great stuff for the audience, but terrifying for Juliet.

The skeletons collapse as suddenly as they'd jumped up; the lighting changes, the interior of the tomb darkens and Paris is spotlighted wandering across the front of the stage, mourning Juliet. He starts singing a sad song, and Juliet, unseen in the tomb, joins in. Paris hears her voice, and terrified of ghosts, hastily exits stage left to tell everyone, which saves him from being killed by Romeo, who enters stage right. Romeo reunites with Juliet, and they sing a duet, another love song, and kiss passionately—again—before stealing away into the night. It's the end, but it also implies a new beginning.

After the show, we join the crush backstage to congratulate the cast. I notice how subdued Dan is. Melanie can't come home with him as she has to attend 'notes' from the director and the 'cast party' afterwards. She is sparkly, bright, euphoric after the standing ovation and curtain calls she and Romeo/Rambo/Roger received—the audience clapping, whistling, cheering and foot-stamping. It's a wonder the floor of the hall didn't collapse.

The event that changed the course of Romeo and Juliet's destiny was the delivery of a letter. Because Romeo received the letter from the friar, he did not buy poison to kill himself, and when Juliet joined Paris in a duet, she not only scared him off, saving his life, but also gave Romeo time to arrive, very much alive, so she had no need to kill herself either. Amazing—the power of a letter. That's all it took to change everything.

Chapter Fifteen

Saturday, 01 April 1995

It's April Fools' Day. Dan and Billy left before dawn to go to
the beach for the weekend, too early to say goodbye. It'll be
Easter in a couple of weeks, and they'll go camping and surfing
with their friends for the whole break and leave me here by myself. Mum will be in her studio, completely immersed. Shaun
will be too busy to scratch himself. A wave of loneliness and
desolation sweeps over me.

'He's leaving me!' Of course, I'm crying. 'In two months,
he'll be *gone!*'

Two months is still a while. Don't waste it being sad. DO something!

I dry my eyes, blow my nose and get dressed in shorts and a
t-shirt over my bikini—a swim in the creek will be something
to do. Maybe Shaun will be picking the last of his produce and
I can help him and persuade him to join me for a paddle and a
dip.

I make a big bowl of muesli, with milk and sliced banana,
and sit on the top back step to eat it, with Cleo, Patra and Anne
for company. I gaze up at *Booyul* on the low hill and visualise
Shaun sitting on *his* back steps eating *his* breakfast. Without Saab
for company, he's probably lonelier than I am.

To think he's twenty-seven and still doesn't know what he
wants to do with his life. At least he's trying to make Antarctica

happen. I need to stop dreaming we'll be together. Tears flow down my cheeks again. I wipe them away with the back of my hand.

At least I've got my schoolwork. Mum picked up my OTEN parcel from the post office containing next term's study notes and assignment topics for all my subjects. I'll enjoy discovering what's next, learning new things and researching new topics.

I decide to walk across the south paddock to the stand of eucalypts growing along the boundary between us and whoever lives next door. I haven't explored that part of our property yet, but now Joe Whittaker has removed his cattle back to *his* property, or the sale yards, all I need to look out for are snakes and wallabies. I'll inspect Dan's vegie patch on the way. I'm curious to know if he's cultivating marihuana. A couple of weeks ago I discovered seedlings sprouting in a tray on top of their wardrobe. They are not there now.

I finish my cereal, go into the kitchen, rinse the bowl and spoon, and make *two* salad and *cheese* sandwiches—*no* ham!

On Wednesday, after burying my parcel of letters, minus one, along with the fake journal, Shaun and I ate the sandwiches I'd made *with* ham. Then we went to look at the piglets. I was amazed to see them already trying out their trotters and squealing and squabbling over their mother's teats. They're so cute when they're little. A vision of suckling piglet served on a tray invaded my mind unexpectedly and I nearly puked! I've never liked pork. Now I'm turned off ham and bacon too.

If I walk along the south boundary down to the creek and then follow the cattle tracks along the top bank north towards *Booyul*, fingers crossed I'll discover Shaun picking produce. We can go for a paddle up the creek to our island, eat lunch together, have a cuddle …

Dream on!

It's hard not to dream and hope. I place my journal, love letter attached, in a plastic bag with a couple of pens, and lie them on the bottom of my backpack along with the condoms and pill packet. I can do some writing and re-reading down by the creek if I don't see him. I add a towel, sunscreen, *Rid*, water flask and the sandwiches in a container, and collect my hat from its hook in the laundry.

Cleo and Patra returned to the west veranda after I went inside. They're lying in the shade, keeping an eye on Mum in the studio. I sit alongside them to pull on my socks and Reeboks, a silly thing to do in front of them as now they think they're invited. I find them some snacks and persuade them to go into their enclosure to eat them. Unimpressed, they obey reluctantly, heads down, tails and ears drooping. I feel mean. I know what it's like to be left behind, to miss out. The wind-chimes ping and ting. A blowfly buzzes past and in a sudden flashback I see—and smell—Saab's decomposing carcass in the marsh behind the billabong and hear the blowflies with sickening clarity.

Upset and tearful again, I go to the studio doorway. No comfort there. All I have is my mother, but there are unspoken gaps between the words we share. She's deep in contemplation, gazing at the first of her triptych panels, dramatically black, white and grey except for a pair of startling blue eyes. She's explained the technique of photo-release to me—how she rubs turps on the back of the photocopy to release the ink onto the expensive, handmade paper—and I can see she's photo-released a photocopy of a blown-up photo of her mask-like drawing of my doll's face and head, with its empty eye-sockets, partly overlaying a photo-release of a photocopy of an enlarged photo of a young child holding a doll: *the* doll. I'm sure the child is an image of me! Her painted blue eyes are wide and intense. The whole thing looks spooky.

'Where would you like *me* to stand? Behind the easel? Holding the doll? So you can photograph me *now*?' I'm dripping sarcasm, but she turns to me, face alight with inspiration.

'That would be *perfect,* Jodie! For the third panel, to indicate the passing of time.'

I grunt, exasperated. 'But what does it *mean*? What are you saying, or implying?'

'I'm asking—can anyone know who we *really* are, behind the masks we wear? We learn to keep secrets from a very young age. How can *anyone* know what's real? Lies conceal truth. Fantasy veils actuality. Dreams are metaphors for reality. Rationality and irrationality lie side by side, separated by a fine line, and to which side does the fine line belong? Sanity overlays insanity, layers separated by surfaces, but where does sanity end and the nightmare of insanity begin?'

She's scaring me to death. Is she talking about me? Herself? Us?

'You should call it *The Big Wank*!'

'Don't mock me, Jodie. Or my work.' Her eyes bore into me. 'You write in a journal with a pen, and I make marks on a different sort of paper using a variety of media.'

Fright surges through me.

'You write words to express your thoughts and feelings and describe what you experience or imagine; I create images for the same reason.'

The hairs on my arms and neck rise in goosebumps.

'Both are equally valid forms of self-expression.'

I'm finding it hard to breathe. 'I'm sorry, Mum. I'm going for a walk. I've locked the dogs up.' Trembling, heart racing, I head for Dan's vegie patch about one hundred metres south of the house. I should have brought my Ventolin.

You write in a journal with a pen … you write words to express your thoughts and feelings and describe what you experience or imagine …

'She found my journal!' I exclaim to Anne. 'She's read it! She's read the letter!' It's like she's plotting. She's been weird and remote, especially since she told me about Dad, and about Lily, and admitted she failed to protect me. 'She's got it in for Dad *and* Shaun!'

Vengeance and retribution. Harm and ruin.

I climb through the splintery grey timber fence of the disused holding yard and step into Dan's garden. Knee-deep amongst the green leaves of the vines, I recover my breath and wait for my heart to slow down. I watch the bees, try to discern the sound of their buzzing as they hover over, and disappear into, the yellow flowers poking up. Peering between the vine leaves, I spy dark green baby zucchinis. Mixed in with the zucchini plants is another vine, and under the broader, variegated leaves are small, round, bright yellow button squash. I keep searching, looking for marihuana seedlings, alert to the possibility of snakes.

'Hah!' I find several seedlings with slender stems and delicate, dark green serrated leaves fanning out at the top. Uncovering Dan's secret gives me a buzz. 'They look like weeds!'

Is that why they call it weed?

'It's marihuana, all right.' I recognise the fronds from photos and drawings I've seen.

I climb through the fence at the other end of the holding yard and continue walking down the paddock towards the southern boundary. The entire *Gwongorella* property is only two hundred acres—eighty plus hectares. I skirt around thistles and watch where I put my feet. Cowpats, wallaby scat and rabbit pellets dot the grass.

A wallaby bounds away from me. Now I'm looking, I notice several resting in the shade of a tall, senescent eucalypt. Some are lying down, others are upright, all watching me, ears flicking.

I continue walking parallel to them and they stay put, as if they know I'm not a threat.

The southern boundary fence runs from the creek to Copmanhurst Road, with eucalypts and scrub growing along its length, on both sides. A cattle track weaves through the trees and undergrowth on the *Gwongorella* side and I follow it towards the creek, enjoying the shade and the breeze, the silence broken by a few last cicadas and occasional bird calls.

Although I'm watching where I put my feet, I nearly trip over an echidna scratching around. The little creature rolls itself into a ball, spines sticking out, and lies completely still. I wait. Just as I think I need to move on, a snout peeks out, the echidna unfurls itself and resumes its search for food, gradually moving away, under the fence into the scrub next door.

I keep walking, the creek ahead glittering between the trees. From time to time, I glance to my right at the fire hazard on the other side of the fence. Then I stop dead. About ten metres in, camouflaged by the scrub, but not well enough, are several oil drums cut in half, each containing a tall, bushy, dark green plant, the serrated fingers of foliage loaded with strange clumps. Around the perimeter of the drums is a makeshift mesh fence— probably to keep the wallabies out.

I'm amazed, scared and elated all at once.

'A dope crop! Is this where Dan and Billy got their seeds?'

Don't hang around. It could be dangerous!

I scurry away from the fence line, towards *Booyul*. Before long, I'm in a patch of blady grass. It's a native grass, birds and wallabies eat the seeds, but it's invasive, like the thistles.

'We could burn it,' I suggest to Anne.

The seeds would still survive.

'But what if it got away from us and became a more generalised grass fire!'

The Grafton Rural Fire Service might help with a controlled burn.

Mum's shown no interest in maintaining the property, or improving it. She fell in love with the tranquillity: the crystal-clear creek, the birdlife, the billabong on Booyul, the huge, old eucalyptus trees in the open paddocks, the homestead with its broad verandas. She needs to employ someone to manage it.

I arrive at the top bank of the creek and continue towards the *Booyul/Gwongorella* boundary. Below the bank, at water level, is a sandy little beach, now covered in debris. I climb through the fence onto the *Booyul* side. From here, access to the creek involves walking down a sandy track parallel to the water, the track separated from the creek by a long, narrow thicket of lantana—another noxious weed, though honeyeaters and blue wrens find shelter in it, and bees and butterflies love the flowers.

Shaun's canoe, camouflaged in the lantana thicket, is tied up in its usual spot. And peering around the canoe and down the track is a small reddish-brown fox with an amazing brush tail. I freeze in mid-stride, hold my breath, don't so much as blink. The fox is unaware of my presence, half-crouching, ears alternately pointing and flattening, nose sniffing, brush drooping, indicating it's seen, heard, smelt something intimidating apart from me.

I look where the fox is looking, not knowing what's around the bend at the end of the lantana thicket either. I'm startled and delighted when Shaun appears, dripping wet, naked except for his watch and battered leather hat, clutching his clothes in one hand, and his boots with socks stuffed in them in the other. Fascinated and amused, I gaze at his naked, muscular body and at his penis—my first glimpse ever. Eyes down, unaware he is being watched, Shaun trudges up the track towards me, until he's almost level with the fox. The little creature doesn't have the nerve to let him pass by; instead, it darts out onto the track in front of him and runs straight at me. It sees me, leaps into the air, twists sideways, lands on all-fours like a cat, dashes up the slope of blady grass on the other side of the track and disappears into the scrub on the top of the bank. Shaun sees the fox and me in the same moment. I'm still in mid-stride and I bring my back foot forward, so my legs are together.

'Bloody hell!' His right hand clutching his clothes moves reflexively towards his belly.

'Don't bother,' I tell him, grinning. 'It's too late for that.'

He hesitates, for just a moment, then lowers his hand, and the clothes, to his side, gazing at me steadily, a sheepish smile on his face. 'Are you trying to give me a heart attack? How come I'm honoured by your unexpected presence?'

'I've brought you some lunch.'

'That's very thoughtful of you. What did you bring?' He drops his clothes and boots onto the track.

I'm still staring at his penis as if in a trance. I tear my gaze away and look him in the eye. 'Salad sandwiches, minus ham.'

'That little fox got a shock. *Two* humans!' Shaun hasn't taken his eyes off me either, but now he bends down, casually picks up his underdaks, gives them a shake and steps into them. 'I've heard strange barks and shrieks in the night—' he shakes the sand off his shorts and pulls them on too '—but that's the first one I've seen.'

'What's the water like?'

'Cold!' He drapes his t-shirt over a still-wet shoulder and picks up his boots. 'Show's over.' He gives me a wry smile as he holds out his free hand. 'Shall we dine?'

I step forward and take his outstretched hand, and we walk down the track towards the creek. He leads me up onto the patch of grass on the top of the bank between the lantana and the water, the canoe just behind us. I'm hoping he'll suggest launching it, but instead he looks at his watch. 'No time for a paddle, I'm sorry, but Wednesday is a promise. Let's eat here.'

I hide my disappointment and remove the towel and the Rid mosquito repellent and the container of sandwiches and water bottle from my backpack, aware, with a thrill of guilt, that my forbidden journal and love letter are lying hidden on the bottom. I spread the towel on the grass and take off my Reeboks and socks. He sits on one end of the towel, and I sit beside him. I offer him his sandwich and start eating my own. It feels familiar and comfortable to be eating lunch together.

'No ham, eh?'

'Nup. I'm off ham.'

'Hmm. We'd better not visit the Baby Animals section at the Grafton Show then … all those little calves, kids, lambs, chickens … and piglets. You'll end up vegetarian if we're not careful! Not that that would be a bad thing.' He bites into his sandwich. 'Cheese is good.'

'Are you saying we can go to the Grafton Show together?'

'If you like.'

'I *would* like—I'd like very much!'

'He chews in silence and swallows the mouthful. 'I loved the Royal Easter Show in Sydney when I was a kid, especially the horses—camp-drafting and high-jumping—and the wood-chopping, and the sheep-dog trials. What about you?'

I shrug. 'I dunno. I've never been to a show anywhere.'

He looks at me with disbelief. 'Never?'

'Never, ever. Not that I remember, anyway.'

'Gosh, that's a shame. We'll have to make up for it.'

'Thank you. But I warn you—I'll want to see and do *every-thing*!'

'Including rides?'

'*Except* rides. I'd be sick for sure.'

'We can visit sideshow alley. Buy showbags and sausage sangers and fairy floss.'

We continue to chat, moving on to *Romeo and Juliet* while we finish our sandwiches. Holding my water flask above my lips so I don't contaminate it, I take a swig and swish the water around my teeth, stand up and spit into the lantana behind us, then swallow a mouthful or two before returning to my towel to pass the flask to Shaun. He copies me—standing up, turning his back, moving towards the lantana, rinsing his mouth, spitting into the foliage, and in that moment madness overtakes me. I whip off my shorts and t-shirt, drop them in the grass, and stand on the towel in my bikini. I pull the strings holding it in place—and the top and bottom fall at my feet just as he turns around.

'It's only fair I even the score,' I tell him.

He is as mesmerised as I was when I saw *his* naked body, but without the amusement. His expression is pure anguish. He is shaking his head, almost imperceptibly, but I can see it.

'Please don't be scared, Shaun. Please hold me. Just this once.' I'm pleading. 'Please.'

'I *am* scared!' His voice is low, pleading with me too. He drops the water flask in the grass, moves towards me and wraps his arms around my back, as if to cover my nakedness and protect me. 'This is *not* a good idea, Jodie.' I can feel him trembling.

I drop my glasses in the grass behind me, hold his head and kiss him with an intensity I can't describe. His penis signals a response, but he pulls away.

'Jodie, we can't. *I* can't.'

'I'm on the pill,' I plead. 'I'm safe.'

'It's not safe for *me,* Jodie!'

'No one will see us …'

His penis, shielded by his shorts, hardens against my body.

'I can't risk it.'

'*Please*, Shaun.'

He glances across the water at the cattle grazing on the swathe of paddock opposite. 'Do you want me to end up in court—and jail?' He breaks free of my embrace, scoops up his boots, socks and t-shirt and flees like the fox.

Utterly mortified, I throw my HAs on the grass next to my glasses, stumble down the bank to the creek's edge, and wade into the water up to my shoulders. The cold does nothing to numb the horrible emotions overwhelming me—the shame and humiliation of rejection; the feeling chastised for being so thoughtless and selfish. I imagine completely submersing myself, expelling all the air from my lungs, and sucking in water so I drown, but I lack the courage to do it. Instead, I return to my towel and dry and dress myself, shivering and crying with shame and regret. Then I sit in the grass and write in my journal to deflect the pain.

April Fools' Day

I'm an April fool all right. To think I forgot to take the pill this morning! Imagine not telling Shaun I'm two months pregnant when he leaves—and by the time my family realises my appearance is more than me being overweight, it will be too late to do anything about it. Imagine introducing him to his son or daughter in ten years' time! I know we can't be together right now. He needs to 'find' himself, travel the path he wants to take in life, and I need to do the same. But ten years from now we will return, resurrect and read my love letters, and forge a life together …

So often I dream I'm lying in the grass with Shaun, making love on the banks of Gwongorella Creek. I learnt what to do watching my father and ex-piano teacher, but in my dreams Shaun and I transcend that ugliness. We hold each other, barely moving, feeling the intensity of our love, coming together in the same moment. I wake up, grief over-riding pleasure as the sensations of orgasm fade away, aching with disappointment because it *is* only a dream …

Now, remembering how I felt when we kissed, his penis hardening against my body, I write a different version on the opposite page.

Love in the grass

We are lying together in the grass, naked, free and exposed. The casuarinas sigh and whisper overhead. We kiss deeply and I reach down, stroke his belly, his thighs, his erect penis. I straddle him, lower myself onto him. He glides inside me easily, my hair a curtain around our faces. My breasts brush his chest, and he cups them in his hands, gently kissing and sucking each nipple in turn. I feel an intense longing, a faraway yearning. I move in slow motion, moaning softly because it feels so good to be this close. An orgasm is building. I move more urgently, pressing myself harder against him, until the intensity overwhelms me. I wail in ecstasy, and he convulses and moans too, again and again. Then we laugh and cry together, sharing the joy and the heartache of forbidden love ….

At the top of the track, weeping again, I agonise with Anne over which way to go home and decide to walk up the track alongside his vegetable patch.

And go over to him. And apologise. And offer to help him.

'Yes. I set him up. I'll tell him I *do* understand his fears and concerns.'

And promise him it won't happen again.

'No! I can't promise that. But he'll probably drop me, anyway; tell me I'm bad news and dangerous to know and he doesn't want to see me anymore!'

He said he'd see you Wednesday for a paddle.

'He'd be having second thoughts after this. He's probably changed his mind.'

Fear of loss, more than courage, urges me up the track towards his vegetable garden, but after all my agonising, Shaun is nowhere to be seen. Feeling like a trespasser, I peer into the silent packing shed. Swallows dart past me, flitting in and out. I walk up the slope towards the stockyards. His utility is not in the lean-to; the tractor is there, but not the trailer. Wendy's car is not in its usual spot beside the house. *Booyul* is deserted. No Saab to bark a warning.

I check on the sow and her piglets, and Big George in his separate pen. The piglets have grown in just a few days. Big George's pen is empty.

Shaun left me naked on the grass beside the creek and took Big George away to be slaughtered. While I wrote erotic imaginings in my journal, Big George had his throat cut. I bend over the fence of his pen and throw up my lunch *and* breakfast.

The realisation I know *nothing* about Shaun's daily activities—his decisions, actions, responsibilities—hits me like a punch in the gut. I don't have a clue about what he has to do, how much work and time it takes to run his enterprise. The one day he takes off each week to be with me is probably a big chunk of his time. Two months have passed since we met, and what have we done together? Shared a paddle on the billabong, half a dozen paddles up the creek with maths and science lessons and picnic lunches on our island; some intense conversations; a couple of 'burials'; two 'dates' disguised as family outings; a few hugs—and even fewer kisses. Two months and he'll be gone. Nine more Wednesdays at the most.

Today I pushed him too far. I frightened him, angered him, turned him off. I've probably ruined our relationship.

Chapter Sixteen

Sunday, 02 April 1995

On the edge of dreaming, I see myself, a very small child, pulling books off a shelf and dropping them, one by one, in a pile at my feet. My first realisation my mother is behind me is her loud, high-pitched, angry voice.

Jodie! Do you hear me? I'm talking to you! Listen to me!

I surface from my dream, heart pounding, and turn over.

'Jodie! Do you hear me? I'm talking to you! Listen to me!'

Bleary-eyed, I see my mother standing in my bedroom doorway. I did not hear her knock—if she did knock. I did not hear the tell-tale squeak my door makes when it is opened.

'What's wrong?' I reach for my hearing aids and glasses on the bedside table and put them on, fumbling in my haste. 'What! What is it? What's the matter?'

'We need to talk!'

Suddenly angry I answer her back, same tone, greater volume. 'Get out of my room! At least let me get dressed!' I'm not going to talk to her naked, in bed. Judging by the expression on her face, there's a good chance I'll need to escape.

'We will continue this conversation on the veranda. Get up and get out there! Pronto!'

The shoulder straps of my backpack are looped over her right arm, my journal and my letter to Shaun clutched in her right hand, her other hand on the doorknob. 'Don't keep me waiting!'

She closes the door with unnecessary force.

While I was asleep and deaf to the world she invaded my room, violated my privacy, snooped around, found my backpack, discovered my journal and letter to Shaun! I leap out of bed in a state of panicked fury, pull on fresh underwear and yesterday's shorts and t-shirt, then look in the back of my desk drawer for the box of contraceptive pills. They're still there, though not precisely where and how I left them. I take today's pill, swallowing it with water from the bottle I keep on my desk. I look under my pillow. The condoms are gone! Since when?

Adrenaline is making me shaky and nauseated. A toxic brew of anger, fury and dread churns in my empty belly. Now the shit has hit the fan I'm determined to have it out with her.

She's on the east veranda, on the sofa, reading—no doubt re-reading—my letter to Shaun, my journal beside her. In her lap are documents and pieces of paper I recognise from my own illicit fossicking in her hiding place, her filing cabinet.

I sit opposite her in the single chair. Her lip curls as she folds Shaun's letter and puts it beside her. She picks up my journal, flips to April Fool's Day and Love in the Grass and thrusts the open pages in my face, clearly appalled by what I've written. 'You're pregnant to him!'

I look her in the eye, shake my head. 'They're just stories I made up.'

'You're not pregnant?'

'I'm not pregnant.' My voice is calm and flat. 'Like I said, it's all made up.'

'On Wednesday, after dropping the boys at school, I returned home, and you were missing—again—so I took the opportunity to fossick around—'

She found my journal and letter to Shaun, hidden behind my textbooks, while I was supposed to be burying them! Shaun trusted me, and I deceived him, betrayed him, put him in harm's way because of my selfishness.

'—to find out what's going on between you and that man. I need to protect you—'

'You should have protected me long before this! How dare you invade my privacy—'

'It was the only way I could find out the truth!'

Amid my fury and despair, I understand her. 'You only had to ask me, Mum. The truth is—none of it is true. It's all make-believe, every word!'

'You're a despicable liar; you're just like Hugh!' Her voice oozes contempt.

'Don't you dare compare me with him!'

'And you are not only a liar. You are also a thief! You disgust me!'

Don't be side-tracked!

'My stories about Shaun are all fantasy stuff—'

'Stop lying to me! It's like walking a tightrope in the dark. I can't stand it—do you want to put me in the madhouse again?'

'Are you saying I put you in the madhouse? Are you blaming me for that? Because I gave you the pink letter?'

She stares at me, deciding whether to answer me. She doesn't. Instead, she says, 'You have a very sick mind, Jodie. Hugh might be a philandering bastard, but he is not a paedophile!'

'You think I'm lying about my father? You'd rather defend him and call me a liar?'

'Well, you are a liar—you've just admitted none of it is true! And judging by what I've read, you are clearly very disturbed! The sooner we get help for you the better.'

'You can't face it, can you.'

She hesitates, but only for a moment.

'You must get real, Jodie. Compulsive lying and fantasising is bordering on psychosis. If you live on the edge of dreaming, between reality and imagination all the time, the edges begin to blur. You lose touch with what is and what isn't. I know. I've been there and it's terrifying not to know the difference. When you tell me you're not having sex with the man next door and I read the opposite, full of pornographic details, and I find condoms under your pillow and in your wardrobe and a box of contraceptive pills in your desk drawer and you tell me it's all fantasy, that what I read and see with my own eyes isn't real, isn't true, isn't happening, I'm just imagining it—and meanwhile you write about Hugh implying he's a paedophile! It's the man next door who is the paedophile!' Her voice has become so strident, so shrill, my hearing aids can't handle it. 'You're sending me round the twist, Jodie. I'm returning you to boarding school, or to live with Hugh—and I'll have that man next door arrested for having sexual intercourse with my daughter! You're still a child, you're barely fifteen, it's carnal knowledge. I can't let you screw up my mind again or your own life!'

I'm stunned by her tirade. She grabs a document off the pile on her lap and shoves it in my hands. I take it and read the highlighted paragraph.

66C. Sexual intercourse—child between 10 and 16

Any person who has sexual intercourse with another person who is of or above the age of 10 years, and under the age of 16 years, shall be liable to penal servitude for 8 years.

I hand it back and look her in the eye. 'I'm telling you the truth, Mum. I have *not* had sex with Shaun. I've wanted to, but he's refused—*for this very reason!*

'I don't believe you! I *know* you're lying! This sudden interest in the pill! Did *he* get them for you? The condom you left in the dryer—'

'I did *not* leave a condom in the dryer! *Jeez!* I didn't have condoms to leave!'

'Then what are these?' She reaches behind her and holds up the string of green packets.

'They're Dan's! He gave them to me. He was sorry he set me up and he heard me say I wanted to own a condom. But I have not used a condom, and I have not had sex!'

'I don't believe you! Oh God help me! I don't know what to believe. You're exactly like Hugh, trying to pull the wool over my eyes.'

'I am *nothing* like my father! Don't you *dare* liken me to my father!'

'I prefer my intuition to your reassurances, Jodie. I'm asking you to know the difference between truth and lies and be *real* with me!'

'I *am* being real. I am telling you the *truth*. Shaun and I are just friends. Nothing's happened between us.'

'Nothing?'

'I've hugged him a few times—so what! We have *not had sex*.'

'He's grooming you. It's just a matter of time and—'

'Why are you *hassling* me like this?'

'He's twenty-seven! You're barely fifteen!'

'What difference does age make!'

'You're under-age!'

'We've done nothing wrong! Shaun takes care of me. He's decent and kind. He helps me with my maths. He helps me in *lots* of ways—'

'What's this then?'

She picks up my letter to Shaun by one corner, as if it is contaminated, her twisted lips indicating disgust, and drops it in my lap. I hold it close to my breaking heart. I don't need to read it, I didn't need to keep it, I know what it says word for word, off by heart. It is a poetic, passionate, detailed expression of my most erotic dreams, hopes and wishes, written as if they were real events that had happened, were happening, and would happen again ….

'It's fiction, Mum,' I tell her wearily, sadly, my voice breaking. 'Just dreams—my imagination. I've not sent it, or given it to him to read, because …'

'I simply don't believe you!'

'I *swear* I'm telling you the truth. And you need to know—with Shaun I'm the safest I've ever been—with *anyone*.' I reach out with both hands and grab the papers from her lap before she can stop me. Riffling through the pages I find what I'm looking for.

'You copied this from somewhere—it's in your handwriting.' I read aloud: *'Under the Family Law Act child abuse can include physical or sexual assault against a child or a sexual activity when a child is used as an object for sexual gratification or witnesses sexual activity between adults for the gratification of the adults.'*

'You copied this because you thought it was significant. You *knew*, Mum, didn't you! You *always* knew. You made me go with him to piano lessons for *years*—'

'I *didn't* know! I didn't have a clue until you gave me the pink letter. I had no idea!'

'*I* don't believe *you*! You *must* have known something wasn't right, and you *still* made me go! My tears should have warned you!' I'm crying now, remembering. 'I couldn't *tell* you why I didn't want to go. Dad said you'd leave us, leave *me*, or send me away if I told you, if you found out. You *should* have known what was happening to me, but you didn't *want* to know! All you ever said to me was, "Jodie! For god's sake top snivelling and blow your nose!" And Dad was right! After five years—in desperation—I gave you hard evidence, the pink letter, and what happened? You *left* me, just like he warned me you would! You *disappeared!* You didn't even say goodbye! And then I was taken away to a boarding school—by strangers—and abandoned there, for *four years!'*

Heat is burning inside me, building as if my thermostat is malfunctioning, as if my blood is coming to the boil. I riffle through the papers again. 'You see this bit here? See the penalty for a person with *intent* to have sexual intercourse with a child under ten, or who's *attempted* to have sexual intercourse with a child under ten? I could put my father away for up to twenty years!' I throw the pieces of paper back in her lap.

The blood has drained from her face. She looks like I've hit her. We stare at each other.

'Mum, I won't blame you for Dad, if you don't blame me for putting you in the clinic. Did you really mean that? Do you *really* think that?'

There are seconds of silence before she shakes her head. 'No. I put myself there, because I didn't love myself enough to quit a toxic marriage.'

'I'm safe with Shaun, Mum, safer than I've *ever* been with *anyone!* I'm repeating myself, because I want you to know it's the *truth.'*

She's trembling. Her face is white. 'And your writings about Hugh, are they just fantasies too?'

I gaze at her, frozen. *Are* my writings about my father true? Everything I've written *feels* true. I *feel* violated. But have I *been* violated? The boundaries—between memory and imagination, between reality and fantasy, between the waking world and the dream world, between conscious awareness and nightmares— have indeed blurred.

She stares back, willing me to answer her, to relieve her. I cannot relieve her.

When she speaks, her voice is constricted, her words slurred, as if her mouth is dry. She tries to moisten her lips to no avail.

'Don't *do* anything, Jodie. Don't *say* anything—not to him, not to the boys, not to *anyone*. There are financial considerations, I mean … I … we all … depend on him for financial support and I don't want it to turn into a-a fight. I'll get my share of our assets eventually, but it could take *years*, even without a legal struggle. I don't want to end up on the Supporting Parents Benefit. We need to work out what to do in our best interests. If he gets nasty about finances *after* the divorce, *then* maybe we could—'

I find my voice. 'We could what? Blackmail him?'

'I guess I'm saying let's not play all our cards at once.'

I feel desolate. Utterly alone. 'You *knew*, Mum, didn't you! You knew and you did *nothing*! And you're *still* choosing to do nothing.'

'Jodie, I *didn't* know. I *swear* I had no idea!'

'Well, *I* don't believe *you*, Mum. *You should have known!* From now on, my life is my own. I don't need your protection. I can do a better job protecting myself.'

Tears spill from her eyes. 'Oh, Jodie, please don't feel like that. I *will* do something, I promise. Just give me time to think it through. Give me time to do the right thing.'

'You've already had my lifetime to do that.'

I take my journal from her and drop it, with my letter to Shaun, along with its envelope, into my backpack. I reach behind her for the string of condoms and put them into the backpack too. I am free. I can end this confrontation. I can walk away.

At the entrance to the hallway, I look back at her.

'While you take time to think,' I speak slowly and clearly, 'I'll take time to be with Shaun. And if you *ever* do *anything* to cause him harm, I will *never* forgive you. I will destroy Dad, and I will destroy you too, because you will be implicated—you *were* complicit—you should have known, and then I will destroy myself.'

I leave her sitting there.

Chapter Seventeen

Monday, 03 April 1995

Late yesterday afternoon the boys came home from Yarrawarra, sunburnt, sandy and stoned. I hardly spoke to them. This morning, Dan was up at dawn picking baby zucchinis and button squash to take to school and watering his 'crop'—I heard the well pump kick in while I was sitting on the loo. I kept out of their way, and they left with Mum without saying goodbye, meaning I stayed in my room with the door closed and didn't say goodbye either.

During yesterday's confrontation with Mum, shame and guilt flooded me when she said, 'You are not only a liar. You are also a thief. You disgust me!' Rifling through my wardrobe and drawers, she must have seen items of clothing she didn't recognise, price tags still attached. It's not like I've *needed* any of the stuff I've pinched.

Last night, in a whispered midnight conference with Anne, I promised to stop shoplifting and to make amends. Anne always tries to talk me out of self-harming behaviour, but if I'm furious or hurt about something, I refuse to listen to her.

This morning, after Mum left with the boys, I placed the stolen clothing, each item neatly folded, into white plastic bags, one bag for each shop, four bags in all, an anonymous note attached to each bag.

*I'm very sorry I stole these items from you.
Now I'm returning them. Please forgive me.*

I know I should deliver each bag in person, but the shopkeepers will accuse me of stealing everything that's ever disappeared from their racks and shelves and call the police.

Tomorrow morning after Mum drops me off at TAFE on her way to the RAG, I'll walk to the Anglican Christ Church Cathedral and leave the bags on the porch of the Dean's residence, with a note addressed to the Dean asking him to return them for me. It's ironical, me who despises religion, choosing a minister of religion to help me, but who else can I ask?

Coward.

Yes, I *am* a coward, but better this way than not at all.

Deed done, I'll return to the TAFE library and tackle some maths before I meet Em and Jacinta at Market Square for lunch. I've opened my parcel from OTEN and checked out my next topics and assignments. I'll find a thorny maths issue I can ask Shaun to help me with, when, if, we meet up on Wednesday.

I set up the card table in its usual spot against the railing and pull up the single chair. I put my maths folder on the table, along with everything else I need, including the binoculars—Shaun might be working in his vegie garden—and stow my backpack beneath it.

I'm panicking Shaun won't want to see me again after Saturday's debacle. I'm still rattled by the experience, as well as by the confrontation with Mum yesterday morning.

Right now, I'm so miserable I need to write a letter to my family to relieve the pain. I need them to understand the cause of my misery, instead of blaming me like it's some sort of defect in my personality.

A LETTER TO MY FAMILY

Dad: *Is it possible to commit the most awful crimes, but with the passing of time forget you ever did them? Like having sex with so many different people you don't remember what you did, or who you did it to?*

I won't be around when you read this letter, but it doesn't make it easier to write. The only thing that makes the pain bearable is knowing it will end. I've started to remember things, Dad, not because I'm ready to face the memories, or deal with your denials or Mum's disbelief, but because I want to make sense of my life before I leave it. But I can't make sense of the fact you've been abusive, unloving and uncaring of me all my life, and cruel to my mother.

Mum: *You were supposed to teach me by example how to love and protect myself. Instead, you developed a 'masochistic personality disorder'—I read a description of that in a magazine somewhere and it fits. By staying with Dad, you failed to love and protect yourself, and that meant you failed to love and protect me.*

I don't want to die believing you never really loved me except for those few hours after I was born. I've read 'The Story of Jodie's Birth' so often, to remind myself you wanted me. When I was younger, you tried to help me with my physical problems, but you had no idea how to help me emotionally—you were too self-absorbed trying to make sense of your own crazy, miserable life, trying to keep track of the women in your husband's life, never imagining he was cheating on you with your own daughter a witness. I don't want to make you responsible for what Dad did to me. He did what he did, not you.

I felt so bad, Mum. I asked him to stop, but he wouldn't. It was his secret, not mine, but he made it mine too. I'm so sorry, even though it wasn't my fault. I was terrified you'd find out and despise me, hate me forever, throw me out, put me in a boarding school. That's what Dad warned me would happen if I told you, or you found out, and he was right!

I used to believe my secret knowledge would 'show' somehow, like a dirty stain. I was sure that you would 'know'. After all, you seemed to know, intuitively, about other women in Dad's life, before you had 'proof'. I couldn't understand why you didn't realise what he was exposing me to. If you did know and you didn't stop him, then clearly you did not love me; I was worth nothing. I cannot cope with that thought. I tell myself we were both victims of his behaviour and his lies.

My brothers: *Not one by one, but two by two, because you are a pair, joined by a bond I cannot share. I'm always on the outside of your lives, looking in, on the edge, of no significance or importance to you at all. I'm separated from everyone by my deafness. It's an 'existential loneliness'. I feel invisible. Worse than invisible. It's as if I don't exist.*

Mum told me you chose to come here with her, instead of staying with Dad, because you wanted to be with me, but I've seen little evidence of that. After four years of separation, I don't know how to interact with you, how to behave around you, how to be friends with you.

Please take me out on your surfboards near the bull-rocks at Yarra-warra, for my first and last surf ever. Being on the waves with you guys will be real deadly as Em would say, and scatter my ashes into the sea. I'll appreciate it for all eternity.

Jodie

Writing the letter was cathartic. I cried while I wrote it, but I feel calmer now it's on paper, in an envelope, instead of festering inside me. I've put it with my letter to Shaun, also restored to its envelope, both letters secured with a paperclip to the inside of the back cover of my journal, which I've stowed on the bottom of my backpack under the four white plastic bags.

I'm curled up on the sofa on the east veranda, having just read parts of Mum's 1990 journal, filched from the bottom drawer of her filing cabinet. 1990 was the year I gave her the pink letter, the year she disappeared. I'll delve into her 1991 journal next; it was written during my first year in boarding school. I know I'm no better than she is, snooping and prying, but I want to know where she was and what she was experiencing, thinking, feeling and doing at the time, just as she's been inquisitive about me and my clandestine life since we moved here. I can't—won't—forgive her for raiding my room and reading my secret writings, but I can relate to her desire to understand my state of mind and find out what I've been up to. I have the same curiosity about her, the same need to know. It's all-consuming, but dangerously upsetting too.

I gaze across the south paddock, horrified and moved by what I've read, about her helplessness against her husband's indifference to her emotional pain; then her incarceration in a clinic for the mentally ill. She's written a vivid record of her dreams, nightmares more like it, and hallucinations; eloquent, lucid descriptions—written with hindsight—about her loss of contact with reality. I'm understanding her abandonment of me in a new light. I just wish I could remember what happened to *me* in 1990. What was it like for Dan and Billy? How did *they* cope? How did our father deal with it?

Cleo and Patra suddenly leap up, claws scrabbling on the veranda boards. They go to the steps and stare out across the south paddock, noses pointing towards the west.

'What is it, girls?' I ask them.

'They glance back at me urgently, before resuming their vigil, ears pricked, tails down. A utility truck suddenly cuts across my vision, followed by another, driving parallel to the south boundary fence towards the creek, followed by two dark grey 4WD vehicles.

'Holy shit!' I instinctively duck below the level of the veranda railing. 'Who are they?' I ask Anne. 'What are they doing on *our* property?'

The neighbours? The cops? They must've had a tip-off!

Through the wrought iron, I watch the cavalcade as it pulls up about where the dope crop is situated. Two dogs on leashes are released from the back of one of the 4WD vehicles.

Sniffer dogs!

They lead their handler down the fence line. 'Good girls!' I tell Cleo and Patra. 'Shh! Come here!' I open the dog-biscuit tin and show them a biscuit each. They follow me as I scramble on hands and feet across the veranda. I persuade them to cross the threshold into the hallway with some cajoling; they're not allowed in the house. They look guilty and unhappy, heads and tails down as they pass my bedroom, the den opposite, and cross the sitting room. Then they act relieved as they follow me out the west veranda door, tails wagging, until they realise they are going into their enclosure. I placate them with the biscuits and a pat each as I lock them in.

Back on the east veranda, I pick up the binoculars from the card table and focus on the activity down the paddock.

They're cutting the fencing wire!

The fence-cutters move out of sight into the scrub, probably to cut away the wire mesh surrounding the crop. Other men follow them. Eventually, they re-emerge, twisting and rolling the obviously heavy half-drums with their tall, leafy, bushy plants through the opening in the fence, and towards the first ute. One of them unlocks the back of the ute's tray and lowers a ramp. He climbs up it, moves towards the back of the cabin and fiddles with something, then pulls on a cable and passes it to one of the men waiting at the bottom of the ramp, who wraps and secures the cable around his half-drum, then steps back while the man on the truck winches the drum up the ramp and onto the tray. Then the man on the ground walks up the ramp and together they manoeuvre the half-drum with its plant into position.

What's the bet they'll come here next—with the dogs and a search warrant!

I know about search warrants from watching *Blue Heelers* and *The Feds* on TV.

'I need to *do* something!' I crawl across the veranda back into the house, grab a couple of white plastic bags from the kitchen, go into the boys' room and systematically hunt out anything that might incriminate them. I know where to look—under their pillows; under their mattresses; under their beds; on top of their wardrobe. I'm so relieved the sprouting marihuana seedlings are no longer there, in their wardrobe, where I go through every pocket in every pair of pants and every jacket. I look in their bedside chests of drawers. I search every shelf, look behind their books and between their magazines. There are probably little plastic bags stuffed under rocks in the snake cages, but they'll have to stay there. I put the incriminating items into one of the white plastic bags: a couple of small, ornate brass pipes; four bongs made of plastic cream bottles and bits of Mum's garden hose—surely she's noticed her hose getting shorter— tallyho papers, matches, and half a dozen small bags of the green stuff. I squeeze the air out of the white plastic bag, twist it, tie the top firmly, put it into the other white plastic bag and do the same. I straighten their beds. I vacuumed their floor on Friday as usual, and they haven't had a chance to mess it up, but if the police bring in the dogs, they'll be able to smell what *was* in here, and now *I'm* contaminated! They'll smell it on *me*, and I'll be in trouble for concealing evidence.

At least my brothers will know I tried. It's too complicated to figure out why that matters. On the west veranda, not visible to the interlopers, I cast around for a hiding place.

Drop it in the well and hope it floats? Throw it on the roof? Hide it in the dog enclosure?

I decide on the enclosure. Cleo's kennel, like Patra's, is raised on bricks—the height of a brick on its side—to keep it off the floorboards. I shove the bag deep underneath. Then I go back inside and get a bone for each of them, a treat, both reward and distraction.

'Good girls!' I tell them.

In the bathroom, I thoroughly wash my hands and arms with soap. Next, I grab Mum's journals from the sofa on the east veranda and put them back in her filing cabinet, exactly where and how I found them. I lock the filing cabinet and return the key to its tack concealed under her dressing gown, which is hanging on the brass hook behind her bedroom door as usual.

Finally, I hunker down in the single chair with the binoculars and watch the men loading half-drums onto the second ute. I give Shaun's vegie patch a sweep with the binoculars too, but there's no sign of him. If the cops use the dogs to look in Dan's patch, he'll be charged with cultivating, same as whoever lives next door!

Chapter Eighteen

Monday, 03 April 1995

I open my maths folder and booklet and begin reading the table of contents, but I can't concentrate or absorb anything; my eyes keep drifting to the south paddock. A couple of the men are repairing the fence. The dogs are being led to their 4WD vehicle. They jump in.

One of the 4WD vehicles moves to the front; the other, with the dogs, takes up the rear. The convoy sets off, slowly driving west up the paddock, parallel to the south boundary fence. As soon as the last vehicle is obscured by the house I hurry inside and peer around the west veranda door. Now they're veering away from the south boundary, heading north towards the lane. They are opposite the west veranda, a few hundred metres away, when the 4WD at the rear—the one with the dogs in it—peels away from the convoy and drives straight towards me, pulling up at the gate in the fence surrounding the house. When the cop in the passenger seat gets out to open it, Cleo and Patra bark ferociously. The vehicle is driven through the opening; the cop closes the gate and climbs back in. They pull up in front of the west veranda in the shade of the kurrajong tree. Both men peer at the dogs' enclosure. Apparently satisfied it's safe to get out of the vehicle, they wind the windows down, climb out, lift the back hatch and drop the tailgate. Their dogs, in a cage, whine and move about no doubt excited by Cleo and Patra.

They're going to get the dogs out!

But no, or not yet. The driver, and the officer carrying papers, approach me as I step onto the veranda. I call out, 'Hey! Cleo! Patra! That's enough! Shush!'

They stop barking, but whine and growl instead.

The officer with the papers seems to be in charge. 'Good morning, ma'am, or is it afternoon?' He consults his watch. 'It's good afternoon.'

'It is. Can I help you?' I'm sure they can see I'm trembling; my heart is beating like a hummingbird's.

'We have a warrant, ma'am, to search the premises.' He waves the documents at me, then holds them out. I take them, briefly peruse them—one is a statement of their powers under the warrant, the other is the warrant itself—before lowering my hands to my sides; I don't want them to see the papers shaking. I'm finding it hard to breathe.

'May we come in?'

'Oh, sorry, yes! Of course.'

They step up onto the veranda and enter the house, me following them.

'Nice piano.'

'Yes.'

'Do you play?'

'Not lately. Too busy with schoolwork.'

'No school today?'

'I do OTEN, distance education through TAFE. I'm hearing impaired.'

He turns, raises his eyebrows, looks at my ears. 'You're deaf?'

'I lip-read.'

'Oh, right.'

'Would you like a cup of tea? Or coffee? Or a glass of cold water?'

'Nice of you to ask, but no thanks. Hopefully this won't take long.'

They begin wandering through the house, like they're thinking of buying or renting it, heading towards the kitchen. I follow them. They look in every cupboard, check every shelf.

'Who else lives here?'

'My mother. And two brothers—they're at school.'

'Where's your mother?'

'In town. She volunteers at the RAG.'

'RAG?'

'The Regional Art Gallery.'

'Oh, right.'

There's a pause, until the other cop asks, 'Where's your father?'

'In the Blue Mountains.'

'Why?'

'Because his business is there.'

'Will he be joining you here?'

'No. They're separated.'

'How do you feel about that?'

I shrug, irritated. I'd retreat, except I don't want to let them out of my sight. They go through the fridge, examining every container. Between the two of them they check out the junk on the top of it, look in the oven, the microwave, the old fuel stove, and go through the rubbish on its top as well. The driver cop looks in the cupboard under the sink, removing and peering into every container.

'Any sign of white ants?' I ask.

Cheeky!

He ignores me.

Now who's deaf.

Finally, after checking everything in the pantry, they move from the kitchen to the dining room, then to the bathroom, again rifling through every cupboard. They check every shelf in the laundry, look in the washing machine and dryer, pull everything out of the linen press. They do put it all back, but not as neatly as it was.

My room is next. My mouth is dry. I pick up the water bottle on my desk and take a swig. They open and search every drawer in my chest of drawers. They scan every shelf of my bookcase. They peer in my wardrobe, stand on my chair and look on the top of it. They examine everything on my desk and in my desk drawers, on my dressing table and in my dressing table drawers. I feel totally violated. My journal, love letter attached, is in my backpack on the east veranda, beneath the white plastic bags full of stolen clothing, the notes attached to each bag confessing my crimes. If they go through my backpack, *I'm* done for, not to mention the risk to Shaun if they read the love letter, and/or pages in my journal.

'What are you looking for, may I ask?'

'Ma-a', mutters the warrant cop.

'Sorry? I didn't hear you.'

He looks at me, points to the documents in my hand, raises his voice and says clearly, 'Evidence of marihuana—and other drugs.'

'Huh! You won't find anything like that in here—I'm asthmatic.' They look at each other, roll their eyes, smirk, then move across the hall to the den. The window overlooking the east veranda is open, the curtains billowing lightly in the breeze. 'This is Mum's office. She's dead against drugs. All she ever takes is Panadol.'

'Izzatso.' The driver checks out the bookshelves, her desk, her in and out trays, the desk drawers. The warrant man tries the filing cabinet. 'Can you open this?'

'Sorry. Mum has the key. She just keeps her personal files in it—papers, documents, letters, accounts, receipts, bank statements—the usual stuff.'

They glance at each other again.

Distract them.

'Don't get a fright when you go into my brothers' room. They're licensed by the NPWS to rescue and release snakes.' I stand in the den doorway and point in the direction of the boys' room up the south hall.

'Is that what I can smell!' says the warrant man, following me into the loungeroom.

'Probably. They burn incense to try and disguise the smell of-of the snakes, but I hate it—the incense I mean—because of my asthma. It's worse than the smell of the snakes! They clean the cages regularly, but—'

Stop babbling!

I point past the piano. 'Mum's bedroom is on the left. Their room is on the right.'

They check out Mum's room. It's cooled and freshened by the breeze wafting through the two open windows, the east-facing one opening onto the veranda, the south-facing one framing a distant stand of senescent eucalypts. They peer in her wardrobe and chest of drawers, and both her bedside table drawers. They look under her bed.

They enter the boys' room. My heart lurches with apprehension. If they find something I've overlooked, I'll act *very* surprised, shocked even, depending on what it is.

'Wow!' says the driver. 'A red-bellied black snake! And hey! A diamond python! And what's this one?'

The warrant cop peers through the glass. 'A Clarence River rough-scaled snake, if I'm not mistaken. And this little fella here is a whip-snake. Oh, and there's a green tree snake.' He seems knowledgeable and genuinely interested, their search for drugs momentarily on hold. 'They all look to be in good nick to me. Rescue and release, you reckon?'

'Yes, they let one go over the weekend.'

Liar.

'They remove ticks and mites from between their scales, and give them vitamins, and feed them mice, or rats, or chickens, and then release them into an appropriate environment.'

'Izzatso. What's in this bag?' He undoes the drawstring.

I shrug. 'Dunno. Probably—'

He reaches into the bag. 'Shit!' he yells and withdraws his hand rapidly. 'There's a bloody snake in there!'

'I was going to say—a snake. Probably one they plan to release when they get home.'

More likely one they caught at the beach yesterday.

I hover by the door, watching them inspect the boys' wardrobe, top to bottom. They look in every pocket of their clothes. They rifle through their chest of drawers, lift their mattresses, peer under their pillows, examine the bookshelves stacked with surfing magazines, feel behind the few books they own, mostly about snakes. They open their guitar cases and look in every cranny. My heart is in my mouth—I forgot to do that! They check out the rat and mouse traps that are lying on the windowsill of the open south-facing window.

Distract them!

'Would your dogs like some water? They must be getting hot out there.'

'They've got water,' the warrant cop says, 'but thanks for your concern.'

The men glance at one another. The warrant cop gives the driver a subtle signal, a slight tilt of his head towards the door, one raised eyebrow. The other responds with the smallest of nods.

Big mouth! They're going to bring in the dogs!

My heart is thumping so hard it hurts my throat.

'I think we've seen enough, for now,' the warrant man says, glancing at his watch.

For now? He said, 'for now'.

'Thanks for your co-operation,' he adds.

'You're welcome,' I respond, like I'm in an American movie on television. According to Murphy's Law, anything that can go wrong will go wrong—not to mention the corollary: if everything's going well, something has been overlooked. They didn't search under the flat rocks in the snakes' cages, or under the cages themselves, or under the house, or under Cleo's and Patra's kennels, or under the vine leaves in Dan's vegie patch. And biggest failure of all, they didn't bother to bring in the dogs.

They'll be back, no warning, and use the dogs next time!

The men return to their vehicle, close the tailgate and hatch, and take their seats.

Clutching the search warrant and powers statement against my chest, I watch them open the gate, drive through, then close it. The 4WD bounces up the paddock towards the lane. I'm expecting it to suddenly stop and do a U-turn. Instead, it arrives at the lane, turns west towards the Copmanhurst Road, and accelerates. Roiling dust rises behind the vehicle and drifts away between the spotted gums.

Later, back on the east veranda with Cleo and Patra, armed with a glass of cold Milo and a handful of Arnott's Orange Cream biscuits, Anne and I rehearse the inevitable conversation with the boys after they discover the makings are missing from their room.

'I'll tell them the police came, with two sniffer dogs! Then I'll produce the search warrant and statement of powers, and they'll assume the *police* found everything and confiscated it for evidence.'

That'll put the wind up them, imagining the charges: possession and use.

'They'll panic, thinking they'll be summoned to appear in court, and be fined at the very least! I'll let them stew while I describe the raid with the sniffer dogs next door.'

Try and discern if they knew about the crop.

'*Then* I'll reveal the fact *I* gathered up the incriminating material in their room and hid it under Cleo's kennel!'

Imagine their relief and gratitude!

'I'll tell them the cops searched every room, until the boss-cop said they'd seen enough *for now*—a warning they'll return with the dogs when we least expect it.'

Why warn them? Why not let them get caught?

'I want them to stop *before* they get caught!'

They could do worse things. Use harder drugs …

'I'm scared they *will* do worse things …'

More important than any of this is what they can tell me about 1990. Having read parts of Mum's 1990 journal, I'm desperate to know about Dan and Billy's experiences during that year, as well as 1991 and later. Was I with them and Dad, without Mum, in 1990—after I gave her the pink letter—and she disappeared? It's very disconcerting to not remember.

'What was *I* doing that year?' I ask Anne. 'Did something so traumatic happen I've blotted it out? How did Dan and Billy cope without Mum around? What did Dad tell them? Did *they* know Mum was in a mental hospital? Did they visit her?'

Anne has no answers.

I do remember being taken away to boarding school early in 1991 by strangers—a man and his wife. The woman told me they were friends of Mum's; she helped me pack. I don't recall saying goodbye to the boys; I guess they were at school. I remember boarding school from then on though, four years of good and bad experiences.

It hurts so much, but I need to know. Why didn't they write to me? Why didn't they answer my letters while I was in boarding school? Why didn't they ever come and visit me?

Mum and the boys arrive home. Cleo and Patra race down the steps and around the west side of the house to greet them, but I stay put on the east veranda, on tenterhooks, wondering how long it will take Dan and Billy to realise things are amiss. Neither they nor Mum poke their heads around the hall doorway, or peer out of Mum's den or bedroom windows to say hullo. Cleo and Patra eventually return and flop down on the boards beside me, panting. It's almost a relief when Dan finally saunters out onto the veranda and parks himself on the sofa in front of Mum's open bedroom window.

'Hi, bro!' I try to sound cheerful and casual. 'How was your day?'

'What game are you playing?' He's not smiling.

'Where's Mum? Is she resting?' I indicate the open den window and Mum's bedroom window behind him.

He shakes his head. 'She's in the studio. So, what's the go?'

'The police came, with a search warrant and two dogs.'

'Holy shit! You're kidding!'

'Nope.' I pull out the search warrant and statement of powers from my maths folder and hand them to him.

'Fuckin' hell!' He kneels on the sofa and calls Billy through the flyscreen on Mum's open window. 'Hey, bro! Come out here, man!'

Billy appears. He scowls at me.

Dan holds out the search warrant and powers statement. 'Police came. With dogs.'

'No shit!' Billy takes the papers, peruses them.

'We're in *deep* shit, man!' Dan corrects him. 'Possession and use. Imagine the fines!'

'And cultivation,' I throw in.

Startled, Dan looks at me, his expression quizzical. 'Did they—?'

'No.' I shake my head. 'But I heard—saw—the boss-cop say, "That'll do *for now*." I'm certain they'll come back with the dogs and *use* them next time.' I nod in the direction of his garden. 'If I were you, I'd stick to zucchinis and button squash from now on. Seriously.'

Dan stares at me, his eyebrows doing the little dance they do when he's caught out.

'*Next* time?' Billy echoes. 'Are you saying they *didn't* use the dogs *this* time?'

'They didn't. They just searched the house themselves—the whole thing started with a raid on the dope crop next door.' I watch their faces, trying to discern if they know about it. I'm certain they do from the way they silently glance at each other. 'The police dogs sniffed *that* out, no problem.' I give them a blow-by-blow description of the raid, and they listen with rapt attention. It's the most I've said to them in one go since I came here. 'That's when I figured I'd better gather up your stuff and hide it, in case we were next on their list.'

Billy's eyes widen as his eyebrows shoot up. 'You *hid* it?'

'I knew the dogs would be able to smell it, but at least there'd be no *visible* evidence.'

'Go *Sis*!' Billy is ecstatic. 'Where'd you—?'

'Under Cleo's kennel. In plastic bags.'

'Wow, Jode!' Dan exclaims. 'Good thinking!' He's grinning from ear to ear, shaking his head like he can't believe his luck. 'You deserve a gold medal!'

Billy also gives me a face-splitting grin and high-fives me before joining Dan on the sofa, where they high-five each other.

Better than winning a gold medal, I've won their trust.

We have a conversation about what, and what not, to tell Mum. We decide I should put off telling her about the raid until tomorrow afternoon, after she picks me up from TAFE and we're on our way to South High, without mentioning their stuff or my hiding it.

'No point ruffling her feathers,' Dan says.

'What she doesn't know can't hurt her,' Billy adds.

Billy's comment unnerves me; I've heard it before in some other context. I let it go.

'Did you know about the dope crop?' I ask them. 'Was that where you got your seeds?'

Dan acts mystified. 'What dope crop?'

Billy acts ignorant. 'What seeds?'

I shake my head at them. 'You're pathetic liars. You'll have to do better than that.'

However, when they answer my questions about 1990 and 1991, I do believe them.

It's nearly midnight. I'm watching a blaze of stars framed by my windows, unable to sleep because of the tumult of emotions inside me after learning my brothers' versions of what happened in 1990 and 1991. I'm mentally exhausted, but wide awake. I turn on the bed lamp, put on my glasses and re-read tonight's entry in my journal.

Monday night, 03 April 1995

This afternoon I told Dan and Billy about the police raid on the dope crop next door and how I hid their stuff under Cleo's kennel, so when the cops arrived here with a search warrant, they didn't find anything incriminating.

After answering Dan and Billy's questions, I asked them about 1990 and 1991. I told them I had no memories of 1990—apart from knowing it was the year of the pink letter, and the year Mum disappeared from my life—and I needed their memories to fill in the gaps.

Dan: 'Mum and Dad were caught up in their own worlds. The upside was, me and Billy had complete freedom. We could ride our bikes wherever we liked. Go bush, find lizards and snakes. Swim in the Grose River, trap yabbies, catch fish and cook them over a campfire.'

Billy: 'It was okay for us, we had each other, but you were on your own pretty much.'

Dan: 'I knew Dad slept around. Mum was always complaining and accusing him.'

Billy: 'Families pulling together are different from families falling apart. The parents are closer to each other, they take an interest in their kids and focus on them together, instead of always doing things separately from each other, outside the family. I used to notice this togetherness in my friends' families. There was very little togetherness in ours.'

Dan: 'Yeah, Mum and Dad were still living together, but they had separate lives. They were wrapped up in themselves, and it affected us kids. Dad either stayed out a lot and did his own thing, or he took us away camping and fishing and four-wheel-driving while you and Mum were left at home. Mum was depressed and lonely and unhappy most of the time.'

I asked, 'What about when she left? Do you remember what happened?'

They looked at each other, each waiting for the other to speak.

Eventually, Dan said, 'It was bad, Jodie. You don't want to know.'

I begged him, 'I DO want to know. I NEED to know! PLEASE tell me what happened.'

Dan said, 'We were in bed. They were arguing downstairs, and it woke us up. You didn't hear it.'

'Just as well,' Billy added.

'What happened?'

Dan folded his arms, shrinking into himself. 'I heard Mum crying, pleading with Dad to stop what he was doing. We snuck downstairs to make sure she was okay.'

Billy: 'Dad didn't seem to give a rat's arse that Mum was upset. He was ridiculing her.'

Dan: 'That's when she opened the kitchen drawer where the knives were kept, and pulled out the long, thin, sharp one.'

Billy: 'Yeah! And I was shit-scared she was going to stab Dad with it!'

Dan: 'But she didn't. She stabbed herself. That's it really. Dad called an ambulance. When you woke up in the morning, Mum was gone, the mess cleaned up. Dad told us Mum would survive, but she'd be away for a while. And he absolutely forbade us to say anything about it to you. I can't recollect anything being said about it again after that.'

Billy to Dan: 'Remember a couple of detectives visited us and asked us what we saw?'

Dan: 'Yeah. Dad was under suspicion that he'd stabbed her himself, but we set the detectives straight. We didn't want to lose him too!'

Billy: 'We didn't see Mum for the rest of 1990, not even for Christmas. Or for the first term of 1991 when I started high school, and you went to boarding school.'

I asked: 'Did anyone tell me anything about what happened?'

Dan: 'We weren't allowed to tell you anything. Dad said you were too young to understand.'

Billy: 'He said, "What Jodie doesn't know can't hurt her."'

Dan: 'I didn't agree, but I wasn't game to go against him.'

Billy: 'I was angry and upset with Mum for what she did and I took it out on you, Jodie. I blamed you, for giving her the pink letter. I'm sorry about that.'

I asked, 'Tell me about 1991.'

Dan: 'School went back. I was in second form.'

Billy: 'I started high school. No uniform. No books. No nothing.'

Dan to Billy: 'I had to lend you my stuff till Dad got his finger out.'

Billy: 'Then you disappeared, Jodie. To boarding school, Dad said.'

I told them about my memories from that time on. How a man and his wife, friends of Mum's apparently, took me away in their car. There were no goodbyes—you were at school. Dad just handed me over to these strangers and then went back to work. It was a long drive to the boarding school. And for the next four years I never saw Dad or you and I never received a single letter from you. Why didn't you write to me? I wrote to you!'

They both reacted, together: 'We DID write to you! YOU never wrote to US!'

Dan said, 'We wrote to you—in 1991, anyway. I was really bummed when you disappeared—first I lose my mother, then I lose my sister! But you never replied. Not once.'

Billy said, 'I was sure you and Mum had both died and Dad wasn't telling us. I was shit-scared to let Dan out of my sight, in case he disappeared too.'

I said, 'But I wrote to BOTH of you! HEAPS of times! BEGGING you to write to me!'

Dan: 'Well, I never received a single letter from you, Jodie.'

Billy: 'Me neither. Not one.'

I said, 'And I never received a single letter from either of you! Or from Mum—or Dad. I was abandoned by ALL of you! Like I was being punished, for giving Mum the pink letter.'

After these revelations, we had a huge talk. According to Dan and Billy, Dad was responsible for posting their letters to me—but obviously he never did—and he must have intercepted the letters I wrote to them as they were addressed to his PO box, so he would have collected them. Did he destroy them all? Or did he hide them in his office desk, at the back of the bottom drawer, the same way he hid the bundle of pink letters Mum found?

I close my journal and tuck it under my pillow, remove my glasses, put them on my bedside table and turn off my reading lamp. I lie back in the dark and think, think, think. There's a lot more Dan and Billy told me—I've only written the bare bones in my journal. The other stuff I want to keep to myself, in my memory, now I remember it—or at least, now I've been *told* about it and I'm remembering what I've been told.

Dan said, 'It was incredibly traumatic to see Mum stab herself, and then watch the paramedics try to save her before they loaded her into the ambulance. There was so much blood! When the siren faded away, I was sure she was already dead.'

Billy said, 'Same—I was devastated, even though Dad tried to reassure us Mum would survive, and we were not to worry about her. He swore us to secrecy. We weren't allowed to say *anything* to ANYONE, *especially* you. You *were* only ten. He reckoned he didn't want you to worry, that it was better for you not to know because you were so highly strung. "No point getting her knickers in a knot," he said.'

Dan said, 'In the morning, when you came wandering downstairs and asked where Mum was, we had to act like we didn't know either. Dad had cleaned up the mess in the kitchen so thoroughly you wouldn't have guessed anything bad had happened if you hadn't seen it with your own eyes. He told all three of us that Mum had gone away to a special clinic so she could get well, because she'd been depressed for a while and wanted to get better. He told us to get on with our lives as usual, and after breakfast he drove the three of us to school as if nothing of any consequence had happened. It was the end of homeschooling for you, Jode. That very morning, he enrolled you in Billy's primary school.'

Hearing this amazed me. I have no memory whatsoever of going to the primary school.

Billy said, 'It was hard to know what was real, what was true. I didn't trust Dad to tell us the truth. *Was* Mum alive? Was she *really* recovering? Why couldn't we see her? Hear from her? I stuck to you and Dan like glue. The only stability we had was each other. After *you* disappeared too, Dan was all I had left. I had some very dark thoughts.'

Dan asked me what *I* remembered. 'I can't remember *anything*,' I told him. 'I don't even remember going to the primary school. It's a complete blank.' And that's what it feels like—a whiteout in my mind. They were amazed; *their* recollections are burnt into their brains.

Billy said, 'We didn't hear from Mum for the rest of 1990. Not even at Christmas.'

Dan asked me, 'Do you remember Dad bringing home a string of women?'

I shook my head.

Both were astonished I couldn't remember. 'They were nice to us, mostly. At first. They'd be bright and cheerful, and cook and clean, trying to impress Dad, making out we were a happy, normal family. Are you saying you don't remember *any* of that?'

'I don't.'

'Lucky you,' Billy said.

'Was he sleeping with them?' I asked.

'Of course,' Dan said. 'Nothing new there. But after a while the complaints would start. We'd hear arguments, and eventually, one after the other, they'd leave him.'

'Only to be replaced,' Billy added.

It is so disconcerting to not remember any of it.

'Did I still go to piano lessons?'

'I don't think so,' Dan said. 'I think that only happened while you were being home-schooled.' He shrugged. 'I'm not sure. We were at school, remember. But after Mum was taken away and you went to the primary school,' he shook his head, 'I don't remember piano lessons. I don't remember you playing the piano again.'

Chapter Nineteen

Tuesday, 04 April 1995

I lift the latch of the wooden gate to the Dean's residence. I open the gate, enter, and close it behind me, very gently. My Reeboks are quiet on the path. Flowers brush me as I pass. I creep up three white marble steps onto the terracotta tiled porch, remove the four white bags from my backpack and place them beside the front door. Apart from the twittering of birds, everything is quiet and serene.

Elated to be released from my ill-gotten gains and bad conscience, I tiptoe down the steps and hurry along the path towards freedom—when a man, armed with secateurs and camellia flowers, suddenly emerges from the shrubbery and stands directly in front of the gate.

'Oh God!' I exclaim.

'Oh no! No, no, no!' He chuckles. 'I'm not God. I'm Richard. You'll find God over there.' He points with his secateurs towards the cathedral, visible through the yellowing foliage of jacaranda trees. Crinkles warm his eyes behind rimless glasses, his smile framed by a grey moustache and beard. 'And what can I do for you?' he asks. 'You've left us a present I see.'

I burst into tears.

'Goodness me!' His tone is both surprised and sympathetic. 'Nothing is so bad it can't be soothed by a cup of tea. Come inside. My wife often provides pastoral care for young people in distress. You can tell us about it, confidentially. I'm sure between the three of us we can work something out.' He closes and pockets the secateurs, takes my arm and leads me back along the path, up the steps and into the Deanery.

It is comforting to discover good, kind people in the world—even religious ones—and it's true, the tea *is* soothing, especially poured from a teapot with a cosy. Richard's wife, Christine, is as kind and unthreatening as he is.

I confess my shoplifting, explain about the contents of the white bags I dumped on their doorstep, and tell them, still sobbing, 'N-now I want to give everything back, b-but I'm t-too scared to do it by m-myself.'

Richard persuades me to let him ring the shops. I agree, though with great trepidation. He does so, in front of me, while I blow my nose and dab my eyes. Each call he introduces himself and asks to speak to the most senior person in charge before explaining the situation.

'They are grateful to be getting their goods back,' he assures me, after the last call. 'And I greatly admire your courage in returning them.' He glances at his watch. 'I have a meeting scheduled for later this morning, but I can come with you, if we leave now.'

Christine gives me a card with their contact details on it. 'Feel free to ring and make a time to visit us again, Jodie. Meanwhile, try to separate issues you *can* resolve, because they *are* your issues—like taking these goods back to their rightful owners—from other issues and situations you *can't* resolve because they belong to other people. She looks at me with a serious expression. 'You don't have to endure other people's bad behaviour, Jodie. *You* can't change their behaviour, only they can do that, but you *can* protect yourself from it, by asking for help. Talking about it with someone you trust is a good start.'

I'm so scared I feel sick. Richard is standing nearby, looking imposing in his scarlet shirtfront and clerical collar, but he's leaving me to deal with the shop owners/managers. They all seem to know him, each addressing him courteously, with reverence even, calling him 'Dean' or 'Reverend' or 'Father', but I certainly don't receive the same respect.

The first woman mutters as she takes the bag—I'm looking at her face and read her lips: 'Never enter my shop again. We don't want thieves on our premises.'

'I'm truly sorry,' I mutter back. 'Please forgive me.'

'Fat chance!'

Not a good start. The second shop owner is no friendlier. She hisses, 'Stay away! If I see you in here again, I'll call the police.'

Outside the last shop I'm trembling, thoroughly chastened and fragile, but Richard just looks at his watch and says, 'Oh dear! My meeting is about to start.'

'Thank you for helping me. They would've eaten me alive if you hadn't been there.'

He chuckles. 'Maybe you can weed our garden as penance.' He climbs into his car.

'I'll do that. It won't be the first garden I've weeded.'

'Excellent! Ring us when you are ready.'

'I will,' I promise him. 'And I swear I won't steal *anything* ever again!'

'Good to hear.' He nods and smiles, then waves as he drives away. I watch him go, weak with relief the ordeal is over. It's too late to go to the TAFE library—I'll hang out in the café near Market Square until it's time to meet Em and Jacinta. In my jeans pocket is the change from the fifty dollars Mum gave me at the Alumy Creek market, plus the ten she gave me for the movie. A soothing hot chocolate and a toasted sandwich is just the fix I need.

Jacinta returns to TAFE for her class, while Em gives the bus and school a miss and takes me for a walk north of Market Square through Fisher Park to show me the waterhole. It looks dismal, choked with hyacinth, surrounded by weeds and lantana and a high wire fence. Nearby, built in 1882, according to a plaque, is the caretaker's cottage, its bricks made of clay from the waterhole. The deserted, dilapidated showground is surrounded by a fence of corrugated iron, rusting tin sheds and stables inside the perimeter. It's hard to visualise that this was once a rainforest inhabited by birds, animals and Em's ancestors. Only two straggly fig trees remain.

We continue north along Villiers to Dobie and Clarence streets, and Em shows me where the vegetable gardens and orchards planted by the early settlers used to be. She tells me how her people were shot in reprisals for losses from the crops. On our way back she points to the street sign. 'See the name of this street? And the next one? Oliver Fry. He was District Commissioner for Crown Lands in the 1840s. Had his own police force—with native police and trackers. Real bad men they were, not from round here. It was war. We fought back, but. Still do, in our own way.'

Thinking about how to wrap up my Aboriginal Studies assignment with reference to 'contemporary issues', I ask Em what changes would help Bundjalung people today.

'It's hard to get your mob to listen to us,' was her response. 'We gotta fight for *everything*. It takes *forever*. But I'm gonna learn your laws, and rules and regulations. I'm gonna learn to read and write and talk all that humbug. I'm gonna study to be a native title lawyer. Your mob don't have to learn *our* language—

maybe you know a few words—but we *must* know how to speak and read and write *your* language. We got no power without it.'

I nod my agreement, my understanding. 'Do you speak Bundjalung at home?'

'Not much. Not enough. The elders are making a Bundjalung dictionary. So our language isn't forgotten. So we can learn it and teach the jarjums.'

Approaching the entrance to TAFE, she says, 'If you wanna know more about us, read the *Koori Mail*. And read our writers! They write about *us*, in *your* language! Like Aunty Ruby. Ruby Langford Ginibi. She won an award for literature. She wrote *Don't take Your Love to Town*. It's in the Grafton library and the TAFE library. It's in *lots* of libraries.'

Waiting for Mum under the mango trees outside TAFE, I'm reliving yesterday afternoon's conversation with Dan and Billy, and my experience with the Dean and the shopkeepers this morning, and my walk and talk with Em this afternoon, while I rehearse the coming conversation with Mum, all at the same time. It's giving me a headache.

Mum pulls up across the road, and I hurry over as soon as there's a break in the traffic. She unlocks the rear hatch. I throw in my backpack, close the hatch, and climb into the front seat. 'Hi Mum.' I sound breathless. 'Thanks for picking me up.'

'No problem.' She pulls out into the traffic and heads for the bridge.

I take a deep breath. Might as well get it over with. 'Mum, I should've told you last night, but you were preoccupied, and I needed to go to bed—'

'Told me what?'

'There was a police raid along our southern boundary, with four-wheel drives and utilities and sniffer dogs and they removed a dope crop—'

'A *what?*'

'A marihuana crop, hidden in the scrub on the neighbour's property. They cut the fence and took the plants away, but two cops in one of the four-wheel drives stopped by our house with a search warrant.'

'A search warrant? For *what?*'

'For drugs. I'll give you the paperwork when we get home. They searched the whole house, but didn't find anything and left.'

'Good grief! What next!' We're driving south across the bridge.

'They were very polite.'

She doesn't say another word. We arrive at South High. She pulls up at a pre-arranged spot—Dan and Billy are there, waiting, talking to other students. They climb in and I glance back at them, answering their raised eyebrows with a nod to indicate she knows, hoping it looks like nothing more than a casual acknowledgment of their presence. Then I sit back, leaving whatever comes next to them.

Nobody says anything.

As soon as we arrive home, I take the search warrant and statement of powers to Mum; she's sitting at her desk in the den, opening the mail.

'Thank you.' She takes the documents, barely glances at them, puts them in her 'in' tray and returns to the mail. Clearly, she has no intention of talking to me about it.

'Would you like a cup of tea?' I ask her.

'That would be lovely,' she responds, as if everything is as it should be. Except it isn't.

Chapter Twenty

Wednesday, 05 April 1995

I'm determined to spend as much time with Shaun as I can, as often as he's willing to see me, now our relationship is no longer secret, but how can I explain what's made it possible? Tell him I tricked him, lied to him, broke my promise to him, betrayed his trust by selfishly and recklessly keeping a letter *and* my journal, both incriminating him, and Mum got hold of them and read them? He'll be appalled—and terrified! He won't accept my apology or forgive me. He'll never trust me or my word again. He'll despise me.

I could bargain with him: 'Don't worry, Shaun, I've blackmailed Mum to prevent her from making accusations against you. I threatened to expose Dad's crimes against me, and imply she was complicit, threatening her financial security and her freedom.' But telling him all that will open another can of worms as he knows *nothing* of my secret shame, *nothing* about what my father did to me. He only knows my father has been unfaithful to my mother and she's divorcing him.

I can't tell Shaun I've threatened suicide and confirmed my intention to do so in a *Letter to my Family*. It all sounds so over the top. He'll think I'm 'mad, bad and dangerous to know'—that's how Lady Caroline Lamb described her lover, Lord Byron. Maybe I *am* mad. Maybe this is what madness is. My brain is so tired. Tired of thinking and ruminating, trying to remember, trying to identify what's true and what's imagined or just a bad dream. Tired of processing new information and trying to work out what to do with it.

I'm physically tired too. Trudging up the slope to *Booyul* my legs feel weak. I'm shaky. I haven't eaten since my hot chocolate and lunchtime toasted sandwich yesterday. Dinner last night was everyone-gets-their-own, and I was too disturbed to prepare anything, let alone eat.

I've deliberately left my journal on my desk, anticipating Mum will come home while I'm with Shaun, snoop in my room again, find it and read my latest entry—my conversation with Dan and Billy—and the *Letter to my Family*. It's a way of communicating with her without having to talk face-to-face. She'll learn about me hiding Dan and Billy's stuff from the cops, and her sons' points of view about what happened in 1990 and 1991, especially their experience of *her* suicide attempt and long absence. And it will bring the mystery of the missing letters into the open.

I've placed a short hair from my hairbrush between the last two pages of my conversation with the boys and left another even shorter hair poking out of the envelope containing the *Letter to my Family*. I've also lined up the journal with my ruler and pen. If I come home and find the hairs moved or missing, or the journal out of place, if only by a centimetre, I'll know she's been snooping and reading.

Thinking about trapping Dad makes me anxious. How can I retrieve my letters? If I demand he explain why he kept them from me, how will I deal with his inevitable lies and denials, or excuses if I find the letters and confront him with them? I've been imagining secretly raiding his desk at his workplace, like Mum did when she discovered the bundle of pink letters. I'll need her help though. Will she be an ally? Or will she try to stop me from taking *any* action? And there's no guarantee they'll be in his desk. He might have destroyed them.

After reading parts of Mum's 1990 journal and learning the horrifying truth from Dan and Billy that she nearly killed herself, I've forgiven her for abandoning me at that time. I'm curious why she didn't write about her attempted suicide in her journal. Was it too painful, or shameful, to record? Did she have amnesia about it? Or has she recorded it somewhere else?

What I cannot understand, cannot forgive her for, is the fact she went back to Dad while I was in boarding school, leaving me there for three and a half more years, with no contact or communication with my brothers—or my father for that matter—and only spasmodic contact with her; I felt punished, abandoned, rejected, neglected and unloved, convinced nobody in my family cared about me except her. I remember occasional awkward weekend lunches with her in cafes in the village near the boarding school, but I can't recall what we talked about. Did we discuss the boys? Did we talk about Dad? Did she ever explain why I never went home? Or did we just talk drivel, nothing worth remembering?

I knock on Shaun's door, a rush of apprehension and guilt flooding my gut. The door opens and he greets me cheerfully. 'Hi Jodie, I'm so glad you've come!' Then his wide, elfin smile leaves his face. He reaches out, puts an arm around me, draws me inside, closes the door and turns me towards him. 'Oh, Jodie!' His voice is soft with concern. 'What's wrong?' He pulls his handkerchief from his shorts pocket and wipes the tears from my cheeks, then puts the handkerchief in my right hand. 'Here. Take it.' He removes the backpack from my shoulders, and leads me into the living room, where he sits down on the lounge and pats the seat beside him. 'Sit down with me for a minute.'

'I feel so *bad*—' I obediently sit alongside him and blow my streaming nose.

'I hope you're not worrying about Saturday—'

'I am, I *am*! I am *so* sorry—' I'm sobbing.

'You don't need to be sorry. Don't cry. It was a learning experience for both of us.'

'But it was my fault—'

He moves my hair back from my face with gentle fingers. 'Jodie, I love your courage and spontaneity. I *want* to respond to you, but you know I can't. It's too dangerous. And I want your mother to trust me. And it's because I care about *you*. We know we care deeply for each other. Lots of lovers through the ages had to wait. We're in illustrious company.'

I can only nod as I sob and blow my nose.

'If we're meant to be together in the future it will happen, but right now—' he shakes his head, '—you *are* only just fifteen. You need to experience a *lot* more of life. Travel. Study. Independence. Friendships. Work. Relationships. I know you can't imagine it now, but you could change your mind about me. Whatever happens though, we'll always be friends.'

'Friends forever.' I feel utterly bereft. I cling to him, my face against his chest.

He hugs me back, kisses the top of my head. 'Right now, we both have things to sort out, even worry about, but our friendship isn't one of them. Let's be confident about that.' He gently sits me up straight, and I release him to mop up and blow my nose yet again.

Looking around the room I notice cardboard boxes—removal boxes, boxes from the packing shed. Some are packed already. 'You're packing? Two months ahead of time?'

'Mum likes to be organised, instead of leaving everything till the last minute. Let's go and see what's happened to our island. Did you bring your maths?'

I nod. I haven't prepared anything, but my maths folder, booklet and assignment sheets are in my backpack, along with our sandwiches and my illicit love letter, secretly stowed away for safe keeping. I don't want Mum reading it again.

The water level has dropped, but the creek is still running faster than usual. Paddling upstream requires effort, and I'm tired. Evidence of the flash flood is caught in every shrub along the lower banks, showing where the water rose to. Our island classroom is littered with debris, the grass flattened. The grevilleas, felled by past floods but still anchored by their exposed roots, have trapped deadwood and detritus caught in them. We tie up the canoe, clear a spot on the grass, spread our towels and sit side by side.

I unzip my backpack. 'I feel woozy,' I tell him. 'I need to eat something first. I missed dinner last night *and* breakfast this morning.' I reach into my backpack for the container of sandwiches and pull it out. My love letter, caught in the container's clips, lands on the towel. Before I can stop him, he picks up the envelope and looks at it. It is addressed to him. Zinging like I'm about to jump off a cliff, I reach out to take it from him. 'You're not meant to see that, Shaun!' His hand, clutching the envelope, disappears behind his back.

'It's one of *those* letters, isn't it?' His deep voice sounds even deeper, accusing, displeased. 'The letters we *buried*?' His emphases speak volumes. 'You thought you'd keep just one, right?' His eyes are ice blue. I cannot handle his disappointed gaze and hang my head.

'Have you kept any others? Have you written more?'

I shake my head. 'No.' It's a whisper—I've lost my voice. 'Just this one. I'm sorry.'

'I'd like to read it. It *is* addressed to me. May I?'

I shake my head again. I think I'm going to faint.

'You're white as a ghost!' He sounds concerned. 'You'd better eat something.' He puts the letter into his backpack, takes the sandwich container from me, opens it and places half a sandwich into one of my hands and my water bottle in the other. 'Here, eat up. Have a drink.' He removes the cap from the water bottle.

I obediently take a swig to moisten my dry-as-dust mouth, take a bite out of the sandwich, chew slowly, swallow with difficulty, sip more water.

'I won't read the letter until you say I can, but I'll hold onto it, if you don't mind.' His tone tells me he's going to hold onto it whether I mind or not. 'C'mon, keep eating! Drink some more water. You're probably dehydrated as well.' He removes a bag of mixed nuts, a box of crackers, slices of cheese and a couple of apples from his backpack. 'This is all good brain food.' He reaches for my backpack, pulls out my folder. 'Anything else in here I should know about?' He peers into the depths.

'No.' I'm *so* relieved my journal is on my desk, but the deceit is a weight in my gut. I finish the first half of the sandwich, drink more water from the bottle, start on the second half. My head gradually clears; the jitteriness, wooziness and weakness dissipate. Inside me is a whirling pool of deception, treachery, betrayal and guilt, along with a thrill of excitement and apprehension about his reaction if—when—he does read the letter.

'Feeling better? You *look* better. I thought you were going to pass out. Low blood sugar can do that to you.' He removes half of his sandwich from the container and offers it to me.

I shake my head. 'I'm full.'

He scoffs it down while we work through my maths topics. We nibble mixed nuts, eat crackers and cheese, and drink water. Finally, Shaun closes my folder and passes it to me.

'Y'know, Jodie, you're exceptionally good at maths. This stuff is too easy for you.'

'You're an exceptionally good tutor,' I tell him.

'Thank you.' He stretches his arms, back and neck, and rotates his shoulders. 'You should consider a degree in science—pure and applied maths, physics, astronomy, computer science. Computers are outdoing and outthinking the human brain when it comes to calculations, using algorithms, along with their capacity to store information. The World Wide Web will become the encyclopaedia of the future. Ask your mum to buy you a personal computer and printer, so you don't get left behind.'

I barely know what the World Wide Web is, but I'm curious, and I like the idea of my own computer and printer.

'The Hubble space telescope is sending back fantastic pictures of distant galaxies. Space is rapidly becoming the next big thing. It's not even forty years since Sputnik first orbited the Earth, and now our little planet is encircled by satellites—communication satellites, weather satellites, spy satellites—all creating the next big problem: space junk. Satellites are orbiting the moon and mapping its surface.' He orbits his fingers in the air. 'Same with Mars. Remember Comet Shoemaker-Levy? How it broke apart and collided with Jupiter last year? Our first observation of an extra-terrestrial collision! The day will come when we'll land a space craft on an asteroid, or on a comet on its way to the sun, or on Mars, or on a moon orbiting a distant planet. Imagine the mathematical calculations required to do any of those things!'

His facial expressions reflect his enthusiasm, his voice his feelings, his enunciation so clear I don't miss a word.

'I reckon Mars will be colonised with robots by 2040. In our lifetime anyway. Robots will take over the Earth. Robot warfare and drone warfare. AI—Artificial intelligence. You could write science-fiction, like Arthur C. Clark, or Isaac Asimov, or Kim Stanley Robinson. What starts off as fiction becomes reality sooner or later. There's a saying: "What the human mind can conceive and believe, it can achieve." I predict we'll soon be chatting or messaging or emailing each other on mobile phones small enough and light enough to carry in our pockets, instead of writing letters! Speaking of which, can I read my letter now?'

'Please don't read it, Shaun. Please give it back. I'll tear it up in front of you, into tiny pieces so you know you're safe. It's the only one I've kept, I swear.'

'I appreciate your offer—it sounds very dangerous.'

He peers into his backpack. 'Hey! It's red-hot! It's burning a hole!'

'It's not funny.'

'What are you afraid of, if I read it first, *before* you destroy it?'

'Your reaction. What you'll think of me.' I want to throw up, I feel so sick.

'You're going to let me read the rest of them in ten years' time. You may as well give me a-a what—a taste beforehand. Something to look forward to.' His eyes are very blue, his expression challenging more than pleading. 'Please?' He takes the letter from his backpack.

I drop my gaze, hold my head in my hands, take a firm grip on my hair as if I'm about to tear it out. 'Alright! Alright!' My voice reflects my anxiety. 'Read it then, if you must!'

Head down, I hang onto my hair like an anchor. In the silence, my hearing aids exaggerate the rustle of paper, the twittering of tiny birds, the creek rippling over stones, the sounds of water and time passing. I know exactly what he is reading. I know every word.

'Wow, Jodie.' His voice is soft. 'It's certainly erotic, but truly beautiful.' From under my hair, I can see his hands; his fingers are trembling slightly as he refolds the letter. 'I'd *love* to keep it. I'd read and re-read it many times over.' He replaces the folded pages in the envelope. 'But it's dynamite, Jodie.' He returns the unsealed envelope to his backpack. 'If it falls into the wrong hands, it'll be curtains for me. It's imperative we bury it with the others.'

What if he unwraps the parcel of letters and discovers the journal is a fake!

I so want to tell him, 'Don't worry, Shaun! Keep the letter! Re-read it as often as you like! My mother has already read it, more than once!' Instead, I say, 'Well, if you must dig up my letters, I want to be there when it happens!'

'Of course. I understand. But aren't they *my* letters? They're addressed to me.'

'They are *not* your letters. They are *my* letters until I give them to you. And I didn't give you this one. You *took* it.' My fear sounds like anger, my guilt like defensive belligerence.

'You're right,' he says. 'I won't bury *your* letter without you. But we *will* bury it. *Now.*'

We drift rapidly downstream, using the paddles to steer, or fend off logs jutting out of the water, or divert the canoe away from overhanging branches. We reach our landing spot, where we pull the canoe up the grass and into the lantana. When Shaun and I arrived here this morning, I was acutely aware I was standing right where I'd stripped naked in front of him last Saturday, but my self-consciousness has faded in the face of this new danger—how to dig up my letters and add this one to them without him discovering my deception with the empty journal.

I do most of the talking as we trudge up the track from the creek, but I'm selective in what I tell him. I leave out my confrontation with Mum, the fact she's read the letter we're about to bury, that I still have my journal, and she's delved into that too. Instead, I start with the raid next door and how the police searched our place afterwards, omitting I hid evidence to protect my brothers. I do tell him about my talk with Dan and Billy concerning Mum's suicide attempt in 1990, the main reason for her absence, and the mystery of the missing letters. When I get to the part where Mum went back to Dad and left me in the boarding school for three and a half more years, with no contact or communication with my brothers, I barely hold myself together.

He reaches across my back and holds my shoulder, pulling me closer as we walk. 'You've had a rough trot, Jodie, no mistake, but you're a true survivor! Your knowledge of literature, your writing ability, your maths skills, are truly impressive. So many kids would've gone off the rails, but not you! Did boarding school shape any of that? Did exceptional teachers promote your love of learning? I think you're amazing!'

'Probably,' I concede, savouring his words.

Apart from our voices, the only sounds I can hear are coming from the pigpen. We arrive to discover squealing piglets bullying each other, competing for teats as they pummel their long-suffering mother.

'They've grown so much!' I exclaim. 'In just a week!'

'These piglets, and their Mumma, have been given a reprieve. I had a phone call from the director of a movie outfit down south—he's a friend of the butcher who bought Big George— he needs piglets for a movie they're making about, guess what: pigs! One pig in particular, and they're constantly having to replace the cast with new piglets because they grow so fast! The butcher gave him my number. Small world, eh? It's all very hush-hush, so don't tell anybody. It will be released in the USA in August and here by Christmas. When you see it, you'll be able to say: "Hey! I know those little pigs!"'

I stride down the hill from *Booyul*, feeling a mix of elation, guilt, bravado and trepidation. Elation, because Shaun read my letter and he wasn't turned off—he was turned on more like it. Elation mixed with guilt, because we dug up my letters, added this one to the 'coffin' without untaping the rest of them, and re-buried them, Shaun none the wiser about the fake journal. Bravado, because I'm spending time with him on my terms. Trepidation as to how Mum will react—she *did* return home instead of staying in town—her car is in the carport, and she's let Cleo and Patra out. They're racing to greet me. I give them pats and hugs and speak soft words to calm them, before I walk past the tank, the well, the carport, the dogs' enclosure and Mum's studio and arrive at the west veranda. I drop my backpack onto the boards.

The studio door is open. Mum is inside, working on the second panel of the triptych. A masked face, also with intense blue eyes, peers out between several photo-released pages of letters and documents seemingly floating. Disembodied female hands face outwards, either rejecting them, or trying to grasp them. I'm too scared to move closer to see if any words on the pages can be read. As Mum turns around, I wipe the grimace off my face and give the work small nods of acknowledgement.

'Looks interesting,' I tell her.

'What've you been up to?' Her light tone tells me she's trying to sound casual.

'Just my usual maths and science lesson with Shaun.' My tone is light too, but my response is loaded with meaning. 'Can I make you a cup of tea?'

'Thank you, that would be lovely. I'll have it in here though. The submission deadline is Monday and I still have a panel to go.'

'Gosh, you'll be busy. Are you picking up the boys this afternoon?'

'No, they're catching the bus.'

'I'll bring your tea.' I turn back to the veranda, pick up my backpack and retreat inside, whispering to Anne, 'She *knew* she was coming home early, telling the boys to catch the bus, but she didn't tell *me*. That means she *planned* it, hoping to catch me out.'

Which she did. Literally!

In my room, door closed, Anne and I check the position of my journal. It is almost, but not exactly, where I left it! I open it, very carefully, to the last two pages of writing. The hair is missing. Not just out of place. Gone!

She's read it!

I turn to the inside of the back cover. The *Letter to my Family* is still in its envelope, attached by the paper clip, but the envelope is not precisely where or how I left it, and the hair that was poking out of it is nowhere to be seen.

'Reading Dan and Billy's reactions to her suicide attempt as well as the *Letter to my Family* would have given her a jolt.'

A familiar sinking feeling is creeping into my gut, about another matter entirely.

'Can I trust her? Does she *already know* about the letters, and whether Dad kept them, or destroyed them?'

Anne remains silent.

We are nursing our hot after-dinner drinks, Dan and Billy lounging, literally, on the lounge, Mum and I sitting in the chairs on either side, watching a TV program about divorce and its impact on kids. I'd like to have a say on one of these programs, instead of having to listen to smug adults airing conflicting opinions, depending on their own experiences and values.

It seems the Family Law Act now focuses on the rights of children and the responsibilities *both* parents have towards them. 'It's a child's right to have a meaningful relationship with *both* of their parents after divorce,' one woman says.

'What if the child doesn't *want* a relationship with the father!' I exclaim.

Mum turns the television off. Dan and Billy protest, but she says, 'I need to talk to you! I've a tight schedule coming up, and I need your co-operation to pull it off. I've got four days to finish my entry for the RAG exhibition. Deadline is next Monday. They'll be making selections before Easter and hanging the entries after Easter. Opening night is Friday evening, 21 April. I hope you'll all come.' She looks at us expectantly.

I hope I'll be well enough to go—Saturday 22 April is the first day of my next period. It will be a test of the pill managing my pain.

'Sure,' says Dan.

'Yep,' says Billy.

I nod.

'Next Tuesday I'm driving to the Blue Mountains, leaving before dawn, so Dan, you can drive Billy to school Tuesday, Wednesday and Thursday. I'll give you money for petrol and leave the fridge full of food. Are you guys planning an Easter break at the beach?'

They both nod.

'Because you'll have to look after Cleo and Patra.'

'I'll look after them!' I tell her indignantly, trying to sound responsible instead of thrilled at the thought of being at home without her, the boys at the beach, and Shaun close by!

Mum shakes her head. 'You're coming with me.'

'Why?'

'Why not?' she counters. 'A change of scene. Some mother-and-daughter time. Besides, there are things we need to talk about. And *do* together.'

Is she talking in code?

'Where will we stay?'

'In a motel.'

The Blue Mountains!

I feel sick. I do *not* want to see my father. But is this trip anything to do with—everything? Everything Mum and I have talked about and fought over? Everything I've written that she's read? Is she an ally, or an enemy? Will she help me recover the letters, or at least find out what happened to them? Or is she planning to leave me there with Dad? It *was* one of her threats on Sunday, and she sure sounded like she meant it.

'Is there a problem?' she asks. 'You look like a scared rabbit!'

Chapter Twenty-one

Thursday, 06 April 1995

I'm standing on the east veranda, in the light of the rising sun, Mum taking photos of me on her polaroid camera for the third panel of her triptych. She dismissed my objections to being photographed, reminding me it was my idea.

'You won't be recognisable,' she assures me, brushing and draping my hair so it cascades down both sides of my face. Instead of cradling my doll, as I'd originally suggested, she's got me holding an enlarged cut-out of the eyeless doll's face featured in the first panel. It truly has become a mask, stuck to cardboard to stiffen it, a nailfile attached under the chin to use as a handle to hold it. 'Imagine you are taking the mask off,' she says, positioning it so it covers my mouth and the lower part of my nose. In my other hand she places a sheet of white paper with black writing on both sides, meticulously arranging how and where I'm to hold it with my fingers and thumb, probably so I don't obscure any words.

'I can't read it without my glasses on.'

'*Look* as if you're reading it,' she says. 'It's more about appearances than reality.'

'Isn't that what this whole thing is about?'

She pauses, momentarily catching my eye. 'You could say that.' She continues to move me around, taking shots from various angles, the backdrop always the lightening sky, checking each photo as it emerges from the camera. I'm dressed in a white, sleeveless summer nightie— it covers me without being a noticeable feature—but the air is nippy and I'm starting to shiver.

'All finished,' she says.

'Can I read the letter?

'Sure. It's only a draft of my Artist's Statement. It'll go on the gallery wall alongside the triptych. I'll take the boys to school and photocopy and enlarge the photos. I won't be long.'

I climb into bed for warmth, put on my glasses and read her Artist's Statement.

Name: Anne Macleod

Title: Unmasked

Development as an artist: I'm amazed how much training she's had, and where, and with whom, and which artists have influenced her work. I had no idea. I'm impressed.

Materials used/methods: I understand that well enough.

Themes, Symbolism, Purpose: I'm not sure what she's getting at, but on the back of the page is a quote: 'For I wear a mask … a thousand masks/And none of them is me.'

**From a poem by Paul Laurence Dunbar.*

Am I being paranoid, narcissistic, self-centred, thinking Mum's triptych is about *me?* Or maybe the triptych is about *both* of us! Although the poem is about *neither* of us! And none of this explains her *Purpose* for creating the triptych in the first place.

I'll research Paul Laurence Dunbar in the TAFE library or the Grafton City Library.

Dan and Billy poke their heads around my door and say goodbye. I'm glad they're friendly, but now the house is silent I'm lonelier than ever. Suddenly hungry, I get out of bed, put on jeans and a pullover, go to the kitchen and fill a bowl with muesli, a cut-up banana and lots of milk.

Eating breakfast on the east veranda, I realise it's Shaun I'm hungry for. I need him to touch me and hold me when I'm *not* crying and vulnerable like I was yesterday morning, blubbering and apologising. I need him to hug me and kiss me when I'm *not* begging for it like I did last Saturday, naked by the creek, trying to seduce him. It's always *me* asking *him* for love and affection. He never initiates contact. He's responded to my requests, but he is so restrained, so afraid!

'I understand he doesn't want to get into trouble, but who would know?' I ask Anne. 'Who'd see us in the bush—like in the cemetery—or hidden by the grevilleas on our island?'

He wants to do the right thing. He doesn't want to lie to, or deceive, anyone. He doesn't want to break the law, even when he's not going to be caught in the act. And he's very afraid of being caught in the act.

Yesterday afternoon, after they walked home from the bus stop at the top of the lane, Dan and Billy cooled off with cold drinks on the east veranda. I was in my room, sitting at my desk. My windows onto the veranda were open, and I was wearing my hearing aids, but I still couldn't understand their mumbling—until Shaun's name was mentioned. Desperate to hear more, I crept across the hall into the den, crouched below the open window, and eavesdropped.

'… I reckon he's gay,' I heard Billy say.

'Nah. He's not gay. He likes Jodie a lot. I can tell.'

'Yeah, but he doesn't have the hots for her that I've noticed.'

'I reckon he does but he's holding back 'cos she's under-age.'

'When did that stop anyone!'

'Yeah, well, I gave her some condoms, didn't I—just in case.'

'Didja? Fair dinkum! That was generous of you!'

'I don't want our little sister in trouble, bro. She's got enough going on.'

'True.'

'Let's repot the seedlings. Hide them in the scrub next door!'

'Back where they came from?' Billy chuckled. 'Okay. Let's do it! Now!'

I darted out of the den and took refuge in the kitchen. When they entered seconds later, I was filling up the electric jug with water from the tank tap over the sink.

They dumped their glasses and lunch boxes on the bench.

I nearly growled, 'Wash them yourselves, you lazy slobs!' Instead, I said, 'Leave them there. I'll wash them for you.' Since our talk we've been allies rather than enemies and it feels good to have them onside.

Mum's back, but she went straight into her studio, no hullo, no nothing. I could drop dead and she wouldn't notice. No doubt she's photo-releasing the photocopies of the photos onto the third panel. I'd love to watch the process, and ask her to explain her *Themes*, *Symbolism* and *Purpose* in plain English, but since Sunday's confrontation we're *both* wearing masks! The silence—what is *not* being said—is daunting, but it's also a relief.

I could refuse point-blank to go to the Blue Mountains with her. Every cell in my body is screaming: *'Danger! Don't go!'* Every cell except in my brain that is. The last person I want to see in the whole world is my father, but my brain knows this trip is my only chance to recover the letters, and where else can I look other than in his office? I can't, won't, go 'home' to the place where it all began. It's bad enough, after a four-year absence, to be in the Blue Mountains *at all*. Even worse to visit his business premises. *Impossible* to drive down the street where I used to live and enter the house of my childhood nightmares.

The night Dan gave me the condoms, I lip-read him as he left my room, *'You owe me!'* I wasn't sure whether he was referring to the twenty dollars missing from his cash box, or to some future favour I could do for him, but I've replaced the twenty from the fifty dollars Mum gave me at the Alumy Creek markets. Now I'm going to ask him to lend me fifty so if Mum does leave me in the Blue Mountains, I can escape on a bus or train and return to *Gwongorella*—though I'd never trust her again or forgive her for abandoning me a second time.

I'm in a cold sweat of anxiety with a thumping headache just thinking about it.

Mum's plan to leave before dawn next Tuesday means I'll not only miss catching up with Em and Jacinta but also forfeit my usual Wednesday with Shaun. I need to talk to him *now*! His mum will be at work today. I pick up the entire phone in the hallway, take it into my room and close the door. I dial his number with trembling fingers, my gut in a twist waiting for him to answer. He finally picks up.

'Shaun? Can I come and see you, please? Now? It's kind of urgent.'

He hesitates. Only for a moment, but long enough for me to notice. 'Yes, sure. How about I come down there?'

'Mum's home. She's in her studio, but … I can come up to yours.'

'Meet me in the packing shed. I'll give you some leftover vegetables.'

He doesn't want me in their house! I noticed yesterday they'd started packing. Doubt and suspicion weigh heavy in my chest. 'Is your mum home?' I ask him.

'No.'

'Speaking of packing—is that what you're doing?'

'Meet me in the packing shed, Jodie.' He hangs up.

I'm dizzy with fear, my chest tightening.

'Jodie?' Mum knocks on the other side of my door. 'I need the phone!'

Breathless and shaky, I open the door and pass her the phone, then pick up my Ventolin and spray puffs into my lungs as I inhale.

Mum gives me a concerned look as she takes the phone from me and restores it to its place on the hall stand. 'Are you okay? You're awfully pale. Are you having an asthma attack?'

I nod and inhale another puff. I feel compelled to ask her, 'Are you ringing Dad?'

'No. My lawyer. To confirm appointments.'

'Does Dad know we're coming?

'No.'

'Are you going to tell him?'

'No.'

Silence ensues while I try to absorb the implications. 'That's good. I'm glad.'

She asks, 'Can we be friends?'

I brush past her and walk unsteadily to the back door. I pause, turn, see she's followed me. I open the screen door, step down three steps, turn to close it again—it's awkward, because there's no landing—and she's right there, on the threshold.

'It's up to you, Mum, but I'd much rather be friends than enemies.' My voice is raspy with emotion and from the Ventolin. I'm still breathless. I close the screen door in her face, very gently, continue down the steps, and walk up the slope towards *Booyul*, taking another puff of Ventolin as I go. I don't look back.

Shaun is already in the packing shed, filling a cardboard box with a medley of vegetables. 'Hi,' he says. He doesn't smile. He hardly looks at me. 'They're all still growing, despite my neglect, though they're starting to go to seed. This is just about the last of them.'

I'm desperate for a hug, but I will myself not to beg, or cry. Instead, I start babbling. 'Mum's submitting her triptych next Monday and driving to the Blue Mountains first thing Tuesday and she's insisting I go with her.' I take a breath. 'I could refuse to go, it's the last place I want to be, but it's a chance to recover the letters I wrote to Dan and Billy and the letters they wrote to me—' another breath '—if Dad hasn't destroyed them. It'll be tricky.'

'How will you go about recovering them?'

'Plan A: Go to his office when he's not there and look in his desk and filing cabinet.'

'And Plan B?' Shaun starts filling the second box with vegetables.

'Confront him, I suppose. Isn't it a crime to steal someone else's mail?'

'I believe so. You could find out easily enough.'

'Mum's seeing her lawyer while she's there. I'll go with her and ask him.' I move closer. 'Shaun, there's something else I'm really worried about. Mum and I had a fight recently, and she said she couldn't handle me. She threatened to send me back to boarding school, or to live with my father. I don't trust her. I can't—I *won't*—live with him again, not under any circumstances! But I'm scared she'll leave in the middle of the night while I'm asleep and I'll wake up in the morning and she'll be gone!'

The tears are so close. I fight them. *I will not cry.* I'm *sick* of crying.

'That's a worst-case scenario. Where will you and your mum stay?'

'In a motel.'

'I can't imagine she'd abandon you in a motel, but what will you do, if she does?'

'Buy a bus or train ticket back here. I'm going to ask Dan to lend me fifty bucks.'

Shaun extracts his wallet from the back pocket of his jeans. 'Consider it a gift, Jodie, not a loan.' He offers me a fifty-dollar note. 'Just in case you *do* need it. But she won't abandon you.'

'Gosh, Shaun! Thank you.' I take it. 'I *will* pay you back. Somehow. One day.' I'm *desperate* for him to hold me. I could reach out and hug him, but I don't.

He extracts a couple of cards from his wallet, returns the wallet to his back pocket, removes his pen from under the flap on his shirt pocket and writes on the back of one of the cards. 'This is my family's address and phone number in Sydney. They're on the north shore. If you catch a train from Central station, take the line to Hornsby via North Sydney. Get off at Turramurra. You can walk to their place from the station. It's easy.' He draws a little map and hands me the card. 'This is just for future reference. It's where I'll be—for a while, anyway.'

He looks uncomfortable. I've seen the look before. Neither of us moves. We're standing close to each other, but in every other way we are far apart. 'Jodie,' he looks into my eyes. 'Mum's itching to leave *Booyul*, now the decision's been made. She's given notice at her workplace. And to Joe. She's figured it will cost more to stay till the lease runs out, than break the lease and hope he finds replacement tenants quickly. She's booked a removalist.'

It's as if he's wrapped an icy cloak around my shoulders. 'Are you saying you'll be gone before I get back from the Blue Mountains?'

'Quite possibly.'

Cold soaks into me as if I've walked into a freezer. I shiver and hug myself.

'You need to ask your mum can you trust her to help you. What have you got to lose?' He continues packing the vegetables into the second box. 'No doubt she's got a few bones to pick with him herself. She's probably more on your side than you realise.'

It's like I've had a massive Novocaine injection. The numbness is not just inside me—it's not only my feelings—it's my entire body. I'm drifting away from myself, and away from him, drifting away … From a distance I can see myself standing beside him, I can see myself watching him filling the box with vegetables, his voice distorted.

'… assume … Mum … you come … the good …'

I see him reach out and touch my arm, but I am not in my body to feel it.

'Jodie?' I hear his voice as if through water. I watch him give my arm a shake.

A savage jolt startles me. My heart palpitates with fright.

'Where did you go? You looked hypnotised or something! Are you okay?'

'Wh-what d-did you say?' I'm back in my body, shivering, teeth chattering so hard I nearly bite my tongue.

'I said, let's assume your mum has no intention of abandoning you in the Blue Mountains, and you come back to Grafton with her. What's the good side of that?'

I make a major effort to comprehend what he is saying, but I'm unable to voice the thoughts in my head and can only stare at him. I finally answer, 'But you w-won't be here!'

'We can write to each other.' He pulls the other card from his shirt pocket along with his pen. 'I know your phone number off by heart, but what's your PO box number?'

I tell him and he writes it down. I watch him return the card and pen to his pocket.

'Shaun, c-can I ring you sometimes? Will you ring m-me?'

'Sure! I'll be staying with my parents for a while. Antarctica won't happen overnight, if it happens at all. I'll always tell you my number, wherever I end up.'

'Is this g-goodbye?'

'It doesn't have to be. Are you free Sunday? For one last paddle up the creek?'

'One last p-paddle.' The pain in my chest is my heart being pulled out of shape.

'Can I hug you, Jodie?' He's looking over my shoulder at the entrance to the shed.

'*Now* you're asking me! You've *never* asked me b-before, that I can remember. It's always b-been *me* asking *you*!'

'Oh, Jodie, I'm so sorry it has to be this way.' He moves towards me, wraps his arms around me, hugs me. I cannot respond. 'I'm sad too. Please look at me.' He's pleading, but I cannot meet his gaze. He sighs audibly, a soft groan, as if he's in pain. He lets me go, turns away, picks up one of the boxes of vegetables and places it in my arms. 'Please give these to your mother, with my compliments. Tell her what's happening; she might want to say goodbye to my mum. And tell her you want to be *here*, with *her*—and Dan and Billy—in Grafton. And *please* come for a paddle with me on Sunday.' His voice cracks. 'I'll be waiting for you, down by the creek, at ten, with our lunch.'

The numbness wears off as the sun goes down, pangs of grief and desolation breaking through. The sensation is physical, all over my body, but especially in my chest, the twisting ache in my heart intensifying. As my bedroom darkens, so does my mood. Shaun is leaving *Booyul* to start something new, something different and exciting, that does not include me.

Alone on my bed, I feel discarded. Dumped. Abandoned. Familiar feelings. Without Shaun, my life—life itself—has no meaning, no purpose.

'He is the only reason I'm still here,' I whisper to Anne.

I scrabble around in the top drawer of my desk for the card Shaun gave me three weeks ago. I read it over and over, but I cannot grasp it, cannot get past *God*, let alone *serenity*—I'm not sure I know the meaning of the word. I don't think I've ever experienced it. Is it a feeling? Is it a state of mind? Is it something around me that I can grasp and hold on to? How can I *accept* the loss of Shaun when I feel so bleak and empty and sad?

I need help. I find Christine and Richard's card and dial the number.

Chapter Twenty-two

'Whose turn is it to mow the grass?' Mum yells, nearly deafening me. She checks the roster on the fridge. 'Billy! It's *your* turn. This afternoon—please!'

'Will do,' Billy replies from the bathroom.

'Time to go, Mum!' Dan shouts from the back steps.

'I'm coming too,' I tell her, as I grab an apple from the bowl on the bench and take a water bottle from the fridge. 'I've got things to do.'

She purses her lips. 'I'm only doing the grocery shopping. I won't be in town for long.'

'I know. I'll catch the school bus home.'

She gives me one of her looks, her eyes narrowed, lips now compressed.

I escape and join Dan at the back door.

'Have you locked the dogs up?' Mum yells.

'Of course!' Dan yells back. He winks at me and grins.

We head for the car—he's carrying his usual box filled with button squash and baby zucchinis in plastic bags, his backpack hanging from one shoulder.

'What are your plans for the day?' he asks me, his tone friendly.

I'd love to confide in him, tell him, 'I'm weeding the Dean's garden in exchange for advice about how to achieve serenity and accept the things I cannot change.' Instead, I say, 'It's complicated. Can we talk this afternoon? I need your opinion—your advice really.'

'Sure. No problem.' Seeing Mum and Billy coming towards us, he climbs into the back behind Mum's seat and settles the box on his knees.

'Dan, did I see you weeding your garden yesterday afternoon?'

He looks at me sideways, with a lop-sided smile. 'Yep. They're back where they came from, until the wallabies find them. When this lot comes to an end,' he eyes his green and gold produce, 'I'm gonna give gardening a rest.'

It's peaceful in the Deanery garden, with small birds flitting and twittering nearby and bees buzzing in and out of the flowers. I've started on the main garden bed that ends at the path. It isn't overrun with weeds and the ones that are there have been easy to remove with the help of a trowel and weeding fork. Christine suggested I work for an hour, then take a morning tea break on the veranda. I check my watch. Ten minutes to go. I'll weed some more after the break, though there's no way I'll finish this garden bed today.

'How are you going?' I look up to see Christine peering down at me through the tall stems, leaves and flower heads of dahlias, daisies, zinnias and chrysanthemums. 'You're doing a wonderful job there. Tea and scones await.'

I stand upright and stretch my back, before stepping carefully between the plants to the pansies, petunias and alyssum edging the path.

'It's a bit of a jungle in there,' she says.

'It's a beautiful garden. There's an *amazing* variety of flowers and shrubs.' I follow her along the terracotta tiled veranda.

'It's a very old garden with a mind of its own, a lot of it self-sown. Unruly, but I love its wildness. Please, sit down.' She indicates a comfortable-looking outdoor chair with a cushioned seat and padded backrest. I sink into it and gaze with pleasurable anticipation at the plate of scones and bowls of jam and cream on the low table between us. She sits on a matching chair opposite, reaches for a paper napkin, plate and knife and passes them to me. 'Please serve yourself.' She pours tea from the now-familiar teapot with its knitted cosy. 'Help yourself to milk and sugar. Richard is attending a conference in Sydney over the weekend, so we have the place to ourselves, but if it's okay with you, I'd like to tell him you came and kept your promise.' She puts down the teapot.

'That's okay.'

'He'll be so pleased. He was very impressed with your courage.'

'I couldn't have done it without his help. I promised him I'd never shoplift again.'

Making promises about my future behaviour is easy when I won't be here. Not being here will solve *all* my problems. I won't have to think about, or feel, anything.

'You decided to change your behaviour, and with help and support it's equally possible to change your reactions to painful experiences. Your thoughts and feelings. I was so pleased you rang me last night.'

She wants to guide me through a maze she's probably never been in. 'On Tuesday, you told me some problems can be solved, but other problems can only be managed.' My voice is wobbly. Tears are stinging my eyes. 'But I can't solve my problems or manage them either.'

'I prefer to call them "issues" rather than "problems". Sometimes, if issues are inter-related, they get tangled up together and seem very complicated. It's useful to identify the issues, separate them and consider them one at a time. But before we talk further, I need to say two things. Firstly, there's the matter of confidentiality. I won't discuss what we talk about with *anybody*, including Richard, unless I have your express permission to do so, or it's clear you are in physical or moral danger. Secondly, I can provide pastoral care by listening to you, and we can untangle and clarify the issues, but I'll encourage you to make appointments with skilled professional practitioners, like psychologists, or counsellors, or mediators. I'll give you names and contact details, but following up will be your choice. Does that sound okay?'

I nod. 'Yes, I think so. Thank you.' I suddenly feel incredibly tired. I take several sips of tea, hoping the caffeine will help me stay awake.

'Please, have a scone.' She pushes the plate closer. I help myself. The silence lengthens while we eat; she's practically mirroring me. We each dab at our mouths with our napkins.

'A top-up?' I nod and she picks up the teapot. 'The toilet is at the end of the veranda, behind that door.' She points. 'Feel free to have another scone.' She re-fills my cup.

'Thank you. I've had enough for now.'

She sits back. 'So, let's imagine there's a basket at your feet, and your issues are in it. Decide which issue you'd like to pull out and look at first—and you don't have to tell me exactly what the issue is, unless you want to. You can call it 'X' or 'Y' or 'Z'. Or 'A' or 'B' or 'C' for that matter. I don't need to know more than you feel comfortable sharing. Figuring out what you can *do* to resolve or manage the issue is the important thing here.'

I peer into the imaginary basket at my feet. Sure enough, I can see issues lurking in it. They don't look like a litter of fluffy kittens, or balls of brightly coloured wool tangled up together. They are murky, dark brown blobs, merging and melting into one another. 'I don't know where to start!' My voice cracks. 'They—they look like … turds.'

'Here are some tongs,' she says, apparently unfazed by my description. She offers me an imaginary tool. 'See if you can extract one issue.' She spreads a paper napkin on her plate and says, as she puts it in front of me, 'Put the issue on here, so we can view it from all sides.'

I reach out for the imaginary tongs and use the tool to pull out a blob, shuddering at the image of a turd on the pristine white napkin on the plate. There's nothing funny about it. It's so embarrassing and disgusting I want to puke!

'What will you call this issue?'

'X'

'Do you have an imaginary friend who can help you with ideas about resolving or managing X?'

Startled, I look into her eyes. Can I trust her? *Nobody* knows about Anne. I nod, cautiously.

'Does she—or he—have a name?'

'Anne, my middle name. My mother's name.'

Christine fetches another, lighter chair from nearby and puts it beside me, facing me. 'This chair is for Anne. She can listen, and if you get stuck, we can ask her for her thoughts.'

I'm intrigued by this make-believe, rather than disconcerted by it. Having Anne beside me is familiar and comforting. I move the basket of issues further away from me though, towards Anne, with one foot.

Christine notices.

'The issues stink,' I tell her. 'And they look horrible.'

'Can you see something around here that looks beautiful to you? Peaceful?' She waves her arm and hand around in an arc, taking in the veranda, the garden, the jacarandas and river beyond. 'Something you can use to anchor yourself to the here-and-now, if it's needed?'

Close by is a gnarled, twisted, sprawling apple tree, its canopy of dark leaves partially shading the veranda. Red apples peer through the foliage. I point to it.

'That tree is over one hundred years old. And it still bears fruit to this day. It never gives up. I may interrupt you and invite you to look at it, to help you return to the here-and-now and leave the there-and-then behind, if it gets too gnarly.'

The tree of knowledge.

I nod my understanding. 'Like a lifebuoy so I don't drown in a whirlpool.'

'Exactly!' She looks pleased, relieved even. 'So—' she gazes at the plate X occupies with an expectant expression on her face. 'If you could have your way, if you had the *power*, what might you do to deal with X? Or at least make X more manageable?'

'I don't know! X is really disgusting! I should never have had to … to see X … I should never have been exposed to-to what was going on … I'm only seven … eight … nine … ten …' My voice sounds high and young. 'It's his dirty secret, not mine, but he's made it mine … he's deceiving my mother … cheating on her … I see them, watch them with my own eyes … but he lies to Mummy … denies it's happening … and I can't tell her … I can't stop him … I ask him to stop but he won't … and I *hate* him! I feel so *bad*! So *ashamed*! So *guilty*!' My voice is a child's voice. I'm hiding under the evil woman's piano, sobbing.

Christine passes me a box of tissues. I take some and dab at the tears sliding down my cheeks. She pours water from a jug into a glass and sets it down close to me. 'Look at the apple tree, Jodie. Tell me what you see.'

I drag tissues from the box, take off my glasses, wipe my eyes, blow my nose, replace my glasses and look at the apple tree. My sobs and hiccups gradually subside as I describe the trunk, the leaves, their shape and colour, and the redness of the apples. One falls as I watch, and I realise there are several apples on the ground. The ancient, twisted trunk, with its rough grey bark and many branches would be easy for a child to climb. I begin to describe myself climbing it, but she gently draws me into the here-and-now—would I climb it now? Now I've grown up? At my age? I get what she's doing.

'I gather it stopped when you were about ten?'

'I don't remember.'

'Have you and Anne ever discussed what you'd like to do about X, now you *are* older and have some agency?'

I shake my head.

'Stay in the present and figure out with Anne what you'd like to do about X *now*, imagining you have *power*. Doing nothing is a legitimate option, but it might not be the *best* option. It's certainly not the only option. Brainstorm some options first, with Anne, then you can look at the pros and cons of each option before you decide what to do.'

'Anne knows I've written a *Letter to my Family*. There's a section in it written to him. But he hasn't seen it, yet.'

'Does Anne think what you've written to him is empowering for you?'

I visualise Anne on her chair, a mirror-image of myself. She's shaking her head.

Saying you're going to kill yourself is hardly empowering.

I shake my head again. 'Um. No. She says no. It's not empowering.'

Christine looks at me, her head tilted, like she's trying to figure out what I mean.

'Jodie, in this letter, what are you saying to him, what are you telling him?'

'I want to *kill* myself!' I wail, and start crying again.

Christine speaks slowly, clearly, matter-of-factly. 'Jodie, have you heard the saying: "Suicide is a permanent solution to a temporary problem"?'

I shake my head, yet again, and blow my streaming nose.

'Think about it for a moment.' She pauses, giving me time to absorb it. 'It's a deadly way to escape from something that may not be happening anymore. Or won't happen forever.'

'I can't deal with the fallout. The memories coming back. Managing my feelings.'

'So, you're dealing with memories, and the feelings associated with those memories?'

'Yes.'

'Is he still around? Do you see him? Do you have to *manage* seeing him?'

'Mum's making me go to the Blue Mountains with her next week, which means I'll probably see him, but I don't want to see him! I don't want to have anything to do with him! Except get my letters back that he stole from me … letters I wrote to my brothers and letters they wrote to me that we never received.' I feel nauseated, but also incredibly angry.

'Now you are older, approaching womanhood, adulthood, maturity, it is possible you can *do* something about it; something really empowering, with help. Can you talk it through with Anne?' She gestures towards Anne's chair. 'Come up with ideas together, no matter how crazy or outlandish or impossible they seem. What might you do *now* about X and this issue of recovering your letters, besides doing nothing, or killing yourself?'

She waits for me to come up with something, but my mind is blank.

'Let's try something,' she says. 'Sit in Anne's chair and Anne can speak through you.'

Obediently I swap chairs, intrigued.

'Anne,' she says, 'what do *you* think Jodie should do?'

I blink rapidly. I've never done this before, put myself in Anne's place, become Anne.

'I think Jodie should confront him. Tell him about the impact of his behaviour, in a letter maybe. Like a victim impact statement she can read to him—or maybe ask him to read it aloud in front of her and whoever she has with her for moral support. And ask him to apologise. And ask him—no, *tell* him—to pay her counselling or therapy fees and any other costs. Tell him she wants him—no, she *expects* him—to pay her legal fees! *And* pay for her university education, however long it takes.' Anne's voice is strong. 'And tell him she wants *all* her letters back or she'll have him arrested and charged with mail theft along with all the other charges. Then tell him she *never* wants to see him or talk to him again ... any communication with her will have to be through her lawyer.'

Christine has been listening and nodding. 'Anne, imagine he acknowledges his behaviour, and apologises, and agrees to all those reparations for Jodie, and asks to be forgiven. Is forgiving him a possibility?'

Anne is silent for a long moment, hands clasped tightly in her lap. 'It's not for me to say. You need to ask Jodie about that.'

'You're right. Jodie—' she gestures towards my chair, '—can you sit in your chair again?'

Back in my chair, I answer Christine's question before she can ask me anything. 'No! I'll *never* forgive him, even if he does apologise, which he won't. He'll never admit to anything. He'll deny any of it ever happened. Or if he's *really* cornered, he'll make excuses, minimise it like it was nothing to get my knickers in a knot about.' I sound furious, because I am, but I'm also feeling vulnerable again, the tears not far away.

Christine says, 'It sounds as if forgiving him is another issue entirely. Z maybe.'

'Z is the *last* issue I want to think about or talk about.'

'So, putting Z aside, Jodie, what are your thoughts regarding what Anne had to say?'

'Anne always has my back. It's as if she's the grown-up part of me, always looking out for what's best for me. Nothing scares her! I agree with everything she said.'

Christine nods again. 'I notice that rather than being angry and aggressive, or timid and scared and tearful, Anne is assertive and mature, the adult part of you. The stolen letters are another issue, Y tangled up with X. Have you heard of mediation? Or dispute resolution?'

The topic was covered in my Legal Studies subject, but I shake my head.

'Mediation is a process for resolving issues and settling conflicts and disputes. You might be seeking damages and reparation from someone who has wronged you and you use mediation instead of taking the person to court. Lawyers help adult survivors of abuse. They help their clients get apologies, and financial reparations—but it can be a long, hard road. Perpetrators rarely admit wrongdoing. It takes courage and fortitude to see it through. Lawyers are useful for advice, but mediation is an alternative to court.'

'Mum is seeing her lawyer in the Blue Mountains. I'll ask him for advice, for starters. He looks after her interests, so he might be willing to look after mine. He might help me get my letters back.'

'Can you confide in your mother? Do you think she'll support you?'

Suddenly overcome by an irresistible urge to flee, I stand up and start walking backwards. 'Thank you, Christine, you've been *very* helpful. I'll do some more weeding, then I have a few things to do in town before I catch the bus.'

'Feel free to ring me, Jodie, any time. I'll gather the information sheets and contact details and bring them out to you in a few minutes.'

'Thank you.' I escape to the garden.

Crouching amongst the flowers I mutter to Anne, my voice low, but emphatic. 'I didn't say *one word* to her about Shaun! Even though him leaving is what compelled me to ring her in the first place!'

Shaun didn't belong in that basket.

'I *can't* tell her about him! I can't trust her confidentiality. She'll think I'm in "physical or moral danger" and report him! I can't talk about him with Mum's lawyer either! Or with a counsellor, or a psychologist or a mediator!' I can't see the weeds for tears. 'I can't talk about him with *anyone!*'

Except Dan. You can talk to Dan.

'I can't survive without Shaun.' Tears, never far away, roll down my cheeks and tickle my nose. I wipe them away with my fingers.

Christine said suicide is a permanent solution to a temporary problem.

'I *know*! I heard! But Shaun leaving me is *not* a temporary problem! It's *permanent!*'

'Jodie? Jodie? Are you okay?'

Christine is on the path. I didn't hear or see her coming. She's holding a large envelope, and she looks worried. I stand up, swipe the tears off my face and exchange the gardening tools for the envelope.

'I'm okay. Thank you.'

Christine takes a tissue from her pocket. 'You've got dirt on your cheeks,' she says, gently dabbing at my tears. She offers me the tissue and I take it. 'Come and see me again, Jodie. Just to chat. About anything at all. I hope you follow up at least one of these referrals.'

I'm grateful she cares, but I'm wary too. I dare not tell her about Shaun. And while she hasn't mentioned religion, or God, or invited me to attend church services or the youth fellowship, or pray, I'm suspicious that's where her offers of help and healing are heading.

Would it be so bad if it was?

At boarding school, I was forced to memorise biblical texts but I learnt to enjoy them for their poetry, same with the hymns and psalms we sang at assembly, without believing they were the gospel truth.

'Thank you, Christine. I will follow up. And I will ring you again. Goodbye.'

I escape out the gate and head for town.

The pharmacist dispenses next month's pill prescription, which I pay for with Shaun's fifty-dollar note. I visit the *Age of Aquarius* shop and buy a new journal and pen, then walk to the café near the bus stop at Market Square and order a mug of hot chocolate and a toasted cheese and tomato sandwich, mentally thanking Shaun.

Melanie is at the head of the bus queue outside South High, with Dan and Billy right behind her. She mounts the stairs, the boys protecting her from being shoved by the mob behind. I'm sitting alone in the front seat on the door side, having boarded the empty bus in town. She slides in beside me, greeting me with surprise and genuine friendliness. I'm flattered. Dan reckons she's a celebrity at school. He acknowledges me with a thumb up, and Billy gives me a salute of sorts before they sit behind us. I can understand why they prefer to get a lift with Mum; the bus is soon chock-a-block, including no-standing-room in the aisle. The air is steamy and stale, the cacophony of voices a painful babble.

We finally set off and the bus whines and chugs through various streets, disgorging kids as it goes, while Melanie and I try to talk. I haven't seen her since opening night.

'Three performances to go—tonight, a matinee tomorrow and then closing night.'

'I'd love to see it again!'

She shakes her head. 'It's completely booked out. We've raised heaps of money for the school's arts and theatre department.'

I'm genuinely glad for her and praise her acting and singing. I'd love to ask her about her relationship with 'Romeo', but with Dan just behind me it's not the right time or place, and anyway, it's too hard to hear her over the noise.

The bus heads west out of town. I gaze through the windscreen and out my side window at the flat paddocks and occasional homesteads, imagining talking with Dan when we get home and hearing his point of view. I have few memories of life with my brothers before I was taken away. How did he and Billy experience Mum's absence? And mine? What was it like once she returned home?

I wish I could persuade them to forego their Easter break at the beach and come to the Blue Mountains with me. The thought of confronting Dad by myself, Anne notwithstanding, is terrifying. I need Mum onside, that's for sure, but can I trust her to support me?

After several kilometres, the bus eventually turns right into Tindal Road and detours through Eatonsville, kids getting off along the way, including Melanie. 'Break a leg!' I tell her. After an interminable side-trip, we're on the home run. Kilometres later, the bus lumbers across Rogan Bridge—*Boorimbah* swirling beneath it—and grinds up the other side.

In due course, Dan and Billy file past me and hover by the door. They remind me of Cleo and Patra, desperate to be released from their enclosure after they've been locked up. I stand up behind them as the bus pulls over. We disembark, wait for it to draw away, then cross the road and set off down our lane.

While Billy mows the lawn, and Mum works on her triptych in the studio, Dan and I wander down the south paddock. We arrive at the fallen tree where I saw the echidna last Saturday, a peaceful, private spot to sit and talk. While we eat our afternoon snacks—apples, cheese and crackers—it's so reminiscent of trysts with Shaun my heart aches.

'What didja wanna talk about?' Dan bites into his apple.

'Shaun and I met up like this every Wednesday. We'd paddle up the creek—'

'Yeah?'

'And he'd help me with my maths and science assignments—'

'Lucky you!'

'—but he and Wendy are leaving *Booyul* while I'm in the Blue Mountains.'

'Fair dinkum?'

I nod.

'For keeps?'

'Yes!' My voice breaks.

'What a bummer!'

'I'm *devastated*!' I start to wail. 'I'll die of loneliness without him!'

'Nah, you won't die.' Dan puts an arm across my shoulders. I can smell the stale sweat in his armpit. 'You'll survive. Life goes on.'

I know he means well, but clearly, he doesn't get it. 'If he forgets about me, I'll *die*.'

'You might *feel* like dying, but you won't—unless *you* do somethin' really stupid! He's probably just as scared you'll forget about *him.*' He gives my shoulder a squeeze. 'But I do understand. Melanie's on her way out.'

'You think?'

'I don't think, I *know*. She's fallen for Romeo. He's going to the Con next year too, to study music and singing. They're on the same wavelength. I can't compete with that.' He removes his arm to fix himself another cracker and cheese. 'They share the same goals and interests. She knows what she wants. And what she wants isn't in Grafton.'

What Shaun wants isn't in Grafton either.

'How will you survive?' I mop up tears with the hem of my t-shirt.

Dan the stalwart, just shrugs. 'I'll survive because I *have* to.' He takes a mouthful of cracker. 'We've had talks and I've tried to—y'know—win her back, but I've met my match. At least I'm free to hook up with someone who likes the beach!' He pops the rest of his cracker and cheese into his mouth, chews and swallows. 'Have you and Shaun agreed to keep in touch? Y'know, ring each other? Write to each other?'

'He says we'll always be friends, and we've swapped addresses and phone numbers.' I blow my nose on a tissue, one of several I had the foresight to bring with me. 'Will you stay friends with Melanie?

'We'll be friend-ly if we bump into each other, like this afternoon. It's not as if we've had a terrible fight or anything.' He finishes his apple and throws the core into the scrub over the fence. 'It doesn't sound like Shaun wants to break up with you though—it's just circumstances. Keep in regular contact. Next year you'll be sixteen, old enough to make your own decisions. What else didja wanna talk about?'

'I want to get our letters back, if they still exist, but I'm so scared of Dad! I don't want to see him, or talk to him, let alone confront him, or challenge him.'

'Why are you scared of him? From what I can make out, you've hardly clapped eyes on him—not since you went to boarding school—apart from a couple of days last Christmas.'

I can't tell Dan why without opening a can of worms, so I shrug, and say, 'I don't know! It's just a bad feeling. He blames me! You know, because of the pink letter.'

'Yeah, well, I feel weird around him too.' He takes a swig from his water bottle. 'But I'm grateful he bought me the old jalopy to get around in. It's a godsend. I'd go stir-crazy without it. I dig how you feel, stuck out here. It's a beautiful place to live, but it's a prison.' He pauses. 'Why do *you* want to get the letters back? I get why, but let me hear it from you.'

He waits while I mop up my tears and control myself enough to answer him. 'Because they're *mine*, Dan! He *stole* them from me! I want them back because they might tell me what was going on for you guys. They might jog my memory. They would've helped me feel like I *had* a family, that I was part of a family, instead of feeling like an orphan, or a state ward. The only thing that stopped me from going completely mental was knowing other boarders were in the same boat. My best friend, Hannah—my only friend, really—was alone too. Her family lived overseas and she rarely heard from them.'

Dan nods. 'At least me and Billy saw Mum being carted off in an ambulance. But, for you, she just vanished. We had the same experience when *you* disappeared; there was no evidence whatsoever you'd gone to boarding school, and Dad refused to take us to visit you. He said it would unsettle you too much. Then later, he said you were settled and didn't need to be unsettled. He was implacable. We felt even worse when you didn't answer our letters. You could've been dead and buried for all we knew; I tell you it did cross our minds! We couldn't understand why we didn't hear from Mum either. We wrote to her, same as we wrote to you, but *she* never replied either.' His voice is suddenly gravelly, and he pauses to clear his throat. 'It was grim, Jode. You and Mum missing, just Billy and me left with Dad, and half the time he'd be gone all night. We learnt not to wait up for him. We'd make something for our dinner, go to bed, then wake up next morning and still no sign of him! We'd have a bowl of cereal, if there was any milk, and make our lunches—if there was enough bread for sandwiches. If there wasn't, we'd raid the pockets of his parka in his wardrobe—we discovered he hid wads of cash there—and take enough to buy our lunches. Then we'd go to school, not knowing if he'd be home that night either.'

'He never warned you?'

'Nup. Never.'

'Do you think Mum *did* write to us, but Dad withheld her letters as well?'

Dan shrugs, then nods. 'It's possible. We were upset with her too. I asked Dad why she didn't answer our letters, and he said she wasn't up to writing, she was too busy getting well and didn't need to be distracted.' Dan shakes his head. 'We didn't know what to believe. We didn't trust a word he said. We half-convinced ourselves you and Mum were dead and he wasn't telling us, but we had no idea who to ask about it. It was scary. Dead-set.' He falls silent, his mouth twisting as if he's in pain and struggling not to cry.

I'm finding it scary just *hearing* about it. I watch him take another sip from his water bottle, composing himself.

'You were gone for months before Mum came back. We arrived home from school one afternoon and there she was! Talk about a surprise! More a shock, really. She wasn't the same person—I mean she was, but she wasn't the Mum *I* remembered.'

Dan is shaking his head. 'She *looked* different. She was skinnier, her hair was longer, she *acted* different. She *was* different. We used to be close; do you remember how she'd tell us stories? And cuddle us?'

I couldn't remember, so I shook my head.

'Well, when she came home, I didn't *want* to cuddle her. I'd changed too. I'd grown. I was taller than she was! My voice had broken. I had a moustache! And dead-set, I was determined never to cry again!' He glances at me. 'I was *angry*. And I've stayed angry. I guess I don't want to be vulnerable, in case she disappears again.'

I nod my understanding. I also grew up in my mother's absence. My periods started without her reassurance. I suffered pain without her empathy. I fear she might disappear again or banish me again. It's a revelation, almost comforting, to know we share the trepidation.

I realise I've not seen either him or Billy give Mum a hug in the four months we've been here. And now he's telling me the distancing started years ago. Is it too late for all of us to love each other and relate to each other again? It won't be easy. Their stand-offishness has become ingrained, habitual. They treat me the same way they treat Mum, keeping me at arm's length. I'm the sister who—apparently—never wrote to them, who never spoke to them for four years, while they became bonded, glued together, supporting and protecting each other, surviving by sharing everything. Now, whether they are behind the closed door of their room or camping down at the beach and surfing the waves, they are a pair, always together. I feel sad, isolated and alone—but hopeful too.

'As soon as Mum came back, Billy 'n' me asked her if *you* were okay, and she said you were fine. That was a relief, I can tell you! We asked her if she'd take us to see you, but she said it was best not to disturb you or make you homesick, and she needed to get well and strong again before she brought you home. It took three more years before that happened! But you know what? I reckon she didn't want you to be around Dad. Or vice versa. I don't know why. Maybe it had something to do with the pink letter. I think she was protecting you.'

I'm suddenly chilled to the bone. My scalp prickles.

'She'd visit you occasionally, by herself, and report back that you were okay. I did ask her why you didn't write to us, but she was so vague I can't remember what she said. I just know I was never satisfied with her answers. Me and Billy quit writing to you during that first year anyway, we just gave up, but we never got over the lack of contact. We always felt uneasy. Truth is, Jode, we missed you!' He puts his arm across my shoulders again and gives me a squeeze.

'Thanks, bro. I missed you guys too.' I mean it.

'Now we know Dad never delivered our letters to you, or your letters to us, I'm thinking you're right; maybe he intercepted Mum's letters too, and she never got ours! What an arsehole! Why would he do such a thing? We've opened a can of worms, figuring it out.'

'Could you and Billy come with me to the Blue Mountains? Please?'

He hesitates, removes his arm from my shoulder. 'Problem is we gotta look after Cleo and Patra. But let's corner Mum over dinner and ask her what she knows, and find out whose side she's on, and whether she can be trusted to help you.'

'Okay.' We sit in silence for a bit, until I ask him, 'Do you suppose Mum *knows* Dad kept our letters, and maybe hers, but she hasn't challenged him about it? Or told us?'

Dan nods. 'It's not impossible.'

'How did they get on after she came back? Did she forgive him?'

Dan doesn't answer me straightaway. He takes a deep breath and holds it, like he's giving my questions some thought, before he lets the breath go. 'Mum always seemed … aloof. Like, she was with us physically, but not mentally, or emotionally. Maybe her medication spaced her out. She took refuge in her art; it consumed her the same as it does here. It seemed like the day after she returned home, she joined an arts centre, and she just about lived there while we were at school, and she'd go away on weekends on painting expeditions. I think the art thing was part of her therapy, to help her make the transition from being in an institution to living at home, but it was like an obsession. I remember Dad struggled to get her attention. He tried to win her back by being nice to her, he'd come home every night, and bring her flowers—and she'd be courteous and calm and polite to him, but—' Dan shook his head, '—she was kind of distant, like she was wary of him, or didn't trust him, or couldn't forgive him or something. She was elusive. He'd try and be affectionate, but she'd move away from him, that sort of thing. Then she announced she'd bought *Gwongorella* and was moving there, with you! Me and Billy were stunned! What about *us*!'

'When Mum picked me up from boarding school we bypassed the Blue Mountains, and Dad, and drove straight here. You and Billy were waiting for us, and I was *so* nervous! It was the first time I'd seen you in *four years*! I barely recognised either of you! And when Dad drove up here for Christmas, in the car he'd bought for you, it was the first time I'd seen *him* in four years! I was so uptight and uncomfortable! All sorts of bad feelings washed over me.'

'It *was* intense. For *all* of us. So much was left unsaid.'

'So much *change*. Boarding school was at least a predictable environment, and I had company. I've been so isolated here, on my own all the time, you guys at school or away at the beach.

Mum in town every day. Shaun saved me from going completely bonkers.' Tears roll down my cheeks again.

'Yeah,' Dan says, adding, after a beat, 'you need to enrol in school.'

I hear him, but I'm not ready to go down that track right now. I ask him, 'Why *are* we here, Dan? I mean—why *Gwongorella?*'

'In the Blue Mountains, me and Billy used to sneak downstairs and eavesdrop on Mum and Dad's conversations, especially when they started arguing, and one night we overheard Mum say she'd bought a property on the north coast. She said she'd paid for it using money from her father's estate, and she'd had a new will drawn up by her lawyer, leaving the property and the balance of Pop's estate to us three kids in the event of her death. Dad was shocked! She'd blind-sided him, well and truly! "Everything else in my will regarding the business stays the same for now," she told him, whatever that meant, "but we need to discuss *your* will, and my share of our joint assets." It sounded like she was planning to separate from him and divorce him, but Dad just tried harder, saying he'd sell the business and come and live with us here on *Gwongorella* and make a fresh start. And Mum fell for it. When she talked with me and Billy about moving to *Gwongorella* it was on the understanding Dad would join us eventually.'

A hot flush permeates my chilled body and I break out in a sweat.

'What about *me?* Was *I* included?'

'Well, you're here now, aren't you?'

'Only 'cos Mum came and got me. Doesn't mean Dad wanted me here.'

'I know it was Mum's idea to bring you here, and me and Billy made it clear we wanted to be with you. No way did we want to stay with Dad in the Blue Mountains without either of you. I guess she was still hanging on to the idea of reuniting the family, so she acted like she forgave him, or she was willing to give him a chance to redeem himself.'

'What a bastard!' I speak softly, but I'm smouldering with rage. 'He ingratiated himself with her, and reeled her back in, and then did it to her *again!* The minute she came here, the minute her back was turned, he *cheated* on her *again.* He's got issues, that man.'

Chapter Twenty-three

Saturday, 08 April 1995

With Mum in the studio and the boys at the beach I've been catching up on schoolwork all day. Now, I'm about to write in my new journal.

I've labelled it PS, for 'Post-Shaun' and 'Private Stuff'. I'm going to keep PS secret. I'll hide it when I'm home and take it with me whenever I leave the house. And I'll write whatever I feel like writing in it.

Anything I want Mum to know about, I'll write in my 'old' journal and leave it on my desk for her to find, seeing as she's probably read most of what I've written in it to date—including incriminating stuff about Dad.

The *Letter to my Family* is still attached to the inside of the back cover. She hasn't said a word about *that* letter, or about the latest journal entries. Truth is, we've hardly said a word to each other about *anything* since our blow-up.

Will we talk, before it's too late to talk about anything at all?

PS
Saturday, 08 April 1995

After Dan and I talked yesterday afternoon, Dan updated Billy, and last night over dinner the three of us asked Mum did she write to us and receive letters from us while she was in the clinic. It turns out she DID write, and felt very hurt we never replied! When we told her the truth, she was so shocked there was no doubting her innocence and ignorance. She was appalled Dad had done such a cruel, mean thing—to her as well as to us.

She challenged the boys: 'Why didn't you tell me, or ask me, when I first came home!'

Dan: 'You weren't in the right headspace to talk to about anything!'

Billy: 'There never was a right place or right time. We were at school weekdays, and weekends you went away on painting trips, or Dad took us camping. The rest of the time Dad was around.'

Mum didn't say anything after that, apart from agreeing to help me retrieve the letters, if they still exist.

The best thing! Dan and Billy invited me, in front of Mum, to come to the beach with them for the weekend! I was thrilled to be asked, even if I didn't entirely trust their motives. Did they REALLY want me to come— a new, bonding experience? Or did they just want me to video them in Melanie's absence? Or did Mum ask them to include me more, after reading the Letter to my Family?

I kept my doubts to myself and said, 'I'd LOVE to come, but I'll need some camping gear, like a tent, a low-allergenic sleeping bag, a bedroll, a torch and eating utensils. Plus Shaun and I are going for our last paddle up the creek on Sunday. But please, please, PLEASE ask me again!'

Mum said, 'We can go to Paddy Pallin's while we're in the Blue Mountains.' Her way of letting me know I can go camping with them in future, and an indication she won't leave me in the Blue Mountains with Dad or send me back to boarding school. Since our confrontation last Sunday, I've been doing my own thing, not asking her permission, and each time she's just given me a look and zipped her lips. It's scary, but it's good she's given up trying to control me and decided to treat me the same as the boys.

I need to ring Em and explain why I can't meet up with her on Tuesday. It's a toss-up between ringing Auntie I or ringing her grandparents. I haven't asked Em who she lives with, or when, or where, or why. It's still too soon to be nosy about that kind of personal stuff. I'm hoping she'll tell me about her home life as we get to know and trust each other more.

So far, most of my time with her has been 'history lessons' because of all my questions. She seems glad I'm interested and I care. She's never tried to make *me* feel sad or bad, or guilty or ashamed, but that *is* how I feel, because even though I wasn't here during Australia's dark past, even though I didn't perpetrate any of the awful things that happened, I am part of 'the dominant culture', one of the 18,000,000 now occupying this land, while Em is one of the 380,000 Aboriginal and Torres Strait Islanders remaining—only 2.0% of the total population. Their country has been invaded alright, and I'm one of the invaders, even though none of my ancestors arrived with the First Fleet, and my parents were born here, making me a second-generation Australian. It's my country too, now.

I want to hear more from Em about how she gets on at school. Find out how other kids treat her. Does she experience racism? Bullying? If she does, how does she cope with it? Are there many other Aboriginal kids at school? What are her teachers like? What is she learning? Is *Aboriginal Studies—Contemporary Issues* part of the curriculum? I'd love to join Em at school and be best friends, like Mum and Lily were friends all those years ago, but she might not want to have anything to do with me at school.

I dial her grandparents' number. The adrenaline rush is wasted. Nobody picks up. I try Auntie I's number before my courage fails me. Auntie I answers, taking me by surprise.

'Hullo?'

'Oh! Gosh. Um. Can I speak to Em, please?'

'She's not here.'

'Oh. Um—is she with—is she at—her grandparents?'

'No. She's at Mala with her mum and dad, and they don't have the phone on.'

'Oh. Okay. Um. Do you know where she'll be on Monday?'

'At school.'

'I mean, like, after school.'

'Here.'

'Oh. Good. Can I ring her here? I mean there? After school?'

'You can try.'

'Well, okay. Thanks heaps. I will try. Thank you, Auntie I.'

'All good, Jodie. Bye.'

She hangs up.

I hang up.

'Did she call me Jodie?' I ask Anne. 'I swear I didn't tell her my name!'

Chapter Twenty-four

Sunday 09 April 1995

The portion of sky framed by my open east-facing window is dotted with stars. I think I can see planets. Red Mars. Venus, or is it *Mir*, the Russian space station? A breeze is wafting over my face, the air cool, but I'm warm and snug under my doona, my toes fiddling with the zipper tabs on my backpack, PS safe inside, the backpack hidden at the bottom of my bed.

I can't see the moon. I watched it rise above the creek yesterday afternoon. It was a bit more than half a moon, so it's waxing gibbous. Gibbous from a fourteenth century word *gibbosus* meaning 'humpbacked'. Shaun told me that. He taught me about the phases of the moon, each phase lasting about seven days. It will be full moon again next Friday—*Good Friday*.

Right now, it's 3:10 a.m., according to the illuminated dial of my alarm clock. I skipped dinner and now I feel empty and hungry, too crazy mixed-up in my mind and heart to sleep.

I need Shaun! I need his arms around me. The first hint he was in love with me was the night of the last full moon, down by the billabong, three or so weeks ago. Six, nearly seven, weeks before that, from the moment we met, I was madly in love with him and he was secretly attracted to me too, but we kept our feelings hidden until the night we lost Saab. And a week or so later, on the east veranda, when I blurted I was in love with him, he confessed he cared for me and was attracted to me too. So much time wasted! Today will be our last day together. While I'm in the Blue Mountains with Mum, dealing with my father, Shaun will be packing up and leaving *Booyul*.

Stop thinking about him—it hurts too much. Get some sleep!

'The distance of the moon from the Earth varies due to its elliptical orbit …. it's around 384,400 km away …. the distance of Mercury from the sun ranges from 46 million to 70 million kilometres; the distance of Venus from the sun is 108 million kilometres; the distance of Earth from the sun 150 million kilometres; the distance of Mars from the sun 228 million kilometres; the distance of Jupiter from the sun 778 million kilometres; the distance of Saturn from the sun 1.4 billion kilometres; the distance of Uranus from the sun 2.9 billion kilometres; the distance of Neptune from the sun 4.5 billion kilometres; the distance of Pluto from the sun 5.9 billion kilometres ….'

It beats counting sheep but it's not helping!

I'm grieving in anticipation. I'm sad, frightened and lonely already.

Shaun is lying on top of me. I can hardly feel his weight; he must be supporting himself on his knees and elbows, because his hands are free and he is caressing my face so lovingly, gazing into my eyes … kissing me tenderly as he slowly enters me … and I am so sensitive to the feel of him it electrifies me … I can feel an orgasm coming … I'm moaning and gasping … arching my back, crying out with ecstasy …

My cries wake me up. I'm in my bed, my tears of joy morphing into despair because it seemed so real—but it wasn't. The orgasm is fading, the exquisite feeling dying away, until I'm left with nothing but the memory of it.

I look at my clock. I've overslept! Shaun is probably already waiting for me down by the creek. If I don't get a move on, he'll think I'm not coming. I climb out of bed, remove a pill from the packet in the top drawer of my desk and swallow it with water from the bottle on my desk. I put on my bikini, find the two loose condom packets—already torn from the string of condoms now hidden in the pocket of my school blazer hanging at the far left-hand end of the rack of clothes in my wardrobe—and place them inside the front of my bikini bottom.

What are they for?

'I don't know!' I hiss tearfully. 'Just in case! Mind your own business!'

My jeans are looser on me. I put on a t-shirt, socks, and my Reeboks. I pull my backpack out from under my sheet and doona, unzip it, and drop a sloppy joe in it in case it's cool up the creek, along with my towel, a tube of sunscreen, a small bottle of Rid and PS.

I open my door quietly. The house is silent with the boys at the beach and Mum in her studio. I'm hoping she didn't hear me moaning in my sleep.

I put cheese slices and crackers into a container and toss it and a couple of apples into my backpack, my water bottle on top. In the bathroom I run a comb through my hair while I sit on the loo. I grab my hat as I go out the door. If Mum eventually notices I'm missing she'll figure out where I've gone. Anxiety and excitement fuel my haste as I half-walk, half-run down our fence line towards the creek.

I arrive breathless and sweaty. Shaun is sitting in the grass on the top of the bank. His back is bare and brown, his elbows resting on his bent knees, his hands clasped together behind his bowed head.

Is he praying? Crying? Meditating? Asleep?

'Shaun?'

'Jodie!' He quickly stands up and turns around.

'Sorry I'm late. I slept in.' I take off my hat and backpack and drop them in the grass.

He moves towards me, his outstretched arms inviting me to come to him, to hug him, but I've lost confidence. Real time feels very different to dream time. He wraps his arms around me and looks down at my face and into my eyes. 'I'm so glad you came. I wasn't sure if you … are you okay now?'

I don't know if I'm okay or not. I nod, but shrug too, uncertain, my eyes downcast.

'Are *we* okay?' he asks, like it matters.

'I don't know.' I shiver. 'Are we?' I glance up at him, make eye contact for a moment.

'We are in my dreams,' he says. 'I dreamt about us this morning.'

'Me too!' I feel a surge in my belly. 'I dreamt about us too! It woke me up!'

'Maybe we went through a wormhole in our sleep and met in a parallel universe. It was amazing. I felt beatific.'

I'm not sure what beatific means, but I can guess, from the tone of his voice and the expression on his face. 'I felt beatific too,' I tell him. 'But terribly sad when I woke up.'

He holds me tighter, and gently kisses the side of my face near my temple. 'Can we keep our Wednesday trysts?' He's pleading with me. 'Take turns to ring each other on Wednesdays?'

I nod, relieved he wants to keep in touch.

'And write to each other regularly, though we'll need to be careful with *what* we write in case someone intercepts our mail. We don't want to give anyone ammunition to shoot us down in flames—but in nine months' time, after your sixteenth birthday, we can write whatever we feel like writing, and when we talk on the telephone, we can say whatever we feel like saying, without fear of retribution.'

I'm mollified by his suggestions, despite his loaded injunction about what to write or not write, but I remind him, 'Until you leave for Antarctica.'

'My chances of being selected this year are remote.'

'It's still possible. *And* we won't be going to the Grafton Show together!' I push him away, just a bit, to make my point.

He loosens his hold, but he doesn't release me. 'We can still go,' he says. 'Unless something cataclysmic happens, I'll drive back up here, and we can go like I promised.'

Instead of goodbye, he's offering me something to look forward to. 'When is it on?'

'The weekend after Easter—Friday and Saturday, 21st and 22nd of April.'

'Oh, no!'

'What?'

'Friday night is the Art Exhibition Opening at the RAG and Mum wants us to go; she's sweating on being selected for hanging. She even used me as a model.'

'Did she now! Will it be for sale?'

'I dunno. I'll ask her.'

'Ask how much.'

'Why?'

'I might buy it, seeing as you're in it—depending on the price tag.'

'You haven't even seen it!'

He chuckles. 'We can do the RAG *and* the Show. The Show is open nine till nine both days. We can go to the RAG exhibition Friday night and the Show on Saturday and Saturday night as well. There's a lot to see, including a fireworks display. I'll ask your mum to invite me to the RAG Opening and give me a preview of the triptych. And can I pitch my tent on her lawn and take you to the Grafton Show, and if she seems the least bit doubtful, I'll suggest she and/or your brothers join us!'

'There's one other thing, though.'

'Sounds like Murphy's Law. What have I overlooked?'

'I'm due the day of the show. Remember my pain last time?' I feel shy mentioning it.

'I do.' His voice is kind and sympathetic. 'You were very miserable.'

'I *was* miserable, about *lots* of things, until you cheered me up!' We gaze at each other, remembering. 'Anyway, I've been on the pill since then; I'm hoping it will stop the pain, but I won't know until Show Day. I'll go anyway—I just don't want to be a drag.' I'm irritated with myself for bringing it up. 'Let's go for a paddle!'

Together we pull the canoe out from under the lantana and carry it down to the water's edge. 'I'll leave the canoe with you, on *Gwongorella*, if you'd like me to.'

I glance at him, momentarily silenced. The canoe, a Canadian, is made of fibreglass, but it's still heavy for one person, cumbersome and awkward on land in contrast to its smooth manoeuvrability in the water. Can I launch and paddle it on my own?

I make myself respond. 'Thank you, Shaun. I'll take good care of it, I promise.'

'I know you will.' He steadies the canoe with one hand and holds out his other arm for me to grasp while I climb in and sit in the bow seat. 'Let's paddle *down*stream for a change. We can check out where to moor it on *Gwongorella* while we're about it.'

He sits in the stern and takes up his paddle. Usually, we take it in turns where to sit. I prefer sitting behind him so I can watch the muscles rippling across his bare back while he paddles, but he's often forced to swap sides with his paddle to steer because I've forgotten to! The stern paddler is responsible for steering, while the bow paddler helps maintain the momentum, looks out for rocks and submerged logs, and enjoys the view!

'Joe's told Mum he's already signed up a family with three kids.' We are skimming smoothly down the creek. 'A two-year lease with an option to buy the place. A teenage boy and two younger girls. They've got horses apparently. You never know, they might be canoeing enthusiasts too. They'll move in as soon as we move out.'

I'm devastated Shaun is leaving, but he's just described a whole new scenario! I *love* horses! I learnt to ride at boarding school. I don't know what to say and end up saying nothing. We paddle in silence until we reach *Gwongorella* where we suss out the most secure place to moor the canoe. I already know the best spot—the little beach still covered in debris after the recent flash flood; the place where I swam in the height of summer before making Shaun's acquaintance. The place where I cried in the grass and wrote about my father in my journal. We beach the canoe in the shallows, and he watches me pull it over the sand, up onto the grass behind the she-oaks and paperbarks and moor it to a low branch.

'No problem!' he says cheerfully.

I drag the canoe back down to the water and settle myself in the stern this time. We continue downstream, and I concentrate on paddling efficiently and steering. As we pass the property next door, I wonder what—if anything—has happened to the owner and his, or her, marihuana crop. Gwongorella Creek is no longer secretive and shadowy, or alive with the flitter and twitter of small birds. Instead, it has become wider and deeper, the banks cleared of timber. Cattle tracks wind down to the waters' edge. Reeds grow rampant in the shallows, a sanctuary for invisible waterbirds; I can hear moorhens calling to each other.

Around midday we moor the canoe on the eastern side of the creek, scramble up the bank and sit on a flat rock above the water to eat the lunch Shaun brought. I'm starving. The sandwich he made me—with avocado, cheese and salad filling—tastes delicious.

It's colder here, the sky clouding over with towering cumulonimbus, the wind chopping up the water. Shaun pulls on his t-shirt and says, 'Let's go back to the calm and peace of our island!'

'You've read my mind!' I'm tempted to take the sloppy joe from my backpack and put it on too, but decide I'll keep warm paddling. We head upstream in silence. Eventually, we pass *Gwongorella* again. As we approach *Booyul*, a twirling twig strikes the crown of Shaun's battered leather hat. He ducks in fright and waves his paddle in the air above his head like he's being assailed by nesting magpies.

I laugh at him, amused by his reaction. 'It was only a twig!'

But he continues to look skyward. He's listening; I can tell from the tilt of his head.

'What?'

'I can hear something.' He resumes paddling, intermittently watching the sky.

I listen and look too. I can't *hear* anything unusual, but the light is becoming very strange. The sky is a sulky purplish-green, like a bruise, a haze dimming the sun. Shadows merge with the general gloom. The creek is no longer glittering and dancing. We're relatively sheltered down here on the water, but the tops of the eucalypts along the eastern escarpment opposite *Booyul* are thrashing about. The cattle below the escarpment are behaving weirdly, bellowing as they run along the fence line parallel to the creek, before turning and stampeding back the other way.

'It's like they're trying to escape from something.'

'You'd think wild dogs were nipping at their heels.'

I sniff the air. 'I can smell rain. Or ozone.' A jagged bolt of lightning surges down the sky from east to west and spears into the earth somewhere on *Booyul*, accompanied by a terrifyingly loud, crackling bang. I yelp and jerk with fright.

'Holy shit! I hope that didn't hit the house!' Shaun says. 'We need to get off the water!' We both paddle furiously towards the bank, leap out of the canoe, drag it across the sand, up the grass and into the lantana. 'Help me turn it over,' he says. 'We'll have to shelter under it.' He points across the creek at the sky above the escarpment. 'We can't escape that. It's hail!'

I look too and see a twisting green curtain sweeping towards us. The cattle opposite have stopped running. They are huddling under a stand of eucalypts, facing us, heads down. The escarpment behind them is blotted out by a white mist. I can hear a metallic drumming.

Shaun is yanking my arm. 'C'mon, Jodie! C'mon! Or we'll be killed!'

Glassy pebbles plummet down into the creek, plinking and plopping like thrown stones. Following Shaun's urgent instructions, I clamber into the prickly lantana, turn around and squat down, my back against the upside-down canoe. Shaun lifts it up and I shuffle backwards under it between the seat struts, leaving a space next to me for him. I hold the canoe up by the gunwale with both hands as he tosses the paddles into the lantana behind it, throws my backpack on the ground beside me and his backpack on the far side of him. He backs in alongside me, his body pressed hard against my side, his knees up to his chin. 'I hope you're strong enough to help me hang onto it in the wind,' he exclaims, his mouth close to my ear.

I'm pumping adrenaline; it's giving me strength. We hang onto the gunwale above our heads and pull the canoe forward and down to shield us in front from the wind-driven rain and hail, but our backs are partially exposed and ricochetting hailstones hit us with stinging force. A sweet leaf and earth smell mixes with an unpleasant pong released by the battered lantana. It's almost dark. We are curled up like embryos in a fibreglass womb, rivulets of icy rainwater running under and around us. I'm shivering with fear as well as cold. Lightning flashes, and the almost simultaneous thunder warns us the strikes are very close, the air reeking of ozone and sizzling with electricity. My chest feels tight like an asthma attack is coming on.

The hailstones threaten to pierce the fibreglass hull protecting our heads as they thud and ricochet off our shelter in an increasing cacophony. The wind buffets us, trying to snatch the canoe away, and I hang onto both the seat strut and gunwale with all my strength. Large, jagged hailstones bounce on the grass at our feet, accumulating along the edge of the canoe. I'm numb, shuddering with cold, yet I feel detached. *How puny we humans are!* I'm visualising our houses in the path of the twisting wind and hail. Was *Booyul* struck by that first lightning bolt? My east-facing windows are probably shattered, a mountain of hailstones piling up on my desk and on the chairs and sofa on the east veranda—if they haven't blown away. Mum is probably cowering under the bench in her studio on the west side of the house. Are Cleo and Patra with her? Or did she have time to put them in their enclosure and they're sheltering in their kennels?

Did the storm start over the ocean like a waterspout? Did Dan and Billy have any warning? Did they come ashore in time, pack up and escape by driving north or south of it? I peer at Shaun; I can hardly see his features in the gloom. He's probably worrying about Wendy.

My fingers hurt, my arms ache, the muscles in my shoulders and neck sting and threaten to spasm with the effort of hanging onto the canoe. My legs are numb from squatting. Bouncing hailstones frequently slam into my back. After an interminable time, the cacophony dies down, the noise receding as the storm sweeps west across our properties, taking the wind with it.

We wait. An eerie silence prevails.

'Murphy won that round,' Shaun declares, raising the canoe like a shutter opening. I help him push it backwards; it drops behind us. We stand up, stretch our cramped muscles and step onto a white wonderland. Hailstones carpet the entire landscape like drifts of snow littered with vast quantities of leaves, bark, twigs, small branches. The trees, and the lantana, are stripped of foliage. Across the creek, the cattle are still packed together, probably injured and in shock.

The storm has blown away any thoughts about a last tryst on our island. The danger has passed, but we are saturated, cold and exhausted. I put on my dripping backpack and follow Shaun up the track behind the lantana, slipping on the melting hail, tripping over the debris. The fallow corn paddock is a white carpet. Not a single bird is visible on the billabong; they've all flown away, hopefully beyond the limits of the storm. Shaun's vegie patch is trashed. The packing shed is minus much of its roofing iron. The lean-to, which sheltered the tractor, trailer and Shaun's ute, has been blown apart. Miraculously, the windows in his ute are still intact, but the roof and the back of the vehicle are pock-marked by the hail. Approaching the house, we notice the chimney has been blasted from its moorings and is lying on the ground shattered, bricks scattered. The water tank has been bowled from its wooden platform and rolled along the ground until stopped by the fence. Wendy's small car is a dented wreck from being flipped over, probably several times, also on its way to the fence. It's pocked by hailstones, all the windows broken.

'Handy it ended up on its wheels,' Shaun says. 'Good thing it's insured.'

We go inside and find Wendy mopping up. She's pale and shocked and very relieved to see us safe and uninjured. After commiserating with her—windows have been broken and the floor is wet from rain and melting hailstones—Shaun quickly changes into dry clothes and escorts me down the slope to check on Mum and the dogs.

Miraculously, *Gwongorella* is undamaged. The hailstones are thick on *Booyul*, but there are only a few scattered remnants around *Gwongorella*, though there are plenty of twigs and leaves blown in from elsewhere littering the space between our houses. My bedroom windows are intact, my desk dry. The furniture on the east veranda is damp, but otherwise undamaged.

'It was a twister,' Shaun tells Mum. '*Booyul* happened to be in its path.'

After making sure Mum and Cleo and Patra are okay, Shaun says, 'I'd like to attend the opening of the RAG exhibition, Anne. Any chance you can wangle me an invitation?'

'Certainly,' she says.

'Can I have a preview of the triptych? Jodie's told me it's unique and a great deal of creative effort has gone into it.'

'Sure,' Mum says. I can tell she's pleased he is interested. She leads the way to the studio. I detour via my room, grab my Ventolin and inhale a couple of puffs, before following them. I stand in the studio doorway, shivering, and watch them interacting. Shaun asks Mum questions about how she created such an arresting piece, what it's saying, and what motivated her in the first place. I can hear his questions and read his lips as he's facing me, but I can't decipher her answers—she has her back to me. When he asks, 'Is it for sale, Anne?' she nods yes, it is. He asks how much, and she tells him, and he says, 'I'd very much like to buy it. Is there a way I can secure it? I don't want to be pipped at the post!'

Mum nods and I hear her say something like, 'If it's hung, I'll put a red sticker on it.' And he says, 'Well, that's a relief.' Then he asks her can he erect his tent on her lawn for that weekend, having vacated *Booyul*, and she nods agreement. Then he asks her can he take me to the Grafton Show on the Saturday, in the same breath suggesting she and Dan and Billy might like to come too! It seems effortless, for Shaun anyway. I can't tell if Mum is acting or being genuinely friendly. She shrugs and says something about the RAG roster, but she doesn't object to me going with him.

'I'll just change into something warm and dry,' I say, and leave them to it.

During my brief absence, Shaun must have invited Mum to come and say hullo and goodbye to Wendy and see the damage done to *Booyul* because they're waiting for me when I emerge from my room. Now the three of us are on our way up the slope. My arms and shoulders and legs are aching, and my lower back feels bruised like I've been punched or kicked. There's a strained feeling in all my muscles. I think I'm in shock too; I'm shivering, with an occasional shudder thrown in, though I'm no longer cold.

'I can't stay long,' Mum says to Shaun. 'I'm under the pump. The triptych still needs some finishing touches. The framer is expecting me first thing in the morning; midday is the submission deadline. Then there's last-minute shopping. And we still need to pack—'

'What will you do with yourself when it's all over?' I interrupt her, then wish I hadn't, because she doesn't answer, and it feels like she's decided to ignore me.

But after a couple of beats she says, 'Good question, Jodie. I've neglected all sorts of important tasks these last few weeks. And I need to get back to Ceramics at TAFE, maybe do another subject in Visual Arts. And I'll still volunteer at the gallery.'

No apology for neglecting us kids!

I listen, and nod, and say, 'That all sounds very positive.' Trying to be positive myself.

Mum and Wendy do an inspection of *Booyul*, talking animatedly to each other, while Shaun and I tag along. I mutter to him, 'I'm *so* sore! All over.'

Shaun nods. 'Me too. We haven't paddled that far before, or for that length of time—and hanging onto the canoe in that wind was another marathon effort. You did well.'

PS
Sunday, 9th April 1995
Late

It's over. So much for our last paddle together. No lying in each other's arms on the grass of our secret island, turning one another on, whispering heartfelt promises to each other. The best we could do, in front of Mum and Wendy, was give each other pats on the back. The only thing saving me from falling into the deepest pit ever dug is knowing—believing—he'll be back in twelve days for the RAG exhibition and the Show.

Dan and Billy provided a diversion though. They survived the hailstorm too, by driving south towards Woolgoolga, but the coast road was so packed with other escapees they couldn't get away fast enough and copped the edge of the hail and Dan's car has dents to prove it. They spun a great yarn about what a close shave they had, and they listened to me rapt when I told them about my experience with Shaun on the creek and under the canoe in the lantana. It was gratifying to have their full attention and Mum was all ears ...

I stop writing and relive the storm in my mind, back there, by the creek, seeing, hearing, smelling it all over again—the rain, the wind, the hail, the lightning and thunder, the trees screaming as the leaves were flayed off them, their arms and fingers bruised and broken. I can smell the ozone, the battered earth, the crushed lantana, the lacerated leaves helpless against the forces of nature, and I'm crying again, always crying, because I'm so sad and hurt, bruised and broken like the trees, my needs and desires thwarted and frustrated ...

I see my door opening and instinctively shove my journal under my pillow. It's Mum, in her nightie and dressing gown. She must've heard me crying. She's brought me a glass of water and a couple of Panadol. I take them from her and swallow them between hiccups, while she gently closes the door.

She sits on my bed and holds my left hand in both of hers. 'You're grieving, and you're dealing with a *double* whammy of grief.'

'How do you mean?'

'You're not only grieving Shaun. I think you're also grieving not having a father you can love and trust and believe in and rely on.'

'I don't give a *stuff* about Dad! Just *talking* about him makes me mad!'

She nods, like she gets it. 'When I was in the clinic, I learnt about the Kubler-Ross model of the five stages of grief. Do you know about it?'

I shake my head.

She grasps my left thumb. 'First there's *Denial*. Wanting to escape from, or not face, the reality of the situation. She moves to my pointer and holds it—it reminds me of this little piggy went to market. 'The second stage is *Anger*. Frustration. Feeling it's not fair. The injustice. Feeling abandoned or wronged.'

'How about *all* of those things!' I growl, sniffling.

She shifts her grip to my middle finger. '*Bargaining* is the third stage—the what if, or if only stuff; feeling guilty, or responsible; praying, promising, wishing for a different outcome ...'

I can relate to that.

'… even though it isn't your fault.'

She moves to my ring finger. 'The fourth stage, *Depression*, is more than sadness. It is feeling hopeless, helpless, powerless to change the situation, no sense of a future, nothing to look forward to. The loss of meaning.'

I've lost my father's love—if I ever had it. And now I'm losing Shaun.

She holds my little finger and wiggles it. 'The last stage of grief is *Acceptance*. It is what it is. We gradually learn to live with it, whatever "it" is. The stages aren't linear though. Meaning we don't go through them one, two, three, four, five. We move back and forth between them, a bit like being lost in a maze, but over time we find our way out.'

I long ago lost my relationship with my father, but I haven't *really* 'lost' Shaun, have I? I'm losing his proximity. But is that *Denial?* Am I *Bargaining?* It's true. I am lost in a maze.

Chapter Twenty-five

Monday, 10 April 1995

PS
Monday, 10ᵗʰ April 1995
Late

Today was hectic. Early this morning, Mum asked me to go with her while she went to the framers and then to the RAG to submit her triptych. She reckoned she needed 'moral support', but I think she was giving ME moral support, meaning she was afraid to leave me at home alone. Next, we did a top-up grocery shop for Dan and Billy's benefit. This afternoon I cleaned and tidied my room (in case the cops come back) and started packing. Mum warned me there's 'a cold snap' in the Blue Mountains and to pack accordingly. I know what 'cold' means, after four winters in the southern highlands!

When I announced I was going to bed, Mum said, 'Don't be writing all night, Jodie!' (How does she know! Does she check up on me? Can she see the light under my door?) 'You need to sleep. We're leaving at dawn— it's a long drive. Set your alarm for five o'clock. Do you want a couple more Panadol? Are you still sore?' When I nodded, she fetched them for me and watched me swallow them down. Then she said, 'Goodnight, daughter. I love you, you know. I want you to be happy here. We need to talk about what will help you to be happy. I want us to be friends.'

Is she reacting to the Letter to my Family? It sounds like she's changed her mind about leaving me in the Blue Mountains with Dad or sending me back to boarding school.

I rang Auntie I's number and Em answered like she knew it was me! I told her about my parents being separated, and I had to go back to the Blue Mountains with Mum to deal with 'unfinished business'. She told me she stays with Auntie I or her grandparents in town and sees her parents and cousins and other extended family some weekends and holidays at 'Mala'—Malabugilmah—a community in the ranges west of here, too far away for her to travel to school and TAFE and back again every day.

I said, 'Thanks for telling me that, Em. Could you tell Jacinta about me, and what I'm doing? And I'll see you both next term.'

'I'll miss you, eh!' she said. Then she sang me a little ditty in a singsong voice:

"When you're in a swamp, don' never look back.
Jus' keep wadin' 'til you reach the other side."

Then she hung up.

Chapter Twenty-six

Tuesday, 11 April 2025

We're sitting in the car at dawn, Mum dishing out last-minute instructions to the boys.

'Make sure you lock up Cleo and Patra every night and any-time you leave the property. I don't want them ending up like Saab. And make sure they've always got water. And a bone each. And feed them every morning and evening, but don't give them too much. And pick up their poo—'

'You're fussing, Mum!' Dan gives her shoulder a reassuring pat.

'Make sure you drive safely, Mum,' Billy chips in, taking her off. 'Don't exceed the speed limit. Check your spare's got air. Take regular breaks. And say hi to Dad for me.'

'Yeah, say hi for me too,' Dan adds, half-heartedly. He winks and smiles at me. 'Look after yourself, sis. Good luck with eve-rything. I wanna hear all about it when you get back.'

'Yeah, have fun, Jode!' Billy gives me a wry grin. 'May *The Force* be with you!'

'Thanks, bros. Seeya.'

Mum lets the clutch out and takes off with a jerk and we're on our way. I get out, open the gate to the lane, wait for her to drive through, and close it. I look to my right and see Wendy's little car a dark shape against their fence, the water tank further along. In the dawn light, *Booyul* with its missing chimney is a desolate silhouette—no Shaun waving goodbye, no barking Saab, no grunting Big George, no squealing piglets … I'm clinging for dear life to his promise I'll see him in ten days' time. It's like a stay of execution.

'Well, it's all happening!' Mum says, driving sedately along the lane, keeping an eye out for wallabies. 'Triptych submitted! What a relief. I just hope it's selected for hanging after all that effort. I'll be *very* disappointed if it isn't.' She glances at me in the half-light. 'Is Shaun serious about buying it?'

'Of course. He never goes back on his word.'

Never? He said he'd be here for the rest of the year. Now it's the rest of the week!

We are silent for several kilometres. Approaching the Gwyder Highway, Mum says, 'I'll go the coast route. We can have breakfast in Port Macquarie.' She turns left. 'There's a pillow and rug behind you; lie your seat back and get some sleep. I'll put a CD on. Are you warm enough?'

'Thanks, Mum.' How to avoid a conversation and tune out. Ahh … *The Seekers* …

Mum wakes me up—meaning she's pulled up and turned off the ignition, and the silence and lack of movement has woken me.

'That was a good sleep! You must have needed it.'

I put my glasses back on and peer at my watch. *Hours* have passed!

'Where are we?'

'Port Macquarie.'

We are parked beside a petrol pump at a roadhouse.

'Time for breakfast. The toilet facilities are over there. I'll just get some petrol. Meet you inside,' she says.

A short while later, in a booth in a quiet corner of the diner, Mum orders omelettes and toast, coffee and hot chocolate. Silence descends. I have so many questions tumbling around in my head I don't know where or even how to start.

'Where are we going to stay?'

'I've booked a family unit in a motel, with a shared bathroom and living area with a minimal kitchen, but separate bedrooms seeing as we'll be staying for a few days. Is your main priority to recover the letters? If they still exist. Have you thought about how you want to go about it?'

'Not really. I mean, no, I haven't. I don't have a clue what to do. Will you help me?'

'Absolutely. We can add the legal ramifications of Hugh stealing your letters to the agenda, and the effect of divorce on the business, and vice versa—among other things. I've made two appointments with Ian, tomorrow afternoon and Thursday morning.'

Ian?

The name sounds familiar.

'Can I come to the appointments too? I'd like to ask about, y'know, other stuff besides the letters.'

'Sure. If one of us wants to talk privately, the other can wait outside.'

'Do I know him?'

'You know him. He and his wife drove you to boarding school.'

'Oh! Right.' I feel very strange in my tummy hearing this. My scalp is prickling. 'His wife helped me pack. But I've forgotten her name—or even what she looked like.'

'Margaret. Ian and Margaret Perry.'

'Whose decision was it, to send me to boarding school?'

'Mine. When I came to my senses. Ian had POA regarding other things, which was useful in the circumstances.'

'POA?'

'Power of Attorney. Meaning he could act for me, on my behalf, as per my instructions.'

'I know what it means. I'm just curious as to why you needed that.'

'I've relied on his advice for a long time. He even chose your school—the most expensive in the state! It was far enough away from you-know-who, with an excellent reputation academically, and for extra-curricular activities, and for looking after its boarders. All I could do was cross my fingers you'd be safe there and become happy and settled. I received regular reports on your progress, and I was assured you were excelling academically. They said you loved horse-riding.'

'True.'

'But you refused to attend piano lessons. Ian told them not to insist on piano lessons.'

Why? Because you said so?

I'm at a loss for how to respond, so I just say, 'Thank you.'

'What rating would you give the school out of ten?'

'Eight.'

'Eight! Why not ten? What was missing?'

'The isolation, Mum. I have no memories of 1990, the year you-you disappeared.' I swallow hard. 'But after I was taken away from Dan and Billy in 1991, I was *totally* isolated, abandoned, for four years! That's the truth. And I remember all of it.'

She wriggles, as if she's uncomfortable, and says, 'I notice you're not including Hugh.'

I give her a momentary intense stare before looking down at my omelette. I carefully cut a piece from it. The silence lengthens while she waits for me to say more, but I'm not going to say more, not here, in a roadside diner.

'So, what was the second missing element?'

'I was bullied. Especially the first couple of years. Usually by seniors.'

'That's no good. What about?'

'Being deaf. Mainly.'

A deaf, fat nerd who talked to herself.

'I wasn't the only victim. We juniors were expected to be their slaves.'

'I'm sorry to hear that. Did you complain?'

I give her another brief, but withering, stare, before looking out at the line-up of trucks, and at the highway beyond. I don't want to revisit those early feelings: the powerlessness, humiliation, fear, helplessness, hopelessness, the intensifying suicidal thoughts.

Hearing her sigh, I glance at her again. She looks sad, defeated, guilty.

'What's on *your* agenda?' I ask her, as I put my mug back down on its saucer.

'File for divorce. I don't know how, or in what order, to do things. What comes first? Property settlement? Financial arrangements? I need to find out how to get the ball rolling.'

'Ask Ian about mediation, instead of going to court.' I pass on what Christine told me, without divulging the source of my information. I can tell from the expression on her face that she's impressed with what I know—and intrigued that I know it.

'I will ask him. Sounds a better option than a protracted, expensive court battle. How come you know all that?'

'I did a year of Legal Studies. Learnt terminology and procedures and how the Australian justice system works.' I stand up. 'I also learnt I don't want to be a lawyer.'

PS
Tuesday, 11 April 1995
Late

This afternoon, after checking in, Mum suggested we drive to chilly, windy Katoomba to buy my camping gear. She brushed aside my concern that she'd done enough driving for one day. Choosing the gear was fun! She also bought me a colourful woollen zip-up jacket with a hood.

Afterwards, we returned to the motel for dinner in the dining room.

The motel is surrounded by tall eucalypts and well-kept gardens. Our suite is old-fashioned, homey and cosy. I'd been dreading having to share a poky little room with Mum, but this set-up, with our own bedrooms, is perfect. What makes it special is she arranged it out of consideration for me. If I wasn't feeling so crazy mixed-up about Shaun leaving, and the confrontation with Dad wasn't looming, I could relax and enjoy this diversion with Mum.

Over dinner, she came up with a plan.

'Tomorrow, very early, we'll park opposite Macleod Chambers and wait for Hugh's secretary Felicity to arrive. We won't see him when—if—he comes in, because he'll drive in the back entrance and park underneath the building, but we can ring Felicity from the phone box at the post office up the road and find out if he's there, or coming in, or not.'

Mum continued, 'When Felicity answers, you do the talking because she won't recognise your voice, whereas she'll know mine for sure. Ask her to put you through to Hugh and if she asks who is calling, give her your ex-piano teacher's name!'

I nearly choked on my mouthful of food.

'It was a long time ago,' Mum said, as if time nullified everything. She was clueless how awful I felt! Felicity might never have spoken to her, or heard her voice, or even met her. Anyway, if Felicity says Hugh is NOT there, tell her you'll ring after Easter and hang up. If he IS there, hand me the phone as soon as she says, "Connecting you now."' Mum chuckled, though she didn't look remotely amused. 'That'll throw him, when he thinks he's about to speak to his long-ago lover and gets me instead!'

I managed to swallow the mouthful, just, but put down my knife and fork. 'What if he's not there?' I asked her, crossing my fingers under the table.

We'll move to Option 2 and enter the building. Bring your Paddy Pallin bag to hold your letters—fingers crossed we find them. I'll be armed with my empty briefcase.'

She sounded aggressive, like she was ready for combat.

'I own half the business, Jodie. I'm Hugh's partner in more ways than marriage. Felicity is in no position to refuse me entry into his inner sanctum. Once we're in, we'll lock the door to keep her out and hopefully find what we're looking for.'

Chapter Twenty-seven

Wednesday, 12 April 1995

We are sitting in Mum's car, across the road from Macleod Chambers. In due course, Felicity arrives and disappears inside. So far so good. As Mum expected, there's no sign of Dad, and she decides it's time to ring Felicity.

In the phone box at the post office, Mum stands close to me, her ear right next to mine so she can hear what Felicity says.

I tell Felicity my first name—the first name of who I'm pretending to be that is—and then I say, trying to mimic my ex-piano teacher's voice, 'Put me through to Hugh, please.'

Felicity's response is astonishingly huffy, impatient and unfriendly.

'You *know* he's not coming in today! You *know* the arrangement is to meet him here, tomorrow, at ten. You'll have plenty of time to talk to him over the Easter break!'

Whoo-ha!

There's no doubting Felicity's tone of voice; she clearly dislikes the woman and disapproves of their relationship, but what truly stuns me is the fact my father and ex-piano teacher *are* still in a relationship! After all these years! After everything that's happened! I'm completely at a loss about what to say next. There is an awkward silence.

'I'm confused!' Felicity says eventually. 'Did you say—am I talking to—?'

Mum is bristling beside me, grinding her teeth! I just manage to hold my roleplay together. I push her away and interrupt Felicity in my poshest southern highlands boarding school voice. 'I think you misheard me. I'm certainly not going away for Easter with Mr Macleod. Whoever he's going away with, it isn't me! But no problem. I'll contact him again next week. Goodbye.' And I hang up on Felicity's disembodied voice still trying to clarify who I am if I'm *not* the woman she thought she heard me say I was …

'Phew!' I look at Mum. I'm shaking.

Mum's response to the news her husband is taking his Easter break with my ex-piano teacher is dangerously brittle. 'Well done, Jodie!' She is icy and glittery-eyed. 'That was an *excellent* recovery!' Her voice could cut glass. She exits the phone box and stalks down the road to the car, me following, our breaths misty in the cold air, her exhalations fast and shallow. 'I suggest we barge into Hugh's office *right now*!' she says. 'I'll tell Felicity I'm collecting personal items he's left for me. We'll be *super* friendly!' She looks and sounds anything but friendly.

She unlocks the car, picks up her briefcase and my Paddy Pallin shopping bag from the back seat. She gives it to me.

We cross the road, and walk up three long, wide, shallow front steps onto a terrace. We pass beneath a portico, and high, automatic, sliding glass doors open, revealing the foyer. Inside, I pause and look around. The layout has a certain familiarity, though five years have passed since I've been here, and I have no memory of specific occasions. It's all very posh.

Mum nudges me and mouths, 'Are you coming?' She points towards a door on the right, directly off the foyer, then marches towards it. I scurry after her.

Mum's display of cheerfulness as she enters the anteroom is admirable. 'Hullo, Felicity, long time no see! Just picking up some personal items from Hugh's office. Won't be long.'

I glance at Felicity sitting behind her desk. Her mouth is open and there's no describing the expression on her face. Surprise? Confusion? She's flummoxed for sure. I follow Mum into Dad's office. She closes the door behind me and locks it and heads straight for the filing cabinet. I try the desk drawers.

'Mum?' I hiss, pointing to the lock. She comes over, finds the desk key on her key ring, and unlocks it.

'Try the back of the bottom drawers. Old habits are often repeated!' She returns to the filing cabinet and unlocks it.

I pull the bottom right-hand drawer out as far as it will go and look inside. At the back is a beige cardboard box, the size of a shoebox. I remove it and place it on the desktop, open the lid, it's attached and bends back, and peer inside. It is full of letters, still in their envelopes. A huge buzz goes through me. I pull out an envelope—it is addressed to the three of us kids, in Mum's writing. My hands start shaking. I pull out another envelope. It's addressed to *me*, in Dan's distinctive scrawl.

'Mum! I've found them!' My voice is a hoarse whisper thick with emotion. The elation I'm experiencing is so intense I feel giddy and hot—giddy with joy, hot with grief and anger.

I sit in my father's over-sized black leather swivel chair, like Goldilocks in Father Bear's chair, and read the envelopes. There are individual letters from me addressed to Mum, to Dan, and to Billy; others are addressed to me from Dan or Billy. Mum's letters are addressed to all three of us. Two envelopes are addressed to Dad in my childish handwriting—so I *did* reach out to him! Did *he* write to *me* though, even if he never sent them? Yes! One envelope, still sealed, is addressed to me in unfamiliar handwriting. The hollow, empty, anxious feeling in my gut is a new sensation. I take the envelope from the box and turn it over and over in my hands, afraid to unseal it, trying to imagine what he's said to me. It's not likely to be an apology. My snatching the pink letter off him five years ago and giving it to Mum was an unforgivable act. I exposed him, blew the whistle, started an extraordinary chain of events—I don't know the half of it— events that are still unfolding, right to this very moment.

And it isn't over yet!

'No, it isn't. Not by a long shot.'

'Pardon?' Mum asks.

'Nothing. Just thinking aloud.'

I return my father's letter to the box with the others and close the lid. I check the contents of the rest of the desk drawers, but nothing else captures my interest.

'Time we weren't here!' Mum says. She locks the filing cabinet and desk. I put the box of letters in my Paddy Pallin bag. Mum unlocks the door and leads the way past Felicity's desk.

'Thanks, Felicity,' she says.

'May I ask what you were looking for?'

Letters! Thank you very much!

'Have a nice break yourself,' Mum says, ignoring the question. 'See you next time I'm down this way.' She strides out of the anteroom into the foyer, briefcase swinging, exits the building, and marches triumphantly across the road to the car, me close behind.

'Time for coffee!' she declares, as she straps herself in. 'It's too early for champagne.'

'Did *you* find what you were looking for?' I fasten my seatbelt and sit back, hugging my backpack *and* the Paddy Pallin shopping bag, hoping she'll tell me what she unearthed.

'Oh, yes!' Her voice is cutting. 'I certainly did.'

During our celebratory brunch, Mum barely discusses the morning's events and dismisses my questions about the documents she took from the filing cabinet. As we prepare to leave the café she says, 'You can have this afternoon's appointment with Ian all to yourself.'

'Why? I'm not at all sure I want to meet Ian by myself or have him to myself!'

'There are things I have to do.'

'Like what?'

'Just—things.'

'*What* things?'

'I need to go through these documents for starters, before I see him.'

What documents did she collect?

Anne is curious, but I know it's useless interrogating Mum when she shuts down like this. Right now, I'm consumed by the thought of meeting Ian again, especially on my own. We return to the motel in silence and retreat to our rooms to recover from the morning's adventures.

I lie on my bed in a nest of pillows with the box of letters, aware that Dad must have read every one of them. It creeps me out, the way he kept them from us and preserved them as if he valued and coveted them. More likely it was some kind of power trip.

I read them all, and re-read them, except for the one he wrote to me. It's still in its sealed envelope. I'm too scared to open it. I'm thinking it could go one of three ways: he's written trite, meaningless sentences about nothing important, pretending all the bad stuff never happened; or he's written something mean; or he's apologised. An apology is the least likely possibility, but it's what I want from him more than anything.

Why would he bother to write a letter with no intention of posting it? I write letters to Shaun but never post them because I'm afraid of his reaction. Is Dad afraid of my reaction?

I can hardly bear to read the letters I wrote to him from my place of exile, but I overcome the cringing feeling and take them out of their envelopes. In the first letter, I beg him to let me come home. I tell him I'm sorry. *Sorry about what, exactly?* My second letter is starkly different; it's formal and standoffish. I describe the school. This time I don't apologise or beg him to reply. Everything that matters is left unsaid.

Not having a relationship with my father feels very strange. We are estranged. Like strangers. *Strange, estranged, strangers.* I'm not anaesthetised though—I'm furiously angry and deeply hurt. He's not worthy of the title 'father'. I'm unspeakably sad I don't have a father I can care about, a father who cares about me, a father I can trust.

The earliest letters were written in the spring of 1990, Mum's letters addressed to the three of us collectively, our letters individually addressed to her. Mine are written in a childish script, and signed by me, but I cannot remember writing them. How scary that is! What else can I not remember? It's as if my brain has holes in it where memories should be.

Mum is heartbroken we haven't responded to her letters. She assumes we are angry with her. She expresses guilt and regret and remorse and asks us to forgive her. I KNOW, now, what happened to her then—after my recent conversation with Dan and Billy—but I cannot REMEMBER anything about that time. Now I'm learning what it was like. The tone of the letters becomes increasingly desperate. Dan asks Mum, 'Are you still alive?' Billy questions, 'Don't you love us anymore?' In my letters I want, need, beg her to come back, unable to comprehend that she could-would-did-disappear, just like that—with no explanation. I ask her, 'Why did you do that? How could you do that!' Although I don't remember writing these early letters to Mum, it's clear her disappearance left me heartbroken, bewildered and distraught. I realise I've been afraid ever since that she'll relapse and disappear again.

How could our father, my mother's husband, shut us off from each other and not care how we felt? Why would he do that?

Once I went to boarding school, I recovered my ability to store memories and recall experiences and events. I remember now the relief I felt then, when Mum turned up at the school—her visits were unpredictable and infrequent—and took me out to lunch.

I also remember, before the fog closed in, snatching the pink letter from my father's hands and running off with it. Do I remember giving it to Mum, or only being told that I did? Billy's voice saying, 'It's all your fault, Jodie!' is the last memory I have of that time.

My nightmares and flashbacks have become more frequent since I moved to *Gwongorella*, like when I dreamt I was struck by a lightning bolt down our chimney and was hurt by the piano; like waking up in the dark convinced someone had come into my room; like the horrible flashbacks of my father having sex with my ex-piano teacher. Has Mum read that entry in my journal, written while I was down by the creek? I don't know what she's read. I only know we've hardly spoken to each other about ANYTHING since our confrontation on the east veranda, when I threatened to expose Dad and implicate her and harm myself. Since then, she's given up trying to control me; she's stopped telling me what to do—or not do.

In their letters to me in 1991, Dan and Billy declare they miss me, that it's a bummer I disappeared, that Dad's an arsehole. 'Please write back, Jodie, so we know you're okay.' I'd just turned eleven when I was whisked away. Billy, thirteen months older than me, was still a kid himself, but Dan, two years and two months older than me, must have been maturing.

In contrast to their scribble, my letters are carefully composed, grammatically correct and always dated. My OCD wasn't entirely self-driven—they were written in the homework room with other boarders on a Sunday night under strict supervision. If our letters weren't tidy and neat, grammatically correct, with accurate spelling, they were attacked with a red pen and we had to rewrite them. They weren't censored for content though, because I describe being kidnapped by strangers and taken to a faraway, forbidding place, how homesick I feel, how much I miss them and Mum. I beg them to write back. I also tell them about horse-riding in groups on forest trails.

I'm so sad we never got to read each other's letters and know each other's feelings. It's incomprehensible that the only witness to, and cause of our growing dismay, was Dad.

Mum drops me off at Ian's chambers. I'm very nervous about seeing him again. I recognise him, and his voice, once we come face-to-face. I tell him I remember he was kind to me, and how his wife Margaret helped me pack, but recalling how distraught I was at the time—the way my father went back to work without saying goodbye, leaving them to deal with my distress—upsets me now and I cry, as I do these days, all too easily.

When I tell Ian how my father stole our mail, he says, as he makes a note of it, 'It's a crime—a commonwealth offence—to interfere with and/or steal other people's mail, with severe penalties, up to ten years imprisonment, depending on the scale of the theft.'

Stealing a shoebox full of kids' letters won't get a slap on the wrist!

Anne is angry and so am I. Emboldened by the rehearsal of my options with Anne and Christine, I declare, 'I'll never forgive my father for the bad things he did to me.' I don't elaborate, and Ian doesn't press me for details, but he notes the fact on his writing pad. 'Nor will I forgive him his infidelities and the emotional and psychological abuse he is STILL inflicting on my mother. I need legal advice. I'd prefer mediation to going to court, but either way, I want compensation and reparations, and an apology would be good too.'

Mum is seeing Ian solo at 10 a.m. tomorrow, but he makes an extra appointment for Mum and me on Good Friday morning, to determine if there are sufficient grounds—and evidence—for a criminal case to be brought against my father. I don't know how I'll go talking about it in front of Mum.

On the walk back to the motel I discuss the day's events with Anne and calm down. I'm expecting Mum to be in our apartment, going through the documents she filched from Dad's filing cabinet, but she is missing, as is her car. I experience a flash of panic, but after checking her belongings are still in her room—they are—I pull myself together, curl up on my bed and write a summary of the day's events in PS. Mum turns up just in time for dinner.

We eat dinner in the motel restaurant in almost silence, both non-committal about how we spent the afternoon; Mum shutting down my questions, me doing the same to her.

Back in our apartment she goes into the bathroom and shuts the door to have a shower, a good moment to ring Shaun and have a private conversation.

He's pleased I've recovered my letters, but blathers on about what *he's* been doing. 'Mum's car is still driveable engine- and tyre-wise, if not windows- or windscreen-wise, so I drove it into town to the insurance panel-beaters this morning. Talk about a windy trip! An assessor is coming up from Coffs tomorrow to decide whether it's salvageable. And Joe is delaying the new tenants from taking possession until he's repaired the chimney and the broken windows and reinstalled the water tank and rebuilt the lean-to and replaced the packing shed roof. Long story short, Mum flew to Sydney this morning, after packing up *every-thing* for the removalists so Dad won't have to drive up, and I'm staying on to help Joe.'

He pauses for breath, or maybe he's giving me space to comment.

'Are you saying you'll be at *Booyul* when Mum and I get back?'

'Yep. All next week, including for the RAG exhibition and the Grafton Show!'

'That's great, Shaun!' I try to sound enthusiastic, but I feel as flat as a doormat.

Chapter Twenty-eight

Thursday, 13 April 1995

This morning I have time to kill while Mum attends her 'private' appointment with Ian. The main street is busy, lots of people doing last-minute pre-Easter shopping. In my jeans pocket is leftover cash from Shaun's fifty dollars, plus a fifty-dollar note Dan was surprisingly willing to lend me 'in case of an emergency', like having to buy a bus or train ticket back to Grafton if Mum does a flit and leaves me with Dad. I no longer believe she'll do that to me—not after discovering the bastard is still seeing my ex-piano teacher and going away with her over Easter. It was almost dark when Mum returned to the motel last night. I don't know where she went or what she did, but she did come back. I must stop obsessing about being abandoned again. Still, it feels good to have money in my pocket.

To fill in time before we meet in her favourite coffee shop in the mall, I decide to walk past Macleod Chambers. It's one street down from the main drag. If what Felicity said on the phone yesterday morning is correct, Dad and my ex-piano teacher are very likely in there. My watch says 10:05. The thought is giving me an adrenaline buzz. I'm almost opposite the building, on the footpath on the other side of the road, behind the parked cars lining the kerb, when the glass doors open and Felicity emerges, rugged up against the chill, holding a bundle of letters!

Whoops!

I instinctively duck and pull the hood of my new jacket further over my forehead, but Felicity barely glances in my direction before she turns left and heads for the post office.

'They'll be in his office alone,' I mutter to Anne. 'I'll creep in and surprise them!'

And do what?

The only weapon I have is my voice, a barrage of words that could come out of my mouth denouncing them. 'Scream at them, accuse them, condemn them, blame them.'

Whoops!

Another shock! I'm frozen to the footpath! My ex-piano teacher is hurrying up the other side of the street towards Macleod Chambers.

She's late!

She arrives, the glass doors open, and she enters the building. My heart is racing from excitement and fear, outrage and injury, but I'm grown up now. I'm no longer a timid, terrified child of ten, nine, eight, seven … I hurry across the road and follow her inside.

The door to Felicity's anteroom is open.

I approach the doorway. My father, perched on Felicity's desk, is kissing my ex-piano teacher with passion. Eventually, she extricates herself. Neither of them notices me. He tries to draw her towards him again as she removes her jacket, but she deftly evades his groping hands and saunters out of sight beyond the anteroom door. He says something to her, and I shiver to hear his voice, and *her* voice as she responds. Then her laugh rings out and for sure I remember her laugh! And when my father throws his head back and laughs in response, happy and carefree, I burn with rage, helpless and mute, ten years old again.

Then my father sees me. Felicity would surely have contacted him and told him about the raid on his office yesterday; he would have checked his desk and found the letters gone and discovered documents missing from his filing cabinet. And yet he looks surprised, his expression confused, uncertain, as if he recognises me, but does not understand why I am here.

The glass doors slide open and I glance sideways. Gliding rapidly towards me on a draught of cold air is a skinny, masked man dressed entirely in black, armed with a crossbow. It is loaded with three red arrows. I recoil, dumb with terror, but he turns towards the anteroom.

My father's face contorts into an expression of horror and panic. Shouting a warning he leaps off the desk. My hearing aids pick up a whistle as an arrow pierces his diaphragm. He grunts, collapses onto the carpet with a thud, gasping for air, gurgling and choking, thrashing his arms as blood oozes and bubbles around the shaft of the arrow, staining his shirt bright red.

The stranger moves swiftly into the anteroom and turns towards my ex-piano teacher, still out of sight beyond the door. Her wail, 'Carl! No!' is recorded in my brain, as is the whistle of the arrow, her deep groan, another thud. He moves towards her, out of my view, and in that instant, I flee. The glass doors slide open, I leap down the steps, turn right, bolt down the street, veer left at the corner, sprint up the side street to the main street and head for the mall, ducking and weaving through the throng until I arrive at the coffee shop, where I hide in a booth and remove my too hot, too colourful jacket and stuff it into my backpack.

The waitress approaches. She recognises me now. 'What would you like?' she asks.

I'm hyperventilating. I can hardly catch my breath to breathe, let alone speak.

'Hot ch-chocolate p-p-p-please.'

I press my hands and wrists between my thighs under the table to subdue the trembling.

'Anything else?'

I shake my head.

'Sure, no problem.' She looks at me strangely as she departs.

The Ventolin is in the side pocket of my backpack. I inhale, trying to steady my breathing between puffs, but with the adrenaline coursing through my body the Ventolin only makes me more jittery. The room is hot and airless. I'm clammy, sweating with exertion and terror. Elbows on the table, supporting my forehead on my fingers, I shield my face. My heart will not slow down. I feel dizzy and faint, my breathing rapid and shallow. I shiver, shudder and shake from head to foot. I try to breathe more deeply, hold each breath, count to three, release it slowly into my cupped hands, breathe the exhalation back in. I do this several times.

My hot chocolate arrives, and I wrap my trembling fingers around the mug, clutching it tightly as I sip the milky sweetness through the foam, trying to soothe myself.

'He had *three* arrows,' I whisper to Anne. 'He could have killed *me*! Did Felicity come back while he was there? Did he kill her too?'

I slowly sip the hot chocolate, shivering, shuddering intermittently, unable to shake the vision of my dying father, or the sound of her panicked cry, *'Carl! No!'*

Beyond the babble filling the cafe I can hear sirens.

Police? Ambulance?

My brain plays and replays the scene. I try to replace it with Felicity discovering them on the carpet pierced by arrows but still alive; I visualise her calling the ambulance as well as the police, but Anne rejects my illusions.

They're both dead. And chances are, Felicity is dead too.

I'm overwhelmed by intense, unnameable feelings.

Mum arrives, pale and shaken.

'A cappuccino, please,' she tells the hovering waitress.

I don't want her questioning me, so I question her.

'Was it upsetting talking to Ian? You don't look too good.'

She shakes her head. 'The police have cordoned off Macleod Chambers with tape like it's a crime scene. Police cars and ambulances are parked outside. Passers-by are congregating. The local press is there. I can't imagine what's happened, but it can't be good.'

I'm staring at her while she's telling me this, but she's looking away and down, spreading and smoothing a paper serviette across her knees.

Tell her!

'Lucky for Hugh and his floozie they've gone away,' she adds, still not looking at me.

No, Mum. Their luck has run out.

'I hope Felicity is okay.' She glances at me momentarily, then looks around the café.

She'll be a mess—if she's alive.

'The police will have CCTV footage.' Mum glances at me again. 'There are cameras everywhere, inside *and* outside. It's like Fort Knox.' She watches the waitress approaching.

Shit! I forgot about the CCTV. I start shaking again. The waitress arrives with Mum's coffee. I notice a tremor in Mum's hands too, as she picks up the cup. She sips carefully. I gulp down the last of my no-longer-hot chocolate.

'You're very quiet,' she says.

'Mum—'

'Hmm?'

'I'll be on the CCTV footage. I was there.'

She stares at me. She looks horrified.

'It's bad, Mum. It's *really, really* bad.'

'Omigod!' She whispers, 'What did you see?'

I don't know how to tell you …'

'Just say it!' she hisses, but I barely begin telling her and the hiss morphs into a wail. 'Why did you enter the building at all, if you saw Felicity leaving? Why did you have to go in there!' She puts down her cup, gags her mouth with her palms, looks around to see if she's attracted attention.

I've barely revealed *anything* and already she's beside herself! I don't know how I manage to keep it together. Telling her about it is like re-experiencing it. Keeping my voice low, I describe what happened. Mum has grasped her jaw, her mouth firmly covered by her palms to stifle any reaction or sound, while she gazes at me wide-eyed.

'She knew him, Mum. She wailed "Carl! No!" But he still shot her. I'm sure they're dead. I don't know about Felicity— he had a third arrow.'

Mum shudders. She takes her hands from her mouth to dab at her eyes with the serviette. 'Oh Jodie, I'm so, so sorry you had to see that.' It's like she's devastated. 'You on the CCTV will really complicate things. We'll have to tell the police right away!' Her hands shake as she takes money from her purse to pay for our drinks. She seems scared, panicky almost. 'They won't appreciate any delay. Carl is her husband's name.'

PS
Thursday, 13 April 1995
Late

The interrogations took forever. I'm shattered. I had to relive the ordeal over and over, answering repetitive questions from police, detectives and social workers, male and female. The CCTV footage verified my story. The images were in black-and-white, no sound.

The CCTV captured both killings. The perpetrator's face was masked, but the fact I heard my ex-piano teacher cry out his name—Carl—her revenge in the last millisecond of her life, was a breakthrough for the detectives. Mum told them it was her husband's name. A huge manhunt is underway.

I asked the social worker what would happen to their children, with their mother dead and their father on the run, but she didn't have an answer. I told the police the name of their street and described the two-storey house where I'd had my piano 'lessons' while she and my father conducted their long-term affair.

When I told the police I'd witnessed their sexual interactions for years, Mum fell apart. Now I'm scared if I tell Ian what happened to me in front of her, she'll relapse and have another nervous breakdown.

Mum volunteered the information to the police that she and I visited Macleod Chambers yesterday morning, 'to pick up personal items'. Just as well she did tell them, because they already knew! Felicity told them while she was being interviewed separately, and when they replayed Wednesday's CCTV footage, there we were, in black-and-white, from the moment we arrived and parked and waited, then walked up the street out of range of the camera towards the post office (if they check the post office's CCTV they'll see us going into the telephone booth!) Then we returned to our car, collected the briefcase and my Paddy Pallin bag, crossed the road and entered Macleod Chambers. And cameras inside the building and in Dad's office recorded us marching past Felicity into his office and going through his desk and filing cabinet.

Mum had to justify why we were on the premises, and our every action. She explained she was Dad's business partner as well as his wife and she needed documents that belonged to her for her lawyer. She told one of the detectives interviewing us, 'I expected Hugh to be there, but when we arrived Felicity said he'd gone away for Easter.'

That was a lie. We *knew* he wasn't there, from the phone call. And Felicity didn't speak a word to us when we marched past her; she was too gobsmacked. I continue writing:

Thursday's CCTV footage showed Felicity leaving the building, my ex-piano teacher entering soon after, me following her, the killer following me. Then the murders, and me running away. Carl fled soon after I did. Was Felicity lucky she'd gone to the PO? Or was it part of the plan? The police were very interested in the fact she was conveniently absent. And they were equally interested in the fact I was there. Their questions implied they thought we both had something to do with it. They also took a dim view of the fact I didn't immediately notify them that a crime had been committed. Instead, I gave the perpetrator time to escape.

The police told Mum we could go home to Grafton, but warned us to expect further questioning in future interviews at Grafton police station. The bodies of the deceased were taken to the morgue in Penrith for autopsies, and they asked Mum was she willing to formally identify them before we left. Turns out Mum and my ex-piano teacher were 'best friends' until five years ago, when the pink letter exposed her affair with my father. Mum knew Carl really well too. And their kids.

A couple of police officers drove us to the morgue. I waited in the car with the driver, while the other officer escorted Mum inside. Poor Mum looked like death warmed up when she came out. They warned us coroners usually take 'quite some time' to complete their reports, and to expect another long wait before the coronial inquest and trial—assuming Carl is captured and taken into custody and depending on how he pleads.

It will cast a shadow over our lives for years to come. Easter will forever be a reminder.

I put down my pen, shake my right arm, and stretch my shoulders, neck and back to untwist my muscles. Writing in bed isn't a great idea, but I'm too scared to sleep, afraid I'll have nightmares. The flashbacks are bad enough. Writing about it helps, surprisingly, like it's one step removed. The motel is very quiet without my HAs in my ears, and with the door to my bedroom closed I don't know if Mum is awake or asleep.

Since leaving the morgue we've steered clear of talking to each other. We agreed to not watch television tonight, in case it was reported on the news. We're both traumatised, in different ways, for different reasons, which neither of us fully grasps, for ourselves or for each other. Mum is beside herself horrified that I witnessed the events, but something else is eating away at her. Maybe she still loved Dad, in spite of everything, and she's grieving. It's awful the way the scene keeps replaying in my head, like a movie I can't turn off. When something distracts me, it stops, temporarily, but the moment the distraction ends, or something triggers it, the scene replays again, in technicolour, complete with sound effects.

The letter from my 'deceased' father—my 'murdered' father, is still unopened. I'm extremely nervous about reading it, but curiosity is outweighing anxiety. It's also a distraction, and I need to be distracted! I open it carefully, to avoid tearing the envelope. There is no date.

Jodie,

You are not my daughter. Ask your mother to tell you the truth. Bored with marriage and motherhood, she had an affair, and you were the result. In March 1979, she farmed out my sons to her parents and escaped to Adelaide to attend Writers Week, saying she 'needed a break'. She abandoned those little boys for eight weeks.

On her return, she initiated a sexual relationship with me immediately, and soon after told me she was pregnant.

When you were born on 15 January 1980, I did the maths. There was no way you were mine. A DNA/PCR paternity test confirmed it.

When I confronted your mother with the results, she told me it was 'Just a fling', but she also said, in the heat and hurt of the moment, that your father was 'the love of her life'. Her excuse: I was too busy working. It's true, I worked very hard, trying to grow the business and build us a home.

I admit I was an absent husband to her and an absent father to the boys much of the time, but I was not having affairs. Not then.

After your birth, when the DNA test confirmed my suspicions, I decided 'what's good for the goose is good for the gander'.

Your mother wanted our marriage to work, but I no longer felt the same commitment. I stayed because of my sons. Also, her father's money had financed the business, and a break up would be messy and expensive. My solution was to 'do my own thing' and keep my 'other life' secret and separate for the sake of peace.

Regardless of my many peccadilloes, your piano teacher has been the love of MY life, and over the years we have maintained our relationship despite your attempt to destroy it.

Involving you in piano lessons with her was a near-fatal mistake. When you snatched the pink letter from me and gave it to your mother you started a train-wreck. After she discovered the rest of the letters, she had a nervous breakdown and nearly died. Secrets are best left unexposed, Jodie. You exposed mine—and you are not forgiven.

I'm glad you are in boarding school, out of sight, out of mind.
It is better without you in my daily life, a constant reminder.
You are NOT my daughter.
I do NOT want you to have a relationship with my sons.
Nor do I want them to have a relationship with you.
They are MY sons. YOU do NOT belong in MY family.

HM

Chapter Twenty-nine

Good Friday, 14 April 1995

In the darkness before dawn, sleepless and desolate, I tiptoe into Mum's room and crawl into her bed, still clutching the letter. I don't know if Mum is awake or asleep, but she wraps an arm around me.

I open my eyes to bright light, realise I'm in the motel, in Mum's bed, and turn over. She's lying beside me, reading the letter! I pull the blankets and quilt up to my eyes, wanting as little of me as possible to be visible. If I could disappear I would. Forever.

She looks directly at me so I can read her lips. She speaks clearly. 'What a stinker of a letter! What a cruel, mean bastard! What an arsehole!' She taps the letter forcefully with a finger. '"Bored with marriage and motherhood", I "escaped", I "needed a break". What I needed was *support*, but I never experienced a scrap of empathy or understanding from him.'

Does she mean he was cruel and mean to me? Or cruel and mean to her?

Probably both.

'Hang on a minute,' I beg her. 'I'll just get my HAs.' I return in seconds, climb back into her bed, and ask her, 'How *were* you feeling with two little ones and no support?'

She looks at me, like she's trying to figure out what, or how, or if, to tell me. 'Desperate! Exhausted. Anxious. Overwhelmed. Trapped. Alone. Lonely. Numb. Tired! *So* tired! Suicidal. Y'know, perinatal and post-natal depression weren't acknowledged by the medical profession until *last year*. When you kids were babies, post-natal depression was called "the baby blues". I was expected to just snap out of it, get over it. Dan was thirteen-months old, barely walking, when Billy was born. My parents were miles away, Hugh worked seven days a week. His mum had her own life. I had no friends I could call on with a little boy and a baby in tow.'

'Why didn't you have friends?'

'When I married Hugh, I moved to *his* part of the world. I knew no one. I started Art School, but I was soon pregnant with Dan and felt too awful with morning sickness to continue. And soon after Dan was born, even though I was breast-feeding him, I fell pregnant with Billy. With Hugh working all the time I was totally isolated and lonely!'

And yet you isolated your own daughter! Why was that okay?

'I tried to be a good housekeeper, wife and mother, looking after Hugh and Dan—and then Billy when he came along.' She pulls and twists her hair, her expression bleak. 'But I just spiralled down into a very dark place I couldn't seem to get out of. Thankfully my parents agreed to look after the little boys and give me a break.'

'Is it true you had an affair in Adelaide? And I'm the result?'

She hesitates, looks at me, her expression a mix of defiance and I'm not sure what. *Shame?*

'Yes,' she says. 'It is true. I'm so sorry you had to find out this way.' She waves the letter about, her other hand reaching for it as if she intends to crush it.

I snatch it from her. 'Don't! It's mine.' I fold it, carefully following the original folds.

'Why do you want to keep it?'

I shrug. 'Because it's about *me*. It's *my* story.'

'I wanted to tell you, but I never quite knew when to, or how to. Hugh was only part of your story. Your biological father was, is, I know he's still alive—the kindest, most intelligent, empathic human being I had the good fortune to meet.' She holds and strokes the heart-shaped opal pendant at her throat. 'You were conceived with love, Jodie, not that either of us knew I'd conceived at the time. I was heartbroken to leave him, I missed him terribly, but I had to look after my two little boys and do my best to make a go of my marriage to *their* father. I tried to reignite the spark with Hugh. I put all my energy into looking after him, and your brothers, and getting through my pregnancy with you, and then managing *three* little kids.'

She gazes out the window into the early dawn light. 'Hugh wasn't remotely enthusiastic about my pregnancy with you, but I put it down to him worrying how I'd manage *three* small children, when I couldn't cope with two. I didn't realise he was harbouring doubts about your paternity. After you were born, he organised the DNA test on the quiet and then confronted me with the results. It was *very* difficult for a while, but I thought we'd got through it. I had no idea he was such an unforgiving man.'

There's a lot my mother has no idea of.

'Hugh *did* do activities with the boys. I thought he was being helpful, trying to give me a break. You *were* left out, but I put it down to your deafness, and your asthma, and the fact you were a bit of a handful. *I* was neglected too! It was often just you and me, kid!' She gives me a brief, rueful smile. 'He was *always* busy; he'd go out, or away, without me, a *lot*. He'd take the boys away for weekends, camping. He taught them to drive off-road. He had many interests that didn't include me. He never introduced me to his friends, or acquaintances, or clients. He'd go away for so-called weekend "conferences" or play in golfing tournaments and leave me at home with the three of you.'

She draws in a breath and releases it with a noisy sigh. 'My artwork saved me. And so did you—homeschooling you was a diversion for me. You *always* loved learning new things. You caught on so quickly, despite your deafness. When Hugh offered to take you to piano lessons, I was delighted he wanted to help me *and* take an interest in you.'

I squirm to escape the horrible feelings crawling over me like cockroaches, but Mum doesn't seem to notice. Her expression is wistful as she gazes into my eyes and strokes an eyebrow with a finger. 'You have beautiful eyes, Jodie. So blue. Your father's eyes are blue.' She twirls a strand of my hair around a finger. 'His hair is blond too—or was. He might be grey by now.'

'What is his name?'

'Paul.'

'Did you tell Paul you were pregnant with me?'

There is a potent silence. I know how to read it.

'No, Jodie, I didn't. Back then, I thought it best not to make things any more complicated than they were. I *had* to stay with Hugh—I had Dan and Billy to think about. I wanted Hugh to believe you were *his* little girl. I was thrilled I was having a daughter, and I wanted him to feel the same way. When he did the DNA test, and proved you *weren't* his child, I was devastated. I tried so hard to make our marriage work and encourage him to accept you. I hoped time would heal the wounds. You were such a beautiful little girl. *I* felt rejected by him as his wife, but I didn't realise how intensely he'd rejected you too.'

'Did you *ever* tell Paul he had a daughter?'

'No. He wasn't married when you were conceived, but he did marry later, and I thought it best not to-not to complicate things for *him*. I know his wife died in a tragic accident a couple of years ago. I also know he has two sons—your half-brothers.'

So, she's kept tabs on him all my life and never told me. And come to think of it, Dan and Billy are also my 'half-brothers'. The realisation shatters my already fragile sense of belonging.

'I'm going to have a shower.'

I spend ages under the shower, but it cannot wash away what I've read and heard, or how I feel.

When it's time to go to our appointment with Ian, Mum says, 'It's a different ballgame now, for *both* of us. I need to ask him about probate, and how to action Hugh's will, which I happen to have in my briefcase—'

'Whatever,' I answer, my head down, pulling on my Reeboks, tears dripping onto the carpet. 'I've got nothing to say to him now, anyway. I just want to go home. Today.'

'I know, Pet. I'm homesick too.' She fetches the tissue box and gives me a handful. 'It's been a rough twenty-four hours. But *Gwongorella* will help us recover and heal.'

We pack up, check out, and go to see Ian. After commiserating with both of us for all of thirty seconds, he talks with Mum about what she needs to do. During their conversation she says, 'I want money from Hugh's estate to be set aside for Jodie: a lump sum in compensation, and for reparations, for her to use in any way she chooses to help her heal from everything that's happened to her over the years, and pay for her education, including university fees.'

I watch Ian make a note of this and smile wanly at Mum. Money can't repair the damage done, but I'm grateful she's acknowledging it.

Ian asks Mum questions and continues to note down her answers. Then he turns to me.

'Regarding the coronial inquest, Jodie, the inquiry will examine the circumstances and facts surrounding the deaths and no doubt the coroner will declare it a case of unlawful killing. Assuming the perpetrator is apprehended, he'll be held in remand—meaning behind bars while awaiting trial—though there may not *be* a trial if he pleads guilty; either way you'll be called as a witness. Felicity will be required to testify too, about what she knew before the event and what she saw after the event. All you need to do Jodie, is tell the truth about what you saw.'

After pulling into the now-familiar truck stop in Port Macquarie, we are on our way again, the near full moon illuminating the highway.

To pass the time, and to avoid dwelling on the events of the last few days, I silently relive—and embellish—my experience with Shaun under the last full moon down by the billabong, trying to rekindle the feeling of connection, the feeling of loving and desiring him. I'm visualising being with him tomorrow night, walking arm-in-arm down the track lit by another full moon, this time to the bank of the creek. No Saab to kill the moment. No irrigation sprays to saturate us. Only my negative, unwanted thoughts and emotions can sabotage me.

Kangaroos leap across the road in our headlights and Mum yelps in fright. One is slower than the rest and she hits the end of its tail with a thump. Is she losing concentration, her mind wandering like mine, reliving the events of the last couple of days? What if she falls asleep!

'Poor 'roo! I hope it's okay,' she says.

Shaken, now hyper-vigilant, I look out for more kangaroos and keep her talking, helping *both* of us to stay awake by asking questions about Paul.

I think she's enjoying reminiscing. His initials are PS, which is cool, because I've called my latest journal PS, meaning 'Post-Shaun', but now it can denote my biological father as well.

Sixteen years ago, Mum tells me, she met Paul at the Adelaide Writers Festival. A professor at Adelaide University, he was launching one of his books. He's still there. He's written university courses on the history and influence of Australian literature, including Feminist, Indigenous and Immigrant literature, and published books, papers and collections of his own poetry.

Realising Mum has kept tabs on him over the years stirs painful emotions inside me. I feel jealous. I've missed out. She's lied to me by omission, keeping this secret locked inside her. Not sharing it with me feels like a betrayal. Cruel. I suppress my anger, hurt and confusion. Maybe, sometime in the future, I'll let her know how I feel, but not now while she's driving, not while I want to extract information from her.

I'll check out Grafton City Library and the TAFE library for copies of his books and any other information I can unearth about him. I'll take another look at the English Language and Literature courses on offer in *The Good Guide to Australian Universities*, which Shaun gave to me, especially Australian literature. Professor Paul S, and his works, might be listed. I'll go to Angus & Robertson and see if they stock his books. If they don't, I'll ask if they can order them from the publishers. Maybe *he* is the reason I love reading and writing, even if my writing so far is limited to letter-writing and journalling and essay-writing. Maybe I've inherited his *literary* genes as well as my eye and hair colour! I'll read and study his published work, especially his poetry, then write to him and ask what inspired him to write certain poems, without letting on I'm his daughter. That revelation can come later, after we've established a relationship through our correspondence. Whatever happens, I'm determined to meet him.

There's no harm in dreaming.

I'm grateful Anne isn't throwing cold water on my plans.

It's late when we turn into the lane. Our farmhouse is a silvery silhouette in the moonlight. We can hear Cleo and Patra barking as we drive towards our gate.

Dan's car isn't in the carport, which is no surprise. They're in for a shock when they get home. I don't envy Mum having to tell them their father is dead. Murdered. They'll be shattered. It's strange how detached from their father I feel. I guess his letter was like an amputation. It severed me from him, body and soul, mind and heart. Instead of being heartbroken by his lack of love, I'm liberated. I don't have to mourn him. I don't have to care. I have my own father. And it's amazing how attached to him I feel; he loved my mother when I was conceived, and I love him now, or the idea of him anyway. At some deep level of my being, I believe we will meet one day and he will love me too.

I rummage around in my backpack for my newly acquired torch from Paddy Pallin so I can visit the dogs and say hello.

They're ecstatic to see me. When I let myself into their enclosure, they nearly knock me over in their enthusiasm. The torchlight reveals their water bowls are full; there are remnants of dried food in their food bowls; a couple of bones are lying on the floorboards along with some doggie toys I don't recognise. Their poo has been removed.

They each select a toy and bring it to me like an offering, a gift.

They must be Saab's toys.

I talk to them and pat them for a while, before encouraging them to go back into their kennels. As I'm leaving the enclosure, I see a scrap of paper attached to the inside of the wire door. It's a note! I read it by the light of my torch.

Welcome home!
See you when you get back.

know it's from Shaun because he's drawn a tiny canoe, with two stick figures paddling upstream, a shining sun on the top left side, and a full moon with a smiley face on the top right.

I feel a twinge of doubt, of uncertainty. Is it fear? If it is fear, what am I afraid of? Having to tell Shaun everything? Having to go through it all again? Having to cope with Dan and Billy's distress? They'll want to hear every detail too. Right now, all I want to do is crawl into my bed and sleep.

Mum is inside the house; the lights have come on in the kitchen and living room. The glow spreads across the grass as she opens the west veranda door and steps out onto the boards. She passes by the dogs' enclosure on her way to the car.

'Hi Cleo, hi Patra. Jodie, please help me unpack the car. I need to go to bed.'

Chapter Thirty

Easter Saturday, 15 April 1995

I've woken up in a bad, sad mood. Unpleasant and half-remembered dreams, nightmares really, linger in my memory. I take the day's pill, then peek into Mum's room. She's still asleep. I'm not surprised after the long drive home. I pull on yesterday's jeans and skivvy; it's chilly and I need to go to the loo before responding to Cleo and Patra's whimpered pleas to be fed and then let out of their enclosure.

I wash and dry my face, insert my HAs, brush my hair, replace my glasses on my nose and over my ears beneath my HAs, when I hear a knock.

Shaun!

My heart sinks. I open the back door. He's already opened the screen door. He drops a bag of dried dog food on the top step, crosses the threshold and takes me in his arms.

I wordlessly push him away, go to the door between the dining room and living room and close it, then retreat into the kitchen, but he follows me, and with Faigan a witness, embraces me again. This time he kisses me, something I've dreamed about, and imagined, and described in my journal and unsent letters to him but never experienced being initiated by him. *And I don't want it!* It's inexplicable. Incomprehensible. It's as if I've fallen out of love.

I extract myself—he lets go of me readily enough—and ask him as I turn away, 'Would you like coffee?' I fill up the electric jug at the sink.

'Yes, please.' Then he exclaims, 'I *missed* you!'

I shrug, don't look at him, put the plug into the jug and switch it on. He is still standing too close for comfort, so I move away and start setting up the tray.

'I stayed to help Joe so I'd be here when you got back.'

I turn my back on him, open the pantry and take out the container of muesli. 'I need to eat. Do you want anything?'

'No, thanks. I've had breakfast.'

I fetch a couple of mugs from the dish drainer and milk from the fridge.

He steps back, out of my way. 'Dan and Billy skipped school and took off for the beach the day you guys left, after asking me to look after Cleo and Patra.'

'You're kidding!'

Apparently not. Disappointment, anger and resentment surge through me. While their father was murdered in front of my eyes, they wagged school and surfed! 'They couldn't come to the Blue Mountains with *me*, for moral support! Oh no! They had to look after the dogs and go to school, didn't they!' I'm radiating sarcasm and hurt. 'Liars!'

'At least *I* had the dogs for company,' Shaun responds mildly. 'They've been with me the whole time, except at night.'

'Well, thanks for that. I'm sure they appreciated it. The dogs I mean.'

'I needed them as much as they needed me!'

'Would you mind giving them some dried food before I let them out?'

'Sure.'

I observe him through the distorting glass panes of the kitchen window as he enters the dog enclosure with the bag of dog food. 'The man I thought was my father—my brothers' father—is dead,' I tell him, knowing he cannot hear me. 'Murdered, two days ago.' There's no way I can say it to his face. Not before Dan and Billy know. Truth is, I cannot bear the thought of another interrogation, another reliving of the trauma. I turn away from the window, spoon coffee grounds into the plunger, shake muesli into a bowl, add milk and cut up a banana.

Shaun returns, places the depleted bag of dog food on top of the fuel stove, and says, 'Thanks for ringing me Wednesday night. It was great to hear you got your letters back. Have you read them?'

'Of course I've read them!' I sound irritable. 'And I'm *very* glad to have them back.'

I know he's trying to get a conversation going, but I'm not in the mood. I say nothing more about the letters or anything else. I sit opposite rather than beside him at the dining room table and deflect him from questioning me further by asking him what *he's* been doing since I left. While I munch on muesli, he describes, yet again, how he and Joe will have to replace the shattered leadlight windows with plain modern glass, and how they manoeuvred the water tank back onto its wooden stand with a hired crane and the tractor, and the insurance assessor has written off Wendy's car. And he and Joe … *boring, boring, boring …*

Mum suddenly appears, dressed, and says, 'Hi' on her way to the bathroom. She must have heard Shaun's voice. She returns, and he offers to pour her a coffee. She accepts and sits at the table while he fetches another mug. They chat, but she too avoids talking about what happened. She catches my eye, raises her eyebrows. I shake my head. We are in agreement. Now is not the time. It is too momentous. Too painful. Too raw.

Shaun, oblivious, invites us to come up to *Booyul* to see the repairs.

I glimpse a vulnerability in Mum. She seems unnerved, like she's adrift, unmoored by events. I'm obsessed with the thought, the suspicion, that she had something to do with it.

How did Carl know they were there?

'I must water my grevilleas and nasturtiums and herbs,' she says, finishing her coffee. 'They'll be desiccated by now.' She disappears out the back door.

In due course, the three of us walk up to *Booyul* together. Shaun chats non-stop to Mum-in-the-middle, while I have a two's-company-three's-a-crowd feeling on the outside edge.

'The chimney is the next big job,' he tells her. 'It's set for Monday, some builder friends of Joe's are coming out to lend a hand.' He and Mum communicate adult-to-adult and I'm aware she's twelve years older than he is—and he's twelve years older than me.

Joe is busy rebuilding the lean-to where his tractor and trailer and Shaun's ute used to be housed. Mum holds planks steady on the sawhorse while he cuts them to size, planes them smooth, and chips out wedges with a mallet and chisel.

I help by picking up bits of the lean-to blown the farthest away across the yard, adding the planks to a pile. Towards lunchtime, I mutter to Shaun, 'I'm going home.'

'Do you feel like a paddle?' he asks me in front of Mum. 'I've made us some lunch.'

Mum doesn't say a word.

We paddle upstream in silence. As we approach our island, Shaun suggests we moor the canoe and eat lunch there. The thought makes me more nervous than the first time a couple of months ago. I didn't like the way he came onto me this morning. It's ironical, considering how I've yearned for his affection and how elusive he's been. It's like a dance. When I chased him, longing for intimacy, he kept a distance between us. Now he's chasing me, *I'm* the one running away! What's changed? Is this the angry stage of grieving? I just want him gone. Him dragging out his departure, putting off the final goodbye, feels like slow torture. I need to get it over with so I can mourn in peace.

We tie the canoe to a grevillea root, sit on his towel and eat in silence. I have so much to tell him, but I cannot bring myself to talk about any of it.

He speaks first. 'Jodie, I'm sorry about this morning. I've not been in a good place since you left and I was looking for reassurance, but I was only thinking of myself.' His apology sounds rehearsed.

I nod, but stiffly, not looking at him.

'I was very lonely before you came to *Gwongorella*. After you left for the Blue Mountains, and Mum flew back to Sydney, I felt the same loneliness all over again.'

I *still* say nothing.

'I *couldn't* leave *Booyul* before you got back. I needed to make sure we were okay.'

I don't—I can't—I won't—look at him.

'But it's obvious we're not okay.' I know he's looking at me. 'What's wrong, Jodie?'

I snap at him in a strange fury. 'You're *leaving* me!'

'I *need* to leave, Jodie.' He sounds desperate, helpless. 'But separation will help us decide if we're meant to be together, if we truly belong together. Let's face it, I'm more likely to lose you than you are to lose me. *My* feelings for *you* haven't changed.' He stows the lunch boxes in his backpack. 'Anyway...' He hesitates.

'Anyway what?'

'I consoled myself by—' He stops.

I finally look at him, curious. He seems embarrassed.

'By what?'

'By reading your letters. I dug them up.'

'You *what?*' A hot wave of rage swamps me.

'You heard.'

'And you *read* them?'

'Yes.'

'*All* of them?'

He nods, sheepish, but defiant. 'They're beautifully written—and very graphic.'

Was that why he was all over me this morning? 'Well, I don't *feel* like that anymore!' I sound as furious as I feel. 'You had *no right!*'

'I *know* I had no right!' His voice has suddenly hardened. 'But it was necessary for my self-preservation, Jodie, knowing *you'd* dig them up the moment I left! I couldn't risk that!'

'You didn't trust me!'

'No! I did *not* trust you. Not. At. All. And my lack of trust was justified!' His voice is emphatic and angry. 'You put an empty, unused journal in with those letters, for no other reason than to deceive me, to lull me into a false sense of security, while you kept the *real* journal, with all its dangerous entries, all sorts of made-up stuff about us written in it—and I know what you're capable of writing, now I've read your letters! Without that journal I'm *still* not safe! How do you think that feels for me? Can you put yourself in my boots for just one minute?'

I'm enraged by his audacity, deeply hurt by his lack of trust, but I hear him loud and clear. I *don't* deserve his trust. I am *not* worthy of it. And we both know it.

'I'm sorry, Jodie—sorry I can't trust you. I lost trust when you kept that letter, after promising me you'd bury *everything*. I'm not apologising for digging up your letters; I feel safer for doing so. And I'm not sorry I read them. I'm *glad* you felt that way about me. I'm *glad* you loved me. I was amazed to read how much you loved me!' His voice sounds like it has a crack in it.

He leans back on his hands and recites: '"How do I love thee? Let me count the ways. I love thee to the depth and breadth and height my soul can reach … I love thee to the level of every day's most quiet need, by sun and candlelight."'

Elizabeth Barrett Browning's sonnet 43. I quoted it in one of my letters. I interrupt him: '"I love thee with a love I seemed to lose with my lost saints. I love thee with the breath, smiles, tears, of all my life. And … I shall love thee better after death."'

At last, we gaze at each other. He reaches for my hand. I don't pull away.

'Please forgive me, Jodie. For leaving you. For reading the letters you wrote to me. Maybe it is over between us. But I'm *glad* I read your letters to me. I'm glad I have them. As for your journal, I have to trust that you will protect me, that you will keep it—and me—safe.'

'My mother is more concerned about the way her late husband behaved towards me than she is about *your* behaviour towards me.'

'*Late* husband? Your father?'

Here come the tears. 'I'm sorry. He's not—I'm not—it's just I'm—I'm not okay.'

'I get that.' His voice is gentle. 'I'm guessing you've had a really hard time.'

'It's a wonder you haven't seen it on the TV news or heard it on the radio or read it in the newspapers!'

'I haven't seen, or heard or read *any* news. The TV and radio are packed up along with everything else. I'm camping in the house! What have I missed?' He's still holding my hand, and he tightens his grip. I don't pull away. Its warmth and strength are comforting. 'What should I have seen, or heard, or read?'

I tell him about the murders, accompanied by floods of tears.

He doesn't interrupt me. He just holds my hand. Sometimes I remove my hand from his to wipe my eyes, or blow my nose— right from the start he produced the ubiquitous clean handkerchief from his pocket, but in between mopping up I replace my hand back into his hand, because it keeps me grounded in the here-and-now, when I could so easily fall into the black hole of the there-and-then, while I tell him all of it. Well, not quite all of it. I don't tell him about the cruel letter rejecting me, written by the man I believed was my father. Nor do I tell him about my mother's infidelity with the man who gave me life.

Chapter Thirty-one

Easter Sunday, 16 April 1995

Headlights are coming along the lane. It'll be Dan and Billy returning home, after six days and five nights camping at the beach. I'm over being mad at them. I want to see them, but right now I'm heading out to meet Shaun. I tell Mum where I'm going, and she follows me to the door, saying, 'Well, I'm looking forward to an early night.' Then she notices the headlights approaching, and adds, 'But I'll tell them about their father first.'

I nod, relieved I don't have to be the bearer of the bad news. I pat her arm wordlessly, trying to convey sympathy, then leave her standing there.

This afternoon, while Mum expanded her garden by the well, planting out her grevilleas and weeding her herbs and nasturtiums, Shaun and I spent time together on the east veranda working on my new maths and science assignments. As he was leaving, he asked me to come for a walk down to the creek, in the moonlight, an experience I yearned to repeat after the first time a month ago when Saab ruined it. But now it's happening, I don't want to be alone with him.

Shaun is waiting for me by the gate. He has a torch too. He holds my hand as we walk down the track. We pass the stockyards and piggery, silent now the piglets and mama have been shipped down south to the film lot. We shine our torches on the newly rebuilt lean-to, the still-unroofed packing shed, and his hail-ruined vegie patch. The billabong, farther away on our left, gleams in the moonlight. The birds returned in skeins after the hailstorm. As we crunch across the corn stubble, indignant lapwings squawk at us. The lantana parallel to the creek is stripped of foliage, the sandy track still littered with twigs, small branches and dying leaves. I'm grateful for the torchlight. We arrive at the creek, and he leads me up the bank and onto the patch of grass in front of the lantana. The canoe is moored behind us. Many times, we have launched the canoe from this spot. I stripped off in front of him right here. I sheltered with him beneath the canoe under the lantana in the hailstorm.

We stand on the bank, side by side, and gaze at the luminous water rippling past. He spreads his large beach towel on the moonlit grass, damp now with dew, and we sit on it. He removes from his backpack a packet of chocolate biscuits, a couple of mugs, and a thermos filled with sweet, milky coffee. It would be perfect, if only I didn't feel so anxious and empty.

Afterwards, he lies down and offers me his right arm for a pillow. I acquiesce, but my nerves are on edge. His left arm supports my back, holding me close. My right arm encircles his back, my left arm and hand squashed between us. We lie entwined. I am intensely aware of the rise and fall of his chest with every breath he takes, and his every heartbeat, but the bonfire that once burned in my belly is reduced to ashes.

My right HA exaggerates some sounds and dulls others. Underlying the night noises is the barely audible swishing of the creek—I'm probably imagining it. A lone frog croaks halfheartedly. Crickets chirrup in the grass. When birds on the billabong call intermittently, the lapwing plovers take exception with strident replies. The eerie echo of a Powerful Owl's repetitive *whoo-hoo* rebounds off the escarpment.

Eventually, I indicate I need to move—my left arm and hand have gone numb; my left HA is squeaking; I've a crick in my neck. Shaun releases me and rolls onto his back. I do the same. We lie side by side on the now damp towel, the ground lumpy, hard and cold beneath us. We gaze at the bright moon. I'm tense, but all he does is reach for my hand and hold it.

'My fascination with the universe started with the moon, but most humans don't care.'

'About what?'

'About what's out there! Do they even notice? They can't even identify visible planets in our solar system.' He waves at the river of stars above us. 'Do they realise our star, our sun, along with our entire solar system, is a miniscule part of the Milky Way, *our* galaxy? Are they awed by the trillions of stars in our galaxy alone? Countless numbers of those stars probably have planets like Earth revolving around them. And there are trillions more galaxies out there, beyond our galaxy. Do they have any idea how *vast* it is?'

I want to ask him, 'So what's your point?' but I don't. Silence ensues.

'I guess I'm trying to say how insignificant we are, and how miraculous it is to be here, to be a part of it, to see it all. That's why human behaviour gets me down. There's so much unfixable hatred in the world. If nuclear war doesn't destroy us, global warming will. Climate change is an all-pervasive threat …'

Anxiety rolls over me like a panic attack. I leap to my feet. 'I need to go home, Shaun!' I'm shivering. 'I want to go home!' My voice is high, like a child's. 'Please take me home!'

Chapter Thirty-two

Easter Monday, 17 April 1995

I felt so awkward and uncomfortable walking home with Shaun last night. We hardly spoke, his unasked questions heavy between us. Once I was safely home, I tried to comfort myself and settle my nerves with a hot shower, but my sleep was disturbed by scary dreams. They left my memory the moment I woke up this morning, but they are still lurking in some dark place in my mind, sure to re-emerge in nights to come.

Mum and I are sharing an early breakfast—the boys still asleep.

I ask her, 'Did you tell them about Hugh?'

She nods. 'I did.'

'How did they take it?'

'Hard.'

I wait for more, but she says nothing else. So after a hiatus, I ask her to tell me more about Paul. Her response is to unlock her filing cabinet and extract an unmarked, brown envelope from the bottom drawer.

'His poems might give you some insight,' she says, revealing a slim volume in the envelope. 'This was published soon after our … encounter.' She smiles at me. 'Most are rather obscure, but you might find a couple of them illuminating. 'Don't spill anything on it. No buttery, sticky fingers. It's precious.'

'I won't!' I wash my hands at the kitchen sink, and dry them carefully, before taking the envelope from her, almost reverently. Emotions well up, coming from a place of gratitude more than sadness. She is sharing a special time in her life with me *now*, and *I* was also there *then*. *'Conceived in a moment of love,'* she said. I want so much to meet Paul. I want to know him. I want a father. I'm enjoying a feeling of completion, of anticipation, knowing he's out there, somewhere. I just wish she'd told me about him earlier, like five years ago.

'One of my artist friends rang last night, to tell me the triptych has been selected for hanging.' She's obviously chuffed.

I'm smiling like the Cheshire Cat. 'You mean *I've* been selected! *I'm* hanging in the exhibition!'

She chuckles as she takes her mug and bowl to the sink. 'I'm off to *Booyul* to watch the chimney being restored. Would you mind washing these?'

'No problem.'

I hear the squeak of the back door as it opens and the click of the latch on the screen door. Then she closes both doors behind her and she's gone.

To watch the chimney being restored? Or to watch Joe restoring the chimney!

'Her husband is dead! She's free!' I whisper to Anne, as I wash up.

I'm curious to know what Mum thinks of Joe. He's not a bad-looking bloke, but he's not a professor type. And he's probably twelve years older than she is! I visualise her walking up the slope to *Booyul* to meet him. It feels like a role-reversal.

I put the envelope containing Paul's poems on my desk and take the day's contraceptive pill. Is it PMT, S, D, or whatever, messing with my head and body? Is that what's causing my irritability and lack of desire, as well as my heavy, achy, bloated belly? Is that why I'm so emotionally withdrawn from Shaun? I couldn't wait to get away from him last night. It's dawning on me I've been short-fused and emotionally reactive *every* month before my period, for a long time.

Dan and Billy emerge from their room. They seem out of it. They are sunburnt; their hair stiff with salt and sand. Neither appears to have used a comb, razor or toothbrush for a week. They eat bowls of muesli on the east veranda and play their guitars between mouthfuls, while I make them coffee and bring out the letters.

I cannot escape the vision of their father's murder. I look elsewhere, but an after-image is burnt into my eyes, imprinted in my brain. The red-tipped arrows, the whites of his terrified eyes, his open mouth, his hands held out like a shield to stop the arrow or plead for mercy, the red blood bubbling, the spreading stain on his shirt ...

My brothers—my half-brothers—read and re-read the letters together, an experience both pleasurable and painful to observe. I withhold their father's letter to me and keep the fact I'm the product of an affair a secret for now. The reality they *are* only half-brothers; they belong to Hugh, and I don't, feels threatening. Will they love me less, accept me less, once they know?

Dan speaks about it first. 'Mum told us about Dad last night. I couldn't sleep for thinking about him.'

I nod.

Billy shivers. 'Same. I'm *still* numb. I can't believe he was ...' He shakes his head.

They are both slow talking and vague, their eyes red. They look wrecked, but I don't know if it's because of the news about their father, or because they're hung over and stoned, or affected by too much sun and salt water. Probably all these things.

'It must've been horrendous for you, Jodie, to see it happen,' Dan speaks with feeling.

'Now I get how awful it must've been for *you* guys, when you saw Mum stab herself.'

They both nod.

Dan asks, 'I wonder how, what's his name, Carl—knew his wife was there, with Dad, in his office? He went there prepared, intending to kill them *both*. It was pre-meditated.'

'Maybe he tapped his home phone somehow, so he could listen in when she made calls. Or he *taped* her calls, and got evidence,' Billy suggests. 'The police will get it out of him.'

'If they catch him.' Dan adds.

'It's not like it was a *new* affair,' I say. I know *so* much more than they do. They have no idea what I've experienced, unless Mum's told them. 'They were seeing each other in secret for *years*! I reckon Carl knew about them all along, and endured it, until something took him over the edge. A kind of last straw.'

They both nod, like they're considering, rather than dismissing, the idea.

'Maybe she was planning to leave Carl to be with Dad—and Dad was planning to leave Mum to be with her—and Carl found out?' Billy offers.

'It's possible,' Dan agrees. 'That could do it.'

'Only a month ago, Mum was mad as a cut snake when she found out he was two-timing her with some *other* woman!' I exclaim.

They both look at me, eyebrows raised, Dan shaking his head. 'He could *not* keep his dick in his pants! He couldn't even be faithful to his mistress!'

'Maybe Carl was afraid he'd lose his kids too, if she left him,' Billy says. 'Men do lose out when it comes to divorce. *Some* men care about their kids.' He sounds bitter.

'If he *really* cared about his kids, and not just himself, he wouldn't have killed their mother!' I retort.

They both silently study me again, until Dan says, 'He might try to contact his kids. But what will they think of him when they learn he's killed their mother?'

'Their house will be under surveillance,' Billy says. 'And their phone will be bugged, in case he tries to ring them from wherever he's hiding out.'

'They've probably been taken to a safe house,' Dan says, picking up his guitar.

Billy nods. 'True. There's no telling how far he'd go.'

I'm horrified. 'Are you suggesting he'd kill his kids?'

Billy also reaches for his guitar. 'It's called "filicide". Before he kills himself. It happens all the time.'

Dan plucks his guitar strings. A familiar Kris Kristofferson melody emerges. Billy strums chords in harmony. I know the song and the lyrics and I'm consumed with melancholy.

Chapter Thirty-three

Tuesday, 18 April 1995

Dan and Billy replenish their supplies and return to the beach; promising Mum they'll be back in time for Friday night's RAG exhibition opening. She probably has no idea they wagged school from the day we left, leaving Shaun to look after Cleo and Patra. Today they invited me to go with them, but I declined, weighed down by an overwhelming tiredness. I wish I could hibernate and switch my brain off. Em will think I'm still in the Blue Mountains unless I ring her. I could ring Christine and make a time to see her—but what can I talk to her about? She'd be horrified to hear what I've been through. My 'issues' are already in the 'too-hard basket'.

Those issues have not lost their relevance; they still eat into me, like an ulcer that will not heal. They are haunting me now. It's shattering to think I'll never have an acknowledgment or apology from him; that all I have is his cruel, miserable letter to remind me I meant nothing to him and didn't belong in 'his' family. The financial compensation for what he subjected me to isn't even his to give; it's really Mum's money from her father's estate. It's like she's placating me for her inaction when I most needed protection.

I crawl out of bed and dress myself—my jeans are looser than ever. I wash my face, eat some muesli, and set up the card table on the east veranda. I place the folder containing my new *English Language and Literature* study notes alongside my father's volume of poetry and my PS journal. I fetch the binoculars from Mum's desk, so I can keep an eye on Shaun and Joe balancing on the packing shed rafters as they replace the sheets of corrugated iron.

Something I wrote in my journal is gnawing at me. I open PS and find it.

Mum told the detective interviewing us, 'I expected Hugh to be there, but when we arrived Felicity said he'd gone away for Easter.'

That's what Mum told the detectives, she even wrote it in her statement, but it's a lie. Maybe she anticipated Hugh would be there *before* we rang Felicity, but after the phone call we *knew* he wasn't there. And Felicity *didn't* speak to us when we barged in—she was too dumbfounded. There's a risk the CCTV footage will show Felicity did *not* speak to us until we were leaving. What if the cops pick up the discrepancy between the CCTV footage and Mum's statement? It's fortunate the CCTV has no sound.

'Why didn't Mum tell the police the *truth*?' I ask Anne.

Anne doesn't have an answer to that, but when I try to recall what Felicity said to me on the phone, thinking she was talking to her employer's mistress, Anne reminds me:

'You know he's not coming in today! You know the arrangement is to meet him here tomorrow at ten. You'll have plenty of time to talk to him over the Easter break!'

'Ouch! *Yes*! And Felicity was *not happy*! And Mum heard her as clearly as I did.'

I get why Mum didn't tell the police about the phone call, but she lied by omission. And I was complicit in the lie. I took my cue from her and didn't mention it either.

Did Felicity tell the cops about the phone call? If she did, they'll surely be curious about the identity of this anonymous caller. Hopefully Felicity was too scared to mention the call or the conversation, in case they thought *she* was complicit in the murders!

Maybe the cops don't know about the call. Or they know but haven't linked *us* to it.

Or maybe they do know, have their suspicions and are just biding their time.

What if Felicity had a flash of intuition, or a suspicion in hindsight, that she was talking to *me*—or Mum—on the phone? After all, we did turn up very soon after the phone call and marched in as if we *knew* Hugh wasn't there! What if she thought our arrival was too much of a coincidence?

Besides, we'll be on the CCTV outside the building, getting out of the car, walking out of range of the camera in the direction of the PO, returning, getting the briefcase and the Paddy Pallin shopping bag out of the car, and entering Macleod Chambers …

And I'm on the CCTV practically alongside the killer the very next day! I followed my ex-piano teacher into the building, and her husband followed me. And I was looking in the doorway of the anteroom to my father's office like I was showing the killer where they were. Different officers asked me why I was there at that time, and I couldn't explain it to their satisfaction or my own. The more I think about how it looks the more scared I feel.

The issue that bothers me most is where Mum went on Wednesday afternoon while I was with Ian. Did she visit Carl? Did *she* tell him his wife was meeting Hugh in his office the next morning? Even if she did tell him, I cannot imagine her thinking—hoping—he'd *kill* them both. The thought chills me. She and Carl, friends in the past, both betrayed by their partners, might have shared a desire for retribution, but not murder, surely, leaving Carl a wanted man—though that's my fault, for telling the police I heard his wife call out his name. But the police would've soon discovered her husband was handy with a crossbow even if she hadn't called out his name and I hadn't blabbed. He'd be their first suspect; husbands usually are.

Mum and I need to co-ordinate our stories. I'm scared because I'm 'a person of interest', 'helping the police with their inquiries' because *I was there,* 'a witness'. One mean detective told me I could be charged 'at the very least' with being 'an accessory after the fact' because I failed to report the crime immediately, giving the perpetrator time to escape while I hid in a coffee shop. At least I was able to tell them she wailed, 'Carl, no!' before he pierced her with an arrow.

Felicity isn't above suspicion either. She knew of her employer's plans. When she thought his mistress was on the phone, her disapproval and contempt were unmistakable. Maybe *she* informed Carl about the arrangements!

I haven't written down these speculations in case PS ends up in the wrong hands.

I pick up the binoculars and peer at Shaun stepping across the packing shed rafters like a long-legged bird. When I told him on our island about what happened, I did not tell him about the letter from Hugh—the man I believed all my life was my father—because of a deep sense of shame. The shame of rejection. Of not belonging. Of being unloved and unlovable. I also kept Paul secret. Why? To protect my mother? After all, she was unfaithful first. She started it.

I put the binoculars down and open the volume of poetry. The poems are intellectual, scattered with literary allusions, but two catch my eye because of their subject matter and relative simplicity. I open PS to a fresh double page and transcribe them.

Transition

*A lone leaf
clings to a wintry morning
afraid to leave the bough
caught between loneliness
and the fear of falling*

*Such is the now
a time to choose between two avenues
and the wind is calling*

I can relate to it, identify with it. I'm caught between staying at home alone and lonely or facing my fears, plunging into the unknown and going to school. Was Paul describing Mum's dilemma? She could stay in her miserable marriage, or let go of that lonely but familiar life, and endure the conflict and turmoil of leaving Hugh to move interstate with her sons to be with Paul. How different my life would have been if she had dared to leave Hugh, if she had made a different choice!

Caring

*It was caring
six yesterdays unbetrayed
sharing the juice
unpossessive of the fruit
paradise regained
unburdened by guilt or grief
consumed to the heart's core
awareness of satisfaction
reborn to live again*

A beautiful thing
a time together
a love so brief
unforgettable link
in the chain of memory
your gift
and you wear mine
remembering me

Is he talking about his time with Mum in this poem? If he is, it is incredibly intimate. I feel like a voyeur reading it.

I'll ask her how many days, or hours, she and Paul spent together. *Was* it only 'six yesterdays unbetrayed'? *Did* they give each other gifts? Or is he writing metaphorically?

He says: '—and you wear mine remembering me'. Mum wears a small heart-shaped white opal pendant on a fine gold chain just below the hollow of her throat. I don't think I've ever seen her without it. Was it a gift from Paul, my father, and she's worn it ever since? And never told me?

It's lunchtime, and Shaun arrives with a couple of sandwiches to share. I push my *English Language and Literature* folder to the back of the card table to make space for the sandwiches, but also to cover my PS journal, Paul's volume of poetry, and the binoculars!

'Come and help me make coffee!' I command him.

In the kitchen he organises mugs and plates and the sugar bowl on the tray and talks to me while I prepare the coffee plunger and wait for the jug to boil.

'Joe's converting the packing shed into stables and a feed shed for the horses.'

'That's nice of him. Are you going to help him?'

'Only during school hours. And not tomorrow.'

'What's tomorrow?'

'Wednesday.'

'So it is.'

'What would *you* like to do tomorrow?'

My mind is blank. I pour the boiling water onto the coffee grounds, replace the plunger, and search for the small milk jug. 'Could you grab some milk?' I ask him.

He fills the jug, returns the milk carton to the fridge.

'Bring the tray. Please.' I pick up the coffee plunger, lead the way out to the east veranda, grab the sandwiches from the card table on my way past and sit on the sofa. He puts the tray on the coffee table and sits, not beside me, but on the adjacent single chair. He's either giving me space, or distancing himself.

I haven't answered him, because I don't know what I want to do tomorrow. Nothing is fun anymore. Everything about him, about us, seems stale and predictable without desire colouring my perceptions. The realisation stuns me. He's so earnest; he goes on and on about serious, depressing topics; he's emotionally restrained, constrained by our circumstances. He's not a rebel, or a risk-taker, or a rule-breaker.

He depresses the plunger and pours coffee into our mugs. 'I need to—can I—' he clears his throat '—ask you what's made you change your mind about me?'

I half-shrug, half-shake my head, drop my gaze, pick up my coffee with shaking hands.

'Jodie, you have a right to feel whatever it is you feel. I just need to understand you. I need to know if it's temporary or permanent; whether to hang in and hope it will pass—or accept that it really is over between us, so I can let go emotionally and move on. For what it's worth, *I* think, after all you've been through, there's no room left for *us* right now. It's like you're in survival mode. Everything else has shut down.' His voice is gravelly, and again he clears his throat. 'But we do need to talk.

I need to know what you want from me going forward. Whether there is anything I can do for you. Anything to make it easier for you.'

I don't know what to say. The silence becomes unbearable.

Shaun finishes his sandwich and coffee and stands up. 'It's time to go. But please, meet me at the billabong at ten tomorrow, Jodie. Even if it is to say goodbye.'

Chapter Thirty-four

Wednesday, 19 April 1995

We are floating on the billabong. I'm sitting arse-about in the bow seat, facing Shaun in the stern seat. Our paddles are resting on the struts. The canoe is drifting gently towards the waterlilies, moved sideways by a light breeze.

I spent hours last night trying to analyse how I felt, writing in a notebook, rather than PS, searching for the right words to express what I wanted to say to him. I didn't write in PS, because I needed the notes in front of me, and PS is secret.

'I made notes too.' He unzips his backpack and pulls out a small sheaf of loose pages. 'But you start.' He gestures at my notebook. 'I won't interrupt you, unless you ask me a direct question or invite me to comment.' He rolls his notes into a cylinder.

'Thank you.' I rest the notebook on my knees to stop the pages from quivering. I'm not sure what to kick off with, so I start with my most formal statement, which I wrote and rewrote a dozen times last night, trying to get it right.

'I should have been protected from the man I believed was my father, but I wasn't. Since his death I've realised I'll never recover my trust in older men by having a sexual relationship with one.'

I don't know what Shaun will make of that. He looks bewildered, surprised and confused all at once. He clearly wants to say, or ask me, something, but I continue.

'You *are* too old for me, Shaun. You've said so yourself.'

He nods, looks out over the billabong.

'I've also realised how pessimistic you are. I'm depressed enough as it is.'

Suddenly, like an epiphany, I realise Shaun is depressed too! Probably as depressed as I am, maybe more so, and I've never acknowledged it, never asked him how he's feeling. He's *told* me—in roundabout ways—but instead of expressing empathy, I've labelled him *pessimistic* to his face and *boring* in my head. I feel ashamed, but it's too late to apologise.

'You're leaving me, now you have better things to do. I've just been a fill-in for you.'

Again, I glance at him. He looks challenged; he's shaking his head.

'You're not *really* attracted to me, Shaun. You're a scaredy-cat. Maybe you're gay. Maybe I've been waiting for an illusion.'

His eyes close, he shakes his head, compresses his lips, breathes out a sigh.

'I've blamed PMT, or PMS, or whatever it's called. I've blamed what happened in the Blue Mountains—is still happening. I've asked myself am I in the angry stage of grieving? I'm grieving the loss of so many things you don't even know about, as well as the fact you're abandoning me!' I shrug. 'Whatever. I'm tired of grieving. It's easier not to care.'

Now he's *really* looking at me, and this time I hold his gaze. I *want* to hurt him. I need him to experience the rejection *I* feel.

'I don't want to go to the RAG exhibition with you, Shaun. And it's okay if you don't want to buy Mum's triptych. It'll probably sell anyway. And if it doesn't, I'd like to keep it for myself, because it's about—it's between—Mum and me. And I won't be going to the Grafton Show with you, for *many* reasons besides knowing I'll be in too much pain to enjoy it.'

There. I've done it. I close my notebook.

'Can I ask you something?'

I nod.

'How much has this got to do with the man you *believed* was your father? You haven't explained what you mean by that. Are you saying he was not your biological father? Or do you mean he didn't behave like fathers are meant to behave—'

'Try both.'

Shaun nods slowly, gazing at me. 'So, you've somehow discovered he was not your biological father, and his behaviour towards you was unspeakably awful.'

I can only nod. I look out over the waterlilies, the breeze trying to lift the strands of hair stuck to the tears rolling down my cheeks.

'And now he's dead. And you're having to contend with that.'

'Yes. And you are going away.'

'I am. But *we* are both alive, Jodie. I'm only a phone call, or a letter, or a car trip, away. We can still be friends. Do *you* want to remain friends? Do *you* want to keep in touch?'

'What's the point? There's nothing to look forward to. Now you've dug up and read my letters, there's no reason to meet here in ten years' time. Or anywhere, anytime, really.'

I just want it to be over. It's hard to breathe. The black rock is back in my chest.

'This is a very sad way to end it, Jodie.' He taps his unread notes against his wrist, then drops them in his backpack.

'Hey! That's not fair, Shaun! I shared *my* thoughts—'

He shrugs, shakes his head. 'My thoughts are superfluous now.' His voice is gentle.

'But I need to know what *you* think—'

'It doesn't matter what I think. What *I* think is irrelevant. I've heard *you*, loud and clear. The removalist is coming early tomorrow morning, and I've still got things to do. I was going to camp on your mother's lawn until Sunday, but I'll leave *Booyul* tomorrow. Here's the money for the triptych. I was buying it for you anyway.' He pulls a fat envelope from his backpack, leans forward and hands it to me. 'Please give this to your mother.' His voice is hoarse. 'Consider the triptych a parting gift. Like the canoe.'

I'm speechless. I can only nod as I take the envelope and put it in my backpack.

He zips up his pack, picks up his paddle and manoeuvres the canoe backwards and sideways out of the waterlilies. He points to the eastern edge of the billabong, then to my paddle, rotating his hand, indicating he wants me to turn around and help him.

'We can lug the canoe back down to the creek, paddle to Gwongorella, and tie up there. Our last paddle.'

Chapter Thirty-five

It's ANZAC Day. We're all at home, having chosen not to go to the Dawn Service, or line up to watch the march. Instead, while Dan and Billy are cleaning out their snake cages and Mum is reorganising her studio in preparation for a new project, I'm walking around the perimeter of *Gwongorella* with Cleo and Patra, recalling and mentally reliving the days since Shaun left.

The removals truck arrived early last Thursday morning, a week after the murders. A couple of hours later I stood on the west veranda and watched it leave *Booyul*, Shaun following in his ute. I crawled into bed, bawled myself into oblivion, and didn't come to until Mum came home and woke me.

Friday, I stayed in bed all day. Mum went to town and did the grocery shopping, and Dan and Billy returned from the beach soon after she arrived home. She bullied me to get up, have a shower and hair wash, and dress for the RAG exhibition opening. She bribed me with her leopard-skin stretch pants, saying, 'They'll fit you better now.'

As we left for the gallery, Billy said, 'Wow, sis, you've made it!'

Dan told me I looked like a million dollars.

At the gallery, caught up in the excitement, I was able to function. Christine and Richard were there, they were VIPs, and

Christine invited me to ring and make a time for a visit. I accepted; I needed something to look forward to, something to keep me anchored and alive. Nobody in Grafton knows, yet, that we're involved in the murders, our names withheld from the press by the police—for now.

To my surprise and delight, Em was at the gallery too, looking elegant and willowy. I felt a surge of comfort when I saw her. We hugged, and she introduced me to Auntie I, who turned out to be an artist too. Her painting, in the Pointillist style, was riveting. It was called *Boorimbah Dreaming* and depicted the Big River and its tributaries and islands, seen from above. The canvas was large, the design intricate, the colours vibrant, yet subtle and harmonious. It must have taken her forever to paint all those dots. A red sticker was on her Artist's Statement, with a sign: 'Gallery Acquisition' above it.

Mum's triptych looked stunning too, in a totally different way. It was hung in a really good position—beautifully lit—also with a red sticker on the Artist's Statement. Mum told me she'd informed Shaun the price was six hundred for him, more if it was sold through the gallery, hoping to put him off, but he hadn't hesitated. When I gave her the envelope with the money in it and told her he'd given the triptych to me, a farewell gift, she was astonished—and thrilled. She'd been in two minds whether to sell it at all. 'It's like having your cake and eating it too!'

Saturday, the shit hit the fan. The cramps were awful! In the middle of one, I wailed to Mum, 'If this is what having a baby is like I don't want one! Never ever!'

Dan and Billy offered to take me to the Grafton show 'to take my mind off everything', but I told them getting out of bed to go to the loo was all I could manage. Mum was rostered on at the gallery, so I was home alone when the phone rang. I agonised over whether to pick up, thinking it might be the Blue

Mountains police, but decided to answer it anyway in case it was Em. It was Shaun! In that first moment hearing his voice I nearly hung up, but I'm so glad I didn't because we talked and talked and shared more about ourselves in that call than in the previous three months. Shaun also told me he'd read, seen and heard that the owner of Macleod Chambers in a town in the Blue Mountains had been murdered in his office, along with a woman, unnamed to protect her children. There was much speculation and he warned me it wouldn't be long before Mum and I were tracked down by journalists.

We agreed each of us would phone the other monthly, meaning we'd talk to each other fortnightly, and write whenever we felt like it. After we hung up, I felt much calmer. Relieved. He was gone but not lost. We were still friends.

Sunday, Dan and Billy again invited me to go to the beach with them, just for the day. I wasn't up to it, but very pleased they'd asked me, and we agreed on next weekend.

Meanwhile, the new tenants moved into *Booyul*. Through the binoculars I watched as three horses were unloaded from the float and introduced to their new stables in the converted packing shed, now inside a timber-fenced yard—Joe having removed the barbed wire. I daydreamed about befriending the family.

Mum had Sunday off. She joined me on the east veranda, with a cup of tea for herself and a mug of hot Milo for me, at a loose end with no art project to engross her.

'What's the significance of that opal you always wear?' I pointed to my own throat.

She reached for the opal, held it between her left thumb and forefinger, and stroked it. 'Your father gave it to me. A parting gift. Something to remember him by.'

I felt a lurch of excitement in my belly. I nodded, pleased, my hunch validated.

'What made you ask?'

'I just wondered, after reading one of his poems.'

'*It was caring, six yesterdays unbetrayed …?*'

'Yes! How long, how much time, *did* you have together? Was it only six yesterdays?'

'It was a month of meeting and eating, and talking and walking, before we actually got together during the last six days—a very short interlude—with monumental consequences.'

'Like what?'

'You, for starters!'

'Are you sorry? Was I more trouble than I was worth?'

'Never. You were my salvation! I'm ever grateful to him!'

For the first time since arriving home we talked about the murders. Mum admitted she was grieving. 'Not for Hugh, though,' she told me. 'After receiving the registered letter from that unknown woman asking me was my marriage over because Hugh had told her it was, and I realised he was *still* cheating on me, *still* lying to me, big time, I finally understood the marriage was dead. But the last straw was discovering he was still involved with your ex-piano teacher. That was the final nail in the coffin! Now he's dead I'm not grieving *him*. I'm grieving the loss of a dream, grieving for what I never had—a trustworthy partner and a happy, fulfilled marriage like my parents had.'

I nodded, trying to convey my understanding and empathy. But I couldn't resist asking her about the other matter consuming me, intensely curious and desperate to know the answer.

'How did Carl know they were there?'

I expected Mum to speculate aloud, to tell me her thoughts and theories. Instead, she was instantly guarded and defensive, her tone bordering on hostile. 'What sort of a question is that! How would I know!'

The fact she thought I was accusing her made me suspicious. My scepticism must have been obvious.

'Do you think *I* told him? Is that what you think?'

'I don't know what to think! *Did* you tell him?'

'If I did, I wouldn't tell *you*! I wouldn't tell anyone. Especially you. The less you know the better. You can't lie to the police if you don't know the truth.'

'How *did* he know they were there, Mum?'

'What are you! The *Stasi* or something? Just drop it!'

'I *need* to know, Mum. I can't get it out of my head. I need to know the *truth*.'

'You don't need to know *anything*! The less you know the better! *Not* knowing is much safer than lying! How could it possibly benefit you if I told you I *did* tell him! What if I told you I rang him from a phone box, or I visited him and we planned it together, or I met him somewhere and told him! Or maybe I arranged to meet him before we even left here—'

'I'm worried, Mum. If you *did* tell him, won't it make you an accessory before *and* after the fact? An accessory to murder? Aiding and abetting? Procuring a hitman? A killer? What if the police catch up with him? What if they ask *him* the same question: "How did you know they were there?" And extract a confession from him? And he dobs you in!'

She shook her head, and I interpreted it to mean he wouldn't dob her in if he was caught.

'Y'know,' she said, 'I did tell Carl—back then. Five years ago. I told him everything I knew. First up, I gave him the pink letter. The one you snatched from Hugh. Then I gave him *all* her letters, the ones I found in Hugh's desk, so he'd *know* it was true! I thought telling him would put an end to it. It caused a shit-storm alright. If ever he was going to kill them it would have been then! He *did* threaten Hugh actually—he warned him there'd be consequences if it ever happened again. They made promises, saying it was over, and they did lie low for a while, but Hugh's word meant nothing! He blatantly lied to me, told me I was paranoid, that I was living an illusion. He accused me of having a mental illness, he treated my suspicions like they were a kind of weakness or sickness. I begged him to stop. Begged him to stop lying to me. Begged him to give me back our marriage, and he laughed at me. That's when I made a choice; you know that instant when you decide? I could have stabbed *him*, right then and there, but I didn't. I stabbed *myself!* Bad decision! *No* man is worth sacrificing your life for.'

I heard everything she said, and it broke my heart, but I still wanted an answer. 'The Wednesday afternoon I was with Ian, and you went missing, did you visit Carl—or contact him—and tell him his wife was meeting Hugh in his office the next morning?'

She twitched like she'd been stung by a wasp. Seriously agitated, she exclaimed, 'For godssake, Jodie! You're not hearing me! Even if I *did*, I wouldn't tell you, to *protect* you. In circumstances like this, ignorance is bliss!'

'Did you know Carl planned to *kill* them both?'

She stared at me, her expression unreadable. When she did speak, her voice was low and emphatic. 'Whether I knew, or didn't know, after what they did to you, I'm *glad* he killed them!' Her eyes pierced mine. '*Especially* after what they did to you. Some things are unforgivable.'

An icy chill swept over me. She and Carl, one-time friends, both betrayed, might well have shared a desire for retribution, but her words implied she was avenging *me*! A month ago, after our confrontation, right here on the east veranda, she declared, *'I will do something, Jodie. I promise. Just give me time to think it through. Give me time to do the right thing.'*

'When the police question you again, Jodie—and they surely will—tell them only what you *know*. Not one thing more. No speculations. No half-baked theories. No assumptions. No suspicions.' Her expression was grim. 'For *both* our sakes! Do you understand me?'

I nodded, my scalp prickling. Without a shadow of doubt, I understood her perfectly.

Chapter Thirty-six

Friday, 26 May 1995

I haven't had an unbroken night's sleep since it happened. My nightmares are so vivid it's hard to separate them from reality. I wake up in a cold sweat, my heart thumping.

Right now, Mum and I are being interviewed yet again, separately, again—in the Grafton Police Station by Blue Mountains detectives. They're asking the same questions they asked me in previous interviews, and I'm endeavouring to give them the same answers, including 'I don't know' or 'I don't remember'.

'Why were you there?'

'I wanted to see my father.'

'How did you know he was there?'

'I didn't. I just hoped.'

'You went to a lot of trouble based on "just hoping".'

'I had nothing better to do. I was just filling in time, waiting for Mum to finish her appointment with her lawyer.'

'Why was she seeing her lawyer?'

A shrug. 'I don't know.'

'You knew who the marksman was?'

'I had no idea.'

'This Carl, you've met him?'

'Nup.' Shaking my head. 'Not that I remember, anyway.'

'But you knew *her*?'

'Of course I knew her, her voice, her laugh. She was my piano teacher for five years.'

The interview continues and it's nerve-wracking. I have to keep my wits about me and not embellish my answers in any way. I have to tell them enough to not appear obstructive, or seem like I'm hiding something, while I keep the secret—so secret I don't know what it is—burdened by an almost unbearable weight of responsibility to protect Mum, certain she has knowledge I'm not privy to.

After the interviews, Mum marches ahead of me to our car. Before I can say a word about anything, she presses her right forefinger against her lips, warning me not to speak. We climb in and belt up in silence, her gestures, grimaces and eye movements indicating she thinks the car has been bugged by the police. She drives away from the police station, pulls up outside the café I've frequented a few times waiting for Em, and says, 'Let's have coffee.' She nods at me, indicating with a gesture of her fingers, that it's okay for me to answer her.

'Good idea,' I respond, cautiously.

Inside the café, Mum orders our drinks at the counter while I claim a corner booth.

'You're paranoid!' I tell her, when she finally sits down. 'Why would they do that?'

'To trap us.'

'Oh, come on!'

'Better to be safe than sorry.'

'The car was locked!'

'They can break into a car in ten seconds.'

'How would they know which car was ours?'

'They can check number plates, registrations.'

'But what could I—we—say?'

'We could say absolutely anything and they'd misconstrue it, read something into it. I don't want to give them *any* ammunition. Did they ask you if you'd heard from Carl?'

'No!' That was unexpected. 'No, they didn't. Did they ask you?'

'Yes, they did. And I told them, "No I haven't heard from him!" And I asked them, "Have *you* heard from him?" They didn't answer me, but they did say he hasn't used his bank cards anywhere, including ATMs, since Thursday, 13th April, implying *someone* has been helping him, sheltering him, feeding him. They didn't accuse me outright, but it's obvious they suspect I'm aiding and abetting him, like I'm an accomplice of some sort.'

'*Are* you? Have you been helping him?'

She doesn't answer me. Instead, she looks around the café at the other patrons, checks them out, scans the room for security cameras.

'Mum?'

She is saved by the café owner approaching with our drinks. She nods thanks, waits till he's back behind the counter before she speaks. 'I'm going to tell you something important, Jodie, but you must forget it as soon as I tell you. It will shock you, okay?'

I draw a deep breath. 'Okay.' I exhale the word slowly, doubtfully. I've had enough shocks. I don't know if I can handle another one. And I'm over-burdened with secrets. At the same time, I desperately want to know whatever it is she is going to tell me. I *need* to know, even though I'm terrified.

'I lied to the police. I *have* heard from Carl. Twice. He rang me one night. And I received a letter from him only yesterday. You saw me weeding the nasturtiums under the water tank soon after I arrived home? I was burying his letter there.' She slowly shakes her head. Her eyes are glistening. 'Those poor kids.'

I gaze at her dumbly, trying to understand.

'There's a popular hiking track in the Blue Mountains; it skirts around the base of a cliff in the Jamison Valley. There's a lookout at the top of the cliff. Paragliders use a nearby launch site. A man's body will be found by bushwalkers, on the track, at the base of the cliff. You must forget I told you, you must forget *what* I've told you; but if you see anything on the television news, or hear anything on the radio, let me know immediately.'

I'm appalled. 'What about his kids? Why didn't you tell the police? They could have stopped him!'

'His letter came too late, Jodie. It was his decision.'

Chapter Thirty-seven

Friday, 30 June 1995

The triptych *Unmasked* hangs on the wall above my bookcase. I have an unobstructed view of it from my bed and I gaze at it frequently, searching for hidden meanings.

I no longer record my thoughts and feelings or anything to do with the murders in PS. Instead, I've been making notes on Paul's literary works and summarising reviews written by his admirers and critics. I've also transcribed, and memorised, several of his poems. I plan to visit Adelaide next year during Writers Week between March 3rd and 8th. Whether Mum comes with me or not, I'm determined to track him down and introduce myself.

I've been spending time on weekends with the family next door. Twelve-year-old Briony is very caring of her fourteen-year-old sister Vicky, who is in a wheelchair with muscular dystrophy. I've become best friends with their sixteen-year-old brother Max—he's quiet and shy, gentle and kind, probably gay, and has amazing rapport with the horses. Vicky can't ride anymore, and she lets me ride her black mare, Star, around *Booyul* and *Gwongorella* with Max riding Sox, his bay gelding with four white socks.

They all go to South High and Mum's persuaded me to go too, three days a week starting next term, to attend advanced— meaning Year 12—maths and science classes and see how I get on. I've been doing Dan's and Billy's maths and science home-work with them and I'm helping them rather than the other way around. Dan reckons if Vicky can go to a new school mid-year in a wheelchair, I should be able to muster up the courage to go to school too. Mum had a discussion with the principal, and the maths and science head teachers, and showed them my distance education results. They were impressed and agreed to take part in the 'experiment'. I'm still studying all my OTEN subjects as well though.

Em and I are like sisters. We visit each other's places; I help her with schoolwork and she teaches me Bundjalung. She's warned me if I'm openly friendly with her at school there might be some kids who won't be friends with me, but I've told her I wouldn't want to be friends with those kinds of kids anyway.

Chapter Thirty-eight

Friday, 17 November 1995

It's been a week of exams for the three of us. Unlike Dan, I had no problems with the HSC maths and science exams. Mum picks us up from school, drives into town and parks opposite the post office. Promising to meet us in Duke Street by the river in an hour, Dan and Billy take off, probably to join their mates for a celebratory game of pool in a nearby pub. I watch Mum cross the road and disappear up the side of the post office to the private mailboxes. It's an imposing building, built of early red bricks the colour of desert sand. On either side upstairs are verandas with ornate, white-painted, cast-iron balustrades, and perched on top of the shingle roof is a white dome with a white-faced clock. Black roman numerals and arrowed hands add to the sense of the past. It's four o'clock, and sure enough, four chimes ring out.

It's ridiculous how scared I was about attending school. I not only have Em as a friend; I've made friends with other girls as well, and I see and talk to Dan and Billy and their mates—and Max—every day I'm there. On school days I work on my OTEN subjects in the school library between maths and science classes. The other days I spend in the TAFE library.

Waiting for Mum, I don't let myself imagine there'll be a letter for me, because nine times out of ten there isn't one, and I'd rather have one surprise than nine disappointments. She returns and waits on the kerb for a break in the traffic, clutching envelopes, a couple big enough to be returned OTEN assignments. I enjoy re-reading them and savouring the positive comments and consistently high marks.

She crosses the road, opens the driver's door, slides easily into the seat and flips through the envelopes. 'A letter for you, and a letter for me. Both from Paul.'

I'm flabbergasted. I take the envelope from her outstretched hand, and gaze at it and at her as the implications hit me. Her expression is a mix of guilt, defiance and amusement. 'I decided to write to him and tell him about you—break the ice, so to speak. I gave him our phone number. And I enclosed a couple of photos, the one you took of me beside the triptych at the gallery, and the one I took of you for the triptych where you look angelic.'

'Oh my God!' I'm horrified. 'What if he doesn't—'

'But he *does*! He does, he does, he does!' She's grinning from ear to ear. 'He was *delighted* to hear from me! He rang as soon as he received my letter. He's *thrilled* he has a daughter! He *very* much wants to meet you and get to know you. And what's more, he can't wait to see *me* again!'

I'm open-mouthed, angry and exhilarated at the same time. A letter from my father! I don't know whether to be outraged or grateful she's pre-empted my own plans for contact. I decide to be grateful.

'And there's *another* letter for you!' She passes it to me. I recognise Shaun's writing. '*Two* letters *and* two returned assignments, probably High Distinctions. What a bonanza! I'll drop you near the river so you can read them.' Mum belts up, drives along Victoria Street and turns right into Duke Street. I clutch the letters against my chest, my heart beating fast and strong under my thumbs.

Which letter will you read first? My father's, of course.

I avoid looking at the police station; it stirs up disturbing memories. We're still waiting for the coronial inquest, but since the dead man on the Blue Mountains hiking trail was identified as the perpetrator, with a letter confessing to the crime in one of his pockets, the police have backed off. I'm really sad his kids have lost both their parents. I feel for Dan and Billy too—their father's death has hit them hard.

It's ironical that as they lost their father, I found mine.

I gaze out the passenger window at the Anglican Cathedral through the trees. Duke Street terminates in a cul-de-sac overhung with jacarandas, and Mum parks rear-to-curb outside the Anglican Dean's residence. She has no idea how familiar I am with both its garden and its occupants.

The jacaranda trees are dropping their blooms; delicate, deep mauve bells constantly float down. The cars parked beneath them are littered with flowers and a mauve carpet covers the road. Light shines through the lilac petals, shades and shadows of a deeper, bluer purple visible inside the bells.

'They were perfect for the Jacaranda Festival parade,' Mum says.

'Yeah, well, my eyes are starting to itch!' I point to a bench seat on the riverbank. 'I'm going to sit over there and get away from them and read my letters.'

'And check out your assignments.'

'Yeah. That too.' I stuff the assignments into my backpack.

'I'll return in an hour, or thereabouts. I've got a few things to do.'

'Okay.' Clutching my backpack and letters, I climb out of the car, close the door and bend down to the open window. 'Thank you, Mum.'

'For what, daughter?'

'For everything.'

***

It's peaceful by the river, with a breeze blowing off the water, playing with my hair, cooling and calming me. I feel the same contentment when we sit on the east veranda after dinner with our hot drinks and watch the moon rise over the escarpment, and sniff the subtle, but unmistakeable whiff of eucalyptus oil and dry grass in the air. Here, though, it's a whiff of rotting jacaranda blooms. Summer is coming.

I gaze at Paul's letter, savouring the moment. I'm not afraid of it, not after Mum said, 'He does! He does!' I open it slowly, then read it, absorbing every word, every sentence. My father wants me, wants to know me, wants to claim me as his own. I lift the pages to my face to smell the ink; he's written with a fountain pen. I'm fascinated by the slant of his words, the shape of his letters, the consistency of his spacing; his writing style is uncannily like my own!

His enclosed photo is not the first I've seen of him, but it's the first one in colour. A while back I borrowed a couple of his publications from the Grafton City Library and studied the photos of him in them so intensely it's a wonder they didn't catch fire! He is so handsome. He wears rimless glasses like mine, his eyes are as blue as mine and his blond hair falls over his forehead with a cowlick just like mine. Without a shadow of doubt, we are father and daughter.

He has invited us to his book launch at Adelaide Writers Week in March next year. And he's offered for us to stay with him and his sons Kari and Finn, my half-brothers, aged eleven and nine, at their residence in Aldgate in the Adelaide Hills. He says the boys are as excited as he is to learn they have a sister. It all seems too perfect to be true, but it is true.

I return Paul's letter and photo to the envelope and put it in my backpack. I want to choose when to share it with Dan and Billy. The fact they are also half-brothers doesn't seem to be an issue, but it hasn't been tested yet. We haven't had a fight in months. But they lost their father just as I found mine. It's complicated.

I open Shaun's letter. It's a very different sort of feeling. Familiar. Pleasant. I no longer write him love letters, and he never has. I just write cheerful stuff, about school and Em, and what I'm studying, and horse-riding and canoeing with Max. I wonder if I make Shaun jealous, sometimes. Too bad if I do. Usually, his letters start newsy and chatty, until his descriptions of his PhD studies deteriorate into depressing commentary about the parlous state of the world.

This time his tone is upbeat all the way through. 'I've sent off a formal application for the AAP, the Australian Antarctic Program, for the 1996 summer intake, in an expeditionary role,' he says. 'It will take months to complete the process, because it involves many assessments, over and above my academic qualifications, like my medical and physical condition, and psychological factors, including my personality and how I'll go being separated from family and friends for such a long time.'

A small jolt jerks my heart reading that last bit, but really, I'm over it now. The separation I mean. The feeling abandoned. We're still friends and that's what matters.

As Anne says, *The future will take care of itself.*

Dan and Billy arrive. 'Move up,' Billy says, plonking himself down beside me and giving me a friendly nudge. Dan sits on the other side of me. 'What's the news?' he asks. Ever since I saved their arses when the cops raided the house, we've been best buddies. It's as if it was some sort of catalyst that brought us together and we bonded. I endure being enveloped in their stale male sweatiness. Their closeness is a kind of love. One of the best kinds.

Acknowledgements

I wrote the first draft of this novel on my computer during 1994–1995. Mobile phones were not readily available, but computer ownership was on the rise and the Internet was growing with it. Windows95 was released by Microsoft in August 1995. The era, and the setting, were my lived experience and became the lived experience of my characters. Thirty years later, in 2024–2025, I decided to revisit the manuscript. The rewrite took on a life of its own, diverting significantly from the original, but I am grateful for the framework and authenticity the first draft provided.

My iPhone, the Internet and the World Wide Web became indispensable research tools, providing me with essential, accurate details about the how, when, where and why of a myriad of matters and events that existed or occurred in 1995, or earlier, providing historical details—and later, in the form of prophesies, such as in the movie *Gaia Strikes Back* or made by my character Shaun. A library and crystal ball at my fingertips!

My long-time friends Sally McDonald and Marilyn Venus became indispensable sounding boards over coffee in our favourite cafes. Later, they became my beta readers. Their feedback and encouragement have been invaluable. Thank you for your time, your insights and observations.

I also thank my daughter, Janannie, for her support and patience through the two years of my writing almost daily amid the growing clutter of books, notebooks and bits of paper around my laptop on the dining room table. I hope when she reads it she thinks it was worth it.

And at the end of all the writing, my heartfelt thanks to Dr Juliette Lachemeier PhD, Managing Editor at The Erudite Pen. Right from the beginning of the publishing journey she has been there for me, with her positive and constructive feedback, wisdom and experience. I know it is a better book because of her editing. I have been truly fortunate to have the benefit of her expertise through the publishing process.

About the author

Heather Farmer is a Cairns-based poet and author. Her latest work, *Shadows of Doubt*, is a compelling and suspenseful novel set on an isolated rural property in Northern New South Wales in the 1990s. Her teenage protagonist Jodie experiences first desire, as she contends with body image, shame, family fracture and the dangerous weight of secrets.

Her professional life has been as diverse as her writing. Heather has taught young children at the Blue Mountains Community School, an innovative school founded on parent participation; English and History to high school students; and adult literacy and tertiary preparation through the TAFE system. She also trained in relationship counselling, mediation and clinical supervision, working in New South Wales with Family Life (now Interrelate) and in private practice, and in Queensland with Relationships Australia. These experiences have given her writing an emotional depth and layered richness, reflected in her ability to craft authentic, complex characters and relationships.

Collected Poems, 1970s–2020s, published in 2021, is a compilation of her poems written over a period of fifty years, in one volume, including poems originally published in *Of Dreams and Discoveries*, and the lyrics of the music album *Peaceful Earth*.

The Longest Decade: a literary memoir of the 1940s, was published in March 2015 after more than five years of research and many drafts. It was launched at the Cairns Tropical Writers Festival in August 2016, and was short-listed for the USA Memoir Magazine Prize in 2022, reviewed by Jerry Waxler, author of Memoir Revolution. It can be purchased online and a number of copies are in the Cairns City Council libraries.

Heather collaborated with renowned nature photographer Steve Parish, to produce *Of Dreams and Discoveries*, a series of connected poems telling the story of a life, enhanced by Steve's nature photographs. The first edition was published in 1979 and a second edition was published fifteen years later in 1994 by Steve Parish Publishing. Both editions were well-received with thousands of copies sold.

The lyrics for *Peaceful Earth* were written in 1996, the music composed by Bruce Vickery and Len E Johnson and the songs sung by Carolyn Ferrie. *Peaceful Earth* is available online on music sites including Amazon, Apple, YouTube, and Spotify. Search Farmer Ferrie Johnson Vickery.

Heather continues to write poetry, short stories and young adult fiction. She is a long-standing member of Tropical Writers Inc. in Cairns, Far North Queensland.

Enjoyed the book? You can connect with the author at:

Email: heatherannfarmer@gmail.com

Facebook: Heather Farmer Author

Twitter/X: HeatherFar22545

YouTube: @heatherfarmer

Please leave a review on Amazon, Goodreads or with the author directly. Reviews are invaluable in supporting an author's hard work and are greatly appreciated.